PRAISE FOR BARBARA MICHAELS

"This writer is ingenious."

—*Kirkus Reviews*

"Miss Michaels has a fine sense of atmosphere and story-telling."

—*The New York Times*

"Simply the best living writer of ghost stories and thrillers."

—Marion Zimmer Bradley

"Michaels' books are the literary equivalent of multiple gin and tonics . . . or double chocolate sundaes with both nuts and whipped cream."

—*Washington Post*

"This author never fails to entertain."

—*Cleveland Plain Dealer*

"Michaels has a fine downright way with the super-natural."

—*San Francisco Chronicle*

Houses of Stone

"Vivid descriptive writing and convincing dialogue."

—*Publishers Weekly*

"Superior Michaels . . . Like the antique gowns the heroine collects, *Shattered Silk* glitters!"

—*Kirkus Reviews*

Here I Stay

"An absolutely first-rate job of summoning up the spooky . . . takes on the added dimension besides that of a very good ghost story."

—*Publishers Weekly*

"Scary, interesting. A winner."

—*Pittsburgh Press*

Into the Darkness

"The suspense builds into a smashing final chapter that does full credit to Michaels' powers of invention."

—*Murder Ad Lib*

Smoke and Mirrors

"Michaels delivers another surefire winner!"

—*Publishers Weekly*

"Her fans will relish the way [Michaels] unveils and manipulates each character's dark secrets."

—*Booklist*

"The perfect curl-up-at-homer for a frosty . . . eve."

—*New Woman*

Books by Barbara Michaels

The Grey Beginning
Here I Stay

Available from HarperPaperbacks

And look for

Stitches in Time

Available in hardcover from HarperCollins*Publishers*

the grey beginning

Barbara Michaels

HarperPaperbacks
A Division of HarperCollinsPublishers

This is a work of fiction. The characters, incidents, and
dialogues are products of the author's imagination and
are not to be construed as real. Any resemblance to
actual events or persons, living or dead, is entirely
coincidental.

HarperPaperbacks   *A Division of* HarperCollins*Publishers*
          10 East 53rd Street, New York, N.Y. 10022

A previous edition of this book was published in 1985 by
Tor Books. It is reprinted by arrangement with Congdon
& Weed, Inc.

Cover photograph by Yagi Studio/Superstock

First HarperPaperbacks printing: June 1995

Printed in the United States of America

HarperPaperbacks and colophon are trademarks of
HarperCollins*Publishers*

10   9   8   7   6   5   4   3   2   1

To Linda, without whom this book and a number of others might not have been completed on time

I know my own way back.
Don't fear me! There's the grey beginning.

—Robert Browning, "Fra Lippo Lippi"

one

From the Piazzale Michelangelo you can see all of
Florence. In the sunlight of late afternoon it looked like
one of the *pietra dura* inlays at which Florentine craftsmen
excelled—a picture shaped from antique gold and semiprecious stones, amber and carnelian, topaz, heliodor, and
chrysoberyl. Few cities are as beautiful; few can boast such
a heritage. The names ring in the mind like trumpets—
Michelangelo, Leonardo, Brunelleschi, Fra Angelico.

I sat sullenly in the car with my back turned to the
spectacular view. I didn't want to be there. I had done my
damnedest to avoid the place, and Florence itself. On the
map the route looked simple. Leave the Autostrada del
Sole at Firenze Est, cross the Arno by the first possible
bridge, and head north toward Fiesole, skirting the inner
city. I never even made it across the river. The map didn't
show the sprawling suburbs with their mystifying mazes of
streets and their inadequate signs. At least when I reached
the Piazzale Michelangelo I knew where I was. I stopped

there because I had a feeling that if I turned the steering wheel one more time I would keep on turning it, around and around, in circles, till I ran into another car or a tree or somebody's front door.

Finger by finger I unglued my sticky hands from the wheel. The weather wasn't hot. It was early spring in Tuscany, crisp and cool despite the brilliant sun. My hands were slippery with perspiration and stiff with cramp. I had held that wheel in a death grip all the way from Rome. But I had made it—so far. If someone had told me three months ago that I would be in the hills above Florence, Italy, after driving a rental car all those miles from Rome, I would have laughed—and laughed, and gone on laughing till a nurse came and gave me a shot.

It had happened, more times than I cared to remember. Even now I wasn't sure what had shaken me up and out of what Aunt Mary called "Kathy's high-priced crazy house." Dear, tactful Aunt Mary. Nobody in our family had ever had a nervous breakdown. Only weaklings had nervous breakdowns. That was how Aunt Mary referred to it; the newfangled jargon of psychiatry was not for her. Call it a crazy house or a nursing home or a psychiatric institution; call it a nervous breakdown or severe depression—or melancholia, as the Victorians did; it hurt just as much by any name.

Aunt Mary was smugly sure that it was her "down-to-earth, no-nonsense" lecture that had shamed me into getting my act together, after weeks of lolling around feeling sorry for myself. Dr. Hochstein took the credit for "curing" me with his new, advanced methods. Dr. Baldwin didn't think I was cured. "We haven't reached the root of the problem, Kathy. Four or five years of intensive psychotherapy. . . ." Baldwin and Hochstein belonged to opposing schools—Baldwin the traditionalist, Hochstein a firm believer in encounter therapy: Never mind what caused the problem, face it and learn to deal with it. Theoretically I've nothing against that approach, but the application of it in my case almost killed me. The first time Hochstein got me into a car I just sat there behind the wheel and sobbed till he let me get out. The second and third times weren't much better. I hated Dr. Hochstein, but it worked for me. I had just proved that it worked. Even in my carefree pre-breakdown driving career I'd have had qualms about driving on an Italian autostrada in a rented car.

I picked up the car at the airport outside Rome, avoiding the city traffic. But it had not been an easy drive. I had to concentrate fiercely on every movement I made and keep a close eye on the movements of other cars, all of which appeared to be driven by people even crazier than I was. I concentrated so hard I was able to forget, for minutes on end, the memory that haunted me—the bright-red Torino looking like a child's toy in the distance, spinning off the road, lifting in dreamlike, impossible flight before it dropped, down into the trees below. Then the sound, splitting the winter stillness, and the leaping column of flame and smoke.

I reached for my cigarettes. I'd quit smoking years ago, started again after . . . Baldwin protested. Baldwin didn't believe in crutches. When he lectured me about emphysema, heart trouble, lung cancer, I laughed and quoted Alfred E. Newman. What, me worry? Why should I worry, Dr. Baldwin? Who cares about heart trouble thirty years from now? The young lives are snuffed out too soon, mangled and crushed and burned. I saw it happen, Dr. Baldwin.

I moved so fast I bruised my knuckles getting out of the car. It was the only way I knew to stop that train of thought. Do something, anything, and do it fast.

I knew what I would see. I had read the brochures and seen the photographs. The view from the Piazzale is *the* view of Florence. But I didn't know it would be so beautiful. I couldn't see crumbling mortar or flaking paint. I didn't know the soft mist in which the city floated like the fairy land of Lyonnesse was auto exhaust. I wouldn't have believed it if someone had told me. It was not a real city, it was a legend suspended above the earth; Avalon, swathed in veils of cloud.

I hung over the parapet for a while playing tourist with the other tourists, trying to see how many landmarks I could identify. Brunelleschi's great dome, with Giotto's bell tower beside it; the slender crenellated tower of the Palazzo Vecchio and the spires of Santa Croce and the Bargello. The gentle curves of the Arno, gilded by sunlight, and the Ponte Vecchio.

The sinking sun furnished me with the excuse I had been unconsciously seeking. I couldn't walk into a house of strangers so late in the day—not on an errand like mine, at any rate. Given my obviously inadequate sense of direction, and the fact that I had only the vaguest idea where I was going, I was bound to get lost again—and again. It had been a wild idea anyway, to plunge in without some preliminary reconnaissance. I'd never have considered doing it if I had not been driven and possessed. Get it over with, get it done—a childish approach to a dreaded but necessary task. I wasn't a child. I was twenty-three, independent, self-supporting, and—relatively—sane. No matter what you say, Dr. Baldwin.

The city became more bewitching with every change of light. Shadows of mauve and lavender and opalescent gray dimmed the rooflines, and I reluctantly turned from the parapet and bade farewell to the two amiable Danish ladies with whom I had been playing "identify the monument."

"I have to find a place to stay," I explained.

The ladies were scandalized. "But, my dear, don't you have reservations?" one asked. "You should have made them in advance. Never travel without reservations."

If they weren't somebody's aunts, they should have been. Their lecture had the familiar ring, but I couldn't resent it. Their concern was too genuine. After they had done fussing at me they admitted that the less time I wasted discussing the problem the sooner I could get to work on it. They insisted on giving me the name and address of the *pensione* where they were staying. It was filled by the tour group of which they were members, but if I found myself in a bind I must come to them, they would think of something.

I had forgotten strangers could be so kind. "Strangers" was the key word; I'd had too much concentrated solicitude from my family, from my doctors—smothering me, imprisoning me in a muffling featherbed of concern. It's easier to accept favors from people you will never see again. Hello, good-bye, it's been nice knowing you. I thanked the Danish ladies and drove away, ready to face the horrors of Florentine traffic at what would have been rush hour back home and probably was here, too.

There is no such thing as rush hour. The traffic in Italian cities is horrendous all the time. I didn't exactly lose my way. I kept seeing things I recognized; it was like a family reunion where there are all those people you've encountered in old photograph albums—"Good Lord, that must be Cousin Jack!" "Good God, that's the Medici Palace!" But I didn't want the Medici Palace, I wanted a hotel. The first two I checked were full up. I was beginning to think I would have to sleep in the car or cast myself on the generous (in every sense of the word) bosoms of the Danish ladies when I got lost again, and this time lost was lucky. I had wandered away from the city center, past the University and San Marco, when I spotted the Grande Albergo San Marco e Stella di Firenze. It wasn't as big as its name—a narrow slit of a building squashed in between two massive piles of stone that might have been medieval palazzi or modern banks. In Florence it's hard to tell one from the other. As soon as I walked in the front door I knew it was my kind of place. Everything was red and white. Red walls and white trim in the lobby, white walls and red trim in the dining room visible through an arch to the right.

I rushed to the desk. "I'm double-parked," I gasped. "Have you got a room?"

The man behind the desk looked up from the magazine he was reading. Its cover depicted a mostly unclad female in the hot embrace of a masked man with a knife.

"For you, signorina, there is a room. All the rooms are yours. For one person or . . ." He paused. "For two?"

"I'll take anything. I'm double-parked—"

A delicate flick of his fingers dismissed the problem as unworthy of consideration. "If you expect a friend, you will want a room for two."

I was about to say I was not expecting a friend when I caught the dark eyes fixed on mine. He was barely a man—seventeen or eighteen at a guess, though his expression of weary cynicism would not have been out of place on an old roué. I hesitated.

Why did I hesitate? I wish I knew. There were several theories. Aunt Mary's is the simplest: "That girl is the worst liar I've ever met." Sister Ursula took a more charitable view, which was rather nice of Sister Ursula, since she had been fighting for twenty-some years to combat the varied vices of the tenth graders of Our Lady of Sorrows High School. It was an uphill fight, and might well have soured her outlook on life. A frown of perplexity wrinkling her smooth, pale brow, she would say, "I'm sure you don't intend to lie, Kathleen. You simply tell people what you think they expect, or want, to hear. But you must overcome this weakness—you really must. One of these days it will get you in serious trouble."

I tried. I really did, and I would like to believe that Sister Ursula's interpretation, not Aunt Mary's, was correct. Sometimes, though, I lied out of cowardice instead of kindness. My reply to the young man behind the desk was compounded of both elements. He so wanted me to have a lover. He expected me to have a lover. And I was afraid that if I said I didn't have one, he would take it upon himself to supply the missing necessity. It was so much easier to say, "My friend has been delayed. For tonight, a single room."

"Delayed? Not coming?"

"Not till later."

"He is a foolish man."

"Thank you," I said, trying not to laugh. "You are very kind. Are you the manager, Mr.—?"

"Angelo. To you, signorina—Angelo. I am everything. I do all things, to learn the business of the hotel. Someday I will own my own hotel. Very fine, very expensive hotel."

After I had registered he carried my suitcase upstairs. The Grande Albergo had no lift, which may have accounted in part for my success in finding a room. Then he asked for my car keys, saying confidently but rather vaguely that he "knew a place." As I unpacked I wondered what other hats Angelo wore besides those of bellboy, desk clerk and car-park attendant.

He was also the waiter—the only waiter. The dining room was small, only six tables, but he was kept busy whizzing back and forth with aperitifs and the endless courses that constituted an Italian dinner. I guess the food wasn't particularly good—in fact I was soon to learn that it was not—but it was all new to me and I enjoyed it. After I had devoured spaghetti alla bolognese, scaloppine, salad, and crème caramel, and finished half a carafe of wine, I began to realize how tired I was. When I looked out my window and saw silver tinsel streaks of rain against the pane, my vague intention of taking a walk was forgotten. I fumbled out of my clothes and fell into bed, confident that tonight at least I would sleep.

I dreamed, of course, but this time I was lucky. I didn't remember the dream.

ii

It was still raining next morning. The streaks on the window weren't silvery tinsel now, they were just rain tracing paths through the dirt on the panes. I was worn out from dreaming and in no mood to face the crowd of twelve in the dining room, so I took advantage of the "service of the room" Angelo had proudly mentioned. "Press the bell, signorina," he had said, indicating the topmost of a row of buzzers next to the door. "And *ecco—la colazione.*"

The buzzers must have dated from an earlier era when hotels had larger staffs. There was one for a chambermaid, one for a porter, and one bafflingly designated *"tutti lavori."* I pressed the top button as directed, and *ecco,* breakfast duly arrived. Angelo, of course. He probably answered all the bells, including the one marked *"tutti lavori."* He gave my wash-and-wear robe a hurried and conventional leer—obviously part of the service. "What hours do you work?" I asked, genuinely curious, as he deposited the napkin-covered tray on a table.

Angelo came to a dead halt. He didn't do any of the obvious things that betoken surprise—roll his eyes or purse his lips or wrinkle his brow—but I could see he was stunned by the question "Hours?" he said.

"Thank you, Angelo."

"Prego, signorina."

The food was foreign enough to tempt my appetite. Two steaming pots, one of coffee and one of milk; rolls hard as a rock on the outside, but silky soft within; strawberry jam thick as glue, and excellent sweet butter. There was also a glass of canned orange juice, as a concession to American tastes. I enjoyed it, even the canned juice, but I was impatient to be on my way. If the sun had been shining I might have been tempted to put off my errand a little longer and play tourist, see some of the sights I had looked forward to seeing under far different circumstances. But if matters went as I expected, I would have plenty of time for sightseeing later. She might refuse to speak to me. I had not been able to reach her by phone. Extracting an unlisted number from Information in a foreign city may not be literally impossible, but it was a complication I had not been able to cope with. She hadn't answered my letters. That in itself suggested that she was unable to face the truth, or that she preferred to have no dealings with a lunatic American. Admittedly, the letters had not been very coherent. Yet I could not dismiss the possibility, however remote, that the mail had gone astray. That she didn't know. I had to make one last effort, for my sake as well as hers.

It was Angelo the omniscient and indispensable who gave me the directions. If I'd stopped to think sensibly I would have realized I could never find the place on my own. I had not been thinking. I had been reacting to stimuli like an animal whose brain is wired to electrical probes.

When Angelo finally replaced the telephone after a long and unintelligible conversation, he appeared slightly perturbed. "Why do you go there, signorina? Is it to look for your friend?"

This time I was not tempted to slake Angelo's thirst for romance. I said wryly, "I don't expect to find a friend, no. It's something I have to do."

"It is very far, signorina. Very hard to find. Stay here. See the beautiful city. I give you a better room, a cheap rate, not expensive. And if you are lonely—"

"That's kind of you. Later, perhaps. You understand, Angelo. It's a job I must do—like all the work you are doing now so that someday you can own your own hotel. How do I get there?"

It wasn't so very far. It might indeed prove difficult to find—I was dismally aware of the fact that maps don't show the complications of actual landscape—but Angelo's directions were clear and concise. I didn't ask him why he had tried to dissuade me. Perhaps if I had . . . But it wouldn't have made any difference, in the end.

I told him to hold my room, that I'd be back. I left my suitcase. If, against all my expectations, she asked me to stay, I would politely decline. This was not a sentimental journey or an attempt to forge lasting ties. It was a dirty job that had to be done before I could get on with my life.

I made one detour before I left Florence. It had stopped raining, but the skies were still a muddy gray, and in the dull light the building looked more like a prison than a palazzo. It presented a frowning face to the passerby; the stones of the wall were rough-hewn rectangles, the windows on the street level were barred by iron grilles. Hard to imagine anyone actually living there—eating and drinking, sweeping floors, playing. . . . It was now a bank. I wasn't tempted to go in. I double-parked for a few minutes, ignoring the infuriated bleats of cars trying to get around me in the narrow street, remembering what Bart had said.

"The palazzo was sold years ago, along with practically everything else that could be turned into cash. If you married me for my money, *cara,* you made a bad mistake. The only thing my profligate grandfather managed to hang on to was the villa. That's where I grew up—an innocent little nobleman in the hills of Tuscany."

And that is where I was going now—to the Villa Morandini in the Tuscan hills where Bart had spent his childhood, to tell his grandmother he was dead.

iii

After my pilgrimage to the former Palazzo Morandini I headed out of town. I made several wrong turns, not because Angelo's directions were faulty, but because I kept finding myself in situations where I couldn't follow them, blocked into the wrong lane by streaming traffic. It took a long time to get out of the city, whose ancient boundaries had now stretched far out into the valley and up the surrounding hills. The outskirts were as unsightly as those of any American city—rows of drab little houses and cheap shops, industrial areas, garages and warehouses. Even after I passed Fiesole and headed north toward the mountains the view was less than inspiring. Patchy fog blurred the higher peaks, and the slopes were bleak and bare. It was a far cry from the sunny, pastoral landscape described in the guidebooks. No teams of white oxen moving in slow dignity across the plowed fields, no vines spreading green ribbons along the curve of the hills, not even a castle crowning a ridge. Bart had warned me; I remembered his snort of contemptuous laughter when I read one of the more fulsome passages aloud. "Better rid yourself of those romantic illusions. You'll see more television antennas than medieval towers and more cheap houses than castles."

The weather matched my state of mind, and my state of mind reflected the weather: gray, all gray, without a ray of light. On the seat beside me was my purse, a brown plastic shoulder bag, shabby and worn like everything else I owned, including my thoughts. Under my raincoat I was wearing the only new outfit I had bought in months—a tailored brown suit whose only virtue was the fact that it didn't hang as loosely on me as my other clothes. The color was all wrong—not the soft, warm russet that matched my eyes, but a drab, dead gray-brown that stripped the color from my face. It was my grudging version of mourning, my halfhearted concession to what she would consider proper. Unsatisfactory, like most compromises; I might as well have bought black and been done with it.

In my purse was a magic potion that could brighten the clouds, and cast a rosy glow of false serenity over the dullness of my thoughts. I had sworn I wasn't going to take any more tranquilizers. Better cigarettes than Valium, I told Baldwin. If cigarettes kill me, at least I'll know I'm dying. I had brought the medication with me, though. If the interview was as painful as I expected, I might succumb. Cheer up, I told myself. It can't be any worse than you expect. Forewarned is forearmed.

I have a sizable collection of tired old clichés. I should have remembered another one: The worst is yet to come.

When I reached the little village of Sanseverino I

stopped to ask directions, as Angelo had suggested. The villa was only a few miles away, but he had not been certain of its precise location. The village was very small. It was the first place I had seen since leaving Florence that resembled my idea of a picturesque Italian town. Small stone houses, a central plaza with a sculptured fountain, now dry except for the drizzling rain—and those inevitable signs of modern life, a red sign admonishing the reader to *"bevete Coca-Cola,"* and a garage with two gas pumps.

There must have been someone in Sanseverino who spoke English but he wasn't working at the garage. The young man who filled my gas tank and tried to tell me where I was going was dressed like an American teenager, in tight jeans and a crumpled khaki shirt. A combination of vigorous gestures, sketches on the back of my map, and a miscellaneous assortment of unconnected words finally got the idea across—at least I thought so, until I drove off and he began yelling and waving his arms, pointing in the opposite direction.

That difficulty having been overcome and the village having been left behind, I looked for the side road the young man had mentioned. *Tre chilometri* past the last house. . . . I almost missed it. The road hardly looked wide enough for two cars, even Fiats, and the entrance was overhung by an enormous oak. The branches scraped taloned twigs across the top of the car as I made a sharp right turn into the lane.

Trees and shrubs on either side cut off my view, but I could tell I was climbing at a steep angle, with abrupt curves to complicate steering. After a while the road's surface dropped, with steep banks on either side. Through the tangle of vines and brush I caught occasional glimpses of brick walls, barriers no more impenetrable than the thorny tangle that had almost enveloped them. If these were the walls of the grounds belonging to the villa, the estate was more extensive than I had supposed from Bart's casual references to the declining family fortunes.

The road was paved, but the surface had deteriorated badly and I was forced to shift down. After a while the steep slope leveled out and the brush on the right-hand side of the road became sparser. The wall was so high I could see nothing above it except clouds and fog, but I thought I must be approaching the entrance. Before long a gatepost emerged from the mist. It was surmounted by a lump of stone that might once have been a sculptured heraldic figure. Beyond it was a pair of ornate wrought-iron gates.

There was enough space in front of the gates for me to pull off the road. The small building beyond them must be the porter's lodge; half hidden by overgrown rhododendron and the branches of overhanging trees, it resembled the witch's cottage in a German fairy tale. The witch did not appear to be at home. A graveled drive curved away from the gates and to all intents and purposes disappeared ten feet away; it was closely lined on both sides by the tall, elegant spires of cypresses, alternating with a lower, shrubbier deciduous tree.

I got out of the car. The gates were immovable. They didn't even creak when I pushed at them. The only visible means of communication with the regions beyond was a rusted button which, when pressed, gave off no sound whatever. I tried yelling. "Hey! Anybody home?" I sounded the horn. I banged on the smaller gate, designed for pedestrians.

There was no response, no sound at all except the drip of water from the branches and the muted chirping of a bird high in one of the cypresses. I got back in the car and lit a cigarette while I considered my next move. I couldn't go through this again. It was now or never, and I wanted it to be now.

It might be never, though, if the villa was as empty of occupation as it appeared to be. Just because it still belonged to the Morandinis didn't mean any of the family were in residence. Bart had not mentioned brothers or sisters, cousins, aunts or uncles; my impression was that he and his grandmother were the last of the family. An old woman might not want to stay in such a remote place. She might be in a nursing home or a hospital. That would explain why she had never answered my letters.

I was on the verge of abandoning the quest when I heard someone coming. Footsteps crunched on gravel beyond the point where the drive curved out of sight. The humid, hushed air distorted the sound in a peculiar fashion, suggesting the approach of something extraordinarily large and heavy, a wild animal rather than a human being. Which was nonsense, of course. I got out of the car and went to the gate.

A man came into view between the trees. He was big enough, over six feet tall and built like a fullback—thick-bodied and muscular, with shoulders like matching boulders and a bullet head sitting squarely on them, with no sign of a neck. He wore dark, shabby clothing and a cap pulled down over his forehead; he carried a thick stick, with which he slashed at branches and weeds as he walked. It was not until he came out from under the trees, into the open space beyond the gates, that I could see his features clearly. They only increased the impression of brutal, formidable strength. His nose looked as if it had been broken and improperly set; it sprawled sideways, overshadowing his coarse lips.

When he saw me, the scowl that had darkened his face changed to an expression I liked even less. He tossed the stick aside. I stepped back as he came toward me, his walk now a slow, sensual swagger. His eyes moved from my face to my feet and back again. I didn't understand what he said. The words might have been in another language than Italian, a harsher, more guttural tongue.

I had prepared a few phrases. *"La contessa Morandini—è a casa?"*

"Sì." I knew that word. It was accompanied by the universal affirmative nod and by a grimace that might have been a smile. But instead of moving to open the gate he just stood there staring at me.

I tried again, with phrase number two. *"Io desidererei vederla."*

The sentence came out of an old Italian phrase book, and I'm sure my pronunciation was all wrong; but he knew what I wanted. His smile became even more offensive. He shook his head, and his lifted forefinger, slowly from side to side. *"No, signorina. La contessa—no.* Would you like to see me? Would you like . . ."

He spoke slowly and simply, as if to a child, using the same words I had used. The only word whose meaning I didn't know was the verb of the last sentence; but his gesture made it perfectly clear.

Every woman, young or old, homely or pretty, who has lived in a large city for any length of time has heard suggestions of that nature. You never really get used to them. You never get over wishing you could reply by heaving a rock at the appropriate part of the speaker's anatomy. But you soon learn that an indignant response only invites more of the same, as in an obscene phone call, and you cultivate an appearance, at least, of cold indifference.

I had not expected it here. The man was a servant in the contessa's employ. What sort of household was this, where the porter felt free to insult his mistress's visitors? I felt the hot color rising to my cheeks. The man laughed hoarsely and embellished his invitation with graphic gestures.

When he started toward the small side gate, I retreated with more haste than dignity and got into the car. I couldn't believe he would actually do anything—but he had already behaved in a way I wouldn't have believed possible, and it was a lonely spot. As I backed out, I saw he was leaning against the gate, convulsed with laughter.

I was so furious and so anxious to get away that I drove blindly on, in the direction in which I'd been going. Another half mile or so brought me to the top of the hill or ridge I had ascended, and, as my temper cooled, I realized I should have gone back the way I came. I had seen no houses or driveways. If this was a private road, leading to a dead end, I would have to turn around.

Before long, however, the road began to descend and a series of tight curves brought me out of the trees. Below lay a valley dotted with houses and farms. It was a through road. I could get directions in the village a few miles ahead.

But I didn't. As soon as I reached a place where I could turn I went back.

I had to give it one more try. Surely the contessa was unaware of her servant's behavior. He had said she was there. Was she alone, with only that animal to care for her? I had heard of old people, friendless and neglected, who were victimized by unscrupulous servants. Could that be the case here?

Over the months a picture of Bart's grandmother had taken shape in my imagination. From his comments about her I got the impression of a dignified aristocrat who commanded his respect as well as his love. She thought of herself as a strict disciplinarian, but as Bart had laughingly admitted, she spoiled him badly. He could always wheedle her out of the punishments she devised.

Another part of my mental picture was created by the word itself. My grandmother had a passion for aerobic dancing and for pizza (the correlation should be obvious), and her hair ranged from bright orange to jet-black, depending on her mood and her hairdresser; yet the Whistlerian image persisted when I thought of the Contessa Morandini. Recent developments had done nothing to dispel that image—a frail, white-haired old woman, swathed in black bombazine and widow's veils. I could see her sitting in her lonely room, rocking, while the slow, senile tears of old age dripped down on the knitting in her gnarled hands.

As I drove back along the rutted road I could feel it coming over me—the impulse my father described, with awful sarcasm, as "Saint Kathleen's holy mission of the week." He was a fine one to criticize, always handing out money to drunks and beggars, bringing home strays, both animal and human, if he thought they looked hungry. . . . All right, Pa, all right, I thought. But I can't just leave her there, until I'm sure she's safe.

I didn't want to approach the gates again. There must be another entrance. I thought I remembered seeing a gap in the brush, at the point where the wall ended or turned. When I reached it I saw a rough, weedy track leading away from the road, paralleling another section of the wall.

I pulled into the track and parked. It might have been meant for service or farm vehicles, but it hadn't been used recently; the sections that weren't covered by weeds were solid mud. It struck off across a stretch of pasture studded with rocks like raisins in a pudding. A sharp wind rattled the dried stalks of last year's weeds. I slung my purse over my shoulder and put my hands in my pockets. Who brings mittens to sunny Italy? Not me. Apparently yester-day's lovely weather had been an unseasonable fluke.

I started slogging down the track. Before I had gone far my feet were soaking wet. Over the wall I could see the tops of trees, but there was no sound and no sign of life. I made a right-angle turn, still following the wall, before I found what I wanted—not a gate, but a section where the bricks had crumbled and fallen. They had fallen outward, forming a rough ramp, up which I scrambled.

At first all I could see was a jungle of tangled branches. I made more noise than I would have liked pushing through them, but in a way I was glad to hear some sound except my own breathing. The place felt like a cemetery. When I got out of the trees I found myself in an enclosed space that had once been a formal garden. I had a hard time finding the way out; if there had been paths or walks, they were buried under the sod. The next ex-garden was larger, and just as disheveled. The next—and the next. . . .

I had only the vaguest idea of what the grounds of a big estate were supposed to look like; this wasn't anything like any of my ideas. There were no sweeping terraces or pools or stretches of lawn, only a maze of enclosed spaces like ceilingless rooms. One had been a topiary garden, its shrubs clipped into the shapes of animals or mythological creatures. They had not been trimmed for a long time. Sometimes it was possible to guess at the original form; the distortions created by new growth made them appear even more monstrous than they had been at first.

At long last I located a gate leading to a space that was comparatively open. The graveled walks were weedy and the shrubs were overgrown, but compared to the jungles I had traversed this area showed signs of recent tending. The shrubs were azaleas and rhododendron; the fresh green of the new leaves pushed impatiently at the old, winter-browned foliage. I started down one of the paths and then froze as a voice cried out in sharp tones. Something whizzed through the air straight at me. Instinctively I put up my hands.

iv

What do you do when you see a big, brown, roughly spherical object hurtling toward you? There is only one sensible answer, especially if you are trespassing. You duck. But if you had two older brothers, both of whom aspired to be quarterbacks, you hear words echoing down the corridors of time—"Get out for that pass, Kathy!"—and you catch the thing.

It *was* a football. My old instincts had recognized it, even before my hands cradled it. It wasn't until I actually held it that the full, Alice-in-Wonderland unlikelihood of the event struck me. I sat down with a thud, hugging the ball to my stomach. ("Don't let go till you hear the whistle, dummy, the other guy's gonna try and strip the ball. . . .")

A child emerged from behind a bush and trotted toward me. He could not have been more than ten, and he looked younger. He was trying not to grin, and not succeeding. "That was a hard one! If I saw you were only a girl I would not have throwed it so hard."

I gaped at him. He wasn't American, despite that semi-spiral pass. His English was stilted and accented, his clothes not just European but old-style European. The ubiquitous blue jeans have conquered the world; but this youngster wore gray flannel shorts, knee socks, and a gray pullover. He needed to wear brighter colors. His skin was sallow. He was too thin. But that wasn't why I stared. He had tumbled dark hair, a thin, sensitive mouth—and eyes of pale silver-gray, the pupils theatrically dark against the irises—eyes fringed with lashes so long and thick and black he looked made up.

Bart's eyes.

His smile faded. "Did I hurt you? You catched it good, for a girl."

I got my breath back. "It was a hard throw. Wow!"

He squatted down beside me. "You have the good hands," he said graciously, and then, with sudden anxiety, "It is right? The good hands?"

"It's the right phrase," I said, laughing. "But my brothers wouldn't agree with you. Butterfingers Malone, they called me. I guess it was a lucky catch."

"Will you catch another?" he asked hopefully.

"Sure. Just wait a minute, I'm a little out of breath."

"Sit on the bench and rest." He helped me up with an old-fashioned courtesy that matched his clothes. He sat down beside me. "I am Pete," he said with an air of defiance.

I gave him my hand, and the football. "I'm Kathy. Pete? That's a good name, but I'd have thought it would be Pietro, for an Italian gentleman."

"I am only half Italian. The other half is American."

"Which half?" I asked, smiling.

"My mother."

I'm not sure how I knew. Maybe it was the way he avoided using a verb—past or present. Maybe it was the way his thick lashes dropped, veiling his eyes.

"And your father?" I asked after a moment. I didn't use a verb either.

"I lived in America for a year," he said evasively.

"Was that where you learned to play football?"

"Yes. Where did you learn? I thought girls did not play."

I told him about Jim and Michael. "They spent all their spare time practicing, from August to December, and when they couldn't get anybody else, they made me play receiver. I was only too happy to oblige; usually they complained when I tagged along. Luckily for me, neither of them wanted to be a linebacker."

He had to think about that one. Then his lips parted in a tentative smile. "To tackle you, you mean. That would hurt, yes."

"Yes."

"I knew you were American," the boy said, swinging his legs. "From the way you caught the ball. No Italian girl could do it."

Feeling it necessary to defend my sex, I said, "Football is an American game. I'll bet a lot of Italian girls can play soccer."

His eyes lit up. "I'll bet. I'll bet . . . I had forgot that. It is a good word. Like 'right on' and 'baad, man.' "

Last year's slang. I didn't want to ask him outright how long ago he had been in America. There was something wrong about his parents—his mother certainly, perhaps his father too. I thought I was safe when I said, "Your English is very good. You must speak it often."

But I made a mistake there, too. His lashes again veiled his eyes. "They do not let me talk English. *'Sempre italiano, Pietro; non parlare inglese.'* " He slid down from the bench, the football extended invitingly. "Will you catch it again? Are you rested now?"

I had actually forgotten how I got there and why I was there. I said with a sigh, "Pete, I wish I could. But I have no right to be here. I climbed the wall. I'm trespassing."

"I thought so," he said coolly. "It is lucky you came here. They do not let the dog here because it is my place."

"The dog? What kind of dog?" I asked apprehensively.

He didn't know the breed, but he measured the dog with his hands. *This* long—*this* high—black, all black, with teeth *this* big. . . . He was right, it was lucky for me I had not met the dog. I got to my feet.

"Well, I'd better go and make my apologies. I came to see the contessa. Is she at home, do you know?"

"I think yes. If you go there—" He pointed to a gate at the far end of the garden. "It leads to the door of the kitchen. You don't mind, to go to the door of the kitchen?"

"Not at all," I said, smiling at the apologetic face looking up at me. "Any door is fine so long as it doesn't lead to the dog's run."

"It is the way I come, so the dog is not there. I would go with you, but I must play for one hour. That is the rule." He glanced at his wristwatch. "It will be twenty minutes more."

I reassured him, resisting the urge to give him a hug or call him honey, or any of the other awful things a boy his age would bitterly resent. He was a darling; those odd, old-fashioned manners in a frustrated football player. . . . I looked back when I reached the gate and saw him standing watching me, the ball cradled in his arms. I smiled and waved before I closed the gate.

Every house, no matter how grand, needs certain humble adjuncts. Garbage is garbage and mops and brooms have to stand somewhere. The path I followed between rows of green sprouts that would one day be peas and carrots, onions and lettuce, led to a paved courtyard with a variety of homely objects scattered around—buckets, rakes, mops, and empty boxes. This wing of the house was humble enough—low-roofed and sprawling, its walls a mosaic of peeling stucco and rough brick. The sun broke through the clouds as I stood there, trying to summon the courage to proceed.

I knocked on the door. My hand was still lifted when the door was flung open by a stout gray-haired woman wearing an apron. Finding my knuckles six inches from her nose unnerved her for a moment; then her alarmed expression turned to a broad, amused grin. My halting apologies only increased her amusement. She replied, but of course I didn't understand a word; I only noticed that her accent sounded softer and more musical than that of the man at the gate.

I produced my memorized sentence. *"La contessa Morandini—io desidererei vederla."* Then I presented my card.

Heaven only knows what I had had in mind when I ordered those cards. They were five years old if they were a day, the product of some long-forgotten adolescent whimsy. I had found the dusty, dog-eared packet a few days before I left for Italy and had put it in my purse. I suppose I had some vague idea that a calling card would increase my aura of respectability. When you call upon a countess—an elderly, European countess—a countess who has never so much as acknowledged the fact of your existence—every little bit helps.

Naturally I had anticipated handing the card to the proper servant at the front door. If I had not been so rattled I'd have revised my plan; for a trespasser who has climbed over a wall to present a visiting card to the cook was nothing less than ludicrous.

The cook wasn't amused. She was flabbergasted. She finally took the card, holding it by the edge as if it might explode any second, and gestured at me to come in.

The kitchen was big and low-ceilinged, with a floor of

red tile. The world's fussiest housekeeper (my mother) couldn't have found fault with it—spotlessly clean, filled with delectable odors from the pots bubbling on the stove. Yet it had an indefinable air of desolation, perhaps because there were only two people occupying a space designed for many times that number. A young girl, slim and black-haired, stood at the sink scrubbing vegetables. She stared at me over her shoulder, her eyes wide with curiosity. The cook turned my card over and over in her fingers; this was a situation she had never encountered, and she didn't know the proper procedure. Finally she shrugged and indicated one of the chairs at a long wooden table. I shook my head, smiling. Again she shrugged, studied the card, and plodded out of the room.

The minutes stretched on. I wished I had had the sense to sit down. I felt like a fool standing there, my hands primly clasped, my feet primly together. The girl at the sink kept glancing at me and giggling. She'd have been the scullery maid in the days when houses like this had dozens of servants. Instead of a uniform she wore a tight skirt that hugged her rounded bottom and a knit blouse that was even tighter. I smiled at her and said, *"Buon giorno,"* and her giggles expanded into a high-pitched laugh.

On the back of the card I had written, "I must see you. It is about your grandson." Eloquent it was not, but it was brief and to the point. By the time the cook returned, I rather hoped she would open the back door and show me out. Instead she beckoned me to follow her.

My heels clicked on bare boards and then were muffled by carpeting before they clicked again, more sharply, on marble. That was all I remembered afterward—the sound of my footsteps, like drumbeats tapping. I could not have described the rooms or corridors or furniture; my heart was pounding and my stomach wasn't too steady either. I expected the cook would hand me over to a butler or footman or parlormaid, but she led me across the marble floor—acres of it—to a door, and threw it open.

I walked into a blaze of sunlight. It filled the room, with its gilded woodwork and white walls, like champagne in a crystal glass. I was too nervous to take in the details then; I saw only the woman seated at a desk near the French doors. She did not rise.

The mental picture I had formed shattered like a window hit by a stone. It isn't easy to guess people's ages these days, but I would have sworn she wasn't a day over forty. That most unflatteringly truthful of spotlights, the sun, fell full on her face. It was exquisitely made-up, but it takes more than makeup to hide the lines carved by years of living. There were no lines visible on her smooth forehead. Her hair was a marvelous shade of silvery copper and her eyes were gray—not silvery bright like Bart's, but darker, tarnished, like old mirrors.

I'm sure I looked as gauche and uncomfortable as I felt. Her lips curled slightly and she said, "You don't speak Italian, I suppose."

"No—I'm sorry. . . ."

"Then I must speak English, much as I dislike doing so. You wrote to me, not once but several times. You might have assumed, when you received no reply, that I had not the desire nor the intention of communicating with you."

I started to answer. She cut me off with a quick movement of her hand. "I did not suppose you would have the effrontery to appear in person. If you came here hoping for money, you will be disappointed. I don't intend to give you a penny. Have I made myself clear?"

"Very clear."

"Good." She turned and touched a bell sitting on the

desk. "No more need be said. Good-bye, Miss"—she glanced at the card she was holding—"Miss Malone."

My father used to say, "Us Malones take no lip from nobody." My father is six foot three. I'm ten inches shorter and a hundred pounds lighter, but so far as my father was concerned, size had nothing to do with it. I said, slowly and deliberately, "Not Miss Malone. Mrs. Morandini. I was your grandson's wife, Contessa."

She leaned back in her chair, fingertips together, face calm. There was no way of telling what effect, if any, my speech had had. Before I could elaborate, the door opened, in response to her ring. It was not the cook, but another woman, heavyset and swarthy, with a perceptible mustache and dead black hair. She glanced quickly, avidly, at me and then looked away.

The contessa spoke to her in Italian. She bowed her head respectfully and went out, giving me another of those quick, unsmiling stares. For some reason I had the impression that the contessa had changed her mind—that the order she had given the servant was not the one she had originally intended to give.

She said nothing to me. I didn't speak either. It was up to her to respond to my challenge. Indignation still boiled in me. I wanted to do something rude—delicately, aristocratically rude, to match her rotten manners. So I sat down, without being invited to do so, on a love seat covered in yellow brocade. It was horribly uncomfortable.

I think the gesture amused her. One arched eyebrow lifted just a trifle. I stared defiantly back at her and we sat like a pair of waxen images until the servant returned.

Pete was with her. I'd not have known him. His thin face was a sullen mask. When he saw me, his eyes lit up and the corners of his mouth quirked, the way Bart's did when he was trying not to smile.

The contessa didn't miss much. "I wondered how you had got in," she said conversationally. "I imagine, however, that you two have not been formally introduced. This is *il conte* Pietro Francesco Morandini. My grandson. My *only* grandson."

two

The weary contempt in her voice was not directed at me.
Her meaning was as plain as if she had spoken the words
aloud: This weakling, this half-barbarian, this insignificant
thing is all I have. And he isn't much, is he?

She was cruel, but not sadistic. She let the boy go,
dismissing him with a flick of her fingers. Another, deliberately more gracious gesture, sent the servant out of the
room after him.

"Well?" she said.

I stood up. "You needn't worry. You'll never see me or
hear from me again. I'm glad I came, if only to find out
what kind of family I have the pleasure of *not* belonging to.
I don't know why you are lying to me, and I don't care. I
married Bart—Bartolommeo Morandini—and we were together for six months before he was killed in a car accident. He told me his grandmother was the Contessa
Morandini. And," I added, "you have a photograph of him
on your desk. There. That's my husband. I don't think

much of your manners, or your morals, or your methods of raising children, but thank God none of those things are my concern. Good-bye."

"Wait." I was almost at the door when that one word cut the air like a whip. "I am beginning to believe you," she went on.

"Thanks so much."

"You do not wear a wedding ring."

"I put it in . . . in with Bart."

"Were you married in the Church?"

"In the . . . No. In a registry office in New Hampshire."

The wry twist of her lips dismissed this as unsuitable, almost illegal. "But you are Catholic?"

It was a reasonable guess, given the good old Irish name of Malone. It was also an impertinent question, by my standards. I said stiffly, "I was raised in the Church."

She studied me thoughtfully. Then she said, "Bartolommeo's mother was my sister-in-law. My husband's sister."

That was when I realized that my increasing queasiness was not caused solely by emotional factors. Change of water, change of air, the milk at breakfast, maybe . . . I must have turned a shade greener, for she said quickly, "You had better sit down."

I had to fumble for the chair. "I'm sorry," I said, swallowing. "I don't feel very . . . Your nephew. Then why did he tell me—"

"He often used the Morandini name. It was not his own, of course. His father was a commoner—a Milanese physician. He was incapable of understanding a child like Bartolommeo. The boy came to me after his mother died. I raised him."

There was no sign of softening in her face or voice when she said that. I wondered why, if she had served as his foster mother, Bart had not claimed to be her son instead of her grandson. Her statement—which, oddly, it never occurred to me to doubt—raised a number of other questions, but I was in no condition to wonder about them. I felt horribly sick. I stood up, hoping I could get outside the house before I threw up.

"Thank you, I'm sorry to have bothered you. Goodbye."

All at once she was beside me, holding me with hard, cold hands that did not so much support as confine me. "Wait," she said again. "Wait. A civil ceremony, but . . . Is it possible? Did you come here because. . . . Tell me the truth. Are you enceinte?"

I could claim the question dealt my reeling brain the final blow that toppled it over into catatonia. But the answer did not require profound thought or elaborate explanations. It required one single, two-letter word. I didn't say it. Something had awakened in the contessa's gray eyes, like an image dimly seen in a dusty mirror. But that wasn't why I let her believe a lie. To respond to that shadowy awakening as I did was not kindness, it was wanton cruelty. If I were superstitious. . . . But I'm not.

Ten minutes later I was lying in a bed the size of a football field in a room the size of a grand ballroom. I was wearing one of the contessa's silk nightgowns, and she was holding my head while I was thoroughly and disgustingly sick.

ii

Some kinds of illness are romantic—consumption, for example. All the best tragic heroines have consumption. Some ailments have at least the dignity of being deadly.

Others are regarded as essentially comic. People always make jokes about seasickness. If I had sprained my ankle or been attacked by the dog; if I had been carried, pale and limp, to that elegant bedchamber—it would have been a fitting episode in one of the romance novels that are all the rage. Even if I had really suffered from what is loosely called morning sickness, as the contessa believed, my "interesting condition" would have glamorized the unpleasant effects. There was nothing glamorous, or romantic, or dignified about my affliction. I had been warned about it, and I knew what it was, and it wasn't one bit funny. I forgot about minor matters like dignity and good manners; I just wanted them to leave me alone so I could die in peace.

They finally did, after making me swallow some revolting stuff that looked and tasted like chalk, and may have been. I didn't die, but I fell asleep; and when I woke I felt much better.

The room wasn't quite as large as a ballroom, but it was big—about four times the size of the Malone living room. Heavy forest-green draperies shrouded the windows, and hangings of the same gloomy shade enclosed the head of the bed. A single lamp burned by the bed. Otherwise the room was as dark as midnight, but a thin finger of light stretching across the floor suggested that I had not slept very long.

For a while I lay still, enjoying the simple pleasure of not feeling sick. Then the full enormity of what I had done struck me. I owed my present position, swathed in silk and occupying what appeared to be the best bedroom in the house, to a lie. The contessa had not played Good Samaritan because I was ill. I had seen enough of her to feel sure she'd have pushed me ruthlessly out the door if she had not misinterpreted the cause of my illness. There was no excuse for what I had done—or rather, had refrained from doing. Even Sister Ursula's boundless charity could not excuse this.

I groaned. "Oh, God," I said aloud.

The dagger-slim streak of light widened. It came, not from the window, as I had supposed, but from the door. A voice said timidly, "Are you going to die?"

It was the first indication I had had that anybody was interested in me, sans embryo. I knew the voice. "Come in," I croaked.

He slid in like an eel, closed the door, and trotted to the bed. "I listened," he whispered. "They sent me to my room, but I listened. Did you throw out?"

"Up," I said automatically. "I'm afraid I did, Pete."

"Up."

"Sorry, I didn't mean to correct you."

"No. You tell me when I say it wrong. I must not forget." His voice rose. "I will not forget!"

I had heard that note in a child's voice before. I said casually, "I hope you won't, because it's great to be able to speak two languages. I wish I could. Tell you what; you teach me Italian, and I'll correct you when you go wrong with English. It'll be harder for you than for me."

His face lit up like a candle. "Are you not going away?"

"Well . . . I'll be here for a while, I guess. Till I stop throwing out."

He could laugh at himself; I suspected it was a rare quality in a Morandini. Then he sobered. "Is it in here"— he pointed—"that you hurt?"

"Right."

"Was it—it is that—I hit you there."

"The football?" I managed to laugh. "Oh, no, Pete, it wasn't that. What kind of receiver would I be if a ball in the midsection made me sick? My brothers would have kicked me off the team if I let a little thing like that bother me."

"Tell me about the brothers. Where do they play the football?"

I had to admit they weren't with the Raiders or the Redskins or even the Pats. It was a blow, but Pete took it bravely. We were deep in a discussion of last year's play-offs when the door opened, without a knock of warning. He flinched, literally and actually, one hand lifting as if to ward off a blow.

Standing in the doorway was the woman who had brought him to the sitting room. She had also helped put me to bed. The contessa had addressed her as Emilia.

She touched a switch and a light went on, somewhere in the galactic reaches of the ceiling. The boy had been sitting on the side of the bed. Now he shrank back into the shadow of the curtains, but the woman saw him and spoke to him in the same harshly accented Italian the man at the gate had used.

"She says for me to get off the bed," Pete whispered. "She says I should not be here."

"Tell her I want you to stay."

When he did so, the woman's scowl darkened. Her eyebrows had not been plucked within recorded history. Some of the hairs were so long they curled back on themselves, and others stood out like the antennae of an insect. She turned on her heel and marched out, leaving the door open.

The boy hastily got down off the bed. "She will bring the contessa. I go now."

I didn't try to detain him. I was feeling queasy again. "Come back and see me later, will you, Pete?"

"You want me?"

"I want you very much. Please."

"O-kay." As he spoke he was edging toward the door. "If I don't come, it is that they lock me in."

He heard the approaching footsteps before I did, and was out the door like a flash.

I lay back against the pillow, trying to control the rising tides of nausea and indignation. It would be foolish of me to overreact. Any boy that age needs discipline, and locking him in his room was a comparatively mild punishment. No doubt the contessa favored good, old-fashioned methods of child-rearing. I might not agree with those methods, but they did not constitute child abuse.

I had been teaching for three years. Not long—but long enough. If, in that length of time, a teacher hasn't caught on to the tricks of her students, she had better find another profession. I knew all the devious wiles the young devise to win sympathy. I knew there were usually—not always, usually—two sides to every question. So why did this situation bother me?

When the contessa appeared and I pleaded the culprit's case, she confounded me by agreeing that he should not be punished for disobedience. "I did not actually forbid him to see you," she said. "I did not suppose you would want him here."

I could believe that. She didn't want him. As she stood there by the bed, she looked as calm and perfect as a wax mannequin in the window of an expensive shop. The folds of her soft wool crepe dress fell in perfect symmetry around her perfect size-six body.

However, when I began making polite noises about getting out of her bed, her house, and her life, she responded with unexpected warmth. "We will discuss that tomorrow. Now you must rest. Call Emilia if you want anything. She understands English, though she speaks it poorly. You are better, I think, but you must not take unnecessary risks."

That was my second chance to set the matter straight. I could have done it then with a minimum of awkwardness—a casual reference to the hazards of travel. I smiled wanly and told her she was very kind.

Pete didn't come·back. I spent the rest of the day dozing, in between trips to the neatly appointed bathroom adjoining my room. Not surprisingly, I did not sleep soundly that night. I woke several times, thinking I had heard voices talking or laughing. But when I went to the door and opened it, there was no sound at all.

iii

My malady turned out to be one of those twenty-four-hour bugs. It lasted just long enough to encourage the contessa's delusion, and then cleared up as rapidly as it had begun. By noon the next day I felt fine. I wondered what she would think when the "morning sickness" didn't appear on schedule. Ah, well, these things are unpredictable.

To say that I had reached a conscious, considered decision about how to resolve the dilemma in which I found myself would not be strictly accurate. At some point I simply knew what I was going to do.

Nothing.

It wasn't my fault if the woman had jumped to the wrong conclusions. The purpose for which I had come to Italy was now accomplished, and if it had raised more questions than it had resolved, that was another problem—my problem. I only lie to other people; I'm reasonably honest with myself. I knew my real reason for visiting

Bart's childhood home had nothing to do with his aunt's needs.

I had known him such a short time. He was already fading, slipping back into a limbo of nonexistence. For weeks after he died I couldn't close my eyes without seeing his face, sharp-cut as a colored photograph. Now the image was only a featureless blur. I had never really accepted his death. That, said Dr. Baldwin pontifically, was one of my problems.

So I knew that. I knew what the other problems were. Unlike the patients in those super-psychology books, I had not solved the problem by identifying it. How I envied those patients, and their moment of truth: "Hey, that's right, Doc, my dad hit me on the head at nine-fourteen on the morning of December 10, 1965." Click, snap, crack, all the pieces whiz into place, and the patient is whole. I knew what had hit me; but there had been no click, snap, crack. Maybe here, in Bart's world, the pieces would start to fit together. That was why I had come—not to console a bereaved old woman, but to heal myself. Whether the visit had done any good remained to be seen. It would be a long time before I knew. But I had made the gesture, and now I could go. Once I got home, I would write the contessa and tell her about my miscarriage. I might even have the courage to tell her the truth.

One thing psychologists tell you is true—any decision, even a wrong decision, is better than none. I stood at the window of my palatial room that bright noontime, feeling an incredible surge of relief.

As if in approval the spring weather presented me with a seductive picture of what Italy had to offer. The sky was the soft, clear blue Fra Angelico used for the robes of his Madonnas, with a few plump clouds hovering like fluffy-winged cherubs. The surrounding hills, decked in young green, resembled one of those dreamy Tuscan landscapes that form the setting for so many paintings of the Cinque-cento. Cutting across the foreground was the wall enclos-ing the villa and its gardens. It should not have been there; nothing straight and geometric should have marred that scene of soft color and gentle rolling curves. In the garden below my window I could make out the pattern of formal beds and walks. Shrubs heavy with rose-pink and scarlet blossoms flung their boughs across the weedy, graveled paths. My windows were closed; Emilia probably had anti-quated ideas about the dangers of fresh air. I wrestled with the catch, opened the windows, and stepped out onto a small, iron-railed balcony.

Immediately below was a flagstoned terrace with a fountain at one end. The fountain was dry; in its center a winged figure, streaked with verdigris and bird droppings, stood on tiptoe, offering a bowl to some dead god.

I left the windows open and was about to turn back into the room when the shrubs at the far end of the garden shivered and shook. Through them came the man I had seen at the gate. He thrust the branches aside with a care-less sweep of the stick he was carrying; petals dropped, covering the ground with a silky pink carpet.

Dark clothes, black scowl on his face, gray cap pulled low over his brow, he was as unseemly in that gentle pastel garden as an ink stain on a Chinese watercolor. He seemed to be pulling something heavy and resistant; his left arm was stretched out behind him, and when I looked more closely I saw he was holding a heavy chain. He gave it a jerk and snapped out a word that sounded like an epithet rather than a command.

I had forgotten about the dog. It emerged from the low-hanging branches in a sudden rush, snarling. It was as big as a calf, all black except for a white patch on the chest.

The man struck it over the head with his stick. The dog stopped, cringing. Another blow; a harsh command; slowly, grudgingly, the animal dropped down and sat still. The handler's thick lips stretched in a smile. The next command must have been "Heel." He walked off, swinging his stick, and the dog fell in behind him. They crossed the garden, treading indiscriminately on gravel and on budding flowers, and passed out of sight.

I let my breath out. It had been a nasty little scene. The dog wasn't a Doberman, it was even bigger, with a massive chest and huge jaws. Had I but known such a creature lurked behind the wall I wouldn't have been so quick to climb over it.

But the man was worse than the dog. I had known a lot of dogs in my time; every stray in the neighborhood gravitated to our house, with or without assistance from Mike and Jim. "Hey, look, Ma, he followed me home." Many had been abandoned, some had been mistreated, a few nurtured a deep and justified suspicion of human beings, but after a few days of good food and kindness they had been slobbering all over us and trying to climb on our laps. I suppose there are some psychotic dogs, just as there are some psychotic people, but in general dogs (and people) aren't vicious unless they are consistently, thoroughly abused, over a long period of time. No doubt the human brute justified his behavior under the pretense of "training" the dog. It wasn't training, it was sadism, ugly and inexcusable.

I had been invited to lunch with the contessa—a formal invitation, written in a delicate, precise hand on notepaper bearing a gilt crest and delivered on a silver tray by Emilia. I'd have dressed up for the occasion if I had had anything appropriate, but I didn't—only the suit I had worn the day before. It had been sponged and pressed; my lingerie and blouse had been neatly laundered. Even my shoes had been shined—and they needed it. The nightgown I had been wearing obviously belonged to the contessa. She was about my size, but a few inches taller; I had to lift the trailing silken skirts when I walked. I had never seen clothes like hers except in windows of fancy shops in New York and Boston. According to Bart, the Morandinis were as poor as church mice, but I was beginning to suspect that "poor" was a relative term. Yet the grounds were untended, the staff inadequate for a place of this size. . . . It was an anomaly, and not the least of the ones that puzzled me.

After I got dressed I stood around waiting for someone to come and escort me to the presence. Nobody came, and after a while I got very bored. I had already inspected the room. It was interesting, like something in a museum. The bed was a magnificent piece of furniture, every inch of its surface carved into intricate patterns, including the posts. For all its splendor it was not very comfortable. The mattress was thin and hard, and a musty smell pervaded it. The dark-green hangings had been looped back, but the effect was rather like lying in a cave whose entrance was fringed with thick grass, a cave in which something had died long ago, leaving a ghostly aroma of decay. This might be the state bedroom, where a long line of counts had breathed their last. I wasn't sure of that, though. Villas and palaces were not my ambience; for all I knew, this could be a minor guest chamber reserved for spinster aunts and unmarried daughters.

The room appeared scantily furnished, but that may have been because it was so big. A huge armoire of heavy dark wood, summoning up Poesian images of hidden corpses—it was large enough to hold half a dozen unwanted wives; a couple of straight chairs with cushioned

seats and backs carved so vigorously a person couldn't
lean back in them; a single overstuffed chair, covered in
faded chintz; a Persian rug or two; a few tables; and a
desk-secretary inlaid in ivory—that was about it. The
bookcase section of the secretary actually contained books.
The glass doors were locked.

I was extremely bored by that time, or I wouldn't have
tried to open the glass doors. It was not polite to investigate cupboards and drawers in other people's houses. My
mother had drilled that into me at an early age, after she
took me to visit Aunt Mary and found me removing that
lady's long underwear from a drawer and festooning it
over the furniture. "Look but don't touch. . . ." No wonder I had not been an outstanding student. My juvenile
mind had been so stuffed with aphorisms and admoni-
tions, by a variety of mentors, there was no room left in it
for facts.

Finally I opened the door and looked timidly out. The
corridor was completely unfamiliar. I hadn't paid much
attention to my surroundings the day before, as I was
towed up the stairs and thrust into bed. I saw closed doors
and a few odds and ends of furniture, but no stairs. I went
looking for them.

I was lost before I had gone fifty feet. I'm good at
getting lost, but in this case there was some excuse. That
house was big. One door looked as if it might lead to a
landing and the stairs I wanted. But I had not gone far into
the regions beyond when I knew I was on the wrong track.
This part of the house seemed older than the rest; the
ceiling was lower, the windows were shuttered. It was very
quiet. I was about to turn back when I heard something
that stirred the hairs on the back of my neck—the sound
of someone laughing.

Impulsively I started forward. A door opened and

closed, and a moment later Emilia came around a turn in the corridor. She was carrying a tray covered with a white cloth. When she saw me, it shifted in her hands with a clash of china and silver. She recovered herself and hurried toward me, almost running.

She did know some English. She had not bothered using it before, but in that moment she found the words she wanted. "Go back—out from here! Go—now—quick, quick."

She kept on walking as she hissed the words, the tray held out in front of her like a weapon. I could have stood my ground, or tried to get past her, but either would have been awkward—and of course I had no business being there in the first place. I let her nudge me away. I must have imagined that laughter. It had only been an echo down the corridors of time. . . .

She was careful to close the door after we left the empty wing. Another gesture indicated the direction I was to follow. She stayed behind me, prodding me with the tray when I hesitated.

The route took us back to the corridor on which my room was located. A few feet farther on, beyond my door, was a wide landing flooded with light, and the stairs. I had gone in the wrong direction.

At this point Emilia decided it was safe to stop herding me away from the forbidden regions. She preceded me down the stairs. The surroundings began to look vaguely familiar. I had crossed that vast expanse of white marble the day before. This must be the entrance hall, and the door opposite the foot of the stairs, flanked by windows, must be the main entrance. The hall was shell-shaped, with fluted niches where plump nymphs cowered, trying to draw their scanty draperies around their nakedness. The effect was more pathetic than erotic. They looked cold. The temperature in the vast unheated room was arctic, and the icy whiteness of floor and walls made it feel even lower.

Then I saw something I had not noticed the other day on my trek from the kitchen across the back of the hall. Between the stairs and the front door an inlaid pattern had been set into the floor—the only color in the room, shockingly, vividly brilliant against the ice-white marble. In my proletarian ignorance I assumed the colored shapes were also of marble, natural or tinted, but as I was to learn, they were semiprecious stones. The deep blood-red of jasper, malachite green as summer, pink and yellow agate formed a spray of roses growing from a central stem. Each petal and leaf had been cut separately; the shading, from soft rose-pink to dark amethyst, created a stunningly realistic bouquet. Bart had given me red roses. . . . They must have had a meaning for him, beyond the conventional language of flowers—red roses for passion, for consummated love.

The door to the left of the stairs was the one I did remember; it led into the room where the contessa had received me. Emilia paused only long enough to deposit the tray on a carved chest before she opened the door and indicated I should enter.

A small table had been opened out and set with crystal and china. I decided I wasn't high-class enough to rate the dining room, or baronial hall, or whatever it was called, but in this I did my hostess an injustice. This was her favorite room, where she spent most of her time. After I had seen the rest of the house I sympathized with her choice. The huge formal *salones* were cold and dismal; most had been closed up, to save money and labor.

The contessa was seated on the brocade love seat leafing through a magazine. On the table before her were a decanter and two wineglasses. She greeted me with a cool smile that quickly changed to a look of concern. "Perhaps you should not have come downstairs. You are quite pale."

"Thank you, I feel fine." I had no intention of telling her what had upset me. It had been nothing more than an auditory hallucination—and not the first one, either. But, said a voice deep down in my mind: If there was no one there, why was Emilia carrying a tray of food?

"I'm afraid I got lost," I went on, squelching the inner voice. "I hope I haven't kept you waiting."

"Lost? Why didn't you ring? One of the servants would have come for you. They were waiting until you were ready."

The gulf between us was never more apparent than when it was illumined by a casual comment like that one. I had never thought of using the bellpull to summon a servant. It had not been too many generations since the Malones had been the ones who answered the bell. Instead of making me feel small and kind of humble, like Tigger, the thought amused me.

"Sorry," I said breezily.

Emilia poured wine like chilled winter sunlight into the glasses and offered them. I took one, with a gracious nod of thanks. The contessa might intimidate me, but I was damned if I was going to be bullied by the maid.

After Emilia had gone we exchanged polite pleasantries for a while. Then the conversation turned to a monologue, as the contessa described the vast antiquity, enormous nobility, and distinguished history of the house of Morandini. As I listened I began to get a feeling that I was missing something—some underlying assumption that colored all her remarks—but I didn't identify it until she said, "If you would prefer another room, that can of course be arranged. Or if there is anything you would like changed . . ."

Fortunately I had finished my wine. The glass slipped; I caught it just in time. "But you mustn't go to so much trouble," I blurted. "I have a room—at the Grande Albergo—"

"Alberto will bring your luggage."

"But—but I—"

"Naturally you will stay here. Bartolommeo's wife cannot stay at a hotel, even one called the Grande Albergo."

A smile touched her mouth as she pronounced the name. It was the first sign of genuine humor she had displayed, and I found it attractive. She added, "You must allow me to make amends for my rudeness. I was under a misapprehension."

I thought guiltily, you don't know the half of it, lady. But less than ever was I moved to confess the truth. The blunt, cruel words would have shattered the porcelain facade of her dignity like a rock tossed through a shop window. Call me coward, call me craven—I couldn't do it.

Without waiting for me to reply she pressed the bell. Emilia promptly appeared carrying a tray and began arranging dishes on the table. The tray was not the one she had been carrying when I first encountered her. It couldn't have been. The soup was still steaming hot.

Emilia served every dish, though the table was so small I could have reached across it. The contessa talked about the beauty of spring and the loveliness of the Tuscan countryside. She quoted Dante—I guess it was Dante. Not until Emilia had collected the dirty dishes and gone out with her tray did the contessa relax. She leaned back, crossed her legs, and lit a cigarette. I was surprised to see such a fastidious woman smoking, and I noticed, as her hands dealt neatly with a gold lighter and gold cigarette box, that those members at least showed signs of age. Veins squirmed like little blue worms across the backs of her hands.

Then she got down to practical matters. We started from the fact that I would be staying at the villa. I never got a chance to protest that basic theorem because I was too busy protesting the corollaries that followed it. Alberto would collect my luggage. . . . No, he wouldn't; thanks very much but I would rather do my own collecting. Alberto would pick me up after I had returned my car to the rental agency. . . . No, he wouldn't; thanks very much, but I preferred to keep the car. She didn't argue; instead she launched into a description of the villa's domestic arrangements. Apparently it had finally dawned on her that I was a barbarian who would have to be instructed in the proper behavior toward servants and other conveniences.

The staff consisted of six people. No wonder the house was closed up and the grounds untended; six people to do the work of forty! Emilia had the impressive title of housekeeper; she also acted as the contessa's personal maid, and I suspected this latter job took most of her time. Emilia's husband Alberto was chauffeur and "head" gardener. A local "half-wit"—the engaging term was the contessa's—was his assistant. The cook was Rosa, the *tuttofare* a local girl named Anna. The contessa didn't translate the second title. I knew just enough Italian to understand; the two words meant "to do everything," and it was an accurate description of a maid of all work. Except for a woman who came in periodically to do heavy cleaning, that was it.

My chief reaction was sympathy for the *tuttofare*. My ignorance of high living kept me from noticing one singular omission in that list. No one for the boy. No nurserymaid, governess, tutor, or nanny. It was some time before I thought of that. I assumed he attended the local school, and that he was too old to need a nurse.

Alberto and Emilia were not local people. They had come from Rome with the contessa when she married. That explained the strange harsh accent I had noticed. Florentine Italian is musical and beautiful; the Roman dialect is considered crude. Maybe so, but I imagined the unpleasant personalities of the pair did not improve the charm of their speech.

The scene I had viewed from my window came back to me, and I said, "I take it Alberto is the man in charge of the dog?"

My hostess glanced unobtrusively at her watch. "Thank you for reminding me. I have an appointment at my hairdresser and must leave shortly; but first you must meet the dog."

The dog got more respect than the servants—she hadn't suggested that I be introduced to them. I was not keen on meeting that dog, but if I had to meet him, I preferred to do so under formal conditions.

A tinkle of the bell brought Emilia, who received her mistress's instructions with a respectful nod and went out. After a few minutes the contessa took her gloves and bag from the desk and we went to the front door.

It was odd to go out a door I had never come in, and see the front of the house for the first time. It was big enough, but compared with the grim palaces of Florence it looked almost homey—if one may use such a word to describe a house that contained twenty or thirty bedrooms, not to mention innumerable reception rooms and *salones*. The facade was a simple rectangle of whitewashed stucco, accented by window frames and piers of the dark-gray stone called *pietra serena*. There were three stories above a high terrace reached by an ornate double staircase.

Open arches in the platform supporting the terrace gave access to a lower, ground-level floor that presumably contained the domestic offices. The huge red-brown pots lining the terrace held small shrubs and trees that might, when the season was farther advanced, put out leaves and flowers and fruit; but they didn't look especially healthy. Small statues alternated with the pots. At the foot of the stairs the drive widened into a semicircular expanse of gravel, with a fountain in the center and a statuary group in the center of the fountain. Bronze muscle men blew soundlessly into verdigrised shells and conches, or clutched coy mermaids to their metal chests. The fountain was dry. The sweep of grass that stretched down to a belt of trees in the far distance was in reasonably good condition and the flower beds had been weeded. I could see why Alberto and his assistant had no time for the rest of the estate. Keeping that four-acre stretch of turf mowed and the flowers weeded and watered was a full-time job in itself.

The car—a Mercedes, what else?—was waiting at the foot of the steps. Alberto had changed into a regular chauffeur's uniform. It didn't do much for his looks. The collar squeezed his bull neck and the buttons strained across his chest. In his polished boots and military jacket he looked like a retired storm trooper.

He held the dog's chain. When the animal saw me, it lunged forward. Alberto let it go the full length of the chain, grinning when I jumped back. The contessa snapped out an order, like a row of ice cubes. Alberto's smile disappeared. He practically genuflected, his manner as servile as that of the dog. He gathered up the chain and brought the animal to heel.

"Walk slowly toward him," the contessa directed me. "Hold out your hand and let him smell it."

I knew the procedure, but I had never seen a dog I was less anxious to try it on. When it was sitting, its head was on a level with my chest. The dog rumbled low in its throat as I sidled toward it. Alberto struck it across the face with the slack of the chain.

"Stop that!" I yelled.

The dog and Alberto appeared equally surprised. I crossed the remaining space in a few strides and thrust my hand at the dog's muzzle. "There, good boy, you're a nice dog. . . . You don't want to hurt anybody. . . ." In the same crooning voice I went on, "Alberto, old boy, I don't know how much English you understand, but I'll bet you know a little, and I am telling you right now to stop beating the dog. *Stupido, cretino,* don't *battere* the *cane.*"

I did not turn to observe the effect of this high-handed behavior on the contessa, but I thought I heard a murmur of musical laughter. Alberto looked black. He understood the insults, at any rate. The dog was not impressed. I let him have a good long smell—his sniffs sounded like an old train engine getting up steam—and dared to run my fingers gently under his jaw before I retreated.

"That man has no more idea how to train a dog than how to solve a differential equation," I said angrily. "Why do you let him—"

"He has his methods," the contessa said calmly. She gestured at Alberto, and he dragged the dog away. The contessa drew on her gloves. "I dine at eight," she said. "I hope you will join me at seven for a cocktail."

She strolled slowly down the stairs. As she reached the car, Alberto appeared out of nowhere in time to open the door for her. It reminded me of the old saying about Queen Victoria—that she never looked over her shoulder when she sat down, because she knew someone would always make sure she had a chair under her.

I watched the car glide smoothly down the drive and vanish into the trees. I felt exhausted, as if I had been trying to walk against a strong wind. I fancied the contessa usually got her way. Or had I yielded, not because she outfought me and won, but because I had not fought very hard?

I got my purse from my room—*my* room—and went in search of my car. Somewhat to my surprise, it was still where I had left it. I got in and headed for Florence.

The drive took almost an hour, long enough for me to think about what I was doing, and decide that what I was doing probably wasn't very nice. My parents would not approve. Sister Ursula certainly would not approve. Drs. Baldwin and Hochstein would disagree; they always did. The hell with Drs. Baldwin and Hochstein, I thought. I was sick of probing into my subconscious searching for motives. This decision *felt* right. It was only for a few days. She had not asked how long I could stay; I had not volunteered the information. If things got sticky, I would make my excuses and leave.

When I reached the Grande Albergo I double-parked in front of the door and went in. No one was at the desk. From the dining room came the clatter of utensils and the murmur of voices. It was still early, and Italians take long lunch hours, lingering over wine and coffee after polishing off their pasta. I was about to reach for my room key when Angelo came darting out of the dining room. He wore his waiter's white apron over his concierge suit, and he was carrying a Tower-of-Pisa stack of cups. Seeing me, he came to a dead halt and stared as if he had never seen me before.

I said, "I'm checking out. There's no hurry—I can see you're busy. I'm going to go up and pack. When you get a minute, could you make up my bill, please?"

"Ah." Angelo pondered. Then he put the cups down

and went behind the desk. Handing me my key, he said, "Your friend has come."

"My . . . Oh. No, I'm afraid not."

"You were not here last night," said Angelo. It was a simple statement of fact; the assumption was implicit, but not judgmental. Angelo made no judgments.

"I was at the villa," I explained. "The Villa Morandini— remember? I'll be staying there for a few days."

"Ah." Angelo thought this over. Then he said, "My brother is a policeman."

"That's nice," I said, wondering what on earth he was getting at.

"It was from him I found where the Villa Morandini is. He knows all, my brother. If your friend does not come, you would like my brother."

"I'm sure I would. But I don't think—"

"He is taller than I," said Angelo. "Taller than you. Very tall." He measured his brother's height with an out-stretched hand. If the measurements were accurate, his brother could have played basketball with any team in the States.

"I'm sure he is very tall and very handsome," I said. "And I'm very grateful to him for his help. I'll let you know, Angelo."

"Ah," said Angelo. Seemingly at random he plucked a sheet of paper from a drawer, scribbled on it, and thrust it at me. *"Il conto, signorina."*

We had a little discussion over the total. It seemed that the rates quoted on the card hanging on my closet door did not include astronomical local taxes, and a few other mysterious but (Angelo assured me) legal charges. I paid the bill and waved away the change. "Thanks for your help, Angelo. Is it all right if I leave my car here for a few hours?"

Angelo assured me I could leave the car anywhere I liked—in the street, in the lobby. "But do not put your suitcase in the car, signorina; leave it in the room, and I will bring it down and keep it at the desk. There are many thieves—many thieves. . . ." And, shaking his head sadly, he picked up the cups and rushed away.

It didn't take me long to pack. Angelo was nowhere in sight when I came down, so I hung my key back on its hook and went out into the street.

I had not intended to do any sightseeing, but in Florence you can't go far without seeing sights, whether you want to or not. I was ambling along, not thinking of anything in particular, when I turned a corner and suddenly found myself in front of the Duomo, with the great dome lifting over it as lightly as a hot-air balloon. I had dreamed of coming to Florence with Bart one day; I had pored over guidebooks and art books, so I knew what the monuments looked like. What they looked like, not what they really were. The reality was overwhelming.

Later, I came by accident on the church of Orsanmichele, with its enshrined, life-sized saints, and there was Saint George, his arm resting lightly on his shield, his head lifted, looking for the dragon. I had fallen in love with Saint George during an art history class. I felt like a groupie gaping at her favorite rock star. Even the bird droppings that whitened George's shoulders and handsome head did not mar his dignity.

Along the way I passed a bookshop. Among the books in the boxes in front of the store were a few in English, and I decided I had better get something to read. Long evenings with the contessa might seem very long indeed. Even if the villa had television, I wouldn't be able to understand the language, and although there was probably a

library—what great house is complete without a library?—
it wouldn't have much in the way of light English fiction.

I rummaged among the books, which had been tumbled haphazardly into the containers—secondhand paperbacks, dog-eared and in some cases missing their covers. It
was a funny assortment; the flotsam and jetsam of the
business, books nobody had wanted—a few mysteries, a
few science-fiction novels, quite a number of romances,
poetry, belles lettres. Among the latter was a copy of *The
Innocents Abroad.* My father was a great fan of Mark Twain;
he had tried to get me to read *The Innocents,* saying it was
one of the funniest books ever written. Naturally I had
refused to read it. Now I picked it up with the feeling that
it was a link, however remote, with home. I selected half a
dozen others, more or less at random.

Eventually I found my way into the Piazza della
Signoria. It was full of tourists and pigeons and fountains
and statues. The copy of Michelangelo's *David* was completely ringed in by tourists, some looking, some conscien-
tiously reading their guidebooks. There were souvenir
stalls all around, even under the beautiful medieval ar-
cades. Oddly enough, the garish banners and cheap copies
of *David* (made in Taiwan) didn't seem out of place. There
had always been crowds in the Piazza della Signoria, and
small tradesmen selling their wares. Yesterday cooking
pots and utensils; today, plastic Davids made in Taiwan.

When I sat down at a table at one of the outdoor cafés, I
had collected several parcels, a small guide to Florence,
and a handful of postcards. I wrote cards to several of my
coworkers: "Having a wonderful time, aren't you jealous?"

The family cards came next. My favorite (and so far,
only) niece couldn't read yet, but she might enjoy eating
the card. I sent one to her and another to her parents, Jim
and his cute wife; and another to Mike, living in bachelor

indigence in Boston. I addressed the last to Mr. and Mrs. Timothy Malone. Then I sat staring at the blank half of the card, my pen poised.

They hadn't wanted me to come. Pa had yelled and pounded on the table, as was his habit. The gist of his argument was, bury the past, forget it, and go on. Ma hadn't said much. It had offended her thrifty soul to see me blow the entire insurance settlement on a trip abroad. It was all Bart had left—the insurance on his car.

Pa never liked Bart. He was too suave, too well dressed, and far, far too handsome. He smiled too much, particularly when Pa asked questions that weren't meant to be funny, such as, "What do you do for a living?" Bart's answer—"As little as possible, Mr. Malone"—didn't go over too well. When I explained that Bart was trying to succeed in one of the most heartbreakingly competitive of all trades, and that establishing oneself as an actor took hard work, talent, *and* luck, my skeptical father just rolled his eyes and sniffed.

I thought I understood his skepticism and his hostility. It isn't easy for a father to give his only daughter, the baby of the family, to another man. And when the man is a stranger, and said baby daughter shows up married, without so much as a preliminary letter of announcement . . . I didn't blame my father for resenting that, but Bart had wanted it that way. I would have agreed if he had suggested we get married in diving suits, with Jacques Cousteau as best man.

I took a firmer grip on my pen and wrote, "It's beautiful here. Everything is fine and I'm having a wonderful time. Love . . ."

It was a cop-out. But what else could I say? I hadn't told the family I hoped to visit Bart's grandmother, as I then believed her to be. They knew he had been born in Italy and they assumed I was on a sentimental journey. That was all they knew. They didn't know Bart's "grandmother" was a countess. That would have finished it for my father. He was a violent egalitarian, and when he started ranting about decadent aristocrats he sounded like the French Revolution. To explain the situation I now found myself in, or even part of it, would have taken more space than half a postcard. And it was not the sort of story I wanted the postman to read. Jack Wilson always read postcards, especially cards from exotic foreign lands. Then he went and told everybody on his route.

Since my father had demanded I give him an address, I wrote down the Grande Albergo San Marco e Stella di Firenze. That took up the rest of the empty space on the card. I was sure Angelo would hold mail for me if I asked him to.

Yet I felt as if I had stopped in the middle of some task I ought to finish. I didn't push the little button that retracted the point of my ballpoint pen. Instead I took the notebook in which I keep addresses and memoranda and tore a couple of pages out of the back. I wrote for five minutes. Then I put the pages in my purse, paid for my espresso, and went on my way.

The sun lay warm and golden on the rooftops. The shops were reopening after the afternoon break. I had not meant to go shopping, but when I found myself in front of a window piled with gloves of all colors and materials, a bizarre impulse came over me, and I went in. According to the guidebook, gloves were one of the things one bought in Florence. I bought two pairs, one brown, one soft cream. I knew I'd probably never wear the cream-colored gloves. Once I got home I would wonder what the devil had prompted me to spend such an outlandish sum on them. But I knew they were a symbol; if the contessa got on my nerves, I would wear my gloves to luncheon next time.

Then the bug bit me and I wanted to buy everything I saw. Mosaic jewelry, straw bags, little wooden boxes, copies of statues and pieces of statues—David's head, David's hands—and other parts of David, meticulously reproduced. I was tempted to get one for Mike.

The only thing I did buy, besides the gloves, was an electronic football game, the kind that can be played by one or more people. It was beautifully crafted, and it cost the earth. I reminded myself that I was saving the cost of food and lodging—and then I remembered my hostess. I ought to get something for her. But what? The gloves I had bought, though more expensive than anything of the sort I had ever owned, weren't of the quality she was accustomed to wear. The truth was, I could not afford to buy her anything of the quality to which she was accustomed. The family fortunes may have declined, but she wore silk nighties trimmed with Valenciennes lace. Even the cigarettes she smoked had monograms and gold tips.

I wandered the streets trying to get an idea, but nothing seemed right for her. The flower market was intoxicating—big fluffy bunches of spring blossoms, pink and pale blue and dazzling yellow and purest white, smelling like heaven and looking like a sunrise. She had flowers—she probably had a greenhouse bursting with orchids. The vegetable market was even more colorful, but I could hardly carry back a bag of tomatoes or an eggplant. Jewelry, perfume, scarves, boxes, handkerchiefs . . . For all I knew, her handkerchiefs were hand-embroidered by particularly superior nuns at a particularly superior convent.

Finally I gave up the hunt. If a brilliant inspiration did not occur to me before I left, I would send her something quaintly plebeian from America when I got back. A copy of the Minute Man at Concord, made in Taiwan.

Angelo was behind the desk when I reached the hotel, reading what appeared to be the same page of the same magazine. His feet rested on my suitcase. I asked him about postage to the States. Not only did he know the amount, he had the stamps. After some searching in the drawers, he also produced an envelope. I put the pages I had written into the envelope and addressed it.

"Angelo, will you do me a favor? It's very important." I reinforced my request by handing over a wad of hundred-lire notes. "Ten days from now, if I don't come back and ask you for this letter, I want you to mail it. Ten days, okay? *Dieci.*" I held up ten fingers.

Angelo was afflicted with the momentary paralysis that struck him whenever he was caught by surprise. "Ten," he repeated, clearing his throat.

"Ten days. You promise?"

He put his hand on his heart and swore by something—I caught the word *madre,* and found that convincing. After he had carried my suitcase to the car, he stood on the step staring after me as I drove off.

I wondered what he was thinking. Did he take me for a spy or a blackmailer, or did he just think I was a little crazy, like all foreigners? *I* thought I was a little crazy. But accidents do happen, even to the young and healthy; no one knew that better than I. If something did happen—it wouldn't happen, but if it did—I did not want to vanish into infinity in the hills of Italy without telling them why I was there. Writing the letter was a catharsis in itself. I made a full confession, as Sister Ursula would have said—or, as my brother Mike would have put it, I spilled my guts out. I told them everything—things they had suspected but had never known, things they had not even suspected. Confession is good for the soul.

And then I gave the letter to Angelo. I knew if I took it with me, I'd get cold feet and tear it up.

Confession was not the only reason for the letter. The other reason was really crazy. Among the books I had bought was a little masterpiece called *Bride of the Madman*. The cover showed a girl running pell-mell down the side of a mountain. She was wearing a long white dress that in real life would have tripped her up before she had gone ten feet; and on the top of the mountain was an Italian villa, surrounded by cypresses. The artist could have used a picture of the Villa Morandini as a model.

I said, sneering, "Move over, Jane Eyre," and, with a defiant twist of the wheel, squeezed into the traffic approaching the bridge.

iv

The setting sun was at my back when I started up the road that led to the villa. I knew the way now, and it was the first time I had driven the road when I was relaxed, so I could appreciate how lovely it was—and how isolated. The lower slopes of the hills framing the Val d'Arno were thickly inhabited—old villas and modern suburbs, small farmhouses and vacation homes, surrounded by gardens and the beautiful, symmetrical cypresses. The small side road might have been in another country. The branches of the trees on either side almost met overhead; sunlight filtering through the new leaves cast flickering gold-green shadows across the car. If there was another house along the road it was invisible—not even a smoking chimney.

The gates were closed. As I glided to a stop, Alberto

trotted out of the lodge, tossing his cigarette aside, and opened the gates. He took his time about it, but when I drove through he touched his cap in a sketchy caricature of the salute that he gave his mistress. I put my nose in the air and ignored him. Perhaps he had not known who I was the first time I encountered him, but that didn't excuse his behavior. And I couldn't forget the way he treated the dog.

The front door opened as I approached. This time it was Emilia who did the honors, with even less enthusiasm than her husband. They made a fine pair, perfectly suited to one another. No wonder Alberto beat the dog. He wouldn't get far bullying Emilia; she was short, but as muscular as a man.

I asked her where I should put the car and she gave me the same look of contemptuous surprise with which the contessa had favored me when I admitted I had not thought of ringing for a servant. It was a look with which I was to become quite familiar. "Alberto will put away the car, signora."

I let her carry my suitcase upstairs, and gave her the car keys.

Now that the room was officially my room, my mother's prohibition no longer applied, so I investigated the drawers and the wardrobe. The doors of the wardrobe stuck when I pulled at them, but there weren't any bodies inside—not even a gown spotted with bloodstains, or a lock of woman's hair. The drawers of the dressing table were lined, rather prosaically, with sheets of *La Nazione,* the local newspaper. What, I thought—no scented, satin fabric? I put my three sets of underwear and my extra nightgown away, and hung my clothes in the wardrobe. They looked lonely, like orphan children in a cold world.

I was amused to learn that the doors of the bookcase had been unlocked; but a survey of the books made me glad I had thought to bring my own reading materials. They were all in Italian, and the most recent had a date of 1933. The added amenities also included a vase of narcissi and hyacinths on the dressing table, and a carafe of water.

Cocktails at seven, she had said. I hoped it was not as formal as it sounded; I hadn't brought the right clothes for a cocktail party. I changed into a cotton blouse and denim skirt and then, having an hour to kill, picked up *Bride of the Madman*. By the time the hour was up I wished the madman would go ahead and strangle the girl and get it over with. She deserved strangling. I tossed the book aside, gave my makeup a final check, and started downstairs.

The contessa was decked out in a long silk gown of a rare and wonderful shade that matched her hair—a blend of soft copper and shimmering silver. After the first critical look she politely ignored my cotton and denim, and when I stumbled, addressing her, she told me to call her Francesca. We dined formally that evening, in a room that made my mammoth bedroom look like a closet. The candles on the table formed an island of light amid a black sea of shadows. On the far-off ceiling was a painting—blue skies, clouds, hovering figures—gods, saints, cherubs, I couldn't tell at that distance. The table could have seated forty people. We huddled at one end, with Emilia serving course after interminable course. The food was superb and so was the wine. "Our label," said Francesca, when I commented.

I had not expected Pete to join us for cocktails, but when we entered the dining salon, in a solemn parade of two, I saw there were only two places set. Of course I had to ask. I got the look again. "Children in America dine with adults, I am told. I fear I am old-fashioned in that respect."

I wondered where Pete ate his dinner. In the kitchen with the cook? Alone in his room? I remembered family dinners when we were kids, still living at home—the boys arguing about fine points of hockey or football, and, as they got older, about politics; Pa yelling out his opinions, my mother correcting our table manners and trying to introduce nice, safe topics of conversation that wouldn't end in a fight. . . . A shiver ran through me. Francesca noticed it, and asked if I would like Emilia to fetch a wrap. I said, no, I was fine, and added, "Perhaps I could go up later and say good night to him. Or read, or play a game."

"Not tonight," said Francesca. "He has been sent early to bed. He did not finish his lessons."

We retired to her sitting room for coffee. Francesca took a piece of embroidery from a brocade bag and inquired whether I had had a pleasant afternoon.

I didn't mention the game I had bought for Pete because I was self-conscious about having nothing for her. I burbled on about the wonders of Florence and she listened with a faint, appreciative smile, as if I were praising one of her possessions. Before long I ran down, and there was a brief silence.

"I'm afraid evenings here are rather quiet," she said. "If you have handwork you would like to do . . . ?"

I had been admiring the flash of her needle as she flicked it deftly in and out of fabric as sheer as a cloud. When she made the suggestion I laughed out loud. My current project was a sweater for Mike. I had already ripped it out three times. She looked at me inquiringly, and I explained, "I'm all thumbs when it comes to handwork. It's very popular back home and all my friends do something—needlepoint or knitting or counted thread. I've tried them all, but I can't seem to get the hang of it."

"But surely you were convent-taught?"

Convent-taught? Our Lady of Sorrows? The sisters counted the year well spent if they got through with nobody pregnant or arrested for drug abuse. I thought of Sister Ursula banging on the desk with her pointer, and tried to picture her sitting in the middle of a circle of demure little maidens, their heads bent over an altar cloth. Imagination reeled.

"Not exactly," I said. "It wasn't like that."

"You ought to learn embroidery. It is a useful skill."

"I admire it; I just can't do it." I tried to see what she was working on. Daisies? White petals on white muslin, with twining stems and tendrils. . . .

"It is never too late to learn." She put her work down and reached into her bag. "Let me show you."

She threaded the needle with bright-red floss; the delicacy of white on white was obviously beyond me—and demonstrated the stitch. I was even clumsier than usual. I had finally identified what she was making. It was a long embroidered dress, like a christening gown, for a small baby.

v

Thank God for Mark Twain. The sight of that tiny white garment punctured my self-esteem and made me feel like a low, crawling worm. After I had excused myself and fled to my room I reached for a book—any book—anything to take my mind off my wickedness.

I couldn't have done better than *The Innocents Abroad*. The buoyant irreverence of Sam Clemens pretending to be unimpressed by the wonders of the Old World was just what I needed. "And now that my temper is up, I may as well go on and abuse everybody I can think of," he wrote, after blasting the Church for building great cathedrals while the poor starved in the streets. "They have a grand mausoleum in Florence, which they built to bury our Lord and Saviour and the Medici family. It sounds blasphemous, but it is true. . . ."

I read on, chuckling to myself, until I got sleepy, and when I finally turned out the light I wasn't feeling quite so wormy. Francesca's tiny garments weren't pathetic, they were only an example of aristocratic snobbishness. She would embroider white gowns for a Morandini baby, but she wouldn't spend five minutes sewing for a child dying of cold and neglect.

I dreamed that night—the same dream that had tormented me for months. The setting and the details might differ, but the theme never changed. I was looking for Bart. They told me he was dead, but I knew it wasn't true. He was alive, but I could not find him. He was a prisoner, held by faceless uniformed guards; he was in a hospital suffering from amnesia; he was in flight, menaced by fantastic dangers—a volcano about to erupt, a tidal wave, a hired killer. I pursued shadows down the dark streets of dreaming, shadows that sometimes paused long enough to give me a glimpse of shining gray eyes, or let me hear an echo of mocking laughter. I never found him. I never touched him. And I always woke drenched with perspiration, as if I really had been running all the long night.

The dream that night was one of the worst. This time I saw him and heard him—the familiar laughter and the shape of his body, tall and slim-hipped, with an eel-like agility. He was so close I could have reached out and touched him when my feet went out from under me and I fell, not to earth, but down, down, through thick fog into infinite depths, lit far below by a ruddy glow of fire.

I woke with the sheets twisted around me like giant

snakes. My face was wet with tears—not of grief, but of rage. I pounded the pillow with clenched fists. Damn him—damn Bart for leaving the way he had; damn God for punishing me this way; damn Sister Ursula for making me believe in the fires of hell, burning, burning for the sinner.

Like Mark Twain, I went on and abused everybody I could think of, and then lay snuffling quietly to myself, the sheets thrown back and the night breeze cooling my fevered body. The breeze carried the scent of fir needles and damp earth—and something else. I sat bolt upright, sniffing. Something acridly sweet, unpleasantly familiar.

I got got out of bed and tiptoed on bare feet to the window. The doors onto the balcony were open. The thin inner curtains swayed gently. Nothing creaked under my feet as I moved; the floors were tiled, even that of the balcony.

The moon had set. A silvery glow behind the pointed silhouettes of the cypresses marked its passing. There was no sound except the soft whisper of the boughs.

Then I saw a small point of glowing red. It moved eerily through the darkness like a satanic firefly.

Someone was on the terrace, by the fountain. I stood motionless, scarcely breathing, as I watched the tip of the cigarette brighten and fade, glide up and down and up again.

Finally the fiery circle soared like a shooting star and disappeared. The shadow enclosing the fountain reached out a long finger across the lighter surface of the starlit stone. He came out of the dark like a swimmer rising from the water—tall and slim, with eel-like swiftness. He glided across the pale grass and was gone.

three

"He's here. I saw him last night, from my window. I heard him laughing."

Through the remainder of that endless night I had told myself that I must state my case as coolly and dispassionately as a judge summing up. I had forced myself to wait until morning before confronting her. I had planned what I intended to say, word for word. But in spite of my resolutions I couldn't keep my voice under control, and I knew the strain of the sleepless hours was visible on my face.

For a moment her face mirrored the shock that had traced disfiguring marks on my own. She burst out, "But that is . . ." and then checked herself. "You dreamed," she said. "You are not yourself. Your condition . . ."

I felt the dangerous, deadly laughter bubbling up my throat and into my mouth. I pressed my lips together and managed to hold it in. My condition? Fresh out of Dr. Baldwin's crazy house, had she but known. I had no intention of mentioning that episode. It would only confirm her picture of the bereaved, neurotic young widow.

I said steadily, "I was not asleep. I was not dreaming. I woke in the night; I went to the window. There was a man by the fountain. He walked across the terrace and. . . ."

Disappeared? Vanished? Neither was a particularly good word, under the circumstances.

Her face cleared miraculously. "You saw a man—but of course you did! My poor child. You must have seen Professor Brown."

"Professor . . . ?" The images created by words are pervasive. I had had professors of all ages and sizes and shapes, yet the suggestion was that of an old man, stooped and white-haired. Nothing like the person I had seen.

"I should have told you about him." She was smiling, speaking quickly, vivaciously. "He is restoring some of the objects in the family collections for me. I gave him permission to walk in the garden at night."

We were at breakfast, in her sitting room. She went on talking about Professor Brown. Occasionally a phrase penetrated the daze of hope and fear, belief and doubt, that filled my mind. ". . . most persistent in his requests . . . the family collections . . . duty to art and science . . . I forget he is here, I see so little of him." Then her smile faded and she actually touched me—a butterfly brush of manicured fingertips across the back of my hand. She said softly, "I should have warned you. I should have remembered. After my husband passed away I saw him often, on the street, in the shops. A chance resemblance, magnified by emotional confusion which is quite normal, quite understandable."

It was an extraordinary speech for her, warm, compassionate. What she had said was true. Other people had told me of having the same experience. Quite normal . . . I wanted to believe it. I wanted so badly to believe it that I dismissed the echo of laughter I had heard in the empty wing. I had heard his laughter a hundred times since that day, awake and dreaming.

"You will want to meet the professor," Francesca said. "Then your last doubt will be dispelled."

"Really, that isn't necessary. I'm sure you're right."

"No, you must meet him. He is an entertaining eccentric; he may amuse you. He spends most of his time in the storerooms. I don't go there. It is very dusty. But you are dressed suitably."

There was a little sting in the words and in the cool glance with which she studied my shirt and jeans. The outfit was shriekingly out of place in the eighteenth-century elegance of her sitting room, but I couldn't wear my brown suit all the time.

We had finished breakfast. She tinkled the little bell, and when Emilia came in she said, "Take Signora Morandini to see *il professore*."

The title jarred me. Signora Morandini . . . That was the name on my marriage license. But she had said it was not Bart's name. What was it? What was *my* name? I wasn't going to become morbid and introspective about my lack of identity. I had a name, a good name, and when I got home I would take steps to make it my legal name.

I followed Emilia up two flights of stairs to what would have been the attic in an American house. It was the floor above the one on which the bedrooms were located, and it was much more than an attic; it was a weird warren of oddly shaped rooms, with stairs intruding for no apparent reason, with zigzag corridors and strange little doorways. Some of the rooms were large and spacious, others were narrow cubicles furnished with scraps of cheap furniture—servants' quarters, I assumed. Some were storerooms or lumber rooms packed with the most astonishing variety of odds and ends. If they were part of the "family collections," Francesca had chosen an inappropriately pretentious term for junk.

Emilia was short of breath when we reached the top of the final stairs, a narrow uncarpeted flight that ended in a closed door. She opened it and stood back. *"Il professore,"* she said.

Piles of clutter stretched out as far as the eye could see. Mountains and hills of boxes and chests and barrels and old furniture formed a landscape as rugged as the terrain outside. The only light came from small windows blurry with dust, and from the door behind me. As I stepped cautiously forward, the door closed, and I found myself in deep gloom, with shadowy objects looming on all sides.

There was no doubt about it; Emilia didn't like me. Her gesture had the subtle malice with which people show hostility when they dare not express it openly. A claustrophobic would have collapsed at finding himself shut in that crowded space. I wasn't exactly happy about it myself. I even tried the door to make sure it wasn't locked.

Presumably *il professore* was in there somewhere. I was afraid to move or call out, for fear of bringing some teetering object down on my head. Damn the woman, she hadn't even offered me a flashlight.

Gradually my eyes grew accustomed to the dimness and I saw a faint glow of light ahead. I started picking a path between the piles of junk. It became a challenge to find a way through, and I thought what a super place this would be for hide and seek, if you were willing to take your chances on being mashed by falling furniture. Only the young and agile could get through; Emilia's stocky frame would never have made it through some of the narrow spaces.

As I drew closer to the light I heard sounds, little chuckles and smothered words. *Il professore* was talking to himself. No wonder Francesca never came here—clutter and dirt and dust and an eccentric professor mumbling to himself—or to the rats? Mice, certainly; there are always mice in old houses. I'm not afraid of mice. I was actually beginning to enjoy myself.

Finally I reached a barricade that seemed impassable—a huge armoire or wardrobe, whose roughly finished back left splinters in my fingers as I explored its surface. The mumbling was louder now, and I deduced that the speaker must be on the other side of the armoire. All at once his voice rose. " 'My scrofulous French novel on gray paper with blunt type! . . . Twenty-nine distinct damnations. . . .' "

There was a gap between the wardrobe and a pile of crates. I tried to squirm through and stuck halfway, hopelessly wedged in at the hips. At least I could see what was beyond.

The mumbles and chuckles had confirmed my picture of a weird little old scholar, and the final outburst—obviously a quotation—nailed it down. The figure I saw was crouched and huddled, and there were streaks of gray in its thick dark hair. He was squatting on the floor, his back to me, his shoulders bowed as he leaned forward, examining some object hidden from me by his body. I wondered how I could possibly have mistaken this middle-aged mumbler for my husband. I decided I had better give him some warning of my presence. My movements had not been noiseless, but obviously he hadn't heard them. I cleared my throat. "Hello," I said loudly.

The crouched figure exploded like a coiled spring. He moved with an admirable economy of motion, displacing nothing except himself and a cloud of dust. That was the gray in his hair—dust. The little old professor vanished, never to return. He was built like Bart—an inch or two shorter, but just as lean and almost as broad-shouldered. There the resemblance ended. His face was as comically homely as that of a gnome—snub nose, wide mouth, rounded cheeks. His jaws were dark with stubble and his ears stuck out. He wore faded jeans and a T-shirt with a design, badly worn, across the chest. He also wore horn-rimmed glasses. The abruptness of his movement sent them skidding down his nose; he caught them at the last second, pushed them into place, and squinted wildly at me through the smeared surfaces.

"I'm sorry I startled you," I said, squirming in a vain effort to free myself. "I'm Kathleen Malone. . . ." And there I stuck, verbally as well as physically. What was my name?

The professor raised his hand in a dramatic gesture. "Of course. Kathleen Malone. Why not? There's everything else in this place; why not a lost Irish colleen? Did you take a wrong turning outside of Dublin, my darling, my serpenting beauty?"

"What?"

"Browning. I'm extremely fond of Browning. And you do look rather serpentine, wriggling through that hole. Here." He shifted a box, took my hand, and yanked me into the open. An ominous ripping sound accompanied the movement.

"Damn it," I said, clapping a hand to the seat of my jeans.

"Sorry. Did I do that?" He didn't look sorry. He was grinning. Even in repose his mouth was not small; when he smiled it stretched like a rubber band, far beyond its original limits. If the length of a smile is an accurate measure of joie de vivre, he had to be the happiest man I had ever met.

"I was snagged on something, as I would have mentioned if you had given me a chance. Do you always act so precipitately?"

"No, no. If I acted precipitately here, I'd be buried under bales and boxes, and I would become a permanent part of the Morandini collections. I doubt that anyone would ever bother to look for me. Here, have a seat."

He swiped ineffectively at a wooden box. I sat down and looked around.

He had cleared a space about ten feet square. At one end was a partition wall, with a door. On one side was a long table covered with papers and office equipment, including a file box of dark metal. The light came from a battery-operated electric lamp.

"I must apologize for disturbing you, Professor," I began.

He interrupted with a hoarse chuckle. It had sounded faintly sinister before; coming from that wide-lipped mouth, it could not be anything but funny. "I'm no professor, love. Just a humble graduate student trying to scrape up material for a dissertation. I thought a title would impress the countess, but I couldn't be lying to you, now could I? How did I miss you? Or did I stumble unawares on Aladdin's lamp and summon up a genie?"

I realized he must take me for a servant. I couldn't blame him, but here, at least, I had to be honest. I was operating under enough false assumptions with too many people as it was. I said, "I'm related to the countess, by marriage. My husband was her nephew."

His smile faded. "Was?"

"He was killed in a car crash a few months ago."

"Killed in . . . But you. . . ." The words burst out like popcorn popping. He clapped his hand over his mouth and stared at me. Then he said, "I'm sorry. Really. Sometimes my mouth gets disconnected from my brain."

I didn't mind. The awkward bluntness of his distress was far more to my taste than polished phrases of formal sympathy. Francesca's dignified acceptance of Bart's death was admirable, no doubt, but it had left me feeling flat and uncomforted. "Cool" is not a quality the Malones appreciate.

"It's all right," I said. "I'd have come up and introduced myself before this if I had known you were here. I think I—I saw you last night, in the garden. The one with the little fountain."

"I'm allowed to walk in the gardens when the gentry are safely in bed. I hope I didn't disturb you."

"No. You didn't. Anyway, I'm not one of the gentry."

"That makes two of us." He held out his hand, blissfully oblivious of the fact that it was as black as a coal miner's. "My name is David."

"Kathy." We shook hands. "What on earth are you doing up here?"

"It's a long, boring story, which I will tell you in complete detail," said David, sitting down on the floor.

"Please do."

"I'm here under false pretenses, actually. What I'm really looking for are nineteenth-century diaries and papers relating to English and American visitors to Italy."

"It sounds very pompous."

"Does it? Good. Doctoral dissertations are supposed to have pompous titles. They are also supposed to incorporate new research, insights, and interpretations. Now I ask you: How the hell is anybody going to find a new topic in the field of nineteenth-century English literature? I mean, my God, they've even done solemn studies on the relative numbers of vowels and consonants in the works of Jane Austen! If an unpublished scrap turns up, every scholar in the field pounces on it like a dog on a bone and tears it to shreds. So I got this bright idea. I decided. . . . Are you sure you want to hear this?"

"I haven't anything better to do."

"If you think that unenthusiastic response is going to keep me from lecturing, you don't know academics. I decided I'd find my own unpublished scraps. As you probably know—and if you don't, I'm going to tell you—Italy became a mecca for English and American writers in the nineteenth century. If you had any pretension to culture, you made the Grand Tour. Henry James, Fenimore Cooper, Hawthorne, the Brownings—"

Not knowing how long the catalog would continue if I did not interrupt, I said intelligently, "I get it. You're doing your dissertation on Browning."

"Don't taunt me, madam." His wide mouth drooped in exaggerated woe. "Oh, sure, I dream of turning up a batch of letters, or a diary describing a visit to Robert and Elizabeth—they lived in the Casa Guidi, in Florence, for almost fifteen years—but Browning has been dissected too many times. The one I'm looking for is Margaret Fuller."

"Who?"

"You've never heard of Margaret Fuller? Good God, the deficiencies of our educational system! She was one of the first female foreign correspondents, and a brilliant scholar at a time when women were not supposed to flaunt their intellectual capacities. Horace Greeley hired her to write for the New York *Tribune*. She was in Italy when the war for Italian independence broke out; she had fallen in love with an Italian nobleman, the Marquis Ossoli, and had a child by him. How's that for being liberated? Unlike most of his peers, the *marchese* was a supporter of the freedom movement, and so was Margaret. During the siege of Rome he fought on the walls while she ran one of the hospitals and sent back dispatches to Greeley—at ten bucks a shot.

He had raised her wages from eight dollars to ten when she threatened to quit. She was also, I hardly need to say, a fighter for women's rights. But maybe that wouldn't interest you."

"What makes you suppose that?" I demanded indignantly.

He looked sheepish. "Ignorant male chauvinism, I guess. We unconsciously assume that a young, beautiful woman—"

"Enjoys being viewed as a charming nitwit? Wake up, buster. Besides, I'm not beautiful."

He adjusted his glasses and stared at me. "No, you aren't. Your lower lip is too full and your nose is too long and your chin sticks out—"

"Only when I'm mad."

David grinned. "Scratch the chin. I don't know why you give the impression of being beautiful. It's an interesting problem. Maybe it's your coloring. Fair hair and brown eyes—and such a nice shade of brown, like a fox's coat. 'Her locks were yellow as gold: Her skin was white as . . .' Oops."

"White as what?"

"Wrong poem," said David, somewhat flustered. "You are a bit pale, though. Have you been sick?"

"Let's get back to Margaret Fuller."

"Oh, sure. Right. Good idea. Uh . . ."

"I'd like to know more about her," I said, relenting.

"I'll send you a copy of my book."

"At the rate you're going, I'll probably be too old and senile to read it. It will take you ten years to sort through all this. Have you any reason to suppose you'll find material about Margaret here, or are you just amusing yourself?"

"It's not a reason so much as a far-out hunch. Like

Margaret's lover, the Count Morandini of that day was a follower of Mazzini and Garibaldi. After the fall of Rome, Margaret and Ossoli came to Florence and were finally married in a little village church, somewhere in Tuscany. It's probable that Morandini knew them, since they moved in the same social and political circles; possible that he mentioned them in his letters or journals. Nobody knows where and when the wedding took place. Imagine the sensation if I could find a written report! I mean, Morandini could have been their best man, or one of the witnesses."

"It looks to me like the proverbial needle in the haystack. You'll have to investigate every box and crate in the villa."

"Right." The prospect did not appear to daunt David. He beamed radiantly.

"Maybe you ought to give up literature and go in for garbage collecting," I suggested.

"It pays better than scholarship," was the bland reply. "Remember the Dickens novel in which the dustman becomes a millionaire?"

"I never read it."

"I can see your education has been sadly neglected. Not to recognize Browning—that's a disgrace." He went on with mounting enthusiasm, "There are tons of junk in this place! It has all the charm of digging for buried treasure without the physical discomforts. You never know what you'll turn up. I found an Aztec mask in a palazzo near Rome last fall—one of the *marchese*'s ancestors had traveled in Mexico and brought back souvenirs. I've only been here a couple of weeks, and already I've found a crate of odds and ends one of the Morandinis collected in Egypt in the 1880's. Most of them are forgeries, but there are a few genuine pieces. I wouldn't be surprised to run across a mummy tucked away in a corner."

The delight in his voice made me laugh. "You'll never write that dissertation. You're having too much fun."

"I'll get tired of junk one day," David said placidly. "But in the meantime, can you imagine a better way to spend your time?"

"Frankly, yes."

"It's a cheap way of getting a European vacation. Free room and sometimes board as well. I'm on good terms with Rosa. I wander into the kitchen twice a day looking pale and wan and she stuffs me with pasta."

"But how do you con people into admitting you to their attics? You can obviously talk the leg off a donkey, but I can't see Francesca giving a damn about Margaret Fuller. Especially Margaret Fuller."

"Oh, that. Well, to be honest with you . . ." David took off his glasses and looked grave. "I got carried away talking to you. It must be your kind, innocent face. You won't split on me, will you?"

"That depends on what deep dark secret you're hiding."

"You already know my deep dark secret. The contessa doesn't. She thinks I'm searching for marketable treasures, like the Aztec mask. Or better—a forgotten Bellini, or an overlooked Botticelli or a Cellini saltcellar that some ignorant former count replaced with a pressed-glass bowl made in Manchester. As you may have observed from the neglected state of the house and grounds and the paucity of staff, the lady's cash flow is none too good. The same thing is true of many of the old families, except the smart ones who have turned to manufacturing cars or clothes. They've already hocked the paintings and the antique furniture and the sculpture. Until I pointed it out, they didn't realize there might be unconsidered gems in the attic. The guy whose ancestor brought back the Aztec mask is a friend of the contessa. An American museum has offered a sum for the mask that dazzles his simple aristocratic soul. Your lady friend thinks I may find something like that here."

"Will you?"

"It's damned unlikely. But one never knows." His eyes rested gloatingly on the heaped-up boxes.

I stood up. "I can see you're dying to get back to work. I won't keep you any longer."

"Not that way." He put out a casual hand to detain me as I turned toward the narrow opening through which I had come. "I don't know how you ever made it through all that stuff. I'll show you my door."

"I don't want to take you from your labor of love."

"It's time for my morning break anyway." He untangled his long legs and got to his feet. "A quick run around the garden, followed by a call on the cook. Come on."

The way out was certainly less complicated than the route I had followed coming in. Uncarpeted stairs and straight passages led down four flights. The last stairs ended in a brick-floored corridor whose walls were of peeling stucco. "Kitchen is that way," David said, lifting a thumb toward the right. "Pantries and storerooms on the other side. All unoccupied now. And this . . ." He opened a door. "This is my exercise yard."

It was a small courtyard, high-walled and rank with weeds. A path had been beaten through the weeds around the walls, presumably by David's feet. A few tangled roses struggled out of the brush to cling to the broken bricks and a half-rotted wooden bench stood against one wall. That was the extent of the amenities.

" 'Run' would be more like it," I said. "You mean this is

the only part of the grounds you're allowed to use during the daytime?"

"Now, now, don't let your democratic indignation get the better of you. I'm here on sufferance, and I take what I can get. It isn't so bad; my room is over the garage, which is through that gate. I can go and come as I please. Anyhow, I'm not anxious to socialize with the gentry or the staff—especially Alberto." His dust-streaked face was grim. I wondered what the chauffeur had done to inspire his silent condemnation, but David did not elaborate.

"That other gate opens into the kitchen garden," he went on. "You can get into the house that way, or go around to the front door."

"Thanks. And thanks for the lecture."

"Any time." His wide smile illumined his face. "If you get bored, come up and help me rummage."

"I might at that. If you get tired of running around this—this outdoor cage—come and play football with me and Pete."

"Pete?"

"I should say Pietro; the contessa doesn't care for American nicknames. Actually he's the Count Morandini, but it sounds silly to call a ten-year-old boy by his title."

"You mean there's a kid living here? A ten-year-old?"

"Haven't you seen him?"

David shook his head.

ii

I left David doggedly jogging around the path. Four circuits made up half a mile; he'd paced it off with a pedometer.

Seeing him in daylight, I realized how distant was the

resemblance I had fancied. He didn't look anything like Bart. They were about the same height and build; that had been enough to deceive me. Even when dusted, David's brown hair was several shades lighter than Bart's; he moved without Bart's smooth actor's grace. Running, he looked like a loose-jointed, long-limbed marionette, a *Petrouchka* puppet with a cheerful clown's face. He should have had freckles. Maybe there were freckles, under the dust. Even if it had been clean, his was not the kind of face women looked at, the bolder staring openly, the well-bred sneaking little sidelong glances. Women did that to Bart. I remembered the smug satisfaction with which I had clung to his arm, watching other women yearn for what was mine.

I made my way to the walled garden where I had found Pete playing. It was quiet and deserted. There was no sign that a child had ever been there—no forgotten balls or toys lying in the long grass, no swing or trapeze hanging from the limb of a tree.

David's blank surprise at the mention of a child had left me with a queer feeling. He kept to his own part of the house and grounds, of course. He was in the attic most of the day. Still, it bothered me to think that the boy was so invisible. Maybe he was away at school. Maybe he had been home for vacation the day I saw him, or he attended a boarding school during the week and was only at the villa on weekends.

I decided I might as well do a little exploring. As Francesca had indicated, I was dressed for it, and I couldn't get any dirtier after my visit to the attic. Besides, I wanted to find out where the garage was located so I could get my car without having to apply to Alberto. I must remember to retrieve my keys, too.

I went back to David's exercise yard. He had finished

his jogging and gone, presumably to beg a snack from Rosa. Through the gate he had pointed out I saw a stone-paved yard with the old stables on the far side. They were part of the house itself, the lower level of a wing that extended away from the central block. The former coachhouse had been turned into a garage. Beyond it, rows of empty stalls stretched forlornly to the far end of the wing.

I didn't go through the gate. The Mercedes was out in the yard, and Alberto was polishing it. Sunlight reflected dazzlingly from the gleaming chrome of the grille. Too bad he wasn't as conscientious about the dog.

I wondered where the animal was kept. It must be nearby, in the work area. I decided it might be a good idea to find out so I wouldn't inadvertently wander into its run. The formal introduction hadn't convinced me of its good intentions.

The obvious course would have been to ask Alberto. Instead I backed quietly away from the gate and began looking on my own. It didn't take me long. I smelled the place before I saw it—not far from the stableyard and, in my opinion, too close to the route Pete followed to reach his bleak playground. The dog's pen was worse than bleak, it was a disgrace. There was a kennel of sorts, tin-roofed and obviously not leak-proof. Though the walls of the pen were ten feet high, the dog was chained. A narrow stretch of beaten earth, liberally sprinkled with piles of dung, marked the limits of its restless pacing. It wasn't pacing now; it lay stretched out, head on paws, next to a cheap plastic bowl containing a scant half-inch of scummy water.

He looked so bored and pathetic I almost did something really stupid. When I touched the gate he started up. The wind must have been blowing the wrong way, for he had not caught my scent. Did he jump with joy at the sight of me, the only person in his life who defended him and spoke gently to him? He jumped, all right—straight at me, jaws gaping. The chain brought him up with a jerk. He strained at it, snarling.

"You have a rotten memory," I said. "Calm down. You're not supposed to eat me; I'm one of the gentry, remember?"

I talked to him awhile, till he stopped snarling and sat down, staring at me like someone trying to remember a face. As I walked away I was so angry I was shaking. It was only sensible to keep the dog chained; he could probably jump the gate with no trouble. But the chain was far too short and Alberto didn't even bother keeping the pen clean. I wondered how often the dog was fed. From the way he had drooled at me, I deduced it wasn't often enough.

I returned to the kitchen garden and went through another gate. I had never seen a place so walled off into little compartments. Once the gardens must have been gorgeous. Even now, after years of neglect, there were signs of the features that had given each enclosure its special character—beds of roses, straggling and unpruned, in one; bulbs forcing brave emerald spears through the weeds in another; a crumbling fountain set in a mosaic-lined grotto in another. The bits of glittering mica and colored stone had been laid in concrete, but the roots of climbing vines had inserted steely fingers, and piles of fallen color littered the fountain's floor. One garden had been walled with marble and adorned with a tiny circular columned temple that must have served as a gazebo. Two of the columns had fallen; I realized that they had been built that way, one of the artificial ruins popular with nineteenth-century landscape artists. And everywhere the untended grass and the weeds were growing, to smother flowers and crack stone.

A final gate of intricate but rusted wrought iron admitted me to the front grounds. They had been splendid in their heyday; the fountain spouting crystal streams from all the Tritons' horns, the lawn like emerald velvet, the flower beds patches of bright color. A stooped figure bent over one of the beds. It must be the man Francesca had mentioned—Alberto's assistant. I assumed he was weeding, though he didn't appear to be working very hard. I hesitated, wondering whether to approach him. There wasn't much I could say except *"Buon giorno,"* nor much I could do except smile. He might not care for my condescending attentions. As I watched he got painfully to his feet, and I realized, with a shock of pity, that the poor creature was physically handicapped. Limping, one shoulder higher than the other, he set off across the lawn away from me.

It was later than I had realized. A glance at my watch confirmed the time suggested by the height of the sun. I would have to shower and change. And, I promised myself, I would ask Francesca where she was hiding her grandson. She could exile the child from her presence if she chose, but there was no reason why I had to treat him like a leper.

However, when I came down to lunch, suitably attired in blouse and skirt, Francesca wasn't there. Emilia poured the ritual glass of wine for me; when I indicated to her that I would wait for my hostess she produced a note from her pocket. The delicate handwriting informed me that I would be lunching alone. Francesca had an appointment she could not cancel. "I meant to tell you this morning at breakfast," she wrote. "I hope you will excuse my rudeness."

I could hardly blame her for forgetting, after the exhibition I had put on.

I waited until Emilia had poured my coffee before I asked about Pete. I called him Pietro, of course.

She repeated the key word. "School?"

"*La scuola.* Is *il conte* at the *scuola* today?"

She shook her head.

"Why not?" She looked blankly at me. I tried again. "Where is he?"

Her shoulders lifted in a shrug. I suspected she would not have committed that vulgarity in Francesca's presence, but vulgarity doesn't bother me; what bothered me was the utter indifference the gesture implied. "You don't know where he is?" I asked.

Another shrug. "In his room?"

I tossed my napkin onto the table with a gesture worthy of a contessa. "Where is his room?"

You'd have thought I had asked the way to the lion house. She didn't try to prevent me or talk me out of it, she simply could not comprehend why I would voluntarily look for the boy.

We started up the stairs. I decided I might as well take advantage of the opportunity to find out the answers to some of the things I was curious about, so I peppered her with questions. Yes, she said, the contessa's room was also on the second floor, at the far end of the same corridor on which my room was located, and near the door into the west wing, which was now unoccupied. Emilia's fractured English became surprisingly fluent at this point, and she went on to explain that the west wing was in a ruinous condition—unsafe, insanitary, and generally undesirable.

It was from this wing I had seen her come with her covered tray. I was tempted to ask if that was where they keep crazy old Uncle Giovanni, but I decided Emilia's

English wasn't good enough for jokes. It was not a very funny joke anyway.

My room wasn't the state bedchamber after all. The suite of the reigning count and his consort occupied the entire second-floor front of the villa.

But the present count was elsewhere. I had taken it for granted that the child's room would be on the same floor as the other bedchambers; however, after I had stopped in my room to pick up the game I'd bought for him, Emilia led me up again. So Pete was in the attic, with the servants and the other junk. I was familiar with the old-fashioned custom of keeping the young as far from the adults as possible, but in this case it struck me as profoundly mistaken, not to say dangerous. That was when it dawned on me that Francesca had not mentioned a governess or nurserymaid. Who looked after him, then, especially at night?

When we reached the head of the stairs Emilia turned in the opposite direction from the one we had taken to reach the storeroom where David was working. Pete's room was on a corridor paralleling the front of the house. It was not far from the stairs, but it was a long way from Francesca's room, which was at the far end of another corridor on the floor below. She wouldn't be able to hear him if he became ill during the night—and that was probably just the way she wanted it.

I asked Emilia where she slept. She gestured—near Francesca's room. "And the *tuttofare*?" I persisted. This time her pointing finger indicated a door not far from the boy's. She added, with a twisted smile, "When she is there. She sleeps away, very often."

I didn't ask any more questions. When I raised my hand to knock on Pete's door, Emilia reached for the key. I had noticed it, but had not thought anything about it. The proper place for a key is in a keyhole. She said, "You wish to go in?"

Not trusting myself to speak, I nodded. Emilia turned the key. "When you come out, you . . ." She gestured, twisting her fingers. Lock him in again when you come out.

I stared at her. She shrugged, smiling insolently. "*Bene, signora.* As you desire."

I waited till she was out of sight. I thought I had heard sounds of movement inside—soft, scuttling, surreptitious movements, like rats in the wall. Then I knocked and called out. "It's me, Pete. Kathy. Can I come in?"

After a moment his voice said, "Please."

The room had been furnished as a nursery, thirty years ago. It may have been pleasant then; there were shelves filled with toys and books, a fireplace with a fender and screen, a rocking horse, a little brass bed. There was nothing wrong with it now, except for its shabbiness and the fact that there was not one object in it that could have amused a ten-year-old boy. The window was barred.

Pete was in bed, a book open on his lap. He sat quite still, his eyes wide and watchful, his lips tight, until I closed the door.

"They didn't tell me you were sick," I said. "I'd have come to see you before if I had known."

"You are alone, signora?"

"Yes." I pulled up a chair and sat down. "How do you feel?"

"Well. I am well. I am not sick."

"I was afraid you had caught something from me. I guess it wasn't catching, though."

The funniest expression spread over his face—sly, almost prurient. It was a horrid look, even worse than the shuttered wariness it had replaced.

I had not missed the significance of the way he had addressed me. He had called me "signorina" before. Some-one must have told him part of the story and hinted at the rest. I said impulsively, "You know I was married to your . . . he'd be your cousin, wouldn't he?"

"Yes, signora."

"I'm not pregnant, though."

The sly little leer vanished in a flood of surprise. He knew the word; after all, he had spent some time in an American school, and there aren't many words those kids haven't heard. I went on casually, "You know, when a woman is going to have a baby, sometimes she gets sick at her stomach. I was sick yesterday. It was just one of those bugs people get when they travel. But I'm afraid someone may have jumped to the wrong conclusion."

I don't think he understood the last word, but the idea got through. His brow furrowed. "You are not—you do not . . ."

"Not pregnant, no. Did someone tell you I was?"

He was still flushed, but his expression was one of normal childish curiosity. He dropped the book and hugged his knees. "I heard them talk—Emilia and Rosa. When Emilia saw I was listening she said I was bad. It was not a thing for children. . . ."

"Never mind, I can imagine what she said. She was wrong on all counts." I smiled at him. "In a way I'm sorry I'm not pregnant. I'd like to have a child."

"You like children?"

"Yes, of course. That's what I do for a living—teach children."

"Like me?"

"A little bit older than you. Junior high school. My students are between twelve and fifteen."

"What do you teach?"

"History."

His face fell. "Not football."

"You know I'm not very good at football, Pete. Oh, that reminds me. I brought you something."

He pounced on the game like a starving man on a bowl of soup. "I had it—like this—before. But it was not so—so—"

"Complicated?"

He tasted the word experimentally. "Complicated . . . Yes. Not so complicated. It was broken. Let us play this now."

It didn't take him long to get the hang of it. I had already accepted the humiliating fact that most of my students could beat the pants off me at any electronic game. He skinned me four games out of six, and he would have gone on playing all day if I hadn't begged off.

"Let's play something else. Darn it, I'd like to win for a change."

"There is nothing else."

"No games—Parcheesi, checkers?"

"Only baby games." He swept the room with a scornful wave of his hand.

"What do you do all day?" I tried to keep my voice neutral. I don't think I succeeded.

"I have a radio. Sometimes I listen to the music. And I am always to study."

He indicated the book he had (not) been reading. It was a thick volume on Italian history, written for adults. There were a few black-and-white photographs.

I couldn't continue the inquisition. I had completely lost my sense of perspective, and that was bad. I had only heard one side of the case. It was hard to imagine there could be another valid point of view, but I had learned through painful experience that one could easily go astray in one's judgments, especially where a child was concerned.

His face changed pitifully when I rose to go, but he didn't ask me to stay. "Maybe you can get up tomorrow," I said. "We might have a game of real football."

"I can get up now. I am not sick."

I felt his forehead. "You haven't got a fever."

He pressed his face against my palm for a moment, then moved away. "I am not sick. They say I have to rest, but I don't. Only . . . only sometimes . . . I have bad dreams."

He must have seen from my expression how that hit me. Not only my own nightmares, but the memory of a voice, smooth and trained: "I could be bounded in a nutshell, And count myself a king of ultimate space, Were it not that I have bad dreams. . . ." Bart had always wanted to play Hamlet. What actor doesn't? And what a gorgeous Prince of Denmark he'd have made in the classic black velvet doublet and tights, with his shock of dark hair and his silver eyes, his high cheekbones and flexible hands.

A small voice stammered, "I said something bad."

"No. No, you didn't." I reached out for him and pulled him close. I needed the warmth, the closeness, as much as he did. "I have bad dreams too, Pete. I know how terrible they can be. But someday they'll go away. When you lose someone you . . . you love, at first all you can feel is anger. But it will pass. The hate and the hurt and the bad dreams, all of it."

As I stumbled through that little speech I knew that Doc Baldwin would have howled with horror at my uneducated attempt at therapy. How dare I meddle with something as deep-rooted and deadly as this child's sense of loss? Was I naive enough to suppose that my ignorant efforts could help?

Yes, I was. And I think they did help. He wasn't ready to let go and cry, but he held me tightly for a few seconds. Then he remembered his age and his dignity and pulled away. "It was bad for you, signora? I am sorry."

"Not as bad as it was for you." I brushed the tumbled hair from his forehead. "I think you are a very brave person."

That opened the floodgates. He started to talk, in a queer mixture of English and Italian. I got a picture of a way of life totally alien to me—a lifestyle I thought of as "jet set" or "beautiful people," for his parents seemed to have traveled constantly, to all the fashionable places. Either there was more money in the family than I supposed, or Mama and Papa had known how to make the most of their income, for Pete made casual mention of maids and tutors and teachers and other luxuries. He had not been left to the care of servants, though. His father had taught him to swim and ski. His mother had taken him to playgrounds and carnivals and zoos. She loved carousels. "Always she rode a white horse. When I was little she took me on the white horse with her. When I was big, I rode another horse, or a lion, or an elephant."

And he had had a dog. Bruno. His eyes filled when he spoke the name, as they had not for his parents. Seeing his distress I braced myself for the worst; but Bruno had not met a sticky end, he had been left behind when Pete came to Italy.

"Maybe you can have another dog," I said, knowing how I would have reacted to that idea if I had been in his shoes.

"I don't want a dog except Bruno. And besides, *she* would not let me have an animal. Not even a bird."

I knew who *she* was.

When the spate of reminiscences finally ran down he

looked limp and exhausted. I knew how he felt; I had been in that state a few times myself. But he didn't look ill. Too thin and too pale, but that was grieving and lack of exercise—mental and physical. Again I prepared to take my leave.

"Tomorrow we'll have that game," I said. "I'll ask your grandmother tonight."

"O-kay," he said, brightening.

I went to the door. "Pete," I said.

"Yes, Signora Kathy?"

"I'm not going to lock the door. Will you stay in your room?"

He thought about it. "If I do not, they will be angry at you?"

I laughed. "Probably."

"Then I will stay. On the word of a Morandini, I swear!" He sat upright, his eyes flashing.

He looked like Bart. Horribly, dreadfully like him. I forced a smile. "See you tomorrow, Pete. Sleep well—and no bad dreams, right?"

"Right! And you, signora."

I went to my room. After ten minutes or so I stopped pacing and sat down and gave myself the lecture Pa would have given me. "Damnation if you're not at it again, rushing in to rescue people who may not need rescuing and may not want to be rescued. You remind me of the Boy Scout dragging the little old lady across the street, and her hitting him with her umbrella because she doesn't want to cross the damn street! Will you never learn to find out the facts before you act?"

I didn't think I would ever learn. Pa never had. But Dr. Baldwin and all the other specialists with whom I had worked, at school, would have said the same. Butt out.

You may do more harm than good. Stop jumping to conclusions, creating imaginary dramas out of nothing.

The boy had not been physically abused. I had seen
that a few times, and the signs are unmistakable. Anyway,
I couldn't imagine Francesca being guilty of that kind of
brutality. Her sins would be those of omission and cold-
ness. I tried to see it from her point of view. She too had
known grief. She had lost an only son. And into her quiet,
ordered life had been thrust a child who was resentful and
angry, confused and disturbed. Perhaps she had tried to
reach out to him and had been rebuffed. It's hard to accept
that treatment even when you understand the reason for it.
Her methods of dealing with the boy were hopelessly
wrongheaded, but they were probably well intentioned.

I put on my brown suit when I dressed for dinner. At
least it was dignified, and I knew the importance of personal appearance when you are planning to start a fight. I
meant to get some plain answers to some plain questions. I
would try to keep an open mind, but . . .

She foiled me again. When I sailed into the ivory-and-
gold sitting room, there were guests.

They were a middle-aged couple, Dr. and Mrs. Con-
dotti. He looked like a baby pig, all pink and plump.
Wisps of graying hair were brushed carefully across his
high forehead. His wife was as thin as he was chubby, with
a head of shimmering blond hair that looked like a carved
wig.

I had learned that Italians were apt to toss titles like
"doctor" and "professor" around rather casually. Dr. Con-
dotti might not have been a medical man. But I thought he
was. His wife's not-so-subtle glances at my stomach were
those of middle-aged female curiosity. The doctor's look
had a decidedly professional gleam.

They were a very dull pair. Only Francesca's smooth

hostess manners kept conversation from limping through a long formal meal. Mercifully the Condottis left early. As soon as the door closed behind them, Francesca leaned back in her chair with a sigh. A less inhibited woman would have kicked off her shoes, run her hands through her hair, and let out a loud "Whew!"

"I hope you weren't too bored," she said. "The Condottis speak English well, that is why I invited them. They are not intellectuals, however."

"Not at all," I said vaguely.

"I must also apologize for leaving you alone all day. Perhaps tomorrow I can show you something of the countryside."

That gave me my opening. "I promised Pete—Pietro—I would spend part of the day with him."

She knew I had visited him. There was no surprise in her look, only a level curiosity. "You did not lock his door."

"No."

"More coffee?" Her hands were steady as she lifted the heavy silver pot. The fact that she had not called Emilia to perform this task told me she had recognized an unpalatable fact—she was going to have to talk to me.

"No, thank you." I had thought I was mad enough to speak plainly, but her superb self-possession weakened my resolve. I said hesitantly, "I suppose you think it's none of my business, but—"

"You teach, I believe."

I had not told her that. I said, "You had me investigated."

"Of course. You would have done the same in my position. When I received your letters I did not know Bartolommeo was married. You might have been . . . anything."

"Fair enough. But—"

"I learned you were precisely what you claimed to be—Bartolommeo's legal wife. Therefore you have a position here. No, I do not believe that Pietro's condition is, as you put it, 'none of your business.' I had hoped you would not be moved to interfere, but I see now that you could not act otherwise. The qualities that lead you to do so are the qualities of youth, and I respect them, though I do not admire them."

I had never been dissected with such cool accuracy, not even by Dr. Baldwin. If she had expressed contempt or anger, I could have responded. Against that dispassionate (and just) assessment I had no defense.

She went on calmly. "You think me harsh in my dealings with the boy. My methods are not yours, and I feel no obligation to defend them. Theories come and go like women's fashions; the truths you hold today will be tomorrow's outmoded theories in their turn. To lock a child in his room is not cruel or unusual punishment. But that is not why I lock his door. I do so because he must be confined for his own safety. Twice in the past weeks he has come close to killing himself. There is insanity in the Morandini line. He has the seeds of it. The child is mad."

four

I said, "I don't believe it."

"What is it you don't believe? That there is such a thing as hereditary insanity, or that Pietro tried to kill himself?"

"Both. Neither."

She smiled. Her teeth looked like icicles. "You are candid, aren't you?"

"I'm sorry. You may be telling the truth as you see it, but . . . You're wrong, that's all."

"My husband died in a hospital in Vicenza," she said. "He was homicidal and raving mad. His uncle—his grandfather—"

The Gothic atmosphere was so thick you could have cut it with a knife. I expected Mrs. Rochester to burst through the door howling curses. "Look," I said desperately, "I don't know much about mental illness—you don't mind if I use that term, I hope, instead of 'raving mad'? I do know there is no surer way of shattering a child's mind than telling him he's doomed to madness."

"I know that too. If I had not known, the psychiatrist Pietro is seeing—"

"You're taking him to a psychiatrist?"

Her glacial calm cracked briefly. "I know I am not your idea of a doting grandmother, Kathleen, but neither am I a monster. Will you allow me to tell you what happened without interruptions or emotional outbursts?"

"You're the one who used the word 'madness,' " I said. "Talk about emotionally loaded—"

"Touché." I expected her to show resentment, but the smile she gave me was almost friendly. "I will try to avoid such terms.

"Pietro's father was my son. My only son. He was always a practical child, intelligent enough, but without a spark of imagination—quite unlike the Morandinis, though I suppose you will frown at that reference to hereditary traits. At any rate, Guido showed some talent for business—investments, that sort of thing. I have never cared for such matters. After matriculating at Bologna he wanted to go to business school. I sent him to Columbia, in the United States. It was there he met his wife. I disapproved of the marriage. I admit it because I am sure you already suspect as much. But my reasons were not what you may suppose. I did not dislike the young woman because she was an American, I disliked her because she was the worst of America—superficial, common, incapable of appreciating another way of life. She was a good wife, however. She accompanied Guido on all his business trips."

So my image of the frivolous aristocrats jetting around the world had been way off base. It ought to have been a lesson to me.

"It was on one such trip that they were killed," Fran-

cesca went on, without the faintest trace of emotion.
"You may have read about the plane crash; it was one of
the worst disasters in recent history. The airliner struck
a school in a small town in Switzerland. The children
were practicing for the Christmas pageant."

I remembered, of course. The media had not spared
their readers and viewers any of the details; there were
endless photographs of the agonized parents trying to
clear away pieces of twisted metal to reach the bodies of
their children. Even Bart's cultivated cool had been
shaken by the story. I remembered his broken exclama-
tions of shock and dismay. . . . Had he known his
cousin was on that plane?

"Pietro had been placed at school in America. Against
my wishes, of course. There is no need for me to tell
you of the painful weeks following his arrival here—"

"You were named guardian in your son's will?"

"There was no will. How many healthy young people
can admit the possibility of dying?"

The answer came readily, with no change in the eyes
fixed steadily on mine; but for the first time I sensed she
was equivocating—not lying, exactly, but not telling the
whole truth.

I could hardly challenge her, though. I nodded, and
after a moment she went on. "I sought psychiatric treatment for him immediately. His behavior was abnormal.
Violent explosions of temper, followed by days of sullen
silence. For a while he showed signs, however small, of
responding to treatment. Then, when he had been here
a little over a month, he ran out of his room in the
middle of the night. His cries woke me. He was shouting
loudly and incoherently, and laughing. By the time I
had roused the servants and followed, he had left the
house and climbed a tree—one of the big oaks by the

gatehouse. I called to him to come down. He said yes, he would come; he would fly. He waved his arms and laughed and shouted, 'I can do it. I can fly. I will show you.' "

She picked up her embroidery. I said unsteadily, "How did you get him down?"

"We didn't. Alberto climbed up after him, but when he reached out for the boy, Pietro jumped. He landed in a mass of shrubbery, with only scratches and bruises to show for his adventure."

I could think of nothing to say. Children do try to commit suicide. Sometimes they succeed. This was worse than I had imagined.

Francesca resumed calmly, "Pietro claimed to have no recollection of the incident. A few weeks ago the second attack occurred. His door was locked—I began locking him in after the first attack. The *tuttofare* was sleeping in the next room. She was awakened by his screams and came for me. He had broken a mirror. Fragments were all around, and he was beating at the empty frame when I entered. There were bloody footprints across the floor. He had raced back and forth, from door to window to mirror, and had, naturally, cut his feet. If one of the shards had severed an artery, or if he had used his hands instead of a book to break the mirror, he might have bled to death before anyone reached him.

"Now perhaps you understand why I lock the child in his room when there is no one in attendance, and why his activities are so restricted. He goes to Firenze three times a week to a psychiatrist, and he is taking medication." She paused to set a stitch, delicately and precisely, before adding, "I may as well tell you that the medication is given to him in his food, without his knowledge. He made such a fuss, it became impossible to give it to him openly. I'm sure you disapprove of my methods, Kathleen; but I hope you will do me the courtesy of not questioning my motives."

ii

It took a large dose of Mark Twain to put me to sleep that night, and for once I was thinking of someone else's problems instead of mine. Maybe that's why I slept like a log, without dreaming. By the following morning my idiot optimism had reasserted itself. Damn it, I just could not accept Francesca's diagnosis. I didn't care if every shrink in Europe and America confirmed it. The child had not demonstrated any symptoms of mental illness before the death of his parents; I felt sure Francesca would have mentioned that, as confirmation of her theory. He was emotionally disturbed—seriously disturbed—I had to admit that much. But a hereditary taint? I felt certain Pete's doctor didn't share that medieval belief. At least I hoped he didn't.

The conversation had cleared up another point I had wondered about. Pietro was the last of the Morandinis—except for the apocryphal embryo Francesca thought I was carrying. No wonder she was so tolerant of my presence and my criticism. I wasn't just an intrusive distant relative by marriage; I, by God, was the mother of the Heir of the Morandinis—with only a "raving madman" between it and the title.

I was in the bathroom brushing my teeth when that occurred to me, and the expression on the face reflected in the mirror was so aghast I couldn't help smiling. "Cheer up, you damned fool," I told my reflection. "Of all the

messes you have got into—and there have been plenty—
this is high on the list."

I couldn't hang on to the smile, though; the situation
was too serious. I had a nasty suspicion I knew what
Francesca was working up to. Oddly enough, our last
conversation had given me a grudging respect for the
woman. I honestly believed she was doing her best. Her
best wasn't good enough, by a long shot, but that was a
weakness, not a crime. She had a number of weaknesses,
not of character but of prejudice and ignorance. She was
intelligent but insensitive, subtle but not complex. Once
you identified the basic beliefs that governed her behavior,
you could understand, and even predict, what she was
going to do. I was as certain of her intentions as if she had
told me point-blank.

She wanted me to stay on. She wanted the Heir of the
Morandinis born in the family mansion, under her matri-
archal eye. If it turned out to be a girl, or a "raving madman," it and I could go to hell, or anywhere else we
wanted to go. If it was what she hoped, then she'd start the
next phase of the campaign. It would be a campaign of
indirection and suggestion rather than command; she
knew by now that I was not easily bullied, and of course
the very idea of physical coercion was absurd in this day
and age. Her methods would be more subtle: Join the
gentry, enjoy a life of ease, servants to wait on you, no
need to work for a living. Now she had another way of
pressuring me—the boy. If I stayed, I might be able to
help him.

The mirrored face was decidedly glum. It had a horrible
premonition of what I was planning to do.

The question was, could I get away with it? I studied
myself critically. If there was such a thing as the glow of
approaching motherhood, I didn't have it. My hair was a

mess. When I met Bart it had been long, falling almost to my waist. He liked it that way; he'd twine it around his hands, spread it across his body. . . . The day after the accident I took a pair of scissors and whacked it off. It was growing out now, too short to be braided or coiled, too long to hold a curl. My face was fuller than it had been, thanks to Rosa—she was a first-class cook. The problem wasn't my face or hair, it was my figure. Bart had been dead for three months. I couldn't be less than three months pregnant. Within a few weeks I should be showing signs of something more substantial than extra calories and the flabbiness of a winter's forced inactivity.

I had a month—six weeks at the outside. So, said my reflection apprehensively—you are going to stay? Saint Georgia on her white mouse, riding out to conquer the dragon and rescue a troubled child? Dr. Baldwin was right; what you need is intensive psychotherapy. Or a padded cell.

If the contessa found out I was not pregnant my departure from the Villa Morandini would be precipitate and unpleasant. I had told Pete; would he tell his grandmother? I doubted that he would tell anyone. He had already been warned off the subject. If he did tell her, then the masquerade was over. I would take my lumps and crawl away. I wouldn't sink so low as to ask him to hold his tongue.

Che sera, sera. With a shrug almost as eloquent as Emilia's, I turned from the mirror.

A remark Francesca made at breakfast confirmed my evil suspicions. We kept up the usual banal chitchat while Emilia served us. Not until we were finishing our coffee did Francesca say casually, "Pietro goes to the doctor today. Would you care to accompany us?" She added, with a faint but cynical smile, "I will arrange for you to speak with him alone."

"Thank you," I said, trying to imitate the smile. "I would appreciate that."

Deeper and deeper in, I thought. Everything I do gets me more involved; everything she does pushes me farther in. I was about to leave the room when she administered another shove. "I am going up now to hear Pietro's lessons," she said. "When he is well enough, he takes physical exercise at eleven. I believe you know where?"

I went looking for David—out and around, and up the back stairs, instead of trying to retrace the route Emilia had shown me. He was hard at work. I could hear his voice, raised in amiable soliloquy, before I opened the door. When he saw me he went right on quoting. It had to be a quote; normal people don't talk that way. " 'Lady, that in the prime of earliest youth, Wisely hast shunned the broad way and the green. . . .' I don't know that it's so wise, though. Why aren't you gamboling on the green this fine morning?"

"I came to invite you to join me—us, rather. The football game is on. Eleven o'clock."

"Oh, yeah? You've got yourself a man. I'm looking forward to meeting *il conte*."

"He's a sweet kid. Lonely. He lost both parents recently in a plane crash."

"I know."

"Yesterday you told me you'd never heard of him."

"Good God, but you're a suspicious wench. After I talked to you, I pumped Rosa for the story."

"Oh. I'm sorry."

"You should be. Anyone with a face like yours ought to

be open, candid, and idiotically trusting. What made you so . . ." He broke off, his smile fading. "I apologize. Always putting my big foot into my bigger mouth."

"It's okay. What are those nasty things?"

The table was covered with scraps of fabric, dark brown and black, ranging from fragments a few inches across to larger pieces.

"Nasty? Nasty! Those, my ignorant innocent, are examples of Coptic and early Arabic embroidery. Not worth their weight in gold, but worth a tidy sum in silver. Part of the count's Egyptian spoils. These bits and pieces weren't popular when he was on tour; he appears to have appreciated the unusual."

"They look awful."

"To me they are as lovely as the sunrise over the Duomo." He picked up one of the scraps. "The best thing about them is that the count had the good sense not to hand them over to the estate washerwoman. Wait till I get through with them."

I sat down on my old seat. "What do you do with them?"

"Wash them, of course—but not with yellow soap and a scrub brush. I'll have to go into town to pick up some chemicals and distilled water. Want to go with me?"

"What did you say?"

"Maybe you're surfeited with the sights of Florence." He didn't look at me as he spoke, but continued to admire the filthy cloth in his hand. "If you aren't—well, I'm a good guide. I know a little bit about a lot of things."

"I'd like that. But I can't go today."

"No sweat. I can wait till tomorrow."

"Fine. Are you planning to walk?"

"Good Lord, no. As an added inducement, I am offering you a ride on my BMW bike—secondhand, but superb."

I thought of the winding, bumpy road, and the carefree habits of Italian drivers. My phobia about driving was pretty well cured, but . . . I said firmly, "I have a rental car. I'll even let you drive."

"Okay. Whatever turns you on."

"I'll see you at eleven, then." I gave him directions to the garden and added doubtfully, "You won't get all wrapped up in your dirty collection and forget, will you?"

"Madam, you cut me to the quick. I'll be there."

In fact, he was there before me. I had gone to my room to compose a letter to my parents. On my next trip to Florence, I must retrieve the incoherent note I left with Angelo. I couldn't remember exactly what I had written, but I could remember the state of mind I'd been in when I wrote it.

The letter took longer than I anticipated. There were so many things I couldn't mention, such as my "condition," and so many others that required careful handling, such as Pete's illness. I had to make Francesca sound like a harmless, lonely old lady who had welcomed me with open arms and affectionate tears, and I had to convince the readers that I was well, happy, and in my right mind. It took three attempts to produce something that succeeded, if only partially, in these aims. I folded the delicate, gold-edged paper and put it in the delicate, gold-edged envelope with the Morandini crest. The stationery had appeared overnight in one of the drawers of the desk-secretary—another of those little amenities to which Francesca assumed I would quickly become accustomed.

When I reached the garden they were both there, sitting on the marble bench. Pete was swinging his legs and talking a blue streak. David leaned forward, arms resting on his knees, listening with intent interest, and nodding occasionally. When I opened the gate Pete jumped up. "Go out for a pass," he yelled.

I had to run forward to catch it. "Not bad," said David critically.

"She has the good hands," Pete said. "Now throw to me, signora."

"Wait a minute, we've got to go by the rules," David said. "Boys against girls?" He grinned wickedly.

"You're a crook," I said.

Pete chuckled. "A crook, a crook. He is. How can there be two against one?"

David said, perfectly deadpan, "She throws the ball, and then runs down and catches it, while we try to tackle her."

Pete broke up. He laughed so hard he had to sit down. David jabbed him in the ribs. "Don't laugh. We might have conned her into it."

After some more low-class clowning from David we decided Pete would play offense with both of us. He was the quarterback, of course. He was also a running back and all the front linesmen. Once when Pete faked and pulled in the ball to run, David tackled him with such gusto I yelped in protest, but Pete loved it. We didn't stop until we were all red-faced and winded. The score was Pete 54 (two missed extra points), opponents 14.

David stayed on the ground after the final play, flat on his back, staring up at the sky. Pete sat on his stomach. "Are you o-kay? Did I hurt you?"

"I could breathe better if you'd get off my diaphragm," David said, rolling the boy off him with a sudden heave. Pete sat cross-legged on the grass beside him. We discussed some of the finer points of the game, and David promised to give Pete some pointers on kicking. Pete nobly admitted that kicking was not one of his best skills. Finally David said, "I'd better get back to work. Thanks for the exercise, gang; that was a lot more fun than jogging."

"We will do it tomorrow?" Pete asked hopefully.

"Sure. Same time, same place."

He ambled off without a backward look. I said, "I guess I had better change for lunch. You too, sport."

"Sport. I like that." But he looked grave, and I knew he was thinking of his visit to the doctor. I had hoped he would mention it, but he didn't; so I took a deep breath and prepared to tackle something a lot heavier than my erstwhile opponent.

"I have a favor to ask, Pete."

"Of course, signora." He looked so pleased at the idea of doing something for me, I hated to tell him what it was.

"Can I go with you to Florence this afternoon?"

His face shut up like a curtained window. "Did *she* say you should come?"

"Yes. You see . . ." I wanted to touch him, but he was so far away from me he might as well have been on another planet. "You see, after Bart died, I was sick. I was in a hospital for several months, and I had to see a doctor—a psychiatrist—every day. I haven't been to my doctor since I left home, and I thought—if you don't mind . . ."

"You were sick? Like—" One finger touched his head.

He hadn't picked that up from Francesca. Probably the *tuttofare*, or Emilia, or the cook. "Right," I said. "Sick in the head. People can get sick there, just as they can get sick in their stomachs or their legs."

"But they get better," Pete said slowly. He picked up a stick and began poking holes in the dirt.

"Oh, sure they do. It takes a while; sometimes it seems as if it takes a very long time. I'm better. But I thought since you were going to see your doctor, maybe I could see him too. Just to make sure—you know—"

He nodded. I was glad he knew. I didn't know what the hell I was talking about. But I had to give him some reason for seeing the doctor alone. I didn't want him to think I was talking about him behind his back—ganging up on him with all the other adults. I knew only too well how that felt.

He went on poking holes—nice, neat holes that formed symmetrical patterns.

I said, "If you don't want me to come, I won't, Pete."

"I want you to come."

"Thank you."

He went on, as if I had not spoken. "I want you to be better."

My breath caught. It wasn't easy to speak lightly, but I tried. "We had better get moving, then. All that exercise has made me hungry. I could eat a horse."

"No, you could not! Could you?"

I held out my hand. "I'm so weak you'll have to help me up."

He did, with much grunting and puffing. It gave me an excuse to hold his hand as we walked to the gate. Francesca wasn't the only one who was pushing me farther in. Already it gave me a pang to think of saying good-bye to Pete. And how ironic that the only person in the house to whom I had told the truth (if not the whole truth) was a ten-year-old boy.

iii

It was too warm to wear my wool suit, so I put on a cotton blouse and skirt. Next to Francesca, cool and slim in pale-green linen, I looked like the *tuttofare*.

As we were finishing lunch, Emilia produced Pete, like a parcel to be taken to the post office. He didn't look like the same child who had laughed and joked and rolled on the grass. Sullen resentment coated his features like a thin, congealed mask.

We went out to the car and Alberto leaped to open the door. His manner toward me was almost as obsequious as it was to Francesca. Her style of living did have an insidious appeal. It would be easy to fall into the habit of treating people like objects, especially when they were people you didn't like. I noticed that Pete kept as far from Alberto as he could when he got into the car. It seemed more like distaste than fear, but it annoyed me, and prompted me to commit another impertinence. When we were ensconced, with Pete, stiff and silent as a doll, between me and Francesca, I said, "Does Alberto have sterling qualities I fail to observe, Francesca? I'm surprised you keep such an unattractive person on your staff."

Pete gave me a startled look. Francesca smiled, as if she enjoyed sparring with me. Fine, I thought; I'll give her plenty of opportunities.

"He does have admirable qualities you have not had occasion to observe, Kathleen. Loyalty, for one. Unquestioning obedience, for another. They are more important to me than a handsome face or fine manners. I don't dine with him, after all."

"He would die for the Morandinis?" I asked, investing the words with ironic quotation marks.

"Yes," she said flatly.

"Isn't that rather medieval?"

"Certainly. I understand he was somewhat rude to you when you first came to the gate. It won't happen again. Naturally, if you have any complaints about him you will tell me."

I wondered if there was anything Francesca didn't know about. Well, yes—there were a few things. Pete was still staring at me with shocked admiration. I winked at him.

Francesca talked to me and occasionally addressed a remark to Pete. I talked to both of them. Pete sometimes spoke to me, but never said a word to Francesca. I could only dimly imagine what those drives must be like when the two of them were alone. Pete must dread the trip as much as he dreaded the doctor.

Dr. Manetti's office was in a building that had once been a Renaissance palazzo, but the office itself was as modern as any I had seen. Like his colleagues the world over, the doctor appeared to be making a good living. The waiting room was furnished with lush plants and handsome pseudo- (or genuine; how would I know?) antiques. We were the only ones there, and when the door to the inner sanctum opened, it was the nurse, who told Pete to come in. Presumably the previous patient had been spirited out a back door. That's how Dr. Baldwin had arranged it.

Pete went with a little squaring of his shoulders that I found infinitely touching. He did not look back.

We waited for the regulation fifty minutes. Francesca looked through the magazines on the table, commenting now and then on an article or a picture. Not until the "hour" was almost up did she say, "I will meet Pietro in the outer office. I have explained to Dr. Manetti why you are here. Take all the time you like, ask whatever you wish. He has been instructed to tell you anything you want to know."

She had timed it perfectly. The last word was hardly out of her mouth when the nurse reappeared. "Signora?"

Francesca put her magazine down, smoothed her gloves, and went out.

I had assumed Dr. Manetti spoke English; there would not have been much point to my seeing him if he didn't. His greeting was not only fluent, it was flawless, with scarcely a trace of an accent. "It is a pleasure to meet you, Mrs. Morandini. May I express my condolences? I had not the pleasure of knowing your husband, but the contessa has often spoken of him."

He was much younger than I had expected, and not at all like the conventional stereotype of a psychiatrist—unless it was the television-movie stereotype. He wore slacks and a white shirt open at the neck, with an emblem on the pocket. It fit his muscular body like a second skin. His face and throat and arms were a gorgeous golden bronze and his hair was only a few shades darker. He was almost as handsome as Bart.

He held a chair for me and then, instead of retreating behind the professional barrier of his desk, sat down on the couch, his pose deliberately casual. "It's good of you to take an interest in the boy," he said. "Do I understand that you have worked with emotionally disturbed children?"

I admitted the limitations of my experience and mentioned Francesca's idée fixe about hereditary mental illness. Manetti laughed good-naturedly. "She is a remarkable woman. Very modern in many ways, and yet these old superstitions linger."

By the end of the hour we were on first-name terms. He was very easy to talk to—subtly flattering in his keen attention, quick to agree with my statements—and then, discreetly, insinuating reservations, or "redefinitions," as he called them. When I found myself moving toward the door I realized I had been given a standard fifty-minute hour. No doubt Francesca would have to pay for it. I can't say that idea upset me very much.

He started to open the door, then paused and said in a sudden change from his professional smoothness, "I wonder . . . Would you perhaps . . . Would you do me the honor of dining with me one evening? I am very proud of my 'home town,' as you say in America, and I like to show it off to visitors."

I was surprised, but not at all averse to the idea. I said I'd be delighted. He said I was very kind. I said not at all, he was kind to ask me. He said he would telephone. I decided not to mention the invitation to Francesca. He probably wouldn't call anyway.

When we got down to the street the car was nowhere to be seen. Francesca looked vexed. "I told Alberto to be here at four."

"He's probably stuck in traffic," I said. "There's a café—why don't we have some ice cream? I think we deserve it, don't you, Pete—Pietro?"

Francesca's expression was that of a woman who has been offered a dish of pickled mice, and it did not change after we took our places at one end of the rickety tables under the faded awning. I must admit I was pushing her deliberately, to see how far I could go, and I must also admit she tried to be a good sport. She even ordered coffee. She didn't drink it, though.

Pete and I had the biggest sundaes on the menu. They weren't called sundaes; I forget the names. We selected them from a card, complete with color photographs displayed next to the door of the café. The flavors were a little peculiar to American taste buds—a touch of black currant, a touch of coconut, and some kind of liqueur. I couldn't finish mine, so Pete kindly offered to finish it for me. He also kindly allowed me to mop his chin with a napkin dipped in the glass of water I had requested. A shudder rippled through Francesca's body, but she didn't say anything.

Except for an occasional wary glance at his grandmother, Pete behaved like a normal child while we ate our ice cream. As soon as the car appeared and we got in, he relapsed into silence. Alberto mumbled apologies for being late; Francesca cut him off with a brusque gesture.

I did most of the talking on the way home. Francesca replied courteously to my questions about the places we passed, but did not volunteer any information until we turned into the narrow, upward road, and I commented on the wildness of the area.

"It's part of the estate," she said. "From the turn to the top of the hill and beyond."

"All that? It must be hundreds of acres."

"We have not yet been forced to give up all that was ours. Many other families have sold the land; it is now occupied by cheap little houses and shops. That may happen here one day, but I hope I am not alive to see it."

For once there was genuine emotion in her voice. She cared more about places than about people.

iv

Sebastiano—Dr. Manetti—did call, the following morning, a little before nine o'clock. He apologized for calling so early. It was a nice touch of flattery, implying that he had awakened at dawn, panting with desire, and had barely managed to control himself until a decent hour. I accepted an invitation to dinner the following evening.

"I don't have any formal clothes with me," I warned him.

He laughed. "It is time you learned something about modern Italy, Kathleen. The only time I wear evening dress is when I must attend some boring professional dinner party."

I said I would look forward to it; and I meant what I said. My social life was certainly improving. Football and rag-picking with David, dinner with the shrink.

Francesca was obviously curious about the call, which had come while we were at breakfast, but she was too well-bred to ask outright. Instead she dropped a sly hint. "It would be courteous, Kathleen, if you would tell Emilia when you plan to be absent at mealtime. Ordinarily I wouldn't ask it of you, but with my small staff . . ."

"I understand. I'll make a point of doing so."

"Dr. Manetti tells me that you are a good influence on Pietro."

She must have telephoned him as soon as we got home. I smiled modestly; she went on, "He approves of the games, and the time you spend with the boy. He said he had cautioned you about certain matters—"

"I'll be careful, Francesca. I'm not as stupid as I look, honestly."

"I don't think you are at all stupid," she said.

After breakfast I went up to the attic to remind David we had a date to tackle each other at eleven. At least that was one of my reasons. There wasn't much else to do. My embroidery bored me, I had read most of the books I had bought, and exploring the desolate gardens had only limited appeal. So I offered my services as assistant scrounger.

He looked at me doubtfully, scratching his chin. He had shaved that morning, but he was just as dusty. "If you're going into this with some expectation of unearthing a box of rubies and diamonds, forget it. There is a method to this apparent madness, and I insist on following proper procedures."

"I will obey orders to the letter."

"Okay. That's what I'm looking for—letters. I found a box of miscellaneous papers that has to be sorted. There's all kinds of stuff here—newspaper clippings, patterns for ladies' bonnets, accounts. I want it sorted, first by category and then by date. If you're in doubt about anything, put it in the miscellaneous box."

The miscellaneous box was overflowing when I finished. I apologized for my lack of skill; David said I'd get the hang of it—which I doubted—and we went to find Pete. He was a little late that morning—a nasty session with Italian history, I gathered—but his glum expression brightened when he saw us waiting, and he put us through a stiff workout. At noon David called a halt.

"I've got to go to Florence to pick up the stuff I told you about," he explained to Pete, man to man. "See you tomorrow?"

"I cannot," Pete said with a glance at me. I gathered that his appointment had been changed, and that he was to see the doctor in the morning.

"The day after, then," David said. "That's Saturday. You don't have lessons on Saturday, do you? We'll start early and have a good long practice."

"O-kay!"

After he had gone David said, "I'm going to do you the

honor of changing my clothes. Meet you in fifteen minutes."

"But I thought—"

"You forgot. Or you changed your mind?"

"Neither. I thought you had forgotten."

"I had planned to leave earlier, but we couldn't disappoint the kid. It doesn't matter; we can have lunch in
Florence and do the shopping later. I know a great trattoria. Cheap."

"O-kay," I said. "I wonder where Alberto put my car.
He's got the keys, too."

"The car is in the garage. I'll extract your keys from
Alberto and pick you up out in front, like a proper chauffeur. Unless you don't want to be seen fraternizing with
the hired help."

"Don't be silly. Make it twenty minutes."

I met Emilia in the hall and was pleased to inform her I
would not be in to lunch. It really was short notice; if I had
been as rude to my mother, Pa would have let me have it,
but Emilia murmured a meek "thank you."

It took me a little longer than twenty minutes. David
was waiting. He came to a snappy salute when I appeared,
but his expression was sour. "What's the matter?" I asked.

"Nothing. I always look like this after I've chatted with
Alberto."

"What did he say?"

"Never mind."

"Something about me?"

"It wasn't so much what he said, it was the way he said
it."

"Oh. I trust you punched him in the nose for insulting a
lady?"

"Are you kidding? I'm the original chicken. He may be
twenty years older than I am, but he is also forty pounds

heavier, with a reach like a gorilla's. Probably learned commando warfare under il *duce*."

"Is he that old?"

"I don't know or care how old he is. Let's not talk about him."

I had such a good time that afternoon I never thought what a good time I was having. David knew the back streets of Florence the way I knew the alleys of Wayford, Massachusetts; and if his casual greetings were any indication, he knew half the inhabitants of Florence, too. Beggars, street cleaners, waiters, guides . . . When I commented he explained solemnly, "I'm a charter member of the fraternity of the poor. It's an international association, confined to people who know what it's like to be hungry—really hungry, not just a little peckish. I can always count on a handout from a fellow member. Generosity is a quality restricted to the impoverished, you know. The rich scatter largesse when they need a tax deduction, and then make pious remarks about how superior they are to the lazy, shiftless recipients of their charity."

It was one of the longest speeches he had made on any subject except Margaret Fuller. I said, "I suspect you are a radical socialist."

"Absolutely."

"You'll have to meet my father."

We had lunch at his favorite trattoria, where the waiter greeted him like a long-lost buddy. We saw some of the standard tourist sights, and some that were not so standard. At the Accademia he lectured me on Florentine sculpture, and when we stood in front of the *David* he flexed his biceps and asked if I noticed the resemblance. He hadn't been boasting when he said he knew a little bit about a lot of things, and his enthusiasm was contagious. It was late in the afternoon before we finally got around to his errands. They took us to a dark little shop in a back street where, after a long discussion, David loaded several armfuls of bottles and packages into the trunk of the car.

"This is really a help," he said as we drove away. "I manage okay with the bike, but its trunk space is limited."

"Stock up on supplies any time."

"Thanks, I may do that. It's none of my business, but are you a rich heiress, despite your demure and modest appearance? I mean, if you want to turn the car in you could save yourself a few bucks, and I'd be glad to take you into town whenever you are reluctant to make use of Alberto's services."

It was a thoughtful and generous offer. There was no sense in my keeping the car; it was costing a small fortune, and I didn't really need it. I don't know why I should have felt a frisson of panic at the idea of giving up a means of escape. . . . Escape? Say rather mobility—independence.

"I'll keep the idea in mind," I said, and was obscurely relieved when he didn't press the point.

I had told him I needed to pick up something at my former hotel, so we went there after we had finished with the chemist. There was no one on duty at the desk; after I banged and yelled, a scrubwoman shuffled out of a back room and informed me that Angelo was not there. I had already deduced that. Thanks to David's superior Italian we learned that Angelo was next door, at the coffee bar, so we went in search of him.

Angelo was drinking coffee as if he were being paid to do so. He probably needed gallons of caffeine to get through his work schedule. When he saw me his face didn't exactly light up, but it became a shade less pensive.

"Ah," he said. "The friend has come."

I looked at David, who looked back at me with amused

curiosity, and decided not to explain. I simply smiled non-committally and introduced them. The title *il professore* did not impress Angelo. After all, his brother was a policeman.

I asked about my letter. Angelo pressed his hand to the pocket of his shirt. "It is here, signorina. Always, next to my heart."

"You can give it back to me, Angelo. I'm very grateful for your help."

"You want it? You don't want I should mail it?"

"No. But thank you."

Angelo's face became, if possible, even blanker. He was thinking. After a while he arrived at some conclusion—I didn't ask what it was; I didn't want to know. He nodded. "Ah. Now the friend has come. . . ."

He handed me the letter. It was somewhat the worse for wear. Apparently he had not exaggerated when he said he always carried it next to his heart.

David suggested another cup of coffee, an offer Angelo was quick to accept. However, he rejected David's suggestion that we sit down. "There is an extra charge, professore. The coffee is the same if we stand; why pay more?"

The two of them entered into an animated conversation, while I shifted from one foot to the other and tried to catch a few words. I wouldn't have blamed David for being curious about the byplay with the letter, but the occasional word I did understand suggested that they were discussing something else. We parted with friendly salutes all around and Angelo's assurance that if I ever again wanted to leave a secret message with him, he would be happy to oblige.

On our way back we were fighting through the traffic at the Piazza della Indipendenza when David waved at the white-uniformed policeman perched on a perilous little platform in the center of the maelstrom of cars and motorbikes. "Was that Angelo's brother?" I asked.

"What gave you that idea?"

"I caught the word *fratello* during your conversation. Angelo is very proud of his brother."

"And rightly so. He's no mere traffic cop, but an honest-to-God plainclothes detective."

Perhaps that explained Angelo's mild obsession with secrets and mysteries. But it didn't explain David's gesture; I persisted, "Do you always wave to traffic cops?"

"I happen to know that guy," David said, grinning. "A slight contretemps concerning the right-of-way in a traffic circle. . . . But I always make friends with cops when I can; you never know when a friend in the force will come in handy."

When we arrived at the villa we found the gates had been closed. David stopped the car. "What do we do now?"

"What do you usually do?"

"Go in the back door, of course. There's a gate on the north side, big enough for the bike."

"Watch." I leaned on the horn.

At first I was afraid my gesture was going to fall flat. Then the shrubs behind the lodge shook violently, as if they had been struck by a miniature, invisible whirlwind. A grotesque figure burst out into the open. Capering and crooning in a tuneless, high-pitched monotone, he wove a fantastic pattern of stumbling steps across the gravel.

"Good God," David breathed. "Who the hell is that?"

"Alberto's assistant. Haven't you seen him before?"

"Never at close range. Do you think he's going to open the gate?"

"I think he's working up to it."

The stooped figure wore clothes that looked like Alberto's cast-offs. They flapped loosely around his body, and the cap came down to the bridge of his nose. From under the cap long, lank hair tumbled onto his neck and over his face. Without interrupting his pathetic travesty of a dance he opened one of the gates, and, after another interval of hopping and singing, dealt with the other.

David reached in his pocket; but when he pulled up a few feet and offered the crumpled bill to the temporary gatekeeper the man let out a screech of terror and fled.

"Don't chase him," I said, as David started to open the door. "You'll only frighten him more."

"I guess you're right." We drove on in silence. I assumed David's thoughts ran along the same path as mine—wondering how Alberto treated his unfortunate assistant—and suspecting the worst.

David put the car in the garage, next to the Mercedes, and handed me the keys. I handed them back. "Hadn't you better unlock the trunk first? I'll help you unload."

"That's okay, I can manage."

"Thanks for today. I had a marvelous time."

"Me, too."

He unlocked the trunk and put the keys into my hand. Our fingers touched, and for a moment we stood without moving or speaking. I hated to have the afternoon end. The Malones are great huggers and kissers; but somehow I couldn't give him the casual, friendly embrace I would normally have offered. We parted formally, thanking one another again in voices that had become strangely reserved.

I treated Francesca to another scathing critique of her servant that evening, describing the condition of the dog's pen and questioning his fitness to supervise a mentally handicapped person. She appeared faintly amused by what she would probably call my "qualities of youthful idealism."

"I assure you that the person to whom you refer is not

abused by Alberto," she said. "As for the dog, discipline is necessary for a guard dog. The animal is not a pet."

"Discipline is one thing, cruelty is another. A dog doesn't have to be vicious to be a good guard dog."

She promised to speak to Alberto and then deftly turned the conversation to a subject she knew would distract me. It was so good of me to take an interest in Pietro. No doubt I had encountered other disturbed children when I was teaching. She would be happy to listen to any advice I cared to give.

There is one form of flattery to which everyone is susceptible: being asked for advice. She let me babble on, interrupting only to ask questions that proved she was listening with close attention. I was feeling pretty full of myself when I went up to bed. Smug is hardly the word. A few more weeks and I'd have everybody straightened out; then I would make a dignified exit, bowing, amid the plaudits of the crowd. The dog would lick my hand, Alberto would apologize and promise reform, Francesca would thank me for showing her the light, Pete . . . I would hate to leave Pete. But he would be o-kay. Thanks to me.

Even youth is no excuse for that kind of conceit.

I had finished Mark Twain. I shuffled through the rest of the books and realized I had read the lot. I should have bought more when I was in Florence. No more Gothic romances, though. The heroine of *Bride of the Madman* was a perfect fool. Sticking grimly to her job in spite of stones that rolled off cliffs, narrowly missing her; in spite of the sinister housekeeper; in spite of the hero, scarred and brooding, who wasn't the type I'd have cared to spend an afternoon with, much less a lifetime. I tossed the book contemptuously aside.

I often thought back on that gesture. As I said, it's a good thing I'm not superstitious.

v

The mattress yielded gently. Bart was sitting beside me. The moonlight streamed in the window, showing every feature in stark detail. The flash of even white teeth as he smiled, the little mole on the sculptured curve of his left cheekbone, the hollow under the bone, the scattering of black hairs across his chest.

His fingers brushed my breast and shoulder in a pattern achingly familiar. He had such smooth hands. Not soft, like a woman's, but smooth like warm ivory, without the tiny calluses and roughness of normal flesh. Brushing and touching, gently at first, then firmer, with little, knowing pressures here, there. . . . Moving up to my throat and cheek, into my hair.

Sometimes I had dreamed of waking into nightmarish reality, and fought to wake again. I had followed his retreating figure down endless shadow streets and wakened weeping with frustration. Now I had found him; and it was worse. My lips parted, my throat tensed to cry out. His mouth muffled the cry. For a split second I felt his lips, tasted them. Then all sensation was blotted out.

I woke with the echo of a scream in my ears and knew it had been my own. The room was almost dark. The moonlight was dim, the gauzy curtains were closed. The straps of my nightgown were pulled down, baring my body to the waist.

* * *

It took me a good five minutes to find my purse and the little bottle lying at the bottom under a jumble of other things. I swallowed one of the capsules and sat down in a chair to wait for it to work. I had turned on every light in the room, but I couldn't force myself to get back into the bed. A faint scent still seemed to linger around it—the scent of the aftershave Bart had used.

Why hadn't Dr. Baldwin warned me this might happen? Well, but he had hinted at it when he questioned me about my sexual impulses. At the time I didn't have any. Not surprising, he said soothingly. (Nothing surprises a psychiatrist.) I was a young, healthy woman. Someday . . .

Fine. But I had not expected that when the day came it would be Bart's ghost that aroused me.

As the drug began to take effect, relaxing muscles and dulling horror, I decided I might survive this too. Maybe it was a stage of convalescence. Maybe I had to dream about Bart making love to me before I could dream of someone else. Maybe my dead husband was a symbol of that someone else. David? Sebastiano? I wasn't conscious of wanting to go to bed with either of them, but they were both attractive men, in very different ways. A lot of people would tell me that was what I needed—a good, satisfying roll in the hay, without emotional commitments. And maybe they'd be right.

I went to the window. The moon hung tangled in the cypress tops, a lopsided ellipsoid, a silver football. I couldn't see David's window, but I pictured him scrubbing his nasty little bits of fabric, or sitting up in bed, reading—culling new scraps of wisdom from the nineteenth-century poets. Somehow it made me feel better to know he was there.

But I spent the rest of the night sitting up in the chair.

five

Sunlight might have improved my state of mind, but there was none the next morning. The skies were a soft pearly gray. Francesca said rain was predicted for that evening.

She seemed a little distraught—nothing definite I could point to, but not her usual self. Always the perfect hostess, she did not fail to notice my hollow eyes, though I thought I had hid the signs of sleeplessness rather well.

I admitted I had not slept well. I hadn't meant to tell her the reason, but her look of concern seemed genuine, and I desperately needed to tell someone—not the whole truth, but part of it. I said, "I had a bad dream. A nightmare, actually. About Bart."

The lines in her forehead deepened. "To dream of someone you love—is that a nightmare?"

"It can be."

"Will it help you to talk about it? I have not asked about him, or about the accident . . ."

"It doesn't really help. I've already . . ." I pushed my chair back and went to the window. "I guess you're entitled to know, though. You were fond of him."

"Yes."

I didn't turn. "When we were married Bart moved in with me." He had moved in before, actually, but why mention that? "I had a little house—it was the guest house of an estate. Only two rooms and kitchen and bath, but I was delighted to have found it—in the country, yet close enough to make commuting feasible. There was even a bus line at the bottom of the hill. Sometimes I took the bus when the weather was bad. The road to my house was a private road, narrow and steep. After a heavy snow it could be dangerous. Bart . . . Bart enjoyed driving it. It was a challenge to him, especially when it was slippery with ice."

"He was an excellent driver," said the calm voice behind me.

"I know. He told me he had driven racing cars. The first time he took me up that road, in a heavy snowstorm, I was scared to death. He was laughing."

"It was on such a snowy day that the accident occurred?"

"We had six inches of snow the day before. It was wet snow, packed down; cold temperatures during the night froze it solid. He—he'd been away. He came back that morning, not to stay, just to pick up some things. I was outside shoveling the walk. When he drove away I stood watching. . . ."

I saw it now, vivid as reality. The sun, blindingly bright on the snowy slopes, the dark band of trees at the foot of the hill. The car, a splash of brilliant crimson in the stark black-and-white landscape, appearing and disappearing around the curves, growing smaller with each appearance.

The road shimmering with colorless brilliance, empty of traffic. The final appearance of the tiny, toy vehicle as it swung—too fast, out of control—into the main road far below.

I turned. "We quarreled. I was angry because he hadn't come home the night before. He said he'd tried to call, that the lines were down because of the storm. But I was angry anyway. I said things. . . . And he wasn't the man to take criticism meekly. The last thing I said to him was—was something hateful. He always drove too fast when he was furious. He was driving too fast that day. I had seen him cope with conditions as bad, or worse. If he hadn't been angry—if we hadn't argued . . ."

I did not expect absolution from her. There was neither sympathy nor condemnation in her voice when she replied. "I thought as much. I won't insult you by pointing out that your feelings of guilt are both normal and unnecessary. Your doctors must have said the same."

"You know about that, too."

"Of course. Are you ashamed of it?" She gestured. "Sit down and finish your coffee."

I needed the caffeine; I was still groggy from taking the Valium so late at night.

Instead of asking more questions she began to talk about Bart. She didn't take out pictures of babies on bearskin rugs or coo about how cute he had been; but the relationship I had pictured became clearer as she went on. Bart had been several years younger than his cousin Guido, but always in their encounters he came out best. His sayings were wittier, his laughter more engaging; he ran faster, hit a tennis ball more accurately, swam more strongly. Guido sounded like a singularly dull lad. When I asked, Francesca showed me a photograph of him, taking it from a drawer. The only photo on display was the one of Bart.

The cousins stood side by side, not touching. Bart must have been about twelve then; he was already almost as tall as his cousin. The contrast between the two was painful. Guido had none of the family good looks. His long, mournful face resembled that of an amiable horse. He stood stiff and unsmiling, arms at his sides. Bart's head was thrown back, laughing.

My preconceptions about Guido couldn't have been more inaccurate. He was probably as dull as he looked—steady, dependable, reliable—all the boring virtues. Pete didn't resemble him at all. Nor, except for those startling silver eyes, did Pete look like the Morandinis. Maybe that accounted for Francesca's indifference to him.

Francesca did not invite me to go with them to the doctor that day. However, she did mention the matter of transportation. Alberto was available to take me to Florence whenever I wished; did I want to return my rental car, or have him do it for me?

I finessed the question, but it bothered me. This was the second time in twenty-four hours someone had worried about that car. It was uncharacteristic of Francesca to do so; why should she care what it was costing me?

After she had gone I jogged around the drive a while, getting some much-needed exercise. The air had the breathless hush that often heralds a storm, but I knew the clouds weren't heavy enough for that; the breathless, restless feeling was not in the air, it was inside me. I wanted to do something, but I couldn't think of anything I really wanted to do. The options were limited: sort junk with David, jog up and down the drive, explore the grounds. Finally I went to my room to review my wardrobe. I didn't want to do that either, but I had to find something to wear to dinner. My clothes were whisked away, laundered and returned, almost as soon as I took them off; even so, I had very little to choose from. I had not been concerned about clothes when I packed, and I certainly had not given much thought to the season. I might have known it would be cold in Florence in April, part of the time at least. Everything I had was too big or too lightweight or too shabby. I should have gone to Florence with Francesca to buy a decent dress. I should go now. I didn't feel like doing that either.

Thoroughly disgusted with myself, I slammed the wardrobe door. I knew what was wrong with me. My treacherous body still tingled with the memory of my dream.

A cold shower is the conventional remedy for what ailed me. I wasn't that Spartan, so I decided to try cold air. It was getting on toward the time when David took his morning break. If he was jogging around his exercise yard, I would jog with him.

I went out the front door and around the house. David wasn't outside. Feeling like a child who has no one to play with, I wandered toward Pete's so-called play yard. A sudden sharp yelp from the dog made me jump, it sounded so close. I heard Alberto's voice and the dog's response—a burst of excited barking. I had never heard it bark before, and curiosity drew me toward the sound. When the dog stopped to draw breath Alberto laughed—either that or he was scraping a rusty metal bar across a stone. They seemed to be having a jolly time, but there was a quality in the dog's barking that made me uneasy—a frenzied note of excitement. If Alberto was teasing him, I'd have a word or two to say. . . .

Then I heard something that made me break into a

headlong run—the high, piercing screams of an animal in pain or desperate terror.

The gate wasn't locked. I burst through it like a cannonball and skidded to a stop. The dog was loose. Its chain lay coiled on the ground beside it. It was facing away from me, crouched, its haunches quivering with eagerness, but restrained by the stick Alberto held. He stood a few feet beyond the dog, the stick in one hand. From the other, raised high above his head, dangled a small ball of bedraggled fur. The ball of fur was screaming. The dog must have already got to it; blood dripped from its side.

The next few seconds were a blur. When I got my wits back, I was standing next to Alberto with the kitten clutched to my chest. All ten of its claws stuck into me, tiny needlepoints pricking. Alberto hadn't moved. The stick still hovered, the other arm was still raised. I used to play basketball with Mike and Jim, but I never made a jump like that one.

How long the tableau would have held I do not know. Alberto was paralyzed by surprise; the dog didn't know what the hell he was supposed to do, if anything; I was so furious I couldn't catch my breath, so furious a red haze clouded my vision. The spell was broken by a bellow of alarm and a flying body. An outthrust arm sent me staggering back. The dog began to bark, the kitten screamed and dug its claws in deeper; David knocked the stick out of Alberto's hand, and Alberto pulled back his fist and hit David in the face. David tumbled over backward. The dog leaped for his throat.

I was afraid to let go of the kitten, or carry it close to the dog. I kicked Alberto in the leg. "Get him off," I yelled. "*Avanti, pronto*—move it, you—you—"

I couldn't think of any name bad enough to call him.

He gave me a startled look and then reached for the dog's collar, lifting it as easily as he had lifted the kitten.

David lay on his back, knees drawn up, arms crossed over his face and throat. He said, "Is it off me?"

"Yes, it's off you. Are you all right?"

David scrambled to his feet. He examined his shirt sleeve and said indignantly, "My shirt's torn."

"Small loss," I said, eyeing the faded garment. Out of the corner of my eye I saw Alberto quietly backing away, dragging the dog with him. Suddenly the full enormity of what had happened swept over me like a huge wave, and I had trouble controlling my voice. "Are you really okay?" I squeaked. "I can't believe—"

"The dog knew me," David said. "I suspect it wouldn't have been long before auld acquaintance was forgot, but he was confused enough to hold back for a few seconds. What a damned fool thing to do!"

"It certainly was. Alberto wasn't threatening me."

David sputtered. "I wasn't referring to myself, I was referring to you. I heard what was going on and was rushing to the rescue. The damned gate stuck, and I was trying to open it when you came barreling in. My God, Kathy, you sailed past that dog's jaws with an inch to spare. You ought to know better than to startle a neurotic animal like that. Not to mention Alberto. He might have—"

"Well, he didn't."

"Don't you ever stop and think before you jump?"

"Not often enough."

His face softened. "Oh, what the hell. Let's see what you've got there."

He held out his hands. I said, "It's stuck to me like a burr. Oh, David, I'm afraid—"

"It couldn't hold on that tight if it were badly hurt," David said reassuringly. "Come on up to my room. I've got some first-aid stuff, and some milk left over from breakfast."

David's voice and touch finally persuaded the little creature to let go. The milk helped too; it practically fell into the saucer, it was so hungry.

The only cute thing about it was its size. Otherwise it was a mess, skinny and dirty, its coat dull and matted and full of burrs. It was so young it didn't know how to drink properly. It kept sneezing and putting its front paws into the milk. David filled the saucer a second time when it had been licked clean. Neither of us spoke. Finally the frantic lapping slowed. The kitten lifted a milky muzzle, and after a moment we heard a faint, uncertain purr. I burst into tears.

A short time later David said, " 'The book of female logic is blotted all over with tears.' "

I mumbled into his shoulder, "I didn't know Browning was such a male chauvinist."

"Thackeray, not Browning. Nor Brown, for that matter. I merely meant to point out that there's nothing to cry about now."

I moved away from him. "Sorry," I said snuffily. "It was just . . ."

"I know." One arm still rested on my shoulders. He gave me a quick, brotherly squeeze, and then took his arm away. "Let's see about some first aid, shall we?"

The kitten was howling again by the time he finished, but its shrieks sounded more indignant than pained. The cut on its side wasn't as bad as I had feared. David smeared on antiseptic lotion from his kit and, despite the kitten's furious struggles, dunked it up to its nose in a basin of warm water. When he took out, the water was black with dead fleas.

"How did you learn to do that?" I asked, as he set about drying and grooming his victim.

"Oh, we always had animals around. My sisters and I dragged home all the neighborhood strays."

"Sounds like my family. Is that your comb?"

"It's the only one I've got," David said cheerfully. "Too bad I don't own a hair drier. I've never gone in for that sort of elegant grooming. But it's a warm day; he won't catch cold. He looks better, doesn't he?"

He had rolled the kitten in a towel; all I could see was a pointed face and two big ears. The eyes had a distinctly resentful expression. The face was prettily marked, however. The dark M of the tabby markings stood out against a silvery gray background, and the pink nose and spiky whiskers were set in a symmetrical frame of white. The eyes blinked and started to close.

"He's pooped," David said. "I guess I'll take him to the vet now, while he's too limp to resist."

"You're nuttier than I am. What are you going to do with it—him?"

"Keep him, I guess. What else is there to do?"

"Bring him to me when you get back from the vet."

"But you can't—"

"I'm going to give him to Pete."

By the time I had fetched the car keys for David and changed my clothes, I was late for lunch. I didn't care. I felt marvelous. There is nothing like a storm of rage to clear away the clouds of depression.

I told Francesca what had happened, without mincing any words. "I don't think it's the first time. I've heard about people who train fighting dogs that way, by letting them kill smaller animals."

Her face wore an expression of fastidious disgust. "Naturally I would never have permitted such a thing had I been aware of it."

I believed her. But she wouldn't have been aware, or made any effort to find out. I said, "Do you mind if I am present when you speak to Alberto about it?"

"You think I will not be forceful enough?"

"I just want to watch him squirm," I said.

She smiled faintly. "I will tell Emilia to bring him here after we have finished."

It was a delightful interview. I enjoyed every minute of it. I couldn't understand what Francesca said, but her voice crackled with anger, and by the time she finished with him Alberto was practically groveling. He had not once looked in my direction.

"Are you satisfied?" Francesca asked.

"One more thing," I said. "Tell him I'm holding him responsible for the cat. If anything happens to it—anything—I will assume he's to blame."

She raised her eyebrows, but did as I asked. Alberto looked at me then, a quick, lowering glance from under his heavy brows. I expected him to show resentment; I was the one who had got him in trouble, and it really wasn't fair to hold him accountable for the animal. It might run away or be injured by some wild creature. But I saw no resentment on his face, only the same fawning humility he gave Francesca.

She dismissed him with a curt command and then looked at me. "You are keeping the animal?"

"I'm sorry. I forgot my manners. I tend to do that when I'm angry. I'd like to give him to Pete, if you have no objection."

"So long as he keeps it out of my way. I do not care for cats. But are you sure it is wise?"

"What do you mean?"

"You seem to be fond of animals. Do you think this one will be safe with Pietro?"

"I know it isn't realistic to expect a child that age to take proper care of a pet; but I'll explain it to him, and the cook—she seems like a kindly person—maybe she could help out—"

"That is not what I meant. I'm sure you believe that my fears about Pietro's mental health are unfounded, and that he needs only a few simpleminded panaceas, such as a pet and a pat on the head, to be fully recovered. But what if you are wrong? Twice he has tried to injure himself. When the next attack comes—and it surely will—he may injure something else."

ii

Naturally—naturally!—I paid no attention to this depressing suggestion. I was waiting on the terrace when David drove up. He leaned across and opened the car door, and I climbed in next to the sleeping cat.

"Here's the loot," he said, indicating a canvas carryall. "Cat food, medicine, the lot. Are you going to take him to Pete now?"

"Why not?"

"Can I come?"

"Why not," I said, laughing.

The kitten woke when I picked it up. It wasn't a beauty, but it looked a hundred percent better. We went into the house through the kitchen and stopped long enough to introduce the new resident to Rosa. She reacted as I had hoped, tickling it under the chin and giving us a saucer and a glass of milk to take up with us. David translated her comment. "It is a good house that has a cat. Better than mousetraps."

"Mice," I said.

"The place is riddled with them. Are you afraid of mice?"

"No. But I don't like to find dead ones in front of my door."

"Better brace yourself. It's a demonstration of affection, I'm told, and this guy sure owes you."

I can't describe Pete's face when he saw the kitten and realized it was for him. I still get choked up thinking about it. I managed to keep my emotions under control, however.

The kitten was not averse to more milk, so Pete fed it, and David explained the proper use of the things he had bought. "Don't try to put the medicine in its ears by yourself, Pete. It's a two-man job. Cats hate the stuff."

"O-kay." Pete stroked the cat's back. It tried to purr and drink at the same time, sneezed, spat, and rubbed its nose irritably. Pete laughed. "Is it a boy or a girl? How old is it? What is its name?"

"Boy," David replied. "About six weeks old. You're the owner; what do you want to name him?"

Pete hesitated. Then he said, "Joe. His name is Joe."

"Namath?" I guessed. "If you're going to name him after a quarterback, there are other—"

"Not a quarterback. Joe is what his friends call my father. His name is not Joe, you understand, but that is what they call him in America."

"That's a very good name," I said, clearing my throat.

"It is not bad, to name an animal for your father?"

"I think it's a great compliment," David said seriously. "I have a pig named after me. He's a very handsome pig."

"I will call him Joe David," Pete said. "I have two

names, so he can have two names. I cannot call him Kathy. He is not a girl. But when I get a girl cat or a girl dog . . ."

"That's a promise," I said. "Don't forget."

"I picked up a few toys too," said David, clearing *his* throat. "Ball, catnip mouse. Here's some string; what you do is, you tie something on the end and—"

"I know." Pete seized the string eagerly. "I know how to do it. My aunt Vera had two cats. I played with them. Like this."

He dangled the string. When we left he was laughing and watching the kitten pounce fiercely on the end of the string. It was the first time I hadn't felt wretched about leaving him alone.

Aunt Vera. His mother's sister? It had not occurred to me that he might have living relatives on that side of his family. The seed of an idea put up a tiny green tendril in my all-too-fertile mind.

"Hey," David said. "We forgot something."

"What?"

"Litter box."

"Oh, lord, you're right. Not that I care if the cat poops on the floor. Emilia will have to clean it up."

"I'll dig up something," David said. "Literally."

We parted with mutual expressions of esteem and a promise to meet next morning for football.

David headed down the back stairs and I went the other way, to the front stairs and my room. When I turned onto the landing I saw Emilia ahead of me, about to start down. Where the devil had the woman come from? She certainly hadn't been with Pete, and there was no other reason for her to be on the top floor.

I called to her to wait. I felt fairly certain she had been spying on me, or on the child. Some people are natural sneaks, and Emilia probably justified her prying and spy-

ing on the grounds that her mistress ought to know what
was going on in her own house. It would have been point-
less to accuse her, though. Instead I told her I was going
out for dinner and asked what time she locked up.

"You will be late, signora?" she asked.

"I don't know when I'll be back. That's why I'm asking."

"*Naturalmente,* I will not lock the house until the signora has returned."

I thanked her and went on down the stairs. Alberto
must have told her about being raked over the coals. He
might not resent my interference, but she did; the sullen
hostility in her eyes was now open instead of half-con-
cealed.

I wondered if she would put snakes in my bed or forget
to clean my room. Probably not; as long as I was on good
terms with Francesca I was safe—hated but sacrosanct. All
the same, I thought, I'll look under the covers before I get
in bed.

iii

Sebastiano was picking me up at seven. I decided to wait
for him downstairs. The idea of being summoned by
Emilia and perhaps being invited to join Francesca for a
drink before we left didn't appeal to me.

I was trying to decide between a bare-shouldered sun-
dress, in which I would freeze, and the inevitable brown
suit, which made me look ten years older, when there was
a knock on the door. "Who is it?" I called.

"Francesca."

"Oh. Come in, please."

I pulled the dress over my head as I spoke. The vexing

question of what to wear was settled, anyhow. The zipper stuck as it always does when you're in a hurry, and when Francesca came in I was squirming around, both hands behind my back, like Laocoön fighting off unseen snakes.

"May I?" she asked.

"Oh; thank you. I'm afraid it's stuck."

It took her about two seconds to free the catch. I thanked her again, and tied the belt. She said nothing more, just stood watching me. I knew what she wanted, but—naive me—I put it down to curiosity, and her habit of authority.

"I hope I gave Emilia enough notice—about not being here tonight," I said after the silence had become embarrassing.

"Yes."

She waited. It was against her principles to ask outright, but this time I was not going to make it easy for her.

"It may be raining before you return," she said finally. "Do you wish Alberto to drive you, instead of driving yourself?"

"No, thanks." There was no sense in stalling; he'd be at the front door in less than half an hour. "Dr. Manetti is picking me up."

"Manetti!"

I decided to go on the attack. "Is there something I don't know about him? Vicious habits, drunk driving, dead wives in the closet, like Bluebeard?"

She was not amused. She began, "Bart is—"

"Bart is dead," I said harshly. "Three months dead. I'm sorry if your notions of propriety are offended, Francesca, but at home we don't go in for formal periods of mourning and I find such observances hypocritical. You needn't worry, I'm not going to . . . do anything you'd disapprove of. I only met the man two days ago. We'll probably spend the evening talking about Pete—Pietro, I mean."

"That is your only interest in Dr. Manetti?"

"I'd be a liar if I said yes, and you'd be very naive to believe me. He's an attractive, interesting man. But I'm not in the habit of jumping into bed with someone the first time I go out with him—or even the second time."

"I see." Lines of worry scarred her forehead. She said, as if to herself, "There is no hope of dissuading you. I can give no reason . . ."

"I'm afraid you can't dissuade me, no. I could meet him on the sly, but I've no intention of behaving like that."

"I see," she repeated. "Well, then . . . Perhaps it will be acceptable. . . ."

And with that peculiar remark she walked out, closing the door softly behind her.

I thought of another old adage: Just because you're paranoid it doesn't mean somebody isn't following you. What a strange interview that had been. It hadn't occurred to me that Francesca might disapprove of a woman so recently widowed dating a man. . . . Well, to be honest, it had occurred to me. I had thought she might not like the idea, but I had not realized it would matter so much. Yet she had seemed more worried than angry. Perhaps Manetti did have a bad reputation. The Florence Strangler? The Marquis de Sade of Tuscany? I felt sure she'd have told me anything to his discredit.

I picked up my purse and my shabby old raincoat, which was all I had, and hurried down the stairs. I caught a glimpse of a black skirt whisking out of sight as I crossed the stairs. Emilia again. Damn the woman, I thought. How does she find time to get her work done? Or is spying on me her chief job?

It felt good to get out of the house, even though the

shadows were closing in and the air was heavy with pent moisture. I had intended to walk to the gate, but after seeing how dark it was I decided not to. I was wearing rather high heels and the gravel was not the best of surfaces for walking.

He was early. I saw the headlights of his car appear and blossom into brilliance. They caught me full-on, and I put up a hand to shield my eyes. He was out of the car before I got over being dazzled.

"What are you doing out here?" he asked, handing me in. "It is dreary, chilly—"

"The atmosphere inside was chillier." I settled back into soft, gray velvet comfort.

"Oh? But I should have known. Was Francesca angry?"

"Not so much angry as upset. It doesn't matter."

"She is difficult to understand," Sebastiano admitted. "So sophisticated, so modern, and yet there are these pockets of traditional belief. I hope you weren't disturbed by her attitude."

"Is that a professional question, Doctor?"

He laughed ruefully. "It is a hard profession, mine. When I ask a simple question, the question of a friend, I am accused of probing. When I don't ask, I am thought cold and unsympathetic."

"You have a point," I admitted.

The big car—it was a Cadillac, brand-spanking-shiny new—went so lightly down the steep road that I hardly felt the bumps. A glare of headlights burst out at us, and Sebastiano pulled sharply to the right to let the oncoming car pass. He swore in Italian, and then said, "I hope you didn't understand what I said. He was coming too fast for such a narrow road. But you need not worry, I am a careful driver."

"I have a mild phobia about fast driving," I said.

"I do not ask why."

"Good for you."

He laughed; then I could laugh too. I was much more relaxed with him than I had expected to be. After a moment he said, "If you don't want to talk, that is fine. If you want to, then talk as you would to any friend. And I won't send you a bill."

It began to rain as we passed through the village, a soft drizzle that barely moistened the windshield. He handled the big car expertly. I don't remember what we talked about, but I remember that we laughed a lot. But it was not until we reached the restaurant, and we had checked our coats, that I really began to appreciate him. I had felt self-conscious about my off-the-rack cotton dress. Sebastiano was wearing an equally unimpressive suit, and his shirt was open at the neck. The other diners were more formally dressed; I had to believe that Sebastiano had deliberately dressed down to my level so as not to embarrass me.

The headwaiter greeted Sebastiano with the enthusiasm reserved for old and valued customers and we were shown to a table in a shadowy corner. I asked him to order for me. It was all superb—the wine, the food, the deft, unobtrusive service, the beautifully appointed table. I couldn't help thinking of the meal I had had with David. Plastic tablecloths instead of snowy linen, coarse white plates instead of fine china, a harsh, biting Chianti instead of—whatever this superb vintage might be. But the two men had one thing in common—the ability to make me feel relaxed and at ease, the ability to make me laugh. And if Sebastiano's charm was practiced and professional, I couldn't have cared less.

I refused dessert, though he urged me to have something. "You are too thin," he said, his fingers tracing a line

along the inside of my arm. "I speak medically, you understand. Doesn't Francesca feed you?"

"Too well. Rosa is a good cook." But there was a reason
why I had enjoyed this meal more than usual. Every bite I
took in that house stuck in my throat. I had not thought
about it until that moment, but it was true. Breaking bread
with another person has time-honored emotional connota-
tions. Offering food is a gesture of friendship; accepting it
is a sign of trust.

"You are thinking thoughts that are not pleasant," Sebastiano said softly. "I don't ask what they are. What shall
we do to take your mind off them? Would you like to go
dancing?"

"I'd rather not, if you don't mind."

"I don't mind at all. Although I am a good dancer. But
not so good as your husband, perhaps."

I looked up from my plate. He clapped his hand to his
mouth in mock consternation and then said, "I can't help
it. Forgive me."

"You're forgiven," I said, laughing. "Bart did love to
dance, and he was marvelous. He was an actor, you know;
every movement he made was trained, graceful."

"I didn't know. Francesca has spoken of him, but only
of his childhood and adolescence. I am something of a
movie buff; I'm surprised I have not recognized the
Morandini name or features."

"He had had a few small parts in television shows, but
most of his work was on the stage."

"Ah. New York?"

"Well . . . It was mostly summer stock, dinner the-
aters, that sort of thing. Luckily he had a private income or
he'd have starved. It takes not only talent, but contacts and
luck, to break into the theatrical profession."

"True." He waited a moment and then said tentatively, "If I were to suggest a film, it would not . . ."

"No, that would be fine. But my Italian is practically nonexistent."

"There is a cinema that shows old British and American films. I don't know what is playing, but we could go there and see."

The movie was an old Marx Brothers film—*A Night at the Opera.* Sebastiano had not martyred himself on my account; he laughed so hard I thought he'd choke. When we came out of the theater it was raining heavily. He suggested a drink, or coffee. "I guess I'd better not," I said reluctantly. "Emilia will be waiting up for me. I can't stand the woman, but it isn't fair to keep her up half the night."

The streets were slippery. He had taken my arm; now he gave it a squeeze. "You are a very kind person, Kathy."

My laugh had more than a touch of wryness.

The gates were closed, but before Sebastiano could sound the horn Alberto came out from the lodge and opened them. The rain had slackened, but he got pretty wet. Sebastiano said, "Is your tender heart concerned for Alberto too?"

"I just wish the rain were boiling oil," I said.

"*Dio mio,* how vicious you are! What has he done to deserve that?"

"Lots of things. I don't understand why Francesca employs a man like that."

"His personal habits would not concern her so long as he performed his duties faithfully. I believe he and his wife have been with her for years. It is hard to keep servants, especially when one doesn't pay high wages." He brought the car to a stop in front of the stairs.

"Don't come in," I said quickly. "I'm sorry, Sebastiano —that sounded awfully rude; I didn't mean it that way—"

"It did not sound rude and I know why you said it. But I must see you to the door."

"It's stopped raining. I'd rather you didn't. Really."

"That bad, eh?" He sat back, his hands resting on the wheel. "Do you mind if I smoke? Will you join me?"

"And you a doctor," I said. "It's very bad for you."

"It is a bad habit. I try to cut down—it is my first of the evening, if you notice."

I accepted a cigarette. I didn't want it, but it seemed boorish just to say thank you and leave after such a nice evening.

"I haven't smoked since I got here," I said proudly. "I don't want to start again; I was smoking too much for a while."

"How long has it been?"

"Since I quit? Only a few days, actually."

"You know what I mean. And you know I am not asking as a doctor."

"Sebastiano—"

"Six months? A year?"

"Three months." I choked on the smoke like a teenager with her first cigarette.

"I didn't know."

"Francesca didn't tell you?"

"No. And that is not strange, for we do not talk of family matters very often. When she called to ask if I would see you she said only that you were her nephew's widow. I was taken aback when I saw how young you were. I knew you could not have been married long, but I had no idea. . . ."

"You wouldn't have asked me to dinner if you had known?"

"Oh yes, I would." The answer was prompt and heartfelt. I laughed a little. Then I said, "Perhaps after all you share Francesca's idea about the propriety of someone so recently widowed going out."

"I don't make rules. All cases are different. In your case, it shows a healthy attitude. One cannot mourn forever."

"How true." I put out my cigarette. "I'd better go in."

"Yes, the poor servants whom you hate so much will be kept waiting," he said mockingly.

"Thank you for a wonderful evening. I really enjoyed it, Sebastiano."

"Then we will do it again. Tomorrow?" Before I could reply, he clicked his tongue and said irritably, "I forgot. I am going away for the weekend. Monday, Tuesday . . . Tuesday for dinner?"

"I'd love to."

"Good. I will telephone." He went on with scarcely a pause, "If I try to kiss you, will you consider it an affront to your hostess?"

I was laughing when he took me in his arms, and the kiss was more intense and prolonged than I had planned. It wasn't at all like Bart's kisses. . . . The fact that I could think of that, in the middle of a thoroughly satisfactory and enjoyable embrace, was not a good sign, but I didn't let it keep me from responding. Not until Sebastiano's hands moved under my loosely belted coat did I pull away.

"Right move, wrong place," I said a little breathlessly. "Emilia is probably looking through the keyhole and Alberto is ticking off the minutes until you drive out."

"Since we will be blamed anyway, why not enjoy it?"

The first fine careless rapture was gone, though. I had a prickly feeling at the back of my neck, as if we were under hidden, intense surveillance. Which was ridiculous. The lantern lights flanking the door of the villa were some distance away, and the interior of the car was dark. When

I drew away the second time, Sebastiano didn't insist. I refused another cigarette. He lit his; the flame trembled perceptibly. "Get out, then," he said lightly. "You won't let me come to the door, you won't . . . Next time it will not be so easy for you to run away."

Despite the light tone and the smile that accompanied the words, I knew he was annoyed—at me, at Francesca, or at both of us. I didn't blame him. He waited until he saw the door open, and then pulled away with a roar of the exhaust.

Emilia had indeed been waiting for me. She had the door open before I reached the top of the stairs. I felt like an adolescent who has violated a curfew, and I found myself self-consciously straightening my coat and tightening my belt as I crossed the terrace. The rain had stopped, but the wet stones were slippery.

Emilia stood back with exaggerated deference, holding the door. I had barely entered the house when I heard it— a scream of tortured metal that seemed to go on forever, and a dull, crunching crash.

For a few seconds I was frozen, flung back into a memory of past horror. But when I turned there was no flame, no column of smoke. I started to run. Emilia followed. I heard a voice call out: "What is it? What has happened?" The voice was Francesca's. She had waited up for me too. I didn't pause to reply.

The Cadillac was halfway between the house and the gates, where the drive curved. The hood was jammed against a tree trunk. The headlights still shone; one went off at a drunken angle, shedding a weird theatrical light up into the leaves.

I saw a man leaning against the driver's side of the car looking in the window and thought it was Alberto, until the gatekeeper came running up, calling out. Sebastiano straightened. He spoke to Alberto, and then started violently as I caught his arm. I stammered out a series of questions, the conventional inquiries, to which he replied that he was unhurt.

Francesca was the last to arrive on the scene. She had delayed to put on a coat and—with her usual good sense—to find a flashlight. She turned it on Sebastiano. He was pale and his hair was disheveled, but his face, at least, was unmarked.

He insisted on inspecting the damage to the car before he did anything else. It might have been worse. One of the headlights was out of line and the hood was crinkled, but there did not appear to be anything wrong with the engine. It would cost a pretty penny to repair the body, though.

We went back to the villa, leaving Alberto trying to straighten the headlight. When Francesca got a good look at Sebastiano she announced flatly, "You have cracked a rib. You had better stay here tonight. I will call a doctor."

"I am a doctor," Sebastiano said, with a forced smile. "It is not broken, only bruised. I was thrown against the steering wheel."

He refused her invitation to stay, or to let Alberto drive him back to Florence. Somewhat to my surprise she didn't insist.

"But you shouldn't drive," I protested. "Even if you are physically able, there may be damage to the brakes or the steering or—"

He cut me short with uncharacteristic abruptness. "I will drive carefully. There is little traffic at this hour. Good night, Kathy—Francesca. I regret having inconvenienced you."

"It is I who should apologize," she said expressionlessly. "The drive must be in poor condition. I will have Alberto look at it."

I don't know how she managed in such innocuous words to convey the impression that the accident was his fault—that he must be drunk, or drowsy, or distracted. I knew he was none of the above, but I couldn't understand how it had happened. The drive was not in first-class condition. There were slippery spots where the gravel had been worn away, but only excessive speed would cause a car to skid out of control.

Sebastiano kissed Francesca's hand, wincing as he bent from the waist, and shook mine with ostentatious formality. His eyes avoided me. He telephoned an hour later, as Francesca had asked him, to let us know he had arrived home safely. Emilia delivered the message. He didn't ask to speak to me.

six

I woke up sneezing. I had not caught cold; there was a cat sitting on my face. Somebody giggled, and a voice said, "You have a mustache. A black-and-white-striped mustache."

I removed the cat's tail from under my nose and sat up. The kitten slid down my front, rolled over, and attacked my knees. I made a grab for it. Pete got to it first and hugged it protectively to his chest.

"Joe did not mean to hurt."

"I was thinking about the sheets." Ruefully I examined the perforated silk. "Your grandmother isn't going to like this. I'm afraid Joe will have to have his claws clipped."

"Clipped?" The silver-gray eyes widened in horror.

"It won't hurt him. A scratching post might not be such a bad idea either." I sank back onto the pillows, yawning. "You little demon, don't you know that people who wake up their friends by putting cats on their faces are not popular?"

"But you sleep too late. Today we have the football, and also washing of David's things. He said we could help. What do you call them—the things from the storeroom?"

"Darned if I know." It had been late before I got to sleep, following the accident and its aftermath, but the beaming face that peered at me from over the cat totally disarmed me. He was reacting to a Saturday off like any child freed from the appalling boredom of studies.

"You have a mustache now," I said. "Okay, buster, scram out of here and let me get dressed. I'll be with you soonest. Am I allowed to eat breakfast first?"

A knock sounded at the door, and the boy's face altered so unpleasantly I reached out a hand to him. Emilia came in before I could reply. "You are ready for breakfast?" she asked. "I have—" Then she saw Pete, who had retired behind the bed curtains, and burst into a tirade in Italian.

"I asked him to wake me," I said sharply. "That will be all, Emilia. I'll be down in fifteen minutes."

"The contessa has eaten an hour ago. I will bring a tray to you."

Pete didn't come out from his shelter until she had closed the door. "You don't have to go," I told him. "Wait for me if you like."

"No, I will put Joe in my room. Then I will go to David. He is in his room, at the garage. You will come?"

"As soon as I can."

He scuttled out, clutching Joe. He didn't want to encounter Emilia again, even with me there to defend him.

When I came out of the bathroom my breakfast tray was on the desk. For all her bulk Emilia could move quietly when she chose. I wasn't sure I liked that idea.

The scientists were hard at work when I arrived. David had put his rags to soak. A row of trays filled with muddy liquid lay on the table. Pete was peering onto one of them with an expectant air that was, in my opinion, hardly justified. All I could see was dirty water.

"Just in time," said David. "The great unveiling is about to take place. Nothing up my sleeve, lady and gent . . ."

He flexed his hand, reached into one of the trays, and came up with a fragment about a foot square. He dunked it in a tray of clear water to rinse it. "Voilà."

The colors seemed to leap up off the surface of the water—bright crimson, clear green and buff against a background of rich dark blue. Careful stitching outlined a woman's face and shoulders. Her features had the big-eyed stiffness of a Byzantine painting, and her hair, of soft auburn, was surmounted by a fillet of twisted gold threads. A border of flowers and leaves framed the portrait. At least David claimed it was a portrait.

"Fifth century if it's a day," he murmured rapturously. "And in perfect condition."

"What do you mean, perfect? The stitching's come undone here—"

He stepped back with a look of horror as I put out my hand. "Don't touch it!"

"I was just pointing. Goodness, what an old granny you are."

"I've been called worse." David deposited his treasure tenderly on a piece of blotting paper and went on to the next. The fabrics—some woven, some embroidered—had a certain charm, especially the squares and roundels with running animals—cats, hares, greyhounds—which, according to David, had been stitched to clothing. I found them mildly interesting, but only mildly, and Pete soon got bored.

"Let us play football," he said.

"Don't tell me you aren't having fun," David said with a grin.

"I like that—" His finger indicated the embroidered cat. "But to wash clothes, it is a woman's work."

"Male chauvinist," I said.

"What is that?"

"Well . . . It's like saying girls can't play football because they're girls."

"But they cannot. Except you," Pete added.

"You'd better quit now while you're ahead," David advised him. "I'll be through in a minute, Pete. Can't stop in the middle of a job, you know. How about getting rid of the used solution for me? No, not out the window, you lazy cuss—in the sink."

He indicated the door behind him.

"You've got plumbing?" I said, as Pete lifted the tray, spilling only a quart or so.

"All the comforts of home. This used to be the chauffeur's quarters. Alberto being a happily married man, and Emilia being vital to the contessa's comfort, they live in the villa."

I helped Pete empty the trays and rinse them. David refilled them with distilled water and mixed some assorted chemicals. "That's the lot," he announced, dunking the next batch of scraps. "Now we can get on to the important business of the day."

Pete had the football with him, of course. He clattered down the stairs ahead of us. "Who called you worse things?" I asked.

"Huh?"

"When I said you were an old granny I was being chauvinist. I apologize. You said—"

"Oh, yeah. Think nothing of it, dearie. My old man had more pejorative comments to make when I took up my profession. He went so far as to impugn my masculinity, if you can believe it."

"What did he want you to do?"

"Follow in the paternal footsteps. He manufactures bolts—those fifty-cent bolts the Pentagon buys for nine hundred bucks."

"Oh." Another stereotype gone west. The starving academic was, or could have been, one of the idle rich. "A matter of principle?" I inquired.

"I don't like bolts," David said.

Pete decided he wanted to practice kicking that morning. I let David talk me into holding, though I ought to have known better. Pete kicked my hand as often as he did the ball, so after a while I persuaded him it wasn't fair for me to have the honor of being the holder all the time, and David and I changed places.

The sun was high in the sky before Pete could be persuaded to stop. I reminded him that Joe would be waiting, and he gave in with reasonably good grace. "To take a nap is not so bad with Joe," he admitted. "Joe must sleep lots, he is young."

After he had gone I dropped onto the bench. David sat beside me. "Nap?" he said. "He's too old for an afternoon nap, isn't he?"

"I would say so. But his grandmother has some idea he's delicate."

"Delicate, my foot." We had ended the session with some passing and tackling. David had been tackled. "Is that why he isn't in school?"

"I guess so." I felt sure David's question wasn't prompted by idle curiosity or love of gossip. But it was not my place to tell him about Pete's emotional problems.

"This is a lousy setup for a kid," David muttered. "He'd be better off in school. Hasn't he got anyone to play with? Not even a pet, until you came up with the kitten."

"I'm working on it," I said briefly.

David's wide, *Petrouchka* smile split his jaws. "I'll bet you are. Little Miss Fix-It."

"I've been called worse than that."

"By your old man?"

"Especially by him. You'd like him," I added after a moment.

"Maybe I'll look him up when I get back."

"When will that be?"

"June, July—whenever the money runs out."

"Oh."

"Any chance that you'll be there?"

"At home with the folks? That depends on the job situation. If I can teach summer school I will; I need the money. If not, I suppose I'll scrounge off my mother and father, and sling hash at the local diner."

"Then you won't be here?"

"Not on your life. I—" His eyes shifted, but not quickly enough. I glowered at him. "Who have you been talking to? Rosa?"

"I was not prying into your personal affairs, if that's what you're thinking. Rosa volunteered the information. She's all excited about it."

"Damn," I said.

David went on, "She keeps talking about what joy it will bring to the house when the baby is born, and all like that. I got the impression you were going to stay until . . . that you were going to stay."

"No."

"I didn't mean to—"

"I don't want to talk about it."

"Okay." He stood up. "See you."

After he had marched off, visibly offended, I regretted having been so brusque. Apparently my interesting and fictitious condition was now public knowledge, and it wasn't his fault if Rosa liked to gossip. I could not imagine Francesca chatting with the cook; presumably Rosa had heard the news from Emilia. I should have known it would happen. It didn't alter the situation, but somehow the fact that David was now one of the deluded majority brought the whole dubious business into sharper, uglier perspective.

I had been kidding myself when I thought I could prolong the lie for another month. Every day brought the possibility of a painful confrontation that much closer. If Francesca asked me flat out I would have to tell her the truth. When the situation first arose she had been a stranger to me, a stranger I didn't much like. Now she was a person I knew, with feelings that could be hurt. I might not sympathize with those feelings; I couldn't even say truthfully that I was fond of her. But when I thought of seeing her face change, her eyes harden with contempt— no, I couldn't contemplate that. I had to leave, soon. I had done all I could for Pete; Lord knows it wasn't much, but there wasn't much I could do except talk. And I had done plenty of that.

As I showered and changed I rehearsed the speech I meant to make to Francesca: graceful thanks for her hospitality, apologies for remaining longer than I had intended. Then she would say something like "Not at all, it was a pleasure." And I'd say, "It's been great getting to know you, but . . ." But I have to get back to my job? But my mother broke her leg and she needs me to take care of her? But I feel another nervous breakdown coming on?

No. That was my guilty conscience thinking I needed an excuse to leave. What I needed was an excuse for barging in and staying so long. A polite hostess doesn't ask a guest when she is planning to go. Maybe my cynical and melodramatic theories about the matriarch and the Heir of the Morandinis were all wrong. Maybe she would be glad to see the last of me.

I revised the dialogue.

"Thank you so much for your hospitality, Francesca."

"Not at all. I've enjoyed having you here."

"I've enjoyed it too. But I've trespassed long enough."

"I'm sorry you must go. When are you leaving?"

"The end of next week."

The end of next week. Set yourself a deadline and stick to it. Don't let an unhappy child or a handsome doctor stop you.

The only trouble with preplanned conversations is that the other guy never says what he's supposed to say.

I went downstairs early, wanting to get it over and done with. Francesca was not in her sitting room. I paced the floor nervously, picking things up and putting them down. Bart's photograph followed me with smiling eyes. I tried not to look at it.

I heard the telephone ring. The instrument was on a table in the hall; I suppose Francesca didn't want such an intrusive, modern vulgarity in her lovely room, where she might have to answer it herself instead of letting Emilia screen the callers.

The door opened. "It is a telephone for you, signora," said Emilia.

It had to be Sebastiano. Who else would be calling? I picked up the telephone and said brightly, "How's the rib today?"

There was a moment of silence. Then a voice said, "Which one? I've got eleven or twelve of the cursed things. They seem to be all there, but I've better things to do than ask them how they are feeling."

"Pa!"

"So you know me, do you? But you weren't expecting

the old man, oh no. Whose ribs was it you were inquiring about so sweetly, may I ask?"

"Oh, Pa, it's so good to hear your voice! How did you find me?"

"With great difficulty. And it's costing me a pretty penny even on a Saturday, so don't be wasting my time in idle chatter."

"Who's wasting whose time? How are you? Is everyone all right? What's wrong?"

"Nothing is wrong *here*," said my father with heavy significance. "It's yourself that must be wrong, I'm thinking, to foist yourself on a poor woman who never saw hide nor hair of you till you turned up on her doorstep. What the devil are you up to? Never mind; don't tell me, I don't dare think about it. When are you coming home?"

"Soon, Pa. Did you get my letter?"

"What letter? I got a postcard with a dozen words on the back, and thank you for the effort. When I telephoned your hotel I had a very strange conversation with a young man who seemed to know more about your affairs than your own father. When is soon?"

"I don't know exactly."

"Aha. You're flat broke, is it, without the means to buy a ticket."

"For God's sake, Pa, I'm not eighteen years old. I have my return ticket—"

"Then use it. When?"

"The end of next week."

"You mean it?"

"Yes. Friday or Saturday—maybe Sunday. I'll call as soon as I get a reservation. Honest."

"Humph," said my father.

"Let me talk to Ma for a minute."

"She's not here."

"I'll bet she doesn't know you called. I'll bet she said, 'Leave the girl alone and don't be treating her as if she was a baby.'"

"Humph."

"I adore you, Pa. I'll call you in a few days."

"You damn well better," said my father.

I heard the click as he replaced the telephone, more than five thousand miles away. I was so homesick I felt dizzy. Friday. I'd try to get on a plane Friday.

Then I looked up and there was Francesca on the stairs, staring down at me.

I said stupidly, "That was my father."

"So I gathered." She came down the stairs. "I apologize. I could not help overhearing."

She walked right past me toward the door of her room. Emilia materialized in time to open the door. I followed, though my first cowardly impulse had been to flee.

We took our seats. Emilia poured wine. I said with forced brightness, "He's mad because I've been gone longer than I planned. As you may have heard, he wants me to come home."

"Friday or Saturday, you said."

"If I can get a reservation. I've trespassed on your hospitality long enough."

I was back on track. Unfortunately she failed to pick up her cue.

"I had assumed you would stay on."

"Oh, my goodness, I don't know what gave you that impression. I haven't any—"

"You are Bartolommeo's wife. This is his home. It is yours, for as long as you like." A faint frown wrinkled the serenity of her brow. "Perhaps I should have made that plain from the beginning. I assumed you would understand."

Worse and worse. She was talking to me the way she would to a simpleminded child. And the kindness, the open-hearted generosity . . . Don't be a boob, I told myself. It isn't generosity. It's the old European assumption that a woman is her husband's property, to be moved from place to place at his convenience. That his child belongs to his family, not his wife's.

"You are very kind," I stammered. "But I must go home. My—my mother . . ."

I verily believe I would have dragged out that stupid lie if she had not interrupted me. "Ah yes. You want to be with your mother. I can hardly hope to take her place at such a time. It would be different, of course, if Bartolommeo were here."

"Oh yes, of course." By that time I didn't know what I was saying. I snatched at the excuse she had offered. "That would be different. But as it is—"

"Friday?"

"If I can get a reservation. Do you mind if I call this afternoon?"

"Emilia will place the call for you," she said abstractedly. "The telephone system is difficult."

My appetite wasn't very good. Francesca did not raise the subject again, but I expected her to at any moment, and my stomach was a mass of fluttering butterflies. It did not improve matters when Emilia came in with a long white florist's box, and Francesca held out her hands, and Emilia said dourly, "For the signora."

I had to open it then and there. The flowers were freesias, a rainbow glory of peach and pale blue, pink and yellow, smelling of springtime. The card said only, "Until Tuesday."

Francesca murmured, "How charming. Give them to

Emilia; she will take them to your room and put them in water."

Emilia took the flowers with a curl of the lip that indicated what she thought of the gift, the giver, and the recipient. No doubt the conventional red roses would have impressed her more; but these soft, fragrant blossoms were more to my taste. That Sebastiano knew they would be—that he wasn't annoyed with me—improved my mood considerably.

I told Francesca I would let her know about the reservation. She only nodded, without speaking. I was on my way out of the room when I thought of something. "Francesca?"

"Yes?"

"I'd appreciate it if you wouldn't tell Pietro I'm leaving. I suppose it's vain of me to think he will care—"

"He will care."

"But he must know I can't . . . Anyway, I'd rather tell him myself, if that's all right with you."

"Certainly." She smiled. "I have not given up hope of persuading you to change your mind."

ii

Welcome back, Jane Eyre, I thought. But that was just my neurotic conscience reacting to what had only been a courteous conventionality. Coming from a sinister housekeeper, or a villain twirling his mustache—or the scarred, brooding hero of *Bride of the Madman*—it might have sounded like a threat.

I decided to go to Florence. It was a beautiful day, a good day for shopping and sightseeing, and a very good day for avoiding the members of the household. There wasn't a single person I could face. I had even been rude to David.

The flowers were in my room, filling the air with their sweetness. I grabbed my purse and coat and went out. Emilia was in the hall when I got downstairs. The damned woman was everywhere. On a sudden impulse I told her I would not be in to dinner. I couldn't endure another meal like the last.

There was no one in the stableyard, no sign of life at David's window. No doubt he was in his beloved dusty attic. It felt good to be behind the wheel of a car again. If no other positive feature had resulted from this visit, that phobia at least seemed to be cured. The car represented freedom, independence, mobility, escape. . . . From my own folly, what else?

When I reached the gates, they were closed. Alberto was nowhere in sight. No reason why he should be on duty; he had not been told I was going out. I got out of the car.

There was a bar on the inside, but after I had hoisted it out of its supports the gates still wouldn't open. I pushed and tugged without result, and then looked more closely. There was a lock. There was a keyhole. There was no key.

Surely Alberto wouldn't carry the key on his person. If he did, I'd have to go back to the garage and look for him, and I was averse to that idea for more reasons than one. I heard something moving in the shrubs behind the lodge. I called, "Alberto?" and went around the shrubs to have a look.

The man behind the bushes wasn't Alberto. He was on his hands and knees, crouched like a beast of prey. Locks of greasy flaxen hair fell over his face; and as I stood watching he began crooning to himself.

I took a grip on my nerves. The poor man couldn't help

it if he looked like a creature out of a horror film. I didn't know his name. I said slowly, *"Pardone, signore. La porta è chiusa. Io desidererei . . ."* I couldn't think of the word for key.

He didn't look up. He started crawling back and forth, snuffling like a dog on a scent. It was really a ghastly performance, and my voice was a trifle unsteady when I began again, *"Scusi—"* That was as far as I got. The man sprang to his feet, arms flailing wildly, and ran straight at me. I caught a flashing glimpse of a face twisted by some strong emotion—fear, perhaps. His eyes were shut, his mouth was an open, gaping hole in his face. He passed within a foot of me and rushed on, limping dreadfully, but moving at surprising speed. A harsh cackle of manic laughter drifted back to me.

I finally found the key hanging on a nail inside the lodge door. It was eight inches long, and I had to use both hands to turn it. Then I had to return the key to its place, drive out the gates, get out of the car, close the gates. I couldn't lock them. I decided that was just too damned bad. Why all the fuss about security, anyway? Barred gates, a vicious killer dog, a surly brute of a human guarding a run-down mansion whose portable treasures had long since gone to the pawnshop. . . .

The green shadows of the tunnel-like road reminded me that I might be unfair to Francesca. The house was certainly isolated. For all I knew, the quiet countryside might be a hotbed of vice and crime. Perhaps she needed the dog and the gates.

As soon as I came out of the trees my spirits improved. Under the spring sun I saw the lovely smiling landscape I knew from photographs and paintings. The hills were flushed with the pale green of new growth; the dark gray-green shapes of the cypresses looked like an ornamental frieze, too symmetrical to be natural. The small piazza in the village was crowded—women shopping, or pushing baby carriages, men filling the tables at the outdoor café. I drove at a crawl, responding to the friendly nods and smiles and the curious stares of passersby.

What a pity my visit had been spoiled by personal difficulties—most of them, I had to admit, brought on by myself. Someday perhaps I could return. I'd like to see Pete again. But Francesca would probably never forgive me when she learned the truth.

I forced Francesca from my mind. This was my afternoon off. I was going to play tourist, shop for souvenirs, see the sights. I had not much time left. Five days, or six.

I had forgotten one little detail until the clerk at American Express reminded me of it. Yes, I could get on a flight from Rome on Friday, if I was willing to pay an extra hundred-plus dollars. My ticket was an excursion-type, with a minimum number of days. If I wanted the lower rate, I would have to wait until Monday.

Luxurious living hadn't blunted my thriftiness. What was a couple of extra days, after all? I made a reservation on a train to Rome Sunday afternoon, and another on the Rome-to-New York flight Monday. There were lots of flights from New York to Boston; I wouldn't need a reservation for that leg of the trip. That job done, I turned to the important business of the day. I had no intention of spending the glorious sunlight hours in the Uffizi or the Pitti Palace. I wanted to go shopping.

Many of the shops were closed; they would reopen later in the afternoon. But the open-air stalls in the Piazza San Lorenzo were doing a thriving business, and I bought presents for everybody—a real leather purse for Ma, a silk shirt for my father (he wouldn't wear it, but he would brag about owning one), toys for the baby, souvenirs for broth-

ers and sister-in-law—and a dress for me. I intended to
dazzle Sebastiano on our next—our last—date. The dress
was peach-colored silk with a jacket trimmed with braid of
the same fabric. My souvenir of Florence.

Later in the afternoon I found myself in my old neighborhood and decided to stop for a cappuccino at the coffee
bar near the hotel. I hadn't been there long when Angelo
came in. I invited him to join me. He glanced doubtfully at
the table and the chair and I said expansively, "I'm buying,
Angelo. Today is the first day of the rest of my life."

"Signorina?"

"Just a figure of speech, Angelo."

"Ah," said Angelo. He looked to my right, to my left,
and then, for reasons known only to himself, over my
head. "The friend is not with you."

"No."

"The friend is gone? My brother—"

"I'm sure your brother is very nice," I said. "But I won't
get a chance to meet him this trip. I'm going home soon."

"He is handsomer than your friend," said Angelo. "Your
friend is nice fellow, but not handsome. You are going
home?"

"I have to work for a living too, Angelo."

"Ah yes. You have more secret letters for me, signorina?"

I thought of telling Angelo I was not a secret agent or an
undercover cop, and decided there was no need to disillu-
sion him. Let him enjoy his fantasy.

"Not at the moment, Angelo. But I appreciate the offer."

"*Prego, signorina.* I am always ready. I am always at your
service. A secret message, a room, if you wish to be private, no one knowing where you are . . ."

"I may take you up on that," I said.

He swallowed two cups of espresso in quick succession

and then announced he had to get back to work. "Any time, signorina. Remember. You take advantage of me."

It was nice to have a friend, even if he liked me for the wrong reasons—as did most of the people I had met recently. Angelo thought I was a spy, Francesca thought I was pregnant, David and Sebastiano . . . I had not been completely candid with them either. They might not like me as well if they found out what I was hiding. Thank heaven for Pete. Pete liked me.

That thought didn't cheer me up one bit.

I took my parcels back to the car, which I had left in a public parking lot. I couldn't return to the villa yet. I had told Emilia I would not be in to dinner. It was too early to eat, but the shops had reopened. I still needed a gift for my hostess, and I wanted something to read. Perhaps I could find a book for Pete too.

Secondhand paperbacks weren't difficult to locate, but I had to go to an expensive foreign-language bookstore to find children's books in English. I had no idea at what level Pete was reading, so I avoided the heavier classics and settled for the Hardy Boys, a book about cats with lots of color photographs, and one real prize—a book called *Famous Quarterbacks of the NFL.* I felt sure he'd struggle through that text, even if it was too advanced for him.

Sometime later I was unconcernedly lost in a maze of narrow streets behind the Duomo. The narrowest were no wider than sidewalks, and here, for the first time, I began to get the feel of the medieval city. The houses were flush with the pavement; occasionally I could see flowers and fountains through open archways. There were a few jarringly modern touches; through the open windows came, not the gentle tinkling of a lute, but blaring rock 'n' roll, from radios whose volume switches had been turned up as far as they would go.

I wandered along, pressing against the wall when a motorbike roared past. Then I saw something in a shop window, illumined by a ray of sunlight that had squeezed through a gap between the high buildings opposite. It was a scrap of embroidery that looked as if it had been cut from a larger piece. A spray of silvery-green leaves and pale-pink flowers curved across a background of ivory silk. The flowers were shaded with such skill that the individual stitches blended, like a painting. On a sudden impulse I opened the door of the shop and went in.

I had tried my hand at the bargaining I knew was customary in the smaller shops, without much success; but I did not have to counterfeit the consternation that seized me when the genteel lady clerk told me the price of the scrap. "It is Lyon silk embroidery, signorina, over two hundred years old. Very rare."

"It's just a scrap," I protested. "Not even big enough for an evening bag, or—"

She looked shocked. "One does not *use* such rare pieces, signorina. One exhibits them. It is a manufacturer's sample, not a scrap!"

I got it for a little more than half the price she had originally quoted, only because I didn't really want it and she knew I didn't really want it. I was almost out the door when she made her final offer. As I filled in traveler's checks I was already regretting my purchase. I must have embroidery on the brain; without David's lectures and Francesca's attempts to instruct me, I'd never have noticed the wickedly expensive trifle. And Francesca would probably consider it a tacky, inappropriate gift.

iii

It was dark when I got back to the villa, and as I drove into the garage I saw that David's window was alight. That surprised me; I had expected he'd be out on the town on Saturday night. I was unloading my purchases when I heard his door open and the clatter of feet down the stairs.

"Hi," he said tentatively.

"Hello."

"Are you still mad at me?"

"No. I was rude, David. Sorry."

"That's okay. Hey, you really went on a shopping binge, didn't you? Let me take some of those things."

"I should have bought a shopping bag. They don't give—" The paperbacks I was trying to balance slipped and fell. David bent to collect them. I had left my headlights on; he examined the books as he gathered them up. One cover was particularly lurid; I seem to remember it featured a decapitated head with tongue protruding and eyeballs rolled up till only the whites showed.

"Tsk, tsk," David said. "Your taste in literature is deplorable."

"Who asked you?"

As we walked toward the back door David said, "Pete was looking for you."

"I didn't tell him I would see him this afternoon."

"Why so defensive? I know you didn't. He's lonesome, that's all. He seemed upset."

"Thanks so much for telling me."

David opened the last gate and we went into the kitchen garden. "There's a carnival in Fiesole tomorrow. We could take the kid."

"What an irresistible invitation."

"Are you sure you aren't still mad at me?" David asked mildly.

"Damn it—" He cringed in mock terror as I turned on him, and I had to laugh. "Sorry again. I'm not in a very good mood, I guess. I'd love to go to a carnival, and I know Pete would get a kick out of it. I'll check with Francesca to make sure it's all right." After a moment I added, "Thanks."

"Prego, signora." He opened the kitchen door.

The room was dark except for a flickering bluish-white light that came from a small television set on one end of the long kitchen table. Beside it sat Rosa, a bottle and glasses in front of her. She called out a greeting in Italian, then saw me and lumbered to her feet. David flicked on a light switch.

"So this is how you spend your evenings, carousing with Rosa," I said. "Tell her to sit down, for goodness' sake. And give me those books; Francesca would have a fit if you took them upstairs."

He handed them to me. "Don't worry, I know my place. Sure you won't join us for a nice lowbrow evening? You haven't lived till you've seen *Dallas* in Italian."

"Each to his own lowbrow tastes, thank you. I prefer to wallow in crime and in chocolates. Have one?" He shook his head. I offered the bag to Rosa, who had returned to her seat and was watching me somewhat warily. She accepted a piece of candy and crunched it between her teeth with such relish that I put a handful of it into a dish. "I can see you're a fellow chocolate fiend, Rosa."

David translated, and Rosa's face broadened into a grin. She nodded vigorously. *"Grazie, signora—molto grazie."*

I patted her on the shoulder. "Enjoy yourselves. *Buona notte,* Rosa. Good night, David."

Before I so much as closed the door they were deeply

involved in the drama. The screen blurred and flickered, but it didn't seem to bother them; Rosa shook with laughter at some quip of J. R.'s and nudged David. I was tempted to stay. They looked so comfortable—so happily lowbrow, like me.

The house was quiet and deserted. I barely saw Emilia's apron fluttering around a corner.

I had to shift my parcels to turn the doorknob. The books slipped again and I made a rush for the bed, reaching it just in time to spill books and parcels onto its surface. Then I jumped back with a gasp. My fingers had touched something wet and slimy.

There was a lamp on the bedside table, but I wanted to get as far from the foul thing as I could. And I had thought I was being morbid when I speculated about snakes in my bed! I found the light switch by the door, and pressed it.

It wasn't a snake. It was the mutilated remains of my pretty flowers, crushed and torn, oozing sap like blood from their broken stems.

seven

My anger wasn't of the speechless variety this time; I
swore at some length, using several expressions of which
my father would not have approved. ("Big as you are, don't
think you can use swear words in my presence, young
lady—and it's no lady you are to say such things.")

Francesca had disapproved of my going out with Sebastiano, but I didn't suspect her of committing this vulgarity.
It was worse than vulgar, it was obscene. The flowers had
been so fragile and pretty. They had been not only
crushed, but wrenched and ripped by hard, spiteful
hands. I was sure the hands had been Emilia's; but was it
Francesca who had prompted the destruction? Like Henry
the Second and Thomas à Becket—"who will free me from
this turbulent priest?"

I couldn't leave the mess, it was smack in the middle of
the velvet spread. I cleared it away, but it left a disfiguring
stain, like the stain of memory in my mind that could
never be forgotten.

The fit of rage on top of an active day and little sleep the night before left me exhausted. I got undressed and climbed into bed with my pile of books and my chocolates and my carafe of water on the table beside me. Eating chocolates always makes me thirsty, and I intended to eat every last one of them. The water had looked stale, beaded with tiny drops and hazy with sediment, so I rinsed it out and refilled it.

The nice proper English detective story or the decapitated head? I sorted through the pile, trying to decide, and realized I had acquired an extra book. As soon as I saw the title I knew how it had got there. *Collected Poems of Robert Browning.* David must have brought it down with him intending to give it to me, and sneaked it into the pile. What a nut he was.

I tossed it aside and opted for the detective story. Decapitated heads were too suggestive of my murdered flowers. But the detective story was dull, and by the time I had eaten my chocolates (filled with peculiar combinations of liquor, nougat, and marzipan) I decided I didn't care who had murdered Lord Billingsgate.

The only Browning I could remember reading was *My Last Duchess.* It had been a requirement one year in high school. I had hated it. At the time I didn't understand why I hated it; it takes a certain experience to comprehend fully the chilling, subtle evil of the Duke. As I leafed through the book I found other familiar lines that I hadn't known were Browning's. "God's in his heaven, All's right with the world." Says who, Robert Browning? With a little snort of laughter I recognized the line I had overheard the first day I met David. "My scrofulous French novel, On gray paper with blunt type. . . ." Poor Brother Lawrence, in his Spanish cloister!

I remembered David saying that the Brownings had

lived in Florence. I must ask him to show me the house, if it was still standing. Although I had never had much use for Robert, I had adored Elizabeth, especially the sloppier, super-romantic sonnets. "How do I love thee? Let me count the ways." Robert must have had some good qualities to inspire those words.

Actually, he wasn't such a bad poet himself, I decided after a while. I read "Andrea del Sarto" and "Fra Lippo Lippi" because I recognized the names—they were Florentine painters—skipping a lot, because the poems were awfully long-winded. There were some good lines, though. The ending of "Fra Lippo Lippi" rather caught my fancy; the old rascal is on his way back to the monastery after an unclerical night on the town when he is stopped by the watch. "No lights, no lights," he begs. "The street's hushed and I know my own way back. Don't fear me! There's the grey beginning. . . ."

I wished I could be sure I knew my own way back. I had taken the first stumbling steps, but the end of the road was lost in darkness, without any sign of the gray light of dawn.

When the sounds woke me it was the dead, silent center of the night. The moon had set; faint starlight delineated the window. The sounds were coming from inside my room. The hair on the back of my neck lifted as I listened.

I sat up in bed and turned on the lamp. He was huddled on the floor just inside the door. Both hands clutched the leg of the chair in a grip that whitened his knuckles. His pajamas stuck to every fragile bone; they were soaking wet, as if he had stood under a shower. The sudden burst of light dilated his pupils to black, hiding the silver-gray.

He forced one word out of his distorted mouth. "Help . . ."

I ran to him and scooped him up bodily. His bones felt like the hollow bones of a bird, and waves of shivering ran through him.

"Pete! For God's sake, honey, what is it? What happened?"

"Don't let them . . ." His teeth were chattering so violently he couldn't get the rest of the word out. His crooked fingers dug into me like the kitten's claws.

"Don't be afraid. I won't let anybody do anything. It's all right. . . ." I went on crooning meaningless words of reassurance as I carried him to the bed, meaning to wrap him in the blanket. Luckily I was still holding him when it happened. Every muscle in his body went into a spasm, hardening like wood. The hands that had clung now struck out at me. His flattened palm cut a stinging slash across my cheek. At first I thought he was having an epileptic seizure. Then I saw his face, and reeled, almost losing my hold, as his fist smacked into the side of my head.

We fell onto the mattress, with me on top. My body pinned his arms to the bed, but he continued to struggle, writhing and kicking with an unnatural strength. I must have outweighed him by fifty pounds, but I could barely hold him down. That was all I could think to do, and all I could manage—hold him, keep him from hurting me or himself, until the attack passed. But every now and then I could have sworn that something flickered behind the eyes that were narrowed with rage—something frightened and bewildered, begging for the help he could not request in words.

The fit passed as suddenly as it had erupted. His eyes closed. I thought he had lost consciousness, and was about to shift my weight when his dark lashes fluttered. He whispered, "Are they gone? Are they gone?"

"There's nobody here but me," I said, fighting to keep my voice calm.

"Signora?"

"Yes. It's all right, honey."

His lashes stuck together in wet points. I rolled over and took him in my arms. "It's all right. Everything is all right now."

It wasn't all right, though. He couldn't look at me. He risked one quick glance, and then scuttled on hands and knees to the farthest corner of the bed, where he huddled against the headboard with his hands pressed to his eyes. When I tried to touch him he let out a thin mewing scream, like a rabbit cornered by hounds.

Sometimes, during that long night, I looked at the clock. The hands didn't seem to move. It was still dark outside when at last he ventured to open his eyes. I was sitting as close as I dared, ready to grab him if he went into another convulsion. But it was over—whatever it was. His chest rose in a sharp sigh. "Signora."

"It's me."

His arm lifted, with painful slowness. I took his hand, but that wasn't what he wanted. His fingers squirmed free and reached for my face. They traced every feature, as a blind person might. He could see, though. His eyes were focused and aware.

"It is you," he said. "I am very sleepy, signora."

"Me too. Get under the covers. You can stay here the rest of the night."

He rubbed his eyes fretfully. "No. I must be there, in my bed. I must see where Joe is."

My heart gave a painful lurch. If Francesca had been

right—if he had struck at the kitten as he struck at me . . . "Okay," I said. "I'll carry you."

I couldn't manage it. He was too heavy and the stairs were too steep. We staggered up them together, leaning on one another. His door was closed but not locked. The kitten was nowhere in sight.

Pete went straight to the wardrobe and opened its door, to be greeted by a reproachful yowl. Like a true philosopher Joe had whiled away the hours of his imprisonment by sleeping. He rose in one of those fabulous stretches only felines can achieve, back arched, tail stiff. Pete dropped to the floor. "He is safe," he murmured. "Joe is o-kay. They didn't . . ."

He fell asleep sitting there. I caught him as he swayed and lifted him onto his bed. With a businesslike air, Joe headed for the litter box. I found clean clothes in a drawer and changed Pete's pajamas. His muscles were relaxed like those of any sleeping child. His lashes lay soft on his cheeks. I had to lift him to get his arms into the pajama top. His eyes opened a slit. A smile curved his lips. "I came to you," he murmured. "I did it. To you."

I spent what was left of the night lying on the rug by his bed. Joe kept me on the qui vive, walking up and down my body and nibbling my hair. Not until the room grew light did I get stiffly to my feet. The child was deeply, peacefully asleep, the cat curled up against his back. Through the barred window I could see the cypresses taking shape against the gray dawn. "There's the grey beginning. . . ." But not here. Not in this room.

ii

I didn't expect to sleep, but I did, instantly, like someone who has been hit over the head. From the angle of the sunlight streaming in when I woke I knew it must be late. Memory returned, total and horrifying. I got out of bed so fast my head swam, and I had to sit down for a minute.

Finally I opened my door and looked out. The house was as silent as a tomb, but Emilia must have been waiting for me to show signs of life, for she appeared instantly. "You are awake, signora. You wish breakfast?"

"Please. Where—where is everybody?"

"*Alla chiesa, signora.*"

Her expression and her tone implied that I should have been at the *chiesa* too. I couldn't have cared less what she thought of my devotional failures. I said, "And Pete—*il conte*—is he at church too?"

"*Sì, signora. Naturalmente.*"

I closed the door, practically in Emilia's face, and collapsed into the chair. Naturally *il conte* was at church. Naturally.

Then he was all right. He was functioning normally. No one had noticed anything wrong.

I sat staring at my bare feet until Emilia came back with my tray. The coffee restored a few of my wits. Could I have dreamed the whole ghastly episode? My aching muscles denied that comforting solution. There were bruises on my shins, where he had kicked me, and a tenderness behind my ear. It had not been a dream. But how could a child go through an attack like that and be fully recovered in the morning? If Francesca was to be believed, there had only been two comparable episodes, weeks apart. Had there been others she didn't know about? Other times when he fought it alone, locked in his room, or sought help and comfort from . . .

From whom? "I came to you," he had said. He had known it was coming. He had shut the cat in the wardrobe, so it wouldn't be hurt, and struggled down the stairs to my room.

I hardly need say that by that point in my meditations the tears were streaming down my cheeks and dripping into my coffee cup. I wiped my face, wincing as my fingers touched another sore spot where his open hand had hit me.

I knew I must tell Francesca. I knew it, and I had no intention of doing it. I should be ashamed to admit that, even in the light of what happened later. It was nothing less than criminal negligence. But I could not bring myself to betray the boy. That was the word that stuck in my mind—betrayal. He had come to me, with God only knew what effort and courage. What would Francesca do if she knew what had happened? Lock him in his room, increase the dosage of the drug he was taking—the same old remedies, only more of them. I couldn't see that her methods were proving particularly effective.

It was a strange coincidence that his door had not been locked last night. But coincidences happen. Someone had forgotten, that was all. Thank God, thank God, he had thought of me. Thank God he had come to me instead of . . .

I was leaving in five days.

By the time I got myself under control my coffee was too salty to drink. I reminded myself that the situation had not changed. He was no worse than he had been before I arrived on the scene. He might even be better. Relapses were only to be expected. It was consummate egotism on my part to think that my half-baked therapy would restore him to perfect health overnight. Things like that happened in movies, not in real life. I would talk to Sebastiano—really talk to him, not exchange compliments. That was all I could do, except make the next few days as happy as possible for Pete.

And then walk away clean, jeered my conscience.

What the hell can I do? demanded my common sense. I'd take him home with me in a second if I could. I can't. I have no right.

My conscience had no answer to that one, but it wasn't satisfied. I could feel it rumbling unhappily, like an empty stomach. An empty conscience is much more uncomfortable.

I was getting dressed when the churchgoers returned. Their arrival was heralded by an altercation in the hall—Pete's shrill voice, and Emilia's growl.

I rushed to the door. She had him by the arm, although he wasn't doing anything except arguing. He looked like a child model for an expensive catalog—shirt and tie, polished shoes, three-piece white linen suit.

"What's going on?" I asked.

"I wanted to see if you were awake," Pete said.

"I told him he must not disturb you, signora."

"You knew I was awake. Let go of him."

"*Si, signora.* As you desire."

The look she gave me didn't match her submissive reply. She walked away.

He looked tired. There were dark stains like bruises under his eyes. He looked at me shyly from under his fantastic lashes. "I dreamed of you last night, signora."

"Did you? What did you dream?"

It was hard to speak casually, but I must have succeeded; he gave me another long, measuring look and then shrugged. "It was a funny dream. I don't remember. Will we do something today?"

I threw caution and common sense to the winds. "How would you like to go to a carnival?"

iii

Francesca agreed to my request that I be allowed to take Pete to the carnival, but expressed some concern that the crowds might be too much for me. She had heard there was a great deal of pushing and shoving at such affairs, coarse language, rude overtures to young women. . . .

I could almost hear Jim and Michael howling with laughter. After Celtics and Red Sox games, with beer bottles, fists and epithets filling the air, I felt sure I could cope with a carnival crowd. I explained that David was going with us.

Francesca nodded approvingly. "Yes, he will do very well. I will see that he is suitably rewarded."

As I withdrew from the presence I told myself I must repeat that condescending comment to David. He would be highly amused.

Not to my surprise I found David hanging around the kitchen. Rosa was baking—some variety of crisp little brown cakes that smelled divine—and he was eating them almost as fast as they came out of the oven.

"You sure took your sweet time," he said when I walked in. "Is Pete—" He broke off, staring.

"That bad?" I said.

"You look like the morning after the night before."

"Your gallantry is remarkable. I didn't sleep well."

"Hm."

"We're all set." I handed him the car keys. "I'll collect Pete and meet you out in front."

Excitement had made Pete so hyper he didn't notice how tired he was. We ate the most awful, indigestible combination of food—"American hot dogs," which didn't taste like hot dogs, but some variety of sausage—slabs of pizza, lemonade, soft drinks, taffy sticks twisted into red-and-white columns. Most of the stalls and rides were typically tawdry affairs, but the carousel was wonderful—real old wooden horses, the kind they put in museums in the States, lovingly repainted and gilded. I had forgotten there would probably be a carousel. By yelling and sliding around on my horse and generally making a spectacle of myself, I managed to keep from waxing sentimental; and if Pete was reminded of his mother he kept his feelings under better control than I did. There weren't any giraffes or elephants or lions, just horses. Some white.

I went bravely on a couple of the rides, the kinds with little cars that bump into each other or swoop sickeningly around a central pole, and then I copped out. David gave me a meaningful look when I said wanly that I would prefer to sit down for a while, but he didn't say anything.

Pete did not want to leave, of course. He whined and complained like any rotten, normal youngster until David said equably, "Cut that out or I'll slug you."

Pete grinned. "Would you?"

"Sure," David said.

"O-kay," Pete said.

He was sound asleep before we had gone a mile, curled up beside me with his head on my lap.

"Now you can tell everybody back home you saw the sights of Fiesole," David said. "It's a popular tourist spot."

"What else is there besides a carnival?"

"Nothing much. A famous cathedral, with frescoes by

Rosselli, tomb sculptures by Mino da Fiesole—boring stuff like that."

"Oh well. Any woman of sense would prefer roller coasters and diseased hot dogs."

"We could go back this evening. Have a quiet dinner someplace, stroll in the piazza under the light of the moon."

"David, I can't. I've been a rotten guest; tonight is my night for being polite to my hostess."

"Some other time, then."

Within another mile I was asleep too.

iv

I woke when the car stopped. The first thing my sleepy eyes saw was Alberto opening the gates. It was not the most auspicious welcome.

I had been able to conquer my forebodings during the horseplay and activity of the afternoon. Now they came back in full measure, and I had to keep telling myself I was being overly protective. There was no reason to suppose that another attack would follow so close on the last, or even that they inevitably occurred at night.

When David stopped to let us out, the front door opened. Emilia was there; and she wasn't the only one. David muttered, "Oh, oh, here it comes," as Francesca's slim, erect figure crossed the terrace and descended the stairs.

But she was smiling. "Did you enjoy yourself?" she asked.

Pete nodded. He never spoke to her if he could help it. He was certainly no advertisement for the quality of my childcare: crumpled, sleepy and sullen, spotted with various foodstuffs. Francesca studied him. "I see you did," she said dryly. "Thank *il professore* and the signora and go with Emilia. You will sleep well tonight."

"I don't know whether he'll eat his supper, though," I said, watching the small, stiff figure ascend the stairs.

"I suppose an occasional orgy of self-indulgence is good for all of us," Francesca said. "I came to thank you personally, Professor, for your kindness. Please join us for cocktails this evening."

I gathered she considered that the suitable reward she had mentioned. It sounded more like an order than an invitation. David said meekly, "Yes, ma'am. Thank you."

"Seven o'clock." She dismissed him with a gesture only slightly less brusque than she used for Emilia and Alberto, and turned away. David winked at me and rolled his eyes in pretended awe.

Francesca waited for me at the door to make sure I didn't linger to chat with the help. I told her I had my reservation, and would be leaving Sunday. "I'll turn my car in at the station," I explained. "So Alberto won't have to drive me."

"Whatever you like."

Her remark about persuading me to stay on had been only a meaningless courtesy after all, and my apprehension had been groundless. "You see?" whispered the shadow of Sister Ursula. "Honesty is the best policy. Now if you will tell her about the other . . ."

Shut up, Sister Ursula.

When I went to my room I found a surprise waiting for me. The vase had been placed near the window and the setting sun struck full upon the flowers, making them shine like carved garnets. Not rubies; the roses were deep, deep red. There was no card.

If they were an apology, they weren't good enough. If

they were a reminder, they were a piece of damned impertinence. I moved them to a dark corner and collapsed on the bed for a nap.

Prompt upon the hour of seven I descended the stairs, washed, brushed, and properly clothed. I hoped David would be the same, and I also hoped he would be able to restrain his irreverent sense of humor.

He was on time, at least. Francesca and I had exchanged only a few words when he appeared, escorted by Emilia. It would have been hard to say which of them looked grimmer. I studied him in exasperation. He was clean—but neat? That depends on how you define the word. From the remains of the once-gaudy scene plastered across the front of his T-shirt I deduced it was a souvenir from one of our national parks. Much of the color had washed out, but I could see the shape of a mountain.

Francesca wasted no time. "How is your work progressing, Professor?"

"Oh, fine. Great. I'm finding all sorts of things."

"What sorts of things?" There was a slight edge to her voice. David looked terrified. He had selected a chair that was too small for him, and he perched uneasily on its edge, knees together, holding his glass of wine as if he were clutching a beer can. The pose and the expression were so exaggeratedly awkward—the country bumpkin in the china shop—that I suspected he was putting on an act.

"Uh," he said. "Well, er . . . I've been working on the Egyptian collection. So far there's nothing particularly interesting except the Coptic embroideries."

"Embroideries?" A spark of interest warmed her face.

David expanded. "The Copts were Christian Egyptians. They used embroidery on robes and clothing for the most part, sometimes for cushions and wall hangings. The surviving pieces date mainly from the third to seventh centuries, though some are as old as the first century A.D. The dry climate explains why so much survived. . . ."

He rambled on, sounding as stiff and dry as a textbook, until Francesca cut him short. "I would like to see them."

"Oh? Oh, sure. I'm cleaning them now. Kathy can tell you. It's a slow process, you have to use special chemicals and distilled water and let them dry—"

"How long will it take?"

I didn't blame her for interrupting, since he appeared prepared to continue talking till someone stopped him; but I was a little surprised at her peremptory tone. David blinked. "A few more days. There's another crate I haven't opened, and it might have—"

"I'm afraid that whatever you are working on will have to be finished by the end of the week," Francesca said. "More wine, Professor?"

"Uh—thanks."

"I am going away for a while," Francesca explained. "The house will be closed."

My astonishment was scarcely less than David's. She had not mentioned her plans to me. A wild and horrid suspicion flashed into my mind. Surely she wouldn't pursue me and the apocryphal embryo into the wilds of western Massachusetts.

Francesca went on, "When you came we left the duration of your stay indefinite. I had no plans at that time, but now the situation has changed. I hope it does not inconvenience you, Professor."

"Yes, yes—I mean, no. I mean—whatever you say, of course. The end of the week?"

"That will give you time to finish whatever you have begun," she said complacently. "And you will let me know when the embroideries are ready for display?"

"Oh, sure," David said bleakly.

She let him finish his wine, and then eased him firmly out the door.

I knew that if I didn't find out what she was planning I wouldn't get a wink of sleep that night. My uneasy conscience might even drive me into premature flight. Sneaking down the stairs at midnight, shoes in hand; hitching a ride to Florence; appealing to Angelo for a room, secret, no one knowing I was there. . . .

With Machiavellian subtlety I said, "Francesca, I hope I'm not interfering with your plans. If you want to get away earlier, I can easily stay at a hotel for a few days."

"That is not the case at all. The idea did not even occur to me until you told me you were planning to go home."

That wasn't reassuring. I abandoned subtlety. "Where are you going?"

She answered readily. "I haven't decided. Switzerland, perhaps. Or Austria. Paris is impossible these days."

I felt so lighthearted with insane relief that I dared make a joke. "Too many American tourists?"

"Too many tourists," she corrected, unsmiling. "I have no prejudice against Americans, Kathleen. I know several who are very pleasant."

"Some of my best friends . . ." I didn't speak the words aloud; her sense of humor wasn't exactly uproarious. A new worry penetrated my selfish euphoria, and I said, "What about Pete?"

"Arrangements will be made for him."

I daresay I would have put my foot in my mouth and asked what arrangements if she had given me time. She pressed the bell, saying pleasantly, "I hope you didn't overindulge in carnival food. Rosa has prepared one of my favorite dishes tonight."

At home we'd have called the dish a seafood casserole, but the seasoning and the delicate wine-flavored sauce made that term too commonplace for such a culinary masterpiece. Francesca was in an excellent mood; she even made a few dry, cynical little jokes. We were finishing dessert, another heavenly concoction consisting primarily of raspberries and whipped cream, when she said, "It is good of you to take such an interest in Pietro, Kathleen. You have strong maternal instincts."

I wanted to get her off that train of thought. "He's a very nice kid," I said.

"You would like to see him again, in the future?"

"Yes, very much."

"We must see if that can't be arranged." She smiled, as if nursing a pleasant little secret.

I excused myself early, saying I was tired, and for once I was telling the truth. It had been a long day and a longer night. Instead of going to my room I went on up the stairs to the top floor. I expected Pete would be asleep by that time, but when I put my ear to the door I heard voices, so I knocked.

A voice I didn't recognize—a woman's voice—answered in Italian. I assumed she was telling me to come in, so I did.

It was the *tuttofare*. I had forgotten her name. She was sitting on the bed watching Pete toy with the contents of a tray lying across his legs. When she saw me she got quickly to her feet.

"Hello," Pete said, sounding pleased. "I was sick."

"You were . . . Oh. I'm not surprised. Eating all that junk food, and then the roller coaster."

"It all came out," Pete said, making a graphic gesture. "The pizza, the hot dog, the *gelato*—"

"Never mind, I get the picture. Only too clearly."

"So now they say I must eat this." He scowled at the bowl on the tray. It appeared to contain some pale substance like mush. "I do not want it."

"I don't blame you. Is it as bad as it looks?"

"Try." He offered an overflowing spoon.

"I will if you will." The *tuttofare* giggled as we finished the mush, turn and turn about. It didn't taste bad, or good. It didn't taste at all. When the bowl was half empty I said, "That ought to be enough. Is she waiting for the tray?"

The boy's eyelids lowered. "Always she waits."

No knives, no glasses that could be broken . . . I gestured at the girl. She picked up the tray, started for the door—hesitated—spoke to me.

"She asks if you stay here?" Pete translated.

"Yes. *Sì*."

The girl started to speak, then broke off with a nervous laugh. "She wants," said Pete, "to tell you to be sure to lock the door."

It wasn't the girl's fault. She was just obeying orders. I dismissed her with a nod and a stiff smile.

Pete got out of bed and opened the door of the wardrobe. Joe emerged, tail high, whiskers indignant. "She made me put him there so he would not eat the food," Pete explained.

"Get in bed and I'll tuck you in. I'll bet you're tired."

"Yes. It was a good day."

Joe thought the tucking-in process was a game for his benefit. He pounced on my hands and rolled himself up in the blanket. His antics cheered us, but I kept thinking of that damned key, and after I had turned out all the lights except one by the bed I said, "I won't lock the door if you don't want me to."

"I want you to."

I couldn't see his face, except as a pale oval beyond the limited circle of the lamp. "Are you sure?"

"Yes. And," he said, "please take the key."

eight

I called Sebastiano the following morning to thank him for his flowers—and for other reasons. The nurse informed me he would not be back until Tuesday. I thanked her and hung up without leaving my name.

Just as well, I told myself. I knew—how well I knew!—that it was difficult to talk with psychiatrists during working hours. I had a lot to talk about. I needed plenty of time and Sebastiano's undivided attention. We had a date for dinner Tuesday. It was only one more day. One more night.

Francesca was working at her desk when I joined her for breakfast. She apologized. "There is so much to do when one is preparing to leave for an extended period. One of the things I would like, Kathleen, is to show you something of the city. What do you say to a thoroughly frivolous view of Florence—shopping, hairdressers?"

I had never seen her look so young and carefree. She's probably happy at the prospect of ridding herself of the woman who came to dinner, I thought.

"I guess I need a beauty shop at that," I said, smoothing my flyaway locks. "My hair needs cutting."

"Only trimming and shaping. You mustn't cut it short; it is beautiful hair."

"I'd love to go to Florence with you," I said, tactfully avoiding the question of how to style my hair. "Let me take you to lunch."

"You are my guest. Today?"

"That would be fine."

After breakfast I left Francesca working on her lists and wandered out onto the terrace. It was a lovely morning. You could practically see the flowers jumping up out of the ground. My fingers itched for a trowel. I love gardening, though I have been accused of not being able to tell a weed from a flower, and one of the charms of my little house on the hill had been its minuscule garden. I looked at my hands. They had become white and soft over the past months. A lady's hands.

The sight of Alberto's unfortunate assistant languidly at work on the front flower beds killed any lingering ambitions at horticulture I might have had. It wasn't his fault he was a pitiable creature, but he made me nervous.

I had returned the key to the lock of Pete's door early that morning, just after daybreak. I had not been able to resist a quick look inside. He was sound asleep, curled awkwardly around the cat, who was, in the manner of cats, lying in the precise center of the bed.

I decided to go up and extract him for an extra hour of football, or washing antiques, or whatever he had in mind. He had no doctor's appointment that day, and it wouldn't hurt him to miss an hour of such schooling as Francesca provided.

His face lit up when he saw me, and I concluded I would postpone telling him I was leaving for another day.

He wasn't studying; the heavy Italian history book lay significantly crumpled against the wall and he was playing with Joe, pulling a string to which a piece of paper had been tied.

"Shall we play football now?" he greeted me.

"You really ought to be studying. Oh, the heck with it. It's too nice a day to stay indoors."

"Shall we find David? It is better with three."

"He's probably in his room washing rags," I said, remembering Francesca's ultimatum. "We could stop by and see if he has time to play."

Joe would have been happy to accompany us. A wail of frustration arose when we closed the door on him. Pete said seriously, "I do not let him go out. I am afraid he will run away."

"You're a good pet owner," I said approvingly.

"David has told me. When an animal is young it does not have good sense, David says. There are many dangers here. Cars on the road, wild animals in the woods, or even . . ."

He didn't finish the sentence. I had not told him about Alberto and the dog, for I felt it was too grisly a tale for a child. Either David had hinted at potential danger from the animal, or Pete was perceptive enough to have figured it out for himself. He went on, "And also, David says, it could climb a tree and not know how to come down. Is that true? If a cat can climb *up* a tree, why can't it climb *down* a tree?"

I explained the physiological mechanism involved, as I understood it, and added comfortingly that most cats managed to get down sooner or later. I did not tell him about a feeble-minded feline we had once owned, who really didn't know how to climb down. We'd once left him up the big sycamore in front of the house for three days, hardening our hearts to his shrieks after all efforts to entice him down had failed. Ma insisted he'd come down when he got hungry, but even she was relieved when Michael finally shinnied up, at extreme risk to life and limb, and retrieved old Bill.

Pete and I stood in the stableyard and yelled for David. At last his head appeared at the window. "What a racket!" he said. "Why didn't you come up?"

"We thought you might be busy," I said.

"Besides, it is more fun to yell," said Pete.

"True. Aren't you guys early today?"

"It is too nice a day to stay inside," Pete informed him.

"True again. I'll be with you in ten minutes. Have to finish this lot first."

I was glad of the interlude because it gave me a chance to ask the boy some questions. I had been puzzling over that enigmatic comment of Francesca's—that she hoped I would have the opportunity to see Pete again—and a possible explanation had occurred to me.

I sat down on the bench, and Pete rambled around kicking at the ball. "You said something about your Aunt Vera," I began.

"Yes. She is the sister of my mother. You go over there and I will kick the ball to you."

"In a minute." I caught his arm and pulled him down beside me. "What's her name?"

"I told you. Aunt Vera."

"Doesn't she have another name?"

"Oh, yes. It is a funny name. It is Hassel-berg. Her husband is Uncle Ben Hassel-berg."

"Where does she live?"

"In America." Pete began to squirm. He wanted down off the bench.

"Where in America?"

I finally pinned him down. Aunt Vera and Uncle Ben lived in or near Philadelphia. "That is where I went to school," Pete said. "Phila-delphia. I had to remember the number of her house, if I was lost."

Aunt Vera sounded like a sensible woman. I wrote down the address and the name. Then I said, "You were living with Aunt Vera when you were going to school in the States? I thought it was a boarding school."

"You mean where you live in the school. I did live there. But I went to Aunt Vera on holidays and on the week endings." He was silent for a moment, remembering. His eyes were wistful, his mouth had a sad little droop to it. "I liked it with Aunt Vera and Uncle Ben. My cousins were older, but on the week endings they played with me sometimes. Evan (he pronounced it with a long *e*, Ee-van) was going to teach me basketball. In his school he was a basketball *star*. And when Uncle Don came, in the summer, he was going to teach me baseball. He was a baseball *star*, when he was in his school. And Aunt Vera let me play with the cats and the dogs, and Bruno was there, and I was going to be a cub."

I assumed they hadn't offered him a position on the Chicago team, so I suggested, "Cub Scout?"

"Yes. They wear clothes like soldiers."

"The eternal male animal," I said.

"What? Oh, there is David! David, hurry, we are ready."

He leaped up to greet his receiver and I sat pondering what he had told me.

It was only a hunch, but I thought I understood why Francesca had equivocated when I had asked her about her son's will. He may or may not have had such a document, but I seriously doubted that he had meant Francesca to be Pete's legal guardian. Guido and his wife might have put the boy in an Italian school, near his grandmother, so he'd have a relative close by in case of illness. Instead they had picked a school near his mother's family. After the death of the boy's parents, Francesca had taken Pete from the Hasselbergs. Had they agreed, or had she simply scooped him up and walked out with him? Possession is nine tenths of the law, and it would be difficult to extradite a child from a foreign country if the person in charge of him was a close relative, and a distinguished citizen of the country in question.

As yet I had no proof of this theory, but it gave me an idea with which to calm my indignant conscience. The minute I got home I would look up the Hasselbergs. If Pete had been taken from them against their wishes, and if they were willing to fight to get him back, I would help them.

It might not be necessary. Francesca's hints could be interpreted as meaning that she intended to return the child to his aunt and uncle. Perhaps she had acted on impulse, not realizing what she was letting herself in for. Finding the boy a burden and a nuisance, she might be willing to let someone else take over.

I surpassed myself at receiving that day. Even Pete was impressed. "Someday you may play quarterback," he promised. "After you have practiced some more. See, you hold the ball like this, with the laces so . . ."

He had the theory down pat, though his hands were too small to encompass the girth of the ball. He remembered his cousins' lectures on sports word for word, though he couldn't seem to get a grip on his history lessons. Not uncharacteristic of boys of any age or nationality; some of my worst students could reel off statistics of prehistoric games played long before they were born, including such crucial details as Bronko Nagurski's height, weight, and yearly stats.

Before we finished the game the skies had clouded over

and a cool breeze was chilling my bare arms. "It's going to rain," said David, with the dour satisfaction some people display when announcing bad news.

"Darn. I guess you always expect the sun to shine when you're on vacation."

"The weather has been very unusual," said David pontifically. "Usually it rains cats and dogs all through April and May. Innocent travelers think of Italy as sunny and semitropical, but the northern parts have the same climate as—"

"It feels like home," I agreed, shivering. "Come on, Pete, we'd better get inside. You're perspiring and I don't want you to catch cold."

"If you two are bored this afternoon you can come up and help me," David offered. "I've got a lot of work to finish before I—"

I shook my head warningly. The boy scampered ahead, and I said in a low voice, "He doesn't know we're leaving. I don't want to tell him until I find out where he'll be going."

"Her ladyship hasn't deigned to inform you?"

"Not yet."

"That's strange, isn't it?"

"Not at all. The decision is hers, and she's not accustomed to discussing her plans with other people."

"Hm," said David.

I read that noncommittal sound correctly. "Look, I'll find out. If she doesn't tell me, I'll ask. She isn't used to children. She doesn't realize they have to be carefully prepared for dramatic changes in their lives. I get the impression she's planning it to be a surprise—a treat—so it must be something he'll like."

"The contessa's idea of a treat may not coincide with the kid's," David said dryly.

"I said I'd find out." I added pointedly, "Even though it really isn't any of my business."

"Or mine?"

"You're a nosy, bossy, impertinent son of a gun, aren't you? I'll talk to Francesca this afternoon. We're going shopping in . . . Good heavens, we're going shopping! I'd better hurry and change."

"Wear your raincoat," was David's parting shot.

It rained, heavily and persistently, all afternoon, but I didn't need my raincoat. Money and status can even protect you from the weather. Alberto drove us from place to place and parked smack in front of the door, in flagrant violation of the traffic signs—to which nobody in Florence seemed to pay much attention anyway. When we had to cross a foot of open pavement he unfurled a big black umbrella and escorted us through the danger zone. Instead of enjoying this, I wanted to grab the umbrella and close it, lift my face to the cold rain.

We lunched exquisitely and leisurely in a small restaurant that made the place Sebastiano had taken me to look like a slum. I think it was a private club; Francesca was greeted like one of the Medicis. I had no opportunity to raise the subject of Pete's future, for there were always at least two waiters hovering.

The next stop was at Francesca's hairdresser. It looked more like a medical clinic than a beauty shop. A grave middle-aged man with the manners of a diplomat inspected me; he and Francesca engaged in serious, low-voiced debate while I sat feeling like a patient who has delayed treatment too long. "If you had only come to me six weeks ago, madam, I might have been able to save your leg." I got the impression the two disagreed, though I could not follow the rapid speech. Finally the diplomat threw up his hands. Francesca smiled at me and vanished into the adjoining cubicle.

When she had gone I had the nerve to tell the diplomat I wanted my hair cut short. Apparently he didn't understand my vigorous gestures. He left it shoulder-length in back, shaking his head firmly when I pantomimed the use of the scissors. I had to give up. The result was certainly a hundred-percent improvement.

Francesca was waiting when I came out. She looked exactly the same as she had when we entered, every hair in place. I guess that was the idea. When I reached for my purse her hand closed over mine. "Please allow me to deal with this, Kathleen."

It's vulgar to argue about money in some circles—not mine—but this was not my ambience, so I gave in. But at the next stop I forgot my manners when I realized what she was up to.

The place was a dress shop. I didn't identify this function at first, for the room resembled a beautifully appointed *salone,* with not a garment in sight. After we had seated ourselves, a series of young women emerged, to posture and stroll, displaying the clothes. I like clothes. I mean, not just as methods of avoiding cold and damp and getting arrested; I like pretty clothes. I had never seen anything like this display. Even my uneducated eye observed the genius of line and tailoring in the most seemingly simple costume. The fabrics were absolutely sensuous—wools soft and light as silk, silk shimmering with imprisoned light, pure linen, even a few humble cottons—for scrubbing floors, I presumed—but they were the sleek, fine cottons I associated with names like Liberty of London.

I enjoyed the novelty of it so much that it took me a while to notice that the women were all about my age and my size, and that the garments did not resemble Francesca's tailored conservative tastes. She consulted me as the parade went on; I thought she was asking my opinion for herself. Then she said decisively, "The apricot suede suit, I think—that is a good shade for you—the blue linen, the amber silk, and the velvet coat."

"Francesca," I said.

"Fittings are so tedious, I know. But it must be done today, if the clothes are to be ready by the weekend."

"No. You . . . Your generosity overwhelms me, I mean it; but I can't let you—"

"I am not making you a gift, Kathleen." She paused just long enough to let a furious blush of embarrassment drench my face, before going on. "As Bartolommeo's wife you are entitled to whatever your position requires."

Such a thing had never occurred to me. Bart always had enough money for what he wanted, but when my father, acting for me, checked out the assets he had owned at the time of the accident, they consisted solely of a few dollars in a bank account and the small insurance policy that had paid for my trip abroad. I stammered, "You mean his father—"

"I will explain it later. Please go now and try on the clothes. If there are any others that appeal to you . . ."

She went into the dressing room with me. So did the fitter and the owner of the establishment. I couldn't go on arguing in front of that audience.

The process dragged on interminably. I turned and pivoted and raised my arms and lowered them, and wondered what the devil I was going to do. It was out of the question for me to accept such a munificent gift; I could only dimly imagine how many million lire the collection would cost. No wonder Francesca hadn't invited any of her friends to meet me—except the doctor, for obvious reasons. Probably she was ashamed of the way I looked.

The suit needed few alterations. Francesca indicated an almost invisible pucker across the shoulders and pointed out that my waistline was half an inch higher than that of the jacket. To me it looked like a perfect fit. I had never tried on an outfit like that, much less owned one. The sight of my image in the mirror sent not one but a few dozen cracks across the surface of my resolve. Maybe there was family money owed Bart. Why shouldn't I take Francesca's word for it, especially since she was determined that I should?

I still hadn't decided what to do when we left the shop. She took my blank-faced, dazed manner for fatigue and proposed a cup of tea. "I hate fittings," she confided, girl to girl. "But it is necessary. These will do for you to go on with."

On with until when? I wondered. Till I visited my favorite couturier in Paris or New York, to pick up my summer wardrobe? At any rate, the fittings proved that Francesca had abandoned her fantasy about my being pregnant. She could count as well as I could. The clothes she had just ordered wouldn't have fit for more than a few weeks, if I had been expecting a baby. Nobody, not even a spoiled aristocrat with more wealth than her run-down living quarters had suggested, would blow a small fortune on clothes that would be outgrown in a few weeks and outdated next season.

Would she?

It didn't matter. The important thing was that she had accepted my imminent departure without argument or hard feelings. Had she something on her conscience that had prompted the expensive gift? I toyed with fantasies. Bart the heir to immense wealth which she had usurped, in her role as Pete's guardian; an aristocratic lover waiting impatiently in the wings for the trespasser to go—to be bribed, so she would not be tempted to change her mind? The first was pure fantasy, but the lover was entirely reasonable. Francesca was still relatively young and more than relatively attractive. Perhaps that was where she was going, to meet *il principe* or *monsieur le comte,* or *Graf von und zu* something, in a Swiss hideaway.

Speculations of this sort kept me preoccupied during the drive home. Francesca was silent, apparently wearied by the effort of selecting clothes, and the view was nothing to brag about in the rain and lowering fog. Mist veiled the dripping tree trunks and swirled in ghostly patterns among the brush. It was pleasant to come in from the dull twilight and the damp air to find a fire burning in my fireplace. I looked forward to a quiet evening with my books.

When I went down to dinner I took the scrap of embroidery I had bought for Francesca. I was tempted to bury it in my suitcase; it seemed so paltry an offering, especially now. "It's not the gift, it's the thought behind it," I quoted to myself—my mother, not Sister Ursula, though the latter would undoubtedly have agreed.

At any rate, Francesca appeared pleased. I expected she would express her thanks graciously, but her reaction was a little warmer than that. She pointed out some of the technical excellences of the stitching and assured me that examples of that kind of work were increasingly rare. "I must start a collection," she said, smiling. "With this and the Coptic embroidery the professor has discovered, I have a good beginning."

She was in such a charming mood I ventured to bring up the subject I had neglected all day. "Have you decided yet what plans you will make for P-Pietro?" I got the Italian name she preferred out with only a slight stutter.

"I have thought he would be better off at school. There are places for such people."

That had an ominous sound. "Yes, but where?" I said. She frowned a little at my peremptory tone, and I added, "The reason I ask is that I know of several excellent schools in the States for children with emotional problems. It occurred to me that you might be thinking of sending him back to his aunt—"

"His aunt! How did you hear of her?"

"Pete—Pietro told me. Of course I don't know anything about his mother's sister or her family; they might not be the proper people to take charge of him, even temporarily. But if you had thought of sending him home—to the States, I mean—I could take him. That would solve one difficulty for you, wouldn't it?"

Her forehead smoothed out as I recited this speech. She listened attentively, nodding from time to time. "You would be willing to have him with you?"

"Of course. I'd love it."

"Such arrangements cannot be made quickly."

I was tempted to ask why she hadn't begun them, then. "I could stay on—as long as you like." The corners of her mouth twitched as if she were trying not to smile. I felt myself flushing. "That sounds as if I'm looking for an excuse to prolong my stay, doesn't it? Honestly, Francesca—"

The smile came into the open. Her eyes shone with amusement—more amusement than my blunder warranted, in my opinion, but if she was enjoying herself, who was I to complain? Actually, I was pleasantly dazed by her reaction to my admittedly high-handed suggestion. I wasn't accustomed to having people respond so amiably to my attempts to run their lives for them. She must be really desperate to get rid of the child.

"You need not explain," she said. "The suggestion certainly has a number of positive aspects. Suppose you let me think it over and take certain preliminary steps before we reach a decision?"

I liked the delicate touch of irony with which she invested the word "we." "Of course," I said quickly. "It's your decision. I only wanted—"

"I understand. I appreciate your concern."

She didn't refer to the subject again, but I hoped I had made an impression. Now the trick was to leave her alone and refrain from nagging. What a marvelous solution that would be—not only for me, selfish creature that I was, but for the boy. He couldn't be worse off than he was here. He'd be with a family, with people who cared about him. And I could see him sometimes.

When I went up to his room there was no sound within. The door was locked. After only a moment's hesitation I removed the key and took it with me.

ii

Another night safely passed, I thought, as I crept back to my room in the gray dawn, after looking in on a sleeping child and restoring the key to the lock. Only a few more nights to go. If Francesca wanted me to stay on I would, but I couldn't see why it would take long to arrange for Pete's return. He must have a valid passport; it had been used within the past year. Communication with his aunt and uncle was only seconds away, thanks to the telephone. Maybe we could make it by Sunday after all. Four more days.

I refused to think about the alternative—catching my plane as I had planned, leaving him behind.

I was so excessively charming to Francesca at breakfast I'm surprised she bothered to add sugar to her coffee. I did not protest about the clothes, even when she coolly informed me that I had an appointment for a final fitting on Thursday. I did not mention my date with Sebastiano. I'd have canceled that—anything to make Francesca think better of me—except for the fact that I wanted to talk seriously to Sebastiano about Pete. I needed all the information I could get if I was to be responsible for him, even for a few days. I even—"The Good Lord curse you for a hypocrite, Kathleen Alice Malone"—I even brought my embroidery down and asked Francesca to straighten out the mess I'd made of it.

She removed the faulty stitches and showed me where I had gone wrong. "I'll never be any good," I said dismally, watching her deft fingers.

"If you don't care to do it, of course you must not. But perseverance and practice will bring skill, and I assure you it is a restful activity. Good for the nerves," she added, her head bent over her work.

The almost-colloquialism of the comment surprised me, as did the sentiment itself. Good for whose nerves? I wondered. Hers? She didn't appear to have any.

She ordered—I suppose I should say asked—me to bring the wretched scrap with me that evening, so we could work on it together. I didn't tell her I would not be there that evening. Assuming that eventually she would inspect the product to see what I had accomplished, I put in a tedious hour pricking myself and taking out more stitches than I put in. I knew the theory, but practice wasn't having any discernible effect on my lack of skill.

When I tossed the damned thing aside I saw that it had

stopped raining. The skies were still swollen with clouds ready to release their burden, and a stiff breeze was blowing; the tops of the cypresses bowed and curtsied. I got my coat and went up to extract the prisoner from his cell. It would do both of us good to get out. If I could persuade him to practice kicking instead of tackling, we wouldn't get quite so wet.

I was surprised to find Emilia with the boy, stuffing him into an assortment of outdoor garments that would have been more appropriate for a winter day in Montana. "He must have the fresh air," she informed me, as I stood staring at the motionless bundle. Between the knit cap and the scarf covering his mouth Pete's eyes blazed with rebellion.

"Oh, I agree, Emilia. A little wet never hurt anybody. You run along. I'll finish—er—dressing him."

She obeyed, shutting the door with a slam. Pete snatched off the scarf and threw it on the floor. "Eevan never wears a scarf. Even in the snow."

"You don't need it," I agreed. "Haven't you got a lighter coat?"

The coat followed the scarf onto the floor. "I will not wear a coat! It does not snow."

I found a light jacket of waterproof material in the wardrobe, and we compromised on that. The cap would have gone the way of the scarf and the coat if I had not agreed to wear its mate. It was too small for me, and I had to tie it on with a babushka. My appearance sent Pete into spasms of laughter, and he forgot to argue about the gloves and the boots.

Joe emerged from under the bed; obviously he had been avoiding Emilia, which only went to show what an intelligent animal he was. He dragged the despised scarf into a corner and began chewing it. Pete was all for that, but I explained wool was not good for cats, and took it away. "He's really getting handsome," I said, stroking the sleek fur on his neck. "A few more weeks and he'll be fat as a tub of butter."

"I comb him every day," Pete said proudly. "And catch the fleas. That is fun, to catch the fleas. They pop when you squeeze them."

We sneaked out the door while Joe was investigating a ball Pete had tossed under the bed. Pete gravely rattled the door to make sure it was latched. He was taking his responsibilities seriously. The kitten had been a godsend. I had hoped it would entertain him—I hadn't thought of the fascination of popping fleas—and increase his self-confidence and self-worth and all those other desirable attributes our school psychologist kept talking about. (I don't disagree with the theory, but sometimes I get awfully tired of professional jargon.)

The boots made a satisfying clatter on the stairs. Pete went up and down a couple of times while I contemplated a problem I had overlooked, the problem of Joe. Pete would kick up a fuss if he had to leave the cat behind, wherever he was destined to go. And he'd be right to fuss. You don't teach a child responsibility by allowing him to discard a living creature if it becomes an inconvenience. I had no idea what formalities were involved in transporting an animal across the Atlantic. There was no six months' quarantine in the States, as there was in England, but Joe would probably need shots and a certificate from a vet. The ticket was no problem. I would happily shell out for Joe's ticket.

You see, I had already assumed that Pete and I would be leaving together. Optimism is an incurable disease.

David didn't want to leave his work. "It's wet out," he protested like a little old lady.

"A little wet never hurt anybody," said Pete, who had a memory like an elephant's for convenient clichés.

"Why don't you come up here and help me?"

"I helped you before. It is boring," said Pete, dancing up and down with impatience.

When David appeared with a shabby windbreaker as his concession to the chill air, I said, "Your work isn't going well?"

"The damned scraps won't dry in this weather," David grumbled. "I promised her ladyship a show tomorrow, and I can't use artificial heat, it warps the fabric."

"Too bad," I said.

"Ha," said David.

"Come *on*," called Pete.

We concentrated on kicking and going out for passes, but we got pretty wet all the same. Once or twice a feeble ray of sunlight tried to struggle through the clouds, but it was quickly vanquished. Thanks to the boots and the jacket, Pete didn't get too soaked, but his pants were drenched, since he kept falling down in dramatic, unnecessary lunges for the ball. I called a halt earlier than I would otherwise have done and sent him in. "Ask Rosa for a cup of cocoa, or something hot," I suggested.

"She's probably baking," David added encouragingly. "She said she meant to this morning."

Pete ran off, promising to save a few cookies for us. "Come up and have a cup of coffee," David said.

He had a small electric heater. We sat in front of it and steamed gently while we drank our coffee. It was instant, and tasted awful after the espresso I had become accustomed to drinking. But it was hot.

"Any news?" he asked, after a while.

"What about?"

"Your imminent departure. Are you really leaving this weekend?"

"I think so. Sunday, possibly."

"What about Pete?"

"I'm working on it."

"Oh, you are, eh? You look awfully pleased with yourself. What have you been up to?"

"I can't tell you till I know for sure. But I am pleased. I think—I hope—something nice is going to happen."

"Nice enough to make you forget your recent bereavement?"

The abrupt brutality of the question took my breath away. He went on in the same savage voice, "You don't look like a grieving widow. What was he like, this husband of yours? Handsome, intelligent, sexy—"

"All those things." I slammed my cup down on the table and stood up. "How dare you!"

"Wait." His fingers wrapped around my arm as I spun toward the door. "I'm sorry, Kathy. Sit down."

I had very little choice in the matter. He kept hold of me after I had seated myself, but the angry contempt had left his face. "Forget I said that, will you? You must know why I said it."

"Innate boorishness, I assume. Let me go."

"Not until you've heard me out. When you showed up that first morning I couldn't believe my eyes. I was only half kidding when I said that about rubbing a magic lamp and getting a free wish. After you told me about your husband, I figured I had better take it slow. But it didn't take long for me to realize that, slow or fast, it was all the same; I was never going to get anywhere. You're still in love with him. You can't get him out of your mind. He was everything I'm not."

"Yes," I said. "You aren't . . . any of the things he was."

"Then you do understand why I spoke out of turn? I didn't mean it. It's only a few more days, Kathy. I'll probably never see you again. Can we go back to what we were, for those few days?"

"We can't ever go back. But I understand."

"It's okay, then?"

"Yes. I think I'd better go now."

"See you tomorrow?" His face was anxious.

"Yes. Sure."

I headed for the kitchen door, so deep in thought I hardly noticed where I was walking. I was in the kitchen garden, treading blindly on baby lettuces and sprouting carrots when the door burst open and Pete came flying out. His face was as gray as his jacket.

He flung himself at me. "Joe. Joe is gone. Did you see him?"

"Why, no. He must be in the house somewhere, Pete. I'll help you look—"

He was off, pelting down the path, water spraying up from the puddles struck by his flying feet. He was out of sight before I could collect my wits.

Then I heard him scream.

I reached the stableyard before the echoes of his cry had died. The kitten flew across the cobblestones like a ball of animated fur, hardly touching the ground. The dog was close behind, but Pete was closer, moving on an oblique line and running as I have never seen a child that age run. Without pausing he scooped up a stone. He pitched it underhand, wildly; instead of hitting the dog, it struck the ground several feet away. But the impact and the sound it made caused the animal to break stride, just long enough.

Pete got through the gate into the garden and slammed it shut.

I didn't stop running, but I was still twenty feet away when the dog crouched to jump. It is difficult to run and yell at the same time. I was trying to do both. Where the hell was David? Pete's first cry should have brought him down from his room.

The dog didn't make it on his first try. The second attempt succeeded. The gate was a wooden grille, I could see through it. My stiff fingers fumbled with the catch. Pete had pulled himself up into a tree. Joe was nowhere in sight. I kept wrestling with the gate, but my racing heart began to slow. They were safe. The cat must have climbed the same tree. My cries had been heard; there were voices, footsteps running.

The dog was snuffling around the trunk of the tree. He jumped again. He missed the boy's feet by a good yard, but Pete lost his head and tried to climb higher. His hands slipped on the wet bark and he fell, landing across the limb on which he had been standing, his legs dangling down.

I could see the drops dripping from the leaves, the quiver of the muscles in the dog's haunches as it crouched, the white terror on the boy's face as he struggled to draw himself up. I could even see Joe, half camouflaged by the leaves where he crouched on a branch high in the tree. All my other senses cut out. I couldn't feel my hands or my feet, I couldn't hear anything except a high, distant ringing. I couldn't hear my own voice; but I must have called to the dog, because it turned to look at me.

The gate opened and I walked into the garden, slowly, not running. The dog stared at me. It knew my voice; but mine was not the voice it had been trained to obey. The words were not the right words of command. I stooped and picked up a fallen branch. With a sudden pop my hearing came back, the way it does when you swallow hard at a high altitude. I heard myself say, "Good dog. Sit. Stay. That's a good boy. . . . Pete, just take it easy. You got up there once, you can do it again. . . . Sit, good boy. Stay."

The dog's hindquarters sank down. It was not sitting; it was getting ready to attack.

The mind works oddly at moments like that. I felt as if I had all the time in the world to decide what to do. I doubted that I could make it to the gate. Better to stand and face what was coming. One arm over my throat, one shielding my eyes. Try to get the stick in its mouth.

The dog was in mid-leap when the shot cracked like a thunderclap. The shock was so great I staggered, feeling as if the bullet had hit me. The dog twisted and spun, and fell in a tangled heap.

I stood as if rooted to the ground, too scared even to faint. My ears rang with the echo of the shot—or had there been several shots? Pete had dropped down out of the tree and was running toward me. When his frantic arms went around me my legs gave way and I sank gently to the ground.

nine

❦

Out of the chaos, faces slowly took shape. Alberto, cradling the rifle and smirking with pride; David, staring not at me but at the twisted body of the dog; Rosa, wringing her hands and invoking a pantheon of saints; Emilia; Francesca, her ashen face contrasting bizarrely with the lacquered perfection of her hair.

Having assured himself I was unharmed, Pete stood up. "I am going to be sick," he announced.

I sat there like a broken doll, my legs doubled up under me. It was David who lifted the boy and held him close. "No, you aren't," he said. "Take deep breaths. You're okay, I'm okay, Kathy is okay. So what's to worry about?"

From the face pressed against his shirt came a muffled voice. "Joe."

"Joe?"

"Joe," I said, in a voice that didn't sound like mine, "is also okay. But I doubt that he'll want to come down out of that tree in the near future."

"I can't say I blame him," David muttered. "Well, Pete, Joe isn't in any danger now. Suppose I carry you up to bed and then I'll come back and—"

"No. Joe will run away."

David looked inquiringly at me. I looked dumbly back at him. My brain had gone as limp as my legs. I just wanted to sit.

Francesca touched my shoulder. "Kathleen. The dog did not . . ."

"Never laid a tooth on me. Thanks to Alberto," I added grudgingly. He had saved me from serious injury, if not worse, but I found it hard to acknowledge his services. Killing the dog had been the kindest thing he had done to it.

"How did the dog slip its chain?" Francesca demanded. "The whole business is unaccountable. I cannot believe—"

A babble of voices interrupted her. Alberto displayed the end of the chain, with its torn link; Emilia praised his quick thinking and superb marksmanship; Rosa raised her hands to heaven and praised the saints and the Holy Mother of God. I leaned toward her interpretation. It was nothing short of a miracle that no one had been hurt.

Francesca ended the uproar with a sharp command and gave orders all around. Rosa took Pete to her ample bosom. David shinnied up the tree and retrieved Joe, and we all went to the house for first aid and sympathy. David was the only one who needed first aid. Joe had not wanted to come down.

I went upstairs to change clothes. My teeth were chattering, not only with cold, and I accepted Francesca's offer of a warm robe, since mine was lightweight cotton. Hers was velvet. Real velvet, not polyester, in the pale ivory she favored, trimmed with what appeared to be mink.

I trailed my mink hem up the stairs and pounded on

Pete's door. Rosa had put him to bed and was trying to coax him to eat. The tray held enough food for three people, every dish steaming—soup, spaghetti, milk, rolls.

"Momentito, momentito," Pete said irritably. He was at work on Joe, rubbing him with a towel and trying to get the tangles out of his tail. Joe was not cooperating.

"That's good," I said. "He can finish the job himself now, Pete. I'll bet he'd like some of your milk."

"Yes, he would." Pete snapped an order at Rosa. He sounded just like his grandmother. She grinned and poured milk into a saucer. Steam rose from it. Rosa blew on the milk so vigorously the surface ruffled into white waves.

"Eccolo," she said, putting the saucer on the floor. Joe sailed into it and Rosa chuckled, her fists on her broad hips.

Before I left I had the satisfaction of seeing Pete eat his lunch with a hearty appetite, having apparently suffered no ill effects from his adventure. I didn't mind leaving him with Rosa. He seemed to like her, and his autocratic attitudes only amused her. It was a pity she couldn't look after him, instead of Emilia.

I exchanged Francesca's gorgeous robe for my suit—the only warm garment I had—before I went downstairs. Francesca exclaimed in surprise when I walked in. "I was about to send Emilia to you with a tray. You ought to rest."

I had forgotten my condition. "I'm fine," I assured her.

"You appear to have taken no harm." She shook her head. "A shocking experience of that nature would have left me completely prostrate."

"I doubt it," I said, before I thought, and then added, "That was meant as a compliment, Francesca, even if it didn't sound like one."

"Thank you, Kathleen."

"I'm sorry about the dog. I hope you won't think I'm impertinent if I suggest you ought to entrust its successor to someone other than Alberto."

"You don't like Alberto. Why?"

"What's to like? He's ignorant, sadistic, crude. . . . I'm sorry. But the dog wouldn't have been so dangerous if he had not mishandled it. A guard dog is a potentially explosive weapon; in my opinion, animals like that shouldn't be in any house where there are children. Proper training and handling can minimize the danger, but the dog wasn't getting it from Alberto. How did it get loose?"

"Apparently there was a weak link in the chain. Seeing the cat, the animal struggled to free itself—"

"And how did the cat get out?" I had no right to quiz her, but remembering Pete's near escape I got queasy all over again. When I feel queasy I yell.

"The child forgot to close the door of his room."

"He didn't. I was with him. I watched him test the latch."

"What are you implying?"

"Someone let the cat out. Oh, it may have been an accident—the cat could have slipped through the door when the *tuttofare* went in to clean. Or someone may have let it out deliberately, hoping it would run away."

"Is it Emilia you are accusing?" she asked coolly.

"I'm not accusing anyone. The culprit won't confess now, when the consequences were so nearly disastrous. I'm only pointing out that you ought to make certain it won't happen again."

"And I might point out that giving Pietro a pet was not a good idea, since it led him into danger."

"You needn't remind me," I said wretchedly. "Don't you suppose I thought of that? But it's part of living, Francesca —at least, that's how I look at it. You take chances every time you give someone, or something, a piece of your heart. They, or Fate, may smash it. But what's the alternative? Not taking risks, not caring—not feeling?"

"I did not intend to accuse you, Kathleen. Your point of view has been argued by others more eloquent than you." She fell silent, her face remote.

I forced a laugh. "This is turning into a morbid discussion. I didn't mean it to. All's well that end's well, after all."

"Trite but true."

"I think I will rest this afternoon," I said. "It's starting to rain again; my room is so pleasant, with the fire and everything."

We were getting along swimmingly when the damned telephone rang. When I heard the far-off shrilling, I had a premonition. Sure enough, it was for me.

Sebastiano apologized for not calling earlier. "I was late getting in last night, and this morning has been busier than usual. Not a free moment! You have not forgotten our engagement this evening?"

"Of course not. Look, Sebastiano, I've been thinking; why don't I meet you? I could drive to Florence—"

"I don't often run the car into a tree, Kathy." The tinny impersonality of the connection robbed his voice of emotion; I couldn't tell whether he was joking or offended.

"I was only thinking of the time," I explained. "It's an hour up here and another hour back—"

"That is not important."

He was offended. I said quickly, "If you don't mind, then. To be honest, I hate driving in the rain on unfamiliar roads."

"Do you need spectacles that you are too vain to wear?" he asked teasingly, his good humor restored. "Never mind, vanity is a sign of mental health. I will pick you up at seven."

I thanked him and hung up. When I turned from the phone, there was Emilia at the door of the sitting room with the coffee tray. What she knew, Francesca would soon know. I decided I might as well get it over with.

"That was Sebastiano," I said, returning to my place at the table. "I'm going to have dinner with him tonight. I hope that doesn't conflict with your plans."

"You must do as you like."

"It will be the last time I see him," I explained. "I want to thank him for his kindness and say good-bye. Besides, there are a few questions I want to ask about Pietro. Supposing I should be able to take him back to the States I ought to know the best way of handling the transition."

"Yes, that is reasonable." Her stiff face relaxed.

Yet as I retreated to my room I felt like a naughty schoolgirl escaping from the principal's office. The strange thing was, I was beginning to like the woman—or rather, not dislike her as much as I had. We had nothing in common, we could never be friends. But if we had met under other circumstances, we might have felt at ease with each other. I had to admit that the present circumstances were mostly my fault.

ii

I waited for Sebastiano in the hall. It was raining so hard I preferred Emilia's not-so-thinly-veiled hostile glances as she passed back and forth between the kitchen and the sitting room. I wondered why she disliked me so much— or rather, why she let it show. Alberto couldn't have any better opinion of me, but he had never been less than obsequious after the first encounter, when he had not known who I was.

As soon as I saw the headlights I pulled the hood of the raincoat over my head and went out. Dusk had fallen; Sebastiano didn't see me till I opened the car door and tumbled in.

"Is this the American liberation I am always reading about?" he demanded. "You can't allow a man to do something for you?"

"It isn't liberation, it's common sense. Why should both of us get wet?"

"I have," said Sebastiano, "an umbrella."

I remained respectfully silent, and after a moment he added, wonderingly, "Why did I say that? I sound like an English butler."

"I'll let you use the umbrella next time," I promised.

He didn't get a chance at the restaurant; the doorman had his own, a perfect monster of an umbrella, the biggest I had seen off a beach. We did not go into the city, but dined at a new restaurant on the outskirts; it had been a monastery, and the restoration was charming and whimsical. Favored patrons, of whom Sebastiano appeared to be one, had tables in miniature white-painted cells, with a discrete wooden grille on the open side.

Since I never can leave well enough alone, I proceeded to spoil the cheerful atmosphere by asking Sebastiano if his ribs had healed. After all, the last time I had seen him, he had been hobbling with one hand pressed to his side as if he expected the contents to spill out. The question brought a frown to his face, and a curt reply: He was fully recovered, thank you.

I took his annoyance for a display of wounded male ego and would have dropped the subject; but then he said, still frowning, "I suppose I must tell you. I have been debating as to whether I ought; but if you are driving yourself, especially at night . . . The reason I skidded is because someone ran out in front of the car."

"Good heavens! Alberto, was it?"

"Not Alberto. This was someone I had never seen before—a truly monstrous figure, like a creature from one of the old horror films. He appeared out of nowhere. I had to slam the brakes on and the car went out of control."

"I think I know who it was," I said. "Francesca has a poor mentally handicapped man working as assistant to Alberto. He has physical handicaps as well."

"Ah, I see. It occurred to me that it was a vagrant—a tramp. But in that first moment I confess I felt a touch of superstitious panic. I was reminded of the great Lon Chaney in some of his masterful performances."

"I know how you felt. I had a brief encounter with the man one day in broad daylight, and I was uneasy too. I don't suppose he realized that he was endangering himself, or you."

"I'm glad you understand. Most of the unfortunates who suffer from such handicaps are the gentlest of people. You probably frightened him more than he frightened you in the encounter you spoke of. It is a shame the public has such a distorted view of mental illness."

"Thanks in part to those horror movies you're so fond of."

"People ought to be able to distinguish between fact and fantasy." He added shrewdly, "Don't you liberated ladies have daydreams of being overpowered by a handsome pirate or highwayman? You wouldn't really want it to happen to you, though."

I didn't resent the touch of malice in his speech. He could not know why it hit so close to home.

I turned my attention to the menu. It was decorated

with amusing little sketches of plump monks doing various things. . . . "Good heavens," I said, blinking.

Sebastiano laughed. "They are clever sketches, aren't they? I hope they don't offend you. Outsiders are sometimes puzzled by what they consider our cavalier approach to religion."

I assured him I was not offended. The approach of adolescent girls to religion is not always conventional, either. I told him about a sign one of the girls had tacked up on her locker, until one of the nuns removed it. "Holy Virgin, who conceived without sin, let me sin without conceiving."

Sebastiano chortled over that one, and we exchanged stories until we were toying with salad, which in Italy, as I had discovered, is served after the main course. I was having such a good time I almost hated to bring up the subject of Pete. I knew I was going to be scolded.

He didn't blow up when I told him about the most recent attack, but the look he gave me was not exactly admiring. "And you didn't mention it to Francesca? Kathy, I can't believe you could be so careless."

I didn't deny the charge. "I'd have called you if you had been available. Oh hell, why not admit it? I don't approve of the way Francesca is handling the child."

"I assume she is following my instructions. You are a sentimental little thing, Kathleen."

I didn't deny that accusation either, though it sparked a tiny flame of resentment. I don't like being treated like a sweet little dumb female. "Is it your idea that he live at home, without a tutor or governess or teacher? Without friends his own age? There isn't one person in that house who shows him affection, except the cook, and he hardly ever sees her."

"I suggested to Francesca that he would be better off at school. There are excellent institutions. . . ."

"Then why hasn't she done it? Why haven't you insisted?"

"Insist? With Francesca?" His laugh was tinged with bitterness. "I sometimes think a hereditary nobility is the curse of any country. They have no power; they are often stupid, uneducated; yet the aura of superiority still surrounds them."

"Francesca would be charismatic if she had been born in a gutter," I said. "I understand your dilemma; she's in charge of the boy, and you can't force her to do anything she doesn't want to do. You'll be glad to hear that she is considering a change. Within the next few days."

"What? She has said nothing to me. But," he added sourly, "she would not consider it necessary. She wouldn't notify her hairdresser or her plumber that she meant to stop his services."

"Come on now," I said. "You're a big, grown-up psychiatrist. Can't you laugh at Francesca's foibles?"

"I may be a psychiatrist, but I am also human." He shook his head. "This news disturbs me. Vanity aside, I would have expected her to consult me as to where the boy should be sent. The doctor who takes over his treatment ought to know what I have done and what results I have achieved. How soon is this change to take place?"

"Maybe I shouldn't have said anything."

"I won't mention that you told me. But I am entitled to know what you know."

He was all business, brisk and professional. I had to agree with him. So I told him what Francesca had said.

"She is closing the villa?" he exclaimed. "But then you—you too are going away."

"You must have known I would, sooner or later. This isn't my home."

"Of course. I don't know why I had the impression you were staying on indefinitely. Something Francesca said, I suppose. Then I won't see you again."

He took my hand and looked deep into my eyes. His disappointment pleased me, but it also aroused feelings I could not encourage. "Now who's being sentimental?" I said lightly. "I'll be back one day. At least I hope I will. This hasn't exactly been a pleasure trip."

We lingered late over coffee and brandy, talking— mostly about Pete, but also about the country Sebastiano loved and his regret that I had seen so little of it. "Surely I will see you another time before you go," he said.

"I had better not plan on it. My schedule is still uncertain. And Francesca doesn't like my seeing you. I won't sneak behind her back, and I don't want to make her angry."

"You are not immune to the aristocratic aura, either."

"It isn't that." I didn't want to tell him my real reasons for wanting to remain on good terms with Francesca. She hadn't actually said she was sending Pete back to the States with me; if I told Sebastiano, he might repeat my statement to Francesca, despite his promises, and she might resent my interference.

Sebastiano didn't give up easily. He continued to press his point as we drove back. "There is so much to see and do in Italy, so much to experience. It is nothing less than an insult that you are leaving so soon. You need not stay with Francesca. There are other places."

Other bedrooms, other beds. He wouldn't make the offer openly unless I responded to his hint. There was enough of the traditionalist under his modern manners to make him a little hesitant about propositioning a widow of three months—a sharer, however faintly, of that aristocratic aura he had mentioned. If it hadn't been for Pete . . . well, I'm not sure how I would have responded. As it was, all I could do was pretend I didn't know what he was getting at, which made me appear pretty simpleminded.

He was still at it when we stopped in front of the villa. "Don't go in just yet," he murmured. "It is still early—see, there are lights in several windows."

Making out in the front seat of a car isn't my idea of comfort. If Sebastiano had yearned to bid me a prolonged and passionate farewell, there had been a dozen places along the way where he could have pulled off the road. I knew his reason for waiting until we reached the villa, and a damned childish reason it was. He had even checked to make sure the inhabitants were awake and watching before . . .

One of the lighted windows was that of my room. The golden rectangle was bisected by a shadow. It was blurred by rain and distance, but I knew what it was doing. Looking down at the car.

Emilia, on her nightly errand of turning down the bed and tidying the room? The shadowy shape looked taller and slimmer than hers.

"I've got to go in," I said.

He took my hand. "I find it harder to say good-bye than I had thought. There is a conference this fall, in New York. . . ."

I agreed to meet him in New York, to call him before I left Italy, to try to find time to see him again. I may have agreed to move in with him or help him rob a bank; I don't know what I said. I didn't linger to make sure he negotiated the drive without incident. The door was unlocked. I closed it and went straight up the stairs.

222   *Barbara Michaels*

My room was empty. The fire had been built up and the bedclothes had been turned back. Across the bed . . . It looked like the sprawled body of a woman, impossibly slender, long skirts trailing, head concealed by the shadow of the curtains.

I found the switch controlling the chandelier and the room sprang into brilliant light. It wasn't a body. It was a nightgown, arranged in the faintly grotesque shape employed by chambermaids in old-fashioned, elegant hotels—waist pinched, skirts carefully spread out. Not that I had ever stayed in such places, but I had read or heard about the custom. The most interesting thing was that it was not my nightgown. It looked like one of Francesca's; silk chiffon, transparent as a drift of cloud, lace-trimmed and embroidered.

I touched the folds of the skirt. The garment looked brand-new, but the truth didn't dawn on me until I saw the other things. They lay in piles on the chair next to the bed, neatly folded, just as they had come from the shop. Bras and panties, nightgowns, slips—the finest batiste and the most delicate silk, tucked and pleated.

When I acted, it was without conscious thought. The emotion that moved me wasn't anger or resentment or pride, it was simple negation—a large, silent NO.

Carrying the nightgown, I marched down the hall to Francesca's room. She wasn't asleep. I could hear voices. The fact that I could hear them through the heavy door suggested that she was berating Emilia about something.

I knocked. Francesca answered: "Who is it?" She must have known who it was, otherwise she wouldn't have spoken English. I answered anyway.

"It's me, Kathy. I'd like to talk to you."

"Just a moment."

It was more than a moment. The seconds ticked by as I

stood there. When Francesca finally opened the door I thought I understood the delay. She wouldn't allow anyone except her maid—a nonperson, by her definition—to see her au naturel. Her makeup had been so hastily applied it failed to cover the deep lines framing her mouth.

She stood back to let me enter. It was the first time I had seen her bedroom. The color scheme was her favorite ivory and off-white; it gave the room an oddly Spartan, almost monkish appearance. But the sheets on the narrow bed were silk, and the top of the dressing table was covered with cosmetics and beauty aids. The only other modern touch was a small clock radio. There was no one else in the room, so I decided I must have heard the radio. Or else Emilia had gone out through the adjoining room, presumably a bathroom, whose door stood slightly ajar.

I held out the nightgown. "I can't take this, Francesca. Or the other things. I appreciate the thought, but I can't."

Her only visible reaction was a tightening of the muscles at the corners of her mouth. Anger, I assumed. I had not been very gracious.

After a moment she said, "Don't you like the . . . things?"

"They're beautiful. But—no, they aren't what I would have selected, even if I had the money. I haven't time to hand-wash and iron lingerie."

"Money," she repeated, with a faint distaste. "As I told you, you have a legitimate claim."

Even in my present mood I was not boorish enough to say that if there was something owed me, I'd rather have the cash. The amount that had been spent on the lacy frivolities would have paid my rent for a year.

So the discussion ended, as it had before, with my giving in—or appearing to. I couldn't afford to alienate her at this stage. I told myself I would leave the clothes in the wardrobe when I left.

As I went out I noticed that the door next to Francesca's was open. So was the door leading into the abandoned wing. Emilia could have gone that way. I had meant to ask her if she had been in my room, but the question was irrelevant now. It must have been Francesca whom I had seen looking down from the window.

A breath of cold air brushed my face from the open door. The darkness at the end of the long, empty corridor seemed to shift and curdle, like shadows trying to shape themselves into a solid form. With the cold air came sound, a breath of soft laughter, trembling on the rim of soundlessness.

When I got back to my room, breathless and shaking, I saw that the fragile silk of the gown was crushed and wrinkled where my hands had squeezed it. I threw it onto the chair and got into bed.

Then I got out of bed. Once again the hated, the too-familiar ritual—a look at a sleeping child, a turn of a key in the lock. The hallway was chilly with dampness, and some of the bulbs had burned out.

iii

I was beginning to count the days—and the nights. Perhaps the weather had something to do with my growing impatience to be gone. Wednesday was another gloomy, dripping day, which meant I couldn't take Pete outdoors. I should have driven to Florence and visited the museums, and the other sights that draw tourists from all over the world; heaven knew when I would be able to afford to visit

Europe again. Hopefully I would come back someday; but at the moment I only wanted to be somewhere else.

I decided I had a legitimate need to know how Francesca's plans were developing. I had promised my father I'd call when I got my reservation. That call had yet to be made. I faced Francesca with the question at breakfast; and, as usual, her unsmiling regard drove me into incoherent and graceless explanations that probably bored her as much as they disgusted me. "I have to let the folks know when I'm arriving. It's a long drive from Wayford to Boston, and my brothers work, and so does my father, part-time anyhow, and my mother hates to drive. . . ."

"I understand. You have not telephoned your father?"

"Not yet. But I told him I would, and he'll be wondering."

"Would it be inconvenient for you to wait until Saturday? You see," she went on smoothly, "I am working on the arrangements we discussed earlier. I have been assured I will be notified by Friday. It may be late in the day, or evening, before I hear, but by Saturday morning you will be able to tell your parents of your plans."

She sounded even more formal and stilted than usual, and the vagueness of her reply irritated me. She must have realized this, for she added, in a more conciliatory tone, "I have every reason to suppose that you will be able to leave Florence as you planned, on Sunday, and that the other arrangement will work out as you desire."

"Oh. Oh, that's wonderful! I'm so pleased."

"You are, aren't you?" She studied me wonderingly. "I too am pleased, of course. To be quite honest, it will be a relief to have someone else take charge of the boy. I know I am not the best of guardians. I really don't care for children."

"Not even Bart?"

"He was different." She didn't say how. Perhaps she didn't know herself. Parents try to love all their children equally, but often there is a quality in one child that brings out a stronger response from one parent or the other, or both.

I didn't hang around after breakfast. Francesca appeared to be preoccupied. She had asked, with only the faintest tinge of irony, if I wanted to accompany her and Pete to the doctor's that morning. It would be his last appointment, so they might be late returning; she had a number of things to discuss with Dr. Manetti. I declined, with thanks, and removed myself.

It looked like a long, boring day. The news had cheered me considerably, but had made me even more anxious to shake the dust of the Villa Morandini off my shoes. I had been mistaken when I hoped the trip would help rid me of Bart. The ghosts of the boy he had been and the man he had become haunted every corridor and moved in the shadows of the gardens. I knew that was foolish, of course. The ghosts that haunt us are in our own minds; they follow wherever we go, unbounded by time and space. But I would find it easier to exorcise that laughing shadow in some other place than this.

For want of anything better to do, I went looking for David. He wasn't in his room. The grubby scraps of Coptic embroidery covered every flat surface. He had placed lamps over some—ordinary table lamps, with ordinary bulbs. Most of the scraps still felt soggy.

The only other place he could be was the attic, so I went there, using the back stairs. As I approached I heard him muttering to himself in his favorite blend of personal commentary and poetic quotation.

I looked in. "How's it going?"

David was holding a handful of papers. He flung them

into the air and said, " 'Shut, shut the door, good girl (fatigued I said), Tie up the knocker, say I'm sick, I'm dead.' "

"That isn't Browning!"

"Pope. How are you getting on with Robert?"

"Slowly." I closed the door. "I can't tie up the knocker, there isn't one, and besides, I don't know how. Are things that bad?"

"Things are worse," David said, stooping to retrieve the scattered papers. "This has really left me in a bind, dammit. I'd counted on six weeks or more."

"I'm sorry."

"Any chance that she'll change her mind?"

"I don't think so. She told me this morning that Sunday would probably be the day. I don't know when she—"

"What about the kid?"

He spoke casually, but I could see he was really concerned. "He's going with me. It's not absolutely dead certain, so don't say anything to him, but it's looking good."

"That's what you wanted?"

"Well, of course. This is a miserable life for a child. Don't you agree?"

He didn't answer, just sat there looking steadily at me, his long, thin mouth drawn down at the corners, his eyes narrowed. I prayed he wasn't going to bring up the subject we had agreed to forget. I hadn't forgotten—I never could—but his manner had been so normal since that one slip that I had been able to behave as usual.

"What's the matter?" I asked. "Is my face turning green or something?"

"Sorry. I am struggling with the impossibility of my own conclusions. Did you come to offer a helping hand?"

"I'll be glad to help if I can."

He put me to work. Real work. Whenever I stopped to

exclaim over a nineteenth-century ball gown, packed in camphor, or an album of family photographs in a fat velvet cover, he yanked this treasure out of my hands and gave me another pile of papers to sort. If effort is any proof of honesty, he really was looking for manuscripts. The rest had just been fooling around. Now that Francesca had given him his marching orders, he wasn't bothering about the family "collections."

I tore myself away, without too much effort, when it was time for lunch. My promptness was wasted, however. Francesca was not there. Emilia gave me another of those exquisite notes, in which Francesca said she would again go out for dinner.

"Is Pietro with her, or did he come back?" I asked Emilia.

"He is here, signora. In his room."

"As usual," I muttered.

"Signora?"

"Nothing. That's all, Emilia. You needn't wait; I prefer to serve myself."

Still she lingered. "Is there any food for which you have a desire, signora? Any special dish?"

She might have been consulting me about the dinner menu. But she wasn't. Her eyes were fixed on my napkin-draped lap, and her smile was sly.

I told her no, and did not thank her for asking.

iv

Now that the time for our departure was imminent, I found myself curious about Pete's academic capabilities. Once a teacher, always a teacher. I had done my practice teaching with fourth graders, so I had a rough—very rough—idea of what to look for. Pete grumbled when I asked him to answer a few questions, but complied; we ran through some math problems and discussed dinosaurs and Pilgrims and George Washington, and read from the cat book. He was deficient in math, but up to grade level on most other subjects. He admitted he had liked history. His mother had read to him every night; he was familiar with most of the children's classics. And he knew one hell of a lot about football.

The rain continued to dribble depressingly, so I had to refuse his invitation to practice kicking. I had a whole bagful of tricks for rainy days, culled from pedagogical journals, but in fact none of them worked well for children over the age of five. Even Joe copped out on us. "Kittens need lots of sleep," I said after Joe had refused an invitation to chase the string. "I have an idea. Why don't we explore? Maybe we can find someplace where we can play ball or hide-and-seek or something."

He agreed, rather listlessly. There were endless rooms, some locked, some open; some furnished, some filled with discarded odds and ends. The unfurnished rooms were too small for strenuous games, the furnished rooms had too many breakables. I was looking for something like a ballroom or a grand gallery. Surely houses of this stature had to have a ballroom? I couldn't find it, and Pete said he didn't know. He was bored and had no hesitation in showing it.

"Maybe it's in this part of the house," I said. We were in the corridor where Francesca's room was located; I indicated the door, now closed, that led to the empty wing.

Pete shrank back. "No. We cannot go there."

"Is it really dangerous? It's broad daylight; we can see if there are holes in the floor, or—"

"I don't like it there," Pete whispered. "Please, signora —don't make me go."

I took his hand. "You're freezing cold," I said, and then, quickly, "So am I. Let's run, okay? I bet I can beat you to the stairs."

So, in the end, we went looking for David. He was at work, mumbling and swearing, but we extracted him for a quick run around the grounds. By that time I had decided I preferred rain to boredom—not to mention whatever it was in the empty wing that had so frightened the child.

The run took quite a bit of time—not the running itself, but the assumption of outdoor garb and the removal of same, the drying of hair and the changing of clothes. Joe was awake and cooperative when we got back, so all three of us entertained him for an hour, and then it was almost time for supper.

David left, with self-righteous remarks about people who had to work while others frittered away their time. I had finally come up with an idea; Pete was sprawled on the hearth rug drawing a picture of Joe. There was no fire, and we could have used one that bleak evening, but even without it the room was cozier than Francesca's immaculate sitting room, and I didn't feel like dining alone with Emilia eyeing my flat stomach and freezing me with her silent criticism of my table manners.

"How about my having supper with you?" I asked.

"Will you?" He beamed with pleasure.

"I'll go ask Rosa. Be back in a minute."

Rosa and I communicated very well. She had three words of English and I had ten words of Italian, but both of us were great at gestures. She thought it would be fine if I ate with Pete. "Tell Emilia?" I suggested. She grinned and made a rude remark—it looked like a rude remark from the gesture that accompanied it. I left it at that. The cook was the one who was chiefly inconvenienced by changes in meals.

When Rosa brought the food she was accompanied by the *tuttofare*, both carrying trays. The covered dishes filled the entire surface of the table. There was milk for Pete and a bottle of wine for me.

"Let's have a toast," I said when we were alone.

"Good. I will have wine," Pete announced, reaching for the bottle.

"No, you will not. You've got to learn to eat American style if you . . ." I stopped just in time. I didn't want to tell him what was in store; according to Francesca, matters were virtually settled, but if the deal fell through, the disappointment would be crushing. "When you're as old as I am you can poison yourself as much as you like," I went on. "Right now it's wine for me and milk for you."

"It is not fair," Pete said. His lower lip went out.

"Life is not fair," I agreed. "Grin and bear it."

"I hate milk. Especially the Italian milk. It is too hot, never cold like American milk. Sometimes when they don't see me, I throw it away."

"Joe doesn't agree with you," I said as the kitten leaped onto the table, his whiskers twitching. "Grab him, Pete, he's heading for the chicken."

Pete thought it was funny. He sat there chuckling, and I reached for Joe. Joe eluded me and bore down on Pete's glass of milk. He didn't get more than a slurp or two before I collared him.

"Well, that gets you off the hook with the milk," I said, trying to sound stern. "Lord knows I'm not fussy, but that cat probably still has several varieties of unsanitary germs."

"I can throw it away?"

"Yes, you had better. But don't get any ideas about

using Joe as an excuse, at least not while I'm around. I'm on to that one now."

Pete came back from the bathroom with a glass of water, so I gathered my lecture on American eating habits had had the proper effect. It was a pretty fiction, but I saw no reason to admit that alcoholism among American teenagers was rising like a rocket. Who should know better than a teacher?

The only way we could keep Joe off the table was by sneaking him tidbits. He particularly relished the chicken, which he gobbled up like a glutton.

It may have saved his life. We were barely finished with dinner when he let out a low moaning mew and began gagging. Saliva drooled from his open mouth.

"Leave him alone," I said to Pete, who was trying to get out of his chair. "He ate too fast. He's just . . ."

The chicken came out, as Pete would have said. That was just the beginning. The cat's back arched in a spasm. He collapsed onto his side, kicking. Pete got to him before I could intervene, and pulled back a hand streaming with blood. Joe jumped high in the air and began racing around the room, ricocheting off the walls, falling and picking himself up again, crashing into the furniture.

I grabbed a blanket from the bed and pounced. The warm bundle under my hands writhed and howled; it felt like a tiger, not a small kitten. I fended Pete off with my elbow. Tears were streaming down his face.

"He'll be all right, Pete. It's okay. Leave it to me."

I hoped I wasn't lying. Fits can be caused by a number of things, from worms to epilepsy. If I had given the child a pet suffering from some fatal disease . . . The contorted lump finally went limp and I cautiously extracted it from the blanket, wrapping it in a fold of the fabric for safety's sake.

He wasn't dead. Not yet, anyway. His half-closed eyes were an uncanny white, the extra eyelid that shows when an animal is sick or comatose. The minuscule pulse was beating wildly and erratically. All I could do was hold him and try to reassure his hysterical owner. By the time we got him to a vet the attack would be over—one way or the other.

I had almost decided we had better make the attempt, at least, when the heartbeat started to steady. Joe opened one eye. He must not have liked what he saw, because he closed it again; but a faint purr began to vibrate through his body. A short time later, still glassy-eyed but seemingly recovered, he was curled up in Pete's arms ready to take a nap.

"What was it? What hurt him?" Pete's face was still sticky with tears.

"Nothing serious. It happens sometimes." What the hell could it have been? I ran over the symptoms in my mind. Vomiting, uneven heartbeat, muscular spasms—like the ones Pete had had that awful night . . .

And then I knew.

I wondered how I could have been so blind. The kitten was the final clue, but I ought to have known before. I had seen it before—in my own classroom, right in the middle of a quiz on the Louisiana Purchase. I remembered how I had paced the floor that night, raging, telling Bart about it, cursing the people who sold the stuff to children.

The balance of that evening reminded me, in retrospect, of a home movie some of my kids had produced for extra credit. One of the characters was the ghost of Abigail Adams. It's an easy special-effects technique and the kids loved doing it. Abigail lay recumbent on her deathbed, while a shadowy similacrum rose from her body and strolled hither and yon, then returned to blend into the original form again. That's how it was with me. I sat on the floor holding Joe, in dumb horror, while my shadow double finished dinner, chatted with Pete, watched the cat play with the remainder of the food, thanked Rosa when she came to take the trays, tucked Pete into bed. . . .

It was the shadow me who kissed Pete good night and closed and locked his door; the shadow who undressed and put on robe and slippers; who stood by the door until she heard Francesca pass down the corridor and enter her room; who continued to wait, counting off the minutes, until the house was quiet; who tiptoed up the stairs and into Pete's room; who locked the door—on the inside.

Not until I lowered myself into a chair did the two parts of me click back together. One of us must have been thinking, because I could see the whole thing now, in all its deadly completeness.

Lysergic acid diethylamide. It could have been one of the other hallucinogenic drugs, mescaline, DMT, morning-glory seeds—but it was probably LSD, a small fleck of which can produce all the symptoms I had seen. There must have been more than a speck in that glass of milk. The cat had only absorbed a minute quantity, but its body weight was so small it had been violently if briefly affected.

Why hadn't I recognized it in the child? That was easy. For the same reasons Sebastiano had never thought of drug abuse as the explanation for Pete's illness. By the time he saw the boy, the physical symptoms had passed. He might jeer at Francesca's melodramatic diagnosis of hereditary madness, but he had only substituted the conventional theories of his own specialty—"infantile death wishes," "transitory manic-depressive state characteristic of mourning," "breaking through of the unconscious at night." Pete's history fit that diagnosis. It didn't fit the pattern of drug abuse. The child had no access to drugs. He was isolated from his peers, from the outside world.

Besides, the symptoms of LSD vary widely, depending on a number of factors—dosage, individual tolerance, psychological strengths and weaknesses. The most common effect of the drug, the one sought by habitual users, is an intensification of sensory impressions. Colors blaze out, textures are magnified, sounds take on a richer meaning. Often there is a phenomenon called synesthesia, the confusion of one sense with another. Users *see* music, *feel* color, *hear* light. During the course of a single episode, extreme mood swings can occur, from ecstasy to terror. Also suspicion and hostility . . .

I had done my homework on drugs; a teacher who doesn't is neglecting part of her job these days. You have to know the facts. The kids can tell when you fake it, and the truth is never quite as bad as the things you imagine. To call LSD a hallucinogen isn't strictly accurate, because the users rarely have genuine hallucinations. They see and feel the real world. They just don't see it in the usual way. They can even control the effects to some extent, if they are fully aware of what is happening. The so-called bad trips are much more likely to occur if the person is anxiety-prone or emotionally disturbed to begin with, or if he doesn't know what to expect.

Pete hadn't known. He was not even aware he had taken a drug. I thought of him waking in the middle of the night with his heart pounding and shudders shaking his body, tô see his familiar room transformed into a crazy house—the red chair humming in a low baritone, the rain shooting rays of bright light through the barred window, his pajamas rubbing his skin like sandpaper. I had read of one case in which the user looked in a mirror and saw his face sag and run, like melting wax. What had Pete seen in his mirror before he smashed it? What ghastly transformation had altered my face when he covered his eyes and refused to look at me?

I had to clench my jaws to keep my teeth from chattering. My thin cotton robe wasn't much protection against the April chill, but it was not cold that made me shiver. My first impulse, an impulse I was still fighting, had been to grab the child and run. Some remnant of common sense had warned me that might be disastrous. There were too many unknowns, and I was too vulnerable—in a foreign country, with no legal right to act for the boy, opposing an adversary who had all the clout and influence I lacked. Many of the options I would have sought if I had been at home were closed to me here. For once in my life I had to stop and think before I acted.

Think. Think. Try to figure out their next move. How many more days? She had talked about the weekend. Wouldn't she prefer to wait until after I had gone—until David was no longer on the premises? Why commit such a vile act with witnesses present, when she could easily rid herself of them?

I wanted to believe that. It would have given me more time. But every scrap of evidence confirmed the probability that Friday was the day. The ambiguous hints that had perplexed me took on a new and dreadful meaning. She had said the final decision as to Pete's future would be made on Friday—"late Friday, perhaps." She had suggested I wait until Saturday before calling home. By that time I would be in a position to tell my parents of my plans. Naturally I would want to stay over for the funeral. . . .

If she had entered the room at that moment I would have gone for her throat. I no longer doubted her intention, even though I did not understand her motive or her reasons for not waiting until I was out of the picture. It would be Friday night. And since she was so certain of the result, the next attempt wouldn't be like the others. It would be brutal and direct.

Don't imagine it was easy for me to believe that Francesca was planning the murder of her own grandson. I kept turning the bits and pieces of evidence over in my mind, trying to find another explanation. One possibility, that Pete was taking the stuff himself, just didn't make sense. The only person from whom he could obtain illegal drugs was Alberto; and in addition to the inherent unlikeliness of such an alliance, I felt sure Alberto wouldn't dare do such a thing without Francesca's approval. Nor was it likely that the boy could have brought a supply of drugs with him. She had made him discard his clothes, his books, his toys; where could he hide the stuff?

I would love to have cast Alberto in the role of chief villain, but that wouldn't wash either. If he wanted to rid himself of an obstacle, he'd use a club or a gun. He and Emilia must be involved. It would have taken both of them to carry out the scheme with the kitten, and it was probably Emilia who drugged the boy's food. But neither was capable of inventing a scheme so diabolically subtle. They were only the tools; the brain directing them belonged to someone else.

Francesca wasn't the only candidate, though. There was another possibility.

David.

I knew nothing about him except what he had told me. Francesca had been satisfied with his credentials, but she wasn't omniscient. Surely it was a strange coincidence that he should turn up now, on a job that was, to say the least, rather unusual. David had taken pains to ingratiate himself with the cook. He couldn't always arrange to be hanging around the kitchen when the boy's food was prepared, but the drug had not been used every night. There had not been time for David to fetch the kitten from Pete's room, but if Joe had escaped by himself and David had spotted him outside, he might have been able to slip in and free the dog.

The most damning evidence against David was the drug connection. The night I saw him in the garden and mistook him for Bart he had been smoking pot. The smell was unmistakable.

I didn't believe it was David. I didn't want it to be David. I had not even thought of him initially. It wasn't until I sat huddled and shivering in the darkness, forcing myself to think before I acted, that the thought occurred to me. Which proved I had been wise not to take Pete and make a run for it. I probably would have run to David.

I had read a lot of books with plots like this. I had often wondered how any heroine could be dumb enough to mistake the villain for the hero. I had often thought contemptuously, Why doesn't the stupid wench go to the police? Now I knew why. I could see myself trying to convince a local cop that a member of one of the most distinguished families in Tuscany was planning to kill her grandson. "And who are you who make this accusation, signorina?" Oh, just a passerby, a stranger, a foreigner—a woman who is fresh out of a mental institution. I'd be lucky if they didn't lock me up.

The night should have dragged on interminably, but it was all too short. The window was a sickly square of cloud-shadowed dawn before I knew what I must do. Get the boy away. By myself, confiding in no one, because there was no one I was certain I could trust. I was not completely without resources. There were people who would testify to my character. I had no criminal record;

I had been sick, but raging paranoia wasn't one of my problems. The boy's aunt and uncle might help. My father . . . He'd hop the first plane if he thought I was in trouble.

Given time, I could marshal those allies and put up a fight, especially if I held the trump card—Pete. The only question remaining was where to hide him. I couldn't get him out of the country without a passport. I think I would have risked a charge of kidnapping with hardly a qualm if I had had that essential document; but after I had considered the pros and cons I realized it wouldn't work. The flight took too long. By the time the plane landed, they would know Pete and I were aboard, and we'd be met by a platoon of assorted law-enforcement agents. Besides, Francesca probably had his passport, and my chances of finding it were slim to nil, with Emilia watching every move I made.

There was only one place I could take him. It had the advantage of being so illogical only an idiot would have thought of it.

ten

I still have nightmares occasionally—not about Bart,
but about that last, awful day. I'm carrying the child and
trying to run through some dark viscous substance that
sucks at my feet. Far ahead I can see the gray light of
morning, but there is darkness all around me and behind,
where the dog is close on our trail. The jingling of its
broken chain gets louder and louder. Dim forms lunge at
us from the side of the path as we struggle forward—
Alberto, aiming his rifle; Francesca, reaching out with
arms that stretch like rubber and end in taloned hands. I
pass them in a desperate burst of speed. I'm gaining on the
dog; the sounds behind grow fainter. The path ahead is
clear. And then *he* is there, blocking the way, laughing,
lank greasy hair covering his face. Almost all his face.

That was the mood of that final day—frustrated desperation, desperate frustration; I wanted to act, and I could
not. The only thing in my favor was that the weather
continued to be cloudy. For once in my life I was praying

for rain. We'd have a better chance of getting away if we waited until nighttime—darkness veiling our movements, hours elapsing before our absence was discovered. It was the best plan, but it was susceptible to change, depending on the circumstances. I dared not assume Pete was safe until Friday night. I had to be ready to make a break for it if he was threatened, or if an unexpected opportunity presented itself.

I dreaded seeing Francesca that morning. I was afraid I wouldn't be able to hide my knowledge, that she'd see my feelings written on my face. It wasn't easy, but I managed it. You can manage anything when you have to. She was distracted too, and that helped. When we sat down to breakfast she had a list in her hand, and the first thing she said was, "You haven't forgotten that you have a fitting today?"

I had forgotten. I was trying to think how to get out of it—for I had no intention of leaving Pete unwatched for that length of time—when Francesca went on, "Unfortunately I will not be able to accompany you. You don't mind going alone, do you?"

"Maybe I'll take Pietro with me," I said. "We could pick up a few things for the trip—games, comic books."

"If you like." The only emotion she displayed was the usual poorly concealed incredulity that I could possibly enjoy the boy's company. So far so good, I thought. I went on, "We'll have lunch in Florence."

She nodded, studying her list. I couldn't believe it. I said casually, "There's no need for Alberto to drive us. I'll take my car."

I might have known it wouldn't be that easy. Francesca looked up, frowning. "That would be foolish," she said sharply. "It is raining and you don't know your way. I won't be needing Alberto this afternoon. I have a great deal to do here."

I was afraid to press the point. I felt as if I were balancing on a tightrope; the wrong word, the wrong look could betray me. She continued to inspect me with a new keenness. "You don't seem your usual self, Kathleen. Did you sleep well last night?"

I was prepared for that one. "I didn't, as a matter of fact. I was worried about Pietro. It seemed to me he was a little high-strung last night. When I went up to look in on him he was awfully restless. I guess it was just overfatigue, but I didn't like to leave him, and . . . Well, I fell asleep in the chair and didn't wake till daybreak."

Stop there, I told myself. Don't explain too much. I had to have some sort of explanation, in case they had discovered I had spent the night in Pete's room. It would have been wiser to avoid that change in routine—the only thing I had going for me was the fact that they believed I was unwitting—but I had simply been unable to face the alternative.

Francesca appeared to buy my excuse. "I admire your conscientiousness. But you mustn't wear yourself out. Your health is important."

I assured her I felt fine, top-notch, in the pink; but I knew I had better get out of that room. There were limits as to how long I could play the game.

So much for the hope of getting him away before nightfall. If I could keep from cracking under the strain, the trip to Florence would give me a chance to make a few essential preparations and throw Francesca off guard.

Pete graciously accepted my invitation. "Will we go to a movie?" he asked hopefully. "I have not gone to a movie since I came here. I like movies about murderers and robbers."

"We'll see."

Pete had a good time, at any rate. I must have put on an adequate performance; he didn't seem to notice anything odd in my behavior. He was bored at the couturier's, but I cut that as short as I could by telling the astonished fitter that everything was fine the way it was. I don't suppose she had ever had such an easy time of it with any customer, especially with Francesca or her kin.

I did derive some satisfaction out of running Alberto ragged. I made him drive all over town looking for the things I wanted, and I dismissed him as cavalierly as Francesca would have done while Pete and I ate lunch and sat through a long movie about bank robbers. I would never have permitted a child to see such a film under ordinary circumstances—when the "hero" wasn't shooting guards or massacring witnesses, he was making love to his girlfriend—but I decided this was no time to cavil at minor moral issues. The important thing was to stay out of the house as long as possible. In the course of the day I managed to complete all my errands—stocking up on games and reading material for Pete, buying a carrier for Joe, and cashing my traveler's checks. I had a little over seven hundred dollars, and I figured I might need it. I also bought Pete a coat and a cap and had the store wrap them. It wasn't much of a disguise, but it was better than nothing.

My last move was to take Pete to a trattoria and stuff him with every filling item on the menu. It was getting late by then and Alberto was obviously resentful of the delay, but I didn't think he was suspicious. He was not smart enough to figure out why I wanted Pete so full he couldn't eat his supper. Pete was big-eyed with delight at the idea of choosing anything he wanted, and I watched benevolently as he finished off his meal with ice cream and an assortment of pastries.

Twilight was closing in when we returned to the villa, and my spirits began to revive. The interminable day was almost over. I would only have to face Francesca one more time, kill a few more hours, and then we would be on our way. The nasty encounters that were sure to follow didn't worry me. There was only one thing that did worry me, and once Pete was safe, I could handle abuse, accusations, and anything else.

Pete went rushing up to show Joe his carrier. I doubted that Joe would share his enthusiasm, and cautioned him about introducing it gradually and tactfully. If Joe started howling when we carried him out, we were in trouble. I took the parcel containing the coat and cap with me and locked it in my suitcase.

My next stop was the kitchen, where I told Rosa Pete had already had his supper and cautioned her not to give him anything more to eat or drink. I was ninety-nine percent sure of Rosa, but she couldn't help me; she was too much in awe of Francesca.

After I had returned to my room I sat down and went over my plans again. Was there anything I had neglected, anything else I could do, any emergency I hadn't anticipated? The answer to the last question was a resounding, depressing yes. The definition of an emergency is something you have not anticipated. But I'd done everything I could and I was now at the point where my thoughts ran around in circles like a hamster on a wheel.

I walked into the *salone* without knocking. Francesca was at her desk. My unannounced appearance startled her so that her pen made an ugly jagged line across the page on which she was writing.

"I'm so sorry," I said.

Slowly and deliberately Francesca crumpled the paper and dropped it into a wastebasket. She was edgy, no question about it, and her nervousness lessened mine. For in spite of all my logic a doubt lingered in my mind. Was I committing the same error of which I had been accused so often and so justly—misinterpreting facts, building fantastic theories on inadequate foundations? I knew myself well enough to know it was possible. The very monstrousness of the plot made it hard to believe. It was not the first time I had faced that possibility, but the answer was simple and incontrovertible. Right or wrong, sane or demented, I had to carry out my plan. I could not take the chance of being . . . right. So I met Francesca's frown with a bland smile, and when she asked if I had completed my errands, I said glibly, "Yes, we had a great time. I cashed a few traveler's checks and bought a carrier for the kitten. I almost forgot that."

"The cat?" Her eyebrows arched. "It can be left with Rosa. She will stay on as caretaker."

"Pietro is very attached to it. You know when a child is facing a big upheaval in his life it helps him to have some familiar object to cling to. The cat won't be any trouble. I thought I would take it to the vet tomorrow and get the necessary papers."

"I see." She shrugged, dismissing the subject. "Was the fitting satisfactory?"

"Oh yes. They said they'd have everything ready by Saturday afternoon."

She nodded. Of course they would have everything ready. Her pen hovered over a fresh sheet of paper, and I said, "I can see you're busy. Please go on with whatever you were doing. Can I help in any way?"

"Thank you, no. Unless you will be good enough to ring for Emilia. I must just finish this note and then I will join you."

Emilia responded to my touch on the bell, and as she

arranged glasses and carafe on the table, I thought how seductive it must be to have such power at one's disposal. A little pressure of a single finger, the contraction of a few small muscles, could produce an industrious bustle of activity. It would be fatally easy to become accustomed to controlling other people's lives with one push of a button.

When Francesca sat down beside me she again apologized for her distraction. "There is always so much to do when one travels."

"I've been trying to get organized too," I said. "Maybe I should return that rental car tomorrow, instead of waiting till Sunday. Would it be possible for Alberto to drive me back?"

"Of course." Her smile was warmer. She approved of that idea. (Don't ask why, don't try to find double entendres and hidden meanings—you're far beyond that now. Just stick to your plan.)

She had left the businesswoman at her desk and was now the charming hostess, but there was a change in her manner—not so much nervousness as suppressed excitement and anticipation. If I hadn't known better, I would have supposed she was looking forward to her trip. (*Il principe, monsieur le comte,* waiting in a secluded chalet in the Swiss Alps.) Her moments of dreamy abstraction and her veiled glances at me—glances that seemed to hold a greedy pleasure—began to wear on my nerves. I wondered if I could get through the evening after all.

Unwittingly, Francesca provided a distraction. "I have asked Professor Brown to join us for dinner. I felt I owed him that, since he will be leaving soon."

I had been careful to avoid David. Guilty or innocent, Francesca's accomplice or independent villain, he was not a factor in my plans, only an obstacle to be avoided at all costs. I was not happy at the prospect of spending an evening in his company.

Francesca saw my reaction and appeared to be amused by it. "I hope you won't be too bored, Kathleen."

"He does tend to go on and on about subjects I find somewhat tedious," I said. "But one last evening won't kill me."

At least I hoped not.

David was wearing a proper shirt, for once, with a relatively respectable jacket over it—probably a concession to the chilly weather rather than a mark of respect for his hostess. He was carrying a brown cardboard box.

"These are the Coptic fabrics you wanted to see," he explained, dropping the box at Francesca's feet.

She studied it with disgust. It was far from clean, and there were cobwebs clinging to its sides. Unaware of his faux pas, David beamed at her. I was reminded of a dog who has just presented his owner with a particularly smelly dead rat.

"Mind if I move this stuff?" David went on, shifting the decanter and wineglasses. "I'll lay the pieces out here. I'm afraid some of them are a little damp."

They were damp, and they smelled of wet fabric, chemicals, and sheer musty age. However, they aroused Francesca's interest; she actually touched one or two, commenting intelligently about the type of embroidery used and questioning David about the age and history of the specimens.

Finally she said, "It is most interesting, Professor. I am grateful to you for rescuing the collection. If you would be good enough to instruct me as to how they should be preserved?"

"Well, see, the problem is they aren't dry," David said. "What they need is a temperature- and humidity-controlled, sealed glass case, but if you put 'em in that environment now, while they're still wet, they will be ruined. I calculate three or four more days—"

"I don't have four days," Francesca said curtly. "Why can't we use heat lamps?"

"That's risky. I don't have the proper equipment—"

"You will have to do the best you can. The house will be closed early next week, perhaps before then. If you can arrange to leave Saturday or Sunday . . ."

"Whatever you say, of course."

It was not a pleasant meal. David was sulky and ill at ease, Francesca abstracted. I need not describe my state of mind. On the surface the interview was precisely what I would have expected: the grande dame dismissing the now inconvenient hireling, but expecting him to accomplish the impossible before she threw him out, and the hireling resenting the whole business. If there were hidden nuances I had missed, then I had missed them, and that was that. I was exhausted by surmises.

Finally the uncomfortable dinner drew to a close. David withdrew, his carton under his arm, presumably to spend the rest of the evening drying his scraps. I sat with Francesca for another hour, massacring my embroidery. My hands were quite steady, but my mind was not on my work.

When the clock chimed ten I got to my feet. It was the usual procedure; she was an early riser, and usually went to her room at ten-thirty. As I stood there saying good night, a strange feeling came over me. Everything in the room—furniture, fireplace, the woman sitting poised and groomed on the couch, her needle in her white hand—went flat and two-dimensional, like a painting. Frozen for all time, but unreal, dead. I suppose she spoke to me, returned my "good night." I didn't hear her. Painted faces cannot speak.

I wasn't nervous or afraid. One good result of that long, agonizing day was that I had used up all those emotions. There was nothing left except a flat calm. I took off my jacket and skirt and put on my robe. I filled the pockets of my raincoat with the things I needed—passport and money, keys and wallet. They were big patch pockets; I stuffed one or two odds and ends of clothing in on top of the other things, to make sure they didn't fall out.

I opened the door and left it ajar. I sat down and picked up a book at random. When I saw it was Browning's *Poems* I almost tossed it away, but it didn't matter; I was incapable of reading print, much less absorbing the content. I sat with the book open, turning pages; now and then a line caught my eye. "Then all smiles stopped together." The Duke, remembering his last Duchess, who had been too indiscriminate in her affections. "Childe Roland to the Dark Tower came." The stuff of nightmares, the dying sunset kindled ahead, the hills crowding in on the quarry at bay. . . . "Grow old along with me! The best is yet to be . . ." I hope so, Robert; I certainly hope so.

I stopped even pretending to read. My watch held the slow time back. The minute hand stayed fixed for eons, then suddenly jumped and stopped again. At a quarter to eleven Francesca came upstairs. Her heels clicked past my door, not pausing; then came the sound of her door opening and closing. Half an hour later it opened again. A brief murmur of voices—Emilia, bidding her mistress *buona notte*. Her heavy footsteps, thudding away. She'd take the back stairs, the servant's path to her room.

I closed the book. Stood up. Turned out the light. Blackness closed over me. The night was clouded, utterly dark. I didn't need light or want it. I took off my robe, put on slacks and jacket, picked up my shoes and the parcel with Pete's clothes. I took my coat out of the closet. I stood by the door waiting. Waiting can be an all-consuming activity, requiring every ounce of concentration. I waited.

At twelve-thirty I opened the door. One light shone at the end of the hall near Francesca's room. Another lit the head of the stairs. I went up into the dark, feeling for each step. The key was in the lock. I turned it and went in.

The dim lamp in the corner of Pete's room made me blink; it seemed bright after the Stygian darkness of the hall. The kitten, curled in the bend of Pete's knees, raised its head with a soft inquiring mew. The light reflecting from its eyes made them glow phosphorescent green.

This was the first hurdle. How do you tell a boy of ten that someone wants to kill him? How do you convince him he must come away with you, a stranger, known for only a few days?

Joe helped me awaken him, pouncing and purring, happy to find an intelligent person who was willing to play with a cat in the middle of the night. When the boy stirred sleepily I spoke. "Pete. Wake up. It's me, Kathy. Don't make a noise."

His hand went out, reaching for the cat. "Signora? Is it morning?"

"Not yet. I have to talk to you, honey. It's important. A secret, just between the two of us—and Joe, of course."

He sat up, rubbing the sleep from his eyes. He looked even younger than ten; his hair stood up in little tufts, and the bones of his arms were as fragile as twigs. I hated what I had to do. I had rehearsed the speech so often that it came out flat and unconvincing. I didn't believe it myself.

"You've got to listen to me, Pete. Listen carefully. Someone is trying to hurt you. You aren't sick. The attacks—the bad times you had—came because they put a drug in your food. You've heard of drugs. They can make people do strange, dangerous things. I want you to come with me—now—to someplace where you'll be safe. You and Joe. I know you find this hard to believe, but you have to. . . ."

Then came the first surprise of the night—the only pleasant surprise. He was nodding his head. His pupils were dilated; his eyes looked like little jet marbles rimmed with blazing silver.

"You believe it," I said, gulping.

"I know it. This drug—I don't know that—but I know I am not sick. I am afraid. Always afraid. Only no one would believe me. Where will we go, signora?"

My icy calm quivered under a burst of relief and thankfulness. Over the first hurdle and still running—and he was a marvel, a miracle, cool and unafraid.

"I know a place, Pete. First get dressed. Something warm and comfortable. . . . Here." I pulled slacks and shirt, sweater and socks from the dresser drawer.

He moved instantly to obey, stripping off his pajamas and reaching for the clothes I handed him. His thin little body quivered, but not, I thought with fear.

"We must take Joe."

"Of course. That's why I got the carrier today. And this coat and hat for you. No one has seen them; if they start looking for you—"

"I know. Like the movie. You were clever to think of it, signora."

Bless him, he was cool as a cucumber—a lot cooler than I was. I watched him entice Joe into the carrier and put his favorite game—the one I had bought him—in his coat pocket. After a moment's thought he stuffed a few of the comic books in the other pocket. "I have not read them," he said. "Now, signora, I am ready."

He stood straight and fearless, the unbecoming cap

pulled low over his forehead, hiding his hair. The coat was too big; it hung below his knees and covered his hands to the knuckles. I knelt beside him and turned back the cuffs. My hands lingered, but I didn't hug him. We were brave adventurers, partners in a daring escape. This was no time for sentiment.

"Okay," I said. "This is the plan. We're going down the back stairs, through the kitchen, to the garage. To my car. Get in the back seat with Joe and crouch down. I hope we can get away without being seen, but just in case—"

"I know. Now, signora, I will lead the way. I know it better than you in the dark."

"Yes, sir!"

He gave me an aloof kindly smile, like a general encouraging a loyal subordinate.

I locked the door and took the key. Anything to prolong discovery. He let me carry Joe. Joe was shifting around and murmuring. I hoped he wouldn't decide to yell, but the carrier had a flap that snapped over the grille at the open end. I had chosen it for that reason. It was our only piece of luggage. We were traveling light, not even my purse to get in the way.

The second hurdle was behind us when we got out of the house without being seen. I had not expected much difficulty there, but the next jump wouldn't be so easy. There was no way I could get the car out of the garage without starting the engine. The stableyard was perfectly level. Alberto and Emilia slept in the house, so David was the only one I had to worry about. He might waken when he heard the car start, but it was not his job to care who came and went. I hoped, and assumed, he would not interfere. But there were so many things that could go wrong. . . .

I swore under my breath when I saw there was a light in

David's window. After a moment's indecision I decided not to wait for it to go out. He might decide to work all night.

Pete put the carrier into the back seat. Then he turned to me. "Signora," he whispered, "will we break the Mercedes?"

I could have kicked myself for not thinking of it. The trouble was, I didn't know how to break the Mercedes. I had no idea how to open the hood. There's one thing any vehicle needs, though, and that's a set of intact tires. I inspected the rack of tools hanging on the wall; there was just enough light from the open door of my car to enable me to select an awl, sharp-pointed and heavy-handled.

"I'll break it," I murmured. "Get in the car and crouch down."

Puncturing the tires wasn't as easy as I had thought it would be. Mine always seemed to go flat when they ran over a pin, but I had to pound and jab before I heard air start to hiss out. I had dealt with the two back tires when a flashlight beam caught me full on.

The shock stopped my heart for a second. I had not heard a sound of warning, and believe me, I had been listening.

"Turn off that light," I said. My voice was ragged with anger and terror.

He turned the light away, but he didn't switch it off. Holding the awl behind me, I edged toward my car.

"What are you doing?" David said. I could hear him now, coming down the stairs.

"I left something in the car."

"Something you need desperately at one in the morning?"

"What business is it of yours?"

"I'm making it my business. Why do I get the strange

impression that you are doing a moonlit flit—without the moonlight? Flitting is easier in the dark, I admit."

I said, "If I want to leave, that's my affair. What do you care?"

"I don't. I don't give a good hearty damn whether you stay or go straight to hell, so long as you are alone. I'll just have a look in the back, and if you have no passenger—"

"Stay away from that car, David. I swear I'll run you down if you get in my way."

He made a soft ambiguous sound that might have been a smothered curse or a jeering laugh. My first miscalculation—and possibly my last. How I had patted myself on the back for having the intelligence and the courage to admit that David might be involved. But I had not really believed it, not in my blood and my bones, my heart and my soul. If I had believed it, I would have known that lighted window raised the odds against us a thousand to one. I'd have thought of some other plan. Too late now. Too late for anything except . . . My fingers tightened around the heavy wooden handle of the awl. Could I use it? I had to. I had to prevent him from stopping us, from giving the alarm. The path to the gates was clear, but the gates would be locked, they always were; by the time I got them open, he'd have caught up with us. And there was his motorcycle. Even if a miracle occurred and we got out of the gates, he could follow.

"Kathy," he said, in a different, softer voice. "Think what you're doing. There is still a way out of this. Maybe you don't realize . . ." He was moving as he spoke. I could tell from the soft sounds his feet made on the stairs. Then I saw him in the open doorway, a featureless shadow against the lighter stones of the courtyard.

He spoke again. "Kathy, please listen to me."

I almost dropped in my tracks. His voice came from the dark at the foot of the stairs. He was still inside the garage.

From the hulking shadow in the doorway came a hoarse laugh. *"No, signora. Eccola—la carabina. Capisce?"*

He wanted to make certain I understood. A switch clicked and lights blazed out. Alberto stood there, his heavy lips parted in a grin, the rifle cradled in his arms.

Every ounce of feeling in me vanished under an overwhelming surge of frigid rage. "God damn you all," I said. "You're not going to touch him. You'll have to shoot me to get at him. At least you may have a hard time convincing the police it was an accident this time."

I wrenched the door open and got into the car. The keys were in my hand. The headlights went on, sending Alberto's shadow darting blackly across the stones. I could hear the child gasping, like a runner after a sprint. We didn't have the ghost of a chance, but I wasn't going to give up until they dragged me kicking and biting out of the car.

I turned the key. At the first cough of the motor Alberto jumped back, moving with the light-footed agility of a boxer. He held the rifle loosely, carelessly. There was no hurry. One shot would do it.

David came out of the garage, across the glare of the lights. I knew who it must be, but I wouldn't have recognized him; he was only a blur of movement, a streak of speed. He tackled Alberto low, knocking him backward. The rifle hit the ground. David made a dive for it, but Alberto was up again, quick as a cat. His booted foot crashed down on David's hand. David's face was a white oval in the glare; his mouth opened in a cry I heard even through the closed window. With his other hand he grabbed Alberto's ankle and pulled. The two bodies closed, writhing in a monstrous tangle of limbs. I slammed my foot down on the gas.

I brushed the gatepost as I turned, felt the car shudder and heard the scream of tortured metal. The car rocked and skidded as it swung around the house and onto the drive. Branches reached out black arms that raked at the windows and clawed at the windshield. The gates loomed up ahead. I hit the brakes, fought the sideways slither of the wheels, and got out, leaving the door open. The key was there, on the nail inside the lodge door. When I ran to the gate I saw Pete was out of the car and started to yell at him; then I shut up. He already had the bar off its supports. After I had turned the key he pulled one section of the gates back while I opened the other. He was crying. His face glistened in the headlights, but he didn't utter a sound.

When we got back in the car I could see the glow of light from behind the villa—not one light but a whole battery of them, all around the stable area. The car splashed through puddles as I sent it down the steep road at a speed I'd never have dared attempt in daylight. We hit a pothole with a jar that jammed my teeth together, and I let up on the gas. I couldn't risk a broken axle or a flat tire.

We had passed through the sleeping village and reached the main road before I could speak. "Okay back there, Pete?"

"O-kay," said a very, very small voice.

"I think we made it. Remind me to tell you someday that you are my number-one draft pick."

His breath caught. "You are the same for me, signora. Joe does not like to ride in a car."

"I noticed that." Joe's protests were piercing and heartfelt. "Most cats hate cars."

"Will I come in the front with you, signora?"

I started to tell him no, it wasn't safe, before I realized he needed to be closer to me. And I needed him closer, too. I was operating in the deceptive calm that follows a shattering shock—or a series of them, in quick succession. I said, "Come up. Be careful."

He tumbled over the seat and rearranged himself. His tears had been dealt with in manly privacy. His face was streaked and grimy, but quite dry.

"Signora?"

"Yes, Pete."

"We will not go to Dr. Manetti?"

"Do you want to go to him?"

"No! He will send me back."

"That's the way I figured," I said. "Pete, did you ever tell Dr. Manetti someone was trying to hurt you?"

"No. He will not believe me."

It made me sick to think of the quiet terror in which the boy had lived for so many weeks. He had only one advantage—a child's fatalistic acceptance of the illogical. He knew they hated him and wanted him dead. He didn't have to know why. The adult world was incomprehensible anyway. This was only another manifestation of its innate senselessness. And with the cunning of all small, hunted animals, he had learned not to trust any of the hunters.

"We aren't going to Dr. Manetti," I said. "For a start, we're going to telephone your aunt and uncle in Philadelphia."

"Maybe they don't want me," Pete said. "I write them letters, but they don't answer."

His voice was flat and unemotional, but I knew that had been another hurt, and not the least of the ones he had endured. I said quickly, "I'll bet they did answer, Pete. Letters don't always reach the people to whom they are addressed. Can you remember what happened after you heard about the plane crash? You were with your aunt and uncle then; did they tell you you were going to live with your grandmother, or did she come and get you, or what?"

He didn't understand the implications of the story he told me, but it confirmed my worst suspicions, and my fondest hopes. No, no one had told him he was to leave until he found Aunt Vera packing his suitcase. She cried all the time she was packing it, though she tried not to let him see. Uncle Ben had been angry, very angry; his face was red and he talked in a deep, growling voice. He had had to leave a lot of his things behind. They could only take one suitcase on the plane, Uncle Bart said.

"You mean Uncle Ben," I corrected. The lights of Florence were a puddle of brightness in the valley below. We were almost there.

"No, Uncle Bart. He said to call him that. He was like a brother to my father, and so—" Pete stopped with a gulp. "Oh," he said. "Oh. I forgot. They made me promise. . . . To say his name will make you sad."

Somehow I managed to get the car off the road and onto the shoulder without hitting anything. There was not much traffic.

"I forgot," Pete whispered. "I made you feel bad."

"No. No. You could never make me feel bad. You've made me better. In fact," I said, "I think I'm completely better now."

eleven

Angelo was at the desk. I had assumed he would be; he always was. He was no more surprised to see me stroll in at two in the morning, accompanied by a child and a cat, than I was to see him. A British butler's demeanor would have been wildly emotional compared to the imperturbability of Angelo.

Yes, of course, he had a room. Had he not said there would always be a room for me? He didn't ask who Pete was, he only nodded affably and admired his tastes in reading materials. He spoke with equal affability to Joe and produced an ingenious makeshift set of sanitary arrangements without batting an eye.

The child was about to drop with exhaustion and even Joe looked a little wilted; he had worn himself out howling for thirty miles. I put them both to bed. Pete was drowsily pleased at being allowed to sleep in his underwear. He had always considered it a frightful waste of time to keep changing clothes. They were both asleep before I closed the door.

I had explained to Pete what he must do in case I didn't come back. Of course I would come back; but just in case . . . When I went downstairs Angelo was back behind the desk. Yes, he knew of an all-night coffee bar. (I felt sure he would.) I took over the desk and a sheet of hotel stationery while he went to get the coffee.

I had almost finished the letter by the time he got back. It was a long letter, but I didn't have to stop to think as I wrote; it was all very clear in my mind. The coffee was strong and black, like the best espresso. I knew I might need an extra jolt of caffeine before morning, although I felt abnormally alert and clearheaded.

I finished writing, put the note in an envelope, and sealed it. "You see," I said. "Another secret letter."

"Ah," said Angelo.

From my pocket I took what was left of my money. I had given most of it to Pete. The remainder came to over a hundred dollars. I handed it to Angelo, along with the letter; and for the first and last time saw his jaw drop in astonished disbelief.

"The money is for you," I said. "The only thing you'll have to pay for is a telephone call to the States. The boy knows the name and the address. If I'm not back here by morning, help him make the call. Keep trying until he gets through. Then take the secret letter to your brother—the policeman."

"Ah," said Angelo.

"It could mean a promotion for him, Angelo. This is a very serious matter—a matter of life and death."

"And the peace of the entire world?"

"Right. I forgot that. Can I trust you?"

Angelo folded the letter and put it in his shirt pocket. He dropped the wad of lira notes onto the counter and delicately, with a flick of his fingertips, pushed it away. It was the most superbly theatrical gesture I have ever seen in my life.

ii

I drove steadily, without haste. The rain had stopped; the clouds were blowing eastward. A star shone bright through a rift in the hills ahead. I wished I could regard it as an omen.

I had known I would go back even before Pete's revelation had torn my world apart as the wind was shredding the storm clouds. David had made the same error about me that I had made about him, and knowing what I now knew, I could understand why he had been so ready to suspect the worst of me. As I reviewed the conversations I had had with him, I realized we had been at cross-purposes from the start, misunderstanding each other's motives, misinterpreting actions and words in the light of our own false preconceptions. It was no coincidence that David was at the villa at this time. He had come for a purpose. He couldn't confide in me because he didn't trust me, and he didn't trust me because I had not told him the one fact that might have changed his mind. How could I tell a stranger what I had tried to hide even from myself?

And now the picture was complete to the last detail. It wasn't like a jigsaw puzzle, made up of fragments meaningless in themselves; it was more like the inlaid roses on the floor of the hall in the villa. Each part was complete—a rose, a leaf, a petal. But the central motif had been missing, the stem to which all the elements were attached. Once I had that, the other pieces formed a perfect pattern. Every ambiguity was resolved, every question answered, even the motive that had eluded me.

The gates were still open, as I had left them. I drove past without slackening speed and pulled off the road at the top of the hill, in the same place where I had parked before. The rain-soaked ground let me pass with little noise as I plodded along the weedy track and climbed the broken wall.

The lights in the stableyard still burned, and as I crept closer I heard the clang of metal on metal. Someone was working in the garage—Alberto, mending the tires of the Mercedes, I assumed. David's window was dark. I didn't expect they'd have taken him to his room but I had planned to have a look. No chance of that now, with Alberto nearby.

I turned and went the long way around, through one garden after another, toward the front of the house.

I'm describing what I did, not how I felt while I was doing it. There are no words for that. The fact that I lost my way is no indication of my state of mind, because I might have done that anyway. The desolation of the abandoned gardens was even worse at night. The boughs moaned as the wind stirred them; the white marble of an armless statue glimmered amid a shroud of strangling vines. Brambles caught at my feet, my hair, my hands. And the walls—walls everywhere, casting shadows deep enough to conceal a dozen enemies, shutting out the normal world, barring the way I had to go. Finally I blundered into a more open space and saw the fallen columns of the little antique temple shining pale in the starlight.

I had to sit down for a few minutes to catch my breath. I tried not to think of the confrontation that lay ahead. I was afraid that if I did, I would turn and run. A soft small voice, the voice of common sense and cowardice, insinuated slyly: You could go back. Go to the police; get help. With what you know now—and other facts, easily obtainable—you can convince them. They'll believe you now. Go. You can slip out the way you came.

Yes, I could probably convince the police—eventually. Eventually was too far away, eventually was too long. They wouldn't harm David if they thought they could use him as a means of retrieving the child; but once the police cars rolled up to the gate, once they knew for certain that Pete was out of their grasp, David was as good as dead. They had no reason to leave a witness alive. A body could lie hidden in the acres of woodland and rough pasture for months, years, forever.

I got stiffly to my feet. Through the delicate grillework of the final gate I saw the front lawn, a sea of silver-gray streaked with shadows. The fountain was a black mass of monstrous shapes, the pitted metal too rough to catch the starlight. The shrouded windows of the formal reception rooms made the place look abandoned, but the lanterns at the front door shone bright, as if awaiting the return of a belated traveler.

I wondered how they would react if I walked boldly up to the door and knocked. I might come to that in the end. Even if I could get into the house without being seen, my chances of finding David were slim. He could be anywhere, in the villa or out of it. But I wasn't ready to face that door and what lay beyond it. Not yet.

The windows of the villa weren't all dark. One section of the terrace was illumined by a glow of light. It came from Francesca's sitting room. Of course. That's where they would be. Planning their next move, trying to find a way out of the dilemma I had created for them.

I had to cross most of the front of the villa to reach that room, for I was at the wrong end. It was a long walk. I kept to the shadows and tried to move quietly, but my feet made little crunching noises on the gravel.

I went up the stairs and crossed the terrace. The windows were closed. The draperies had been pulled back. Though thin curtains blurred the scene inside, I had no difficulty in recognizing Francesca. She was wearing a long, flowing robe and she sat on the love seat, facing the windows. She was talking to someone. Her hands moved in quick gestures. I couldn't see the other person, only a black-clad arm and a hand, resting on Francesca's shoulder.

She stopped speaking. After a moment she rose, gathering the folds of her robe more closely around her. She moved toward the door, her steps slow and dragging, her shoulders bowed.

The figure of a man came into view. He stood with his back to me, watching Francesca. I had not meant to move but I did, step by slow step, drawn by fascinated horror. I may have made a sound. He may have caught the flicker of movement out of the corner of his eyes. He spun around. I stood full in the light, staring, unable to move.

He came to the doors and threw them open.

"I knew you'd be back, Kathy."

Marveling at the steadiness of my voice, I said, "Hello, Bart."

iii

He hadn't changed. Slim as a panther in black slacks and turtleneck, silver eyes gleaming, he was tanned and fit and as incredibly handsome as ever.

I walked into the room. He closed the window behind me. "You don't look surprised, *cara*. I thought you'd swoon with astonishment and joy."

"I never really believed you were dead. Somehow I always knew."

His eyes narrowed with laughter. "Yes, that was your trouble, wasn't it? When I think of those stupid shrinks trying to cure you of your neurotic obsession . . . Well, I'm sorry about that, darling. I simply couldn't risk telling you the truth."

"Of course you couldn't risk it. What was my sanity compared to your . . . your what, Bart? Your life? Your freedom? What were you running away from?"

He didn't like my choice of words. His level dark brows drew together. Instead of defending himself, he hit back. "Maybe it was you, Kathy. Did you ever think of that?"

"Often."

It was a simple admission of fact, but to Bart it was something more—an admission of ignorance. He thought I had accepted his devastating, hurting excuse, that I had no suspicion of any other motives. His frown cleared and he said magnanimously, "I might have acted differently if I had known. Why didn't you tell me you were pregnant?"

It was a good thing he had reminded me. That little matter had slipped my mind—and yet it was probably the strongest card in my hand. I said, "I didn't know . . ." and without willing the movement, stepped back as he started toward me.

He smiled. "You're still afraid of me, aren't you, Kathy? You always were."

"I always was," I said. "You enjoyed that, didn't you?"

"Of course. And so did you. Don't pretend you didn't."

He took me in his arms. A shudder ran through me, and Bart laughed softly. He turned my face up toward his; his fingers were hard, painful. As his mouth covered mine I wondered why it had taken me so long to realize that for Bart a kiss was a demonstration of mastery, not of love.

He let me go with a quick, careless movement that sent me staggering, one hand to my bruised mouth. "That will have to wait," he said. "You've made a pretty mess of things, as usual. Where's the boy?"

"Really, Bart." I pouted prettily. "You make me so mad, you really do. I guess I did go off half-cocked, but damn it. It's your fault. You've been here all along, haven't you? Playing your little tricks, getting me all worked up—"

"I couldn't resist. You're so susceptible, *cara*. Did you like the lingerie?" His smile broadened. "The time you caught me, down by the gate, I almost whisked off my wig and my hump and confronted you. But I wasn't quite ready for that."

"You—you were—"

"The imbecile, yes. You never suspected, did you?"

I ought to have suspected, though. What had Sebastiano said? Lon Chaney, the *Hunchback of Notre Dame*? Bart's roles were always derivative. He was an excellent mimic, but a rotten actor.

I said, "No, I didn't. That was quite a performance."

"Too good a performance," Bart said complacently. "Was it the imbecile you were fleeing tonight? What the hell possessed you to pull a stupid stunt like that?"

"I was running away from Alberto." I let some of my rage and disgust spill out. "Damn you, Bart, I'm not as stupid as you think. That so-called accident of Pete's was pretty clumsy. Alberto shot the dog because I got in the way."

"Alberto? That clod couldn't hit the side of a barn. It was your loving husband who saved your life—and that of his unborn son."

"Thanks," I said.

"Don't be sarcastic, Kathy. It doesn't suit you. So you thought Alberto wanted the kid out of the way?"

"I thought it was Francesca," I admitted.

Bart threw his head back and shouted with laughter. "Francesca? You really have slipped a few cogs, sweetie. Francesca doesn't like the brat; he's too much like his father. I was always the golden boy around here. But she wouldn't . . . No one would hurt the kid. Where is he?"

"Where is David?"

As soon as I spoke I knew I had blundered. Bart was a wholehearted supporter of the double standard. It was all right for him to have other women, I was expected to tolerate that. But I couldn't even smile warmly at another man without arousing a storm of rage—filthy accusations, even physical violence—but in the latter case, only against the poor devil who had been decent to me. Bart had never struck me. He didn't have to. He could hurt me a lot worse in other ways.

I had to convince him that I didn't care about David, and pray he didn't know David was anything more than an innocent bystander. Slowly and deliberately I seated myself, leaned back, crossed my legs. He watched me with narrowed eyes. I said casually, "Bart, you always were too impetuous. What was that poor wimp supposed to think when he saw Alberto waving a gun at me? He jumped in, playing hero, and now I suppose you've got him locked up somewhere, bleeding all over the carpet. If you don't explain and apologize and get him out of here before he has time to brood about his bruises, he'll slap an assault charge on you."

"Wimp?" Bart repeated. "How unkind, darling. I thought you had taken a fancy to the man."

I laughed. "He reads Browning," I said.

Bart's head turned. He was looking at himself in the mirror. Smiling at his reflection.

"That might be the best solution," he said. "But I'll let you do the apologizing."

"I'll be damned if I will. You always expect me to—"

"While I fetch my poor little cousin home. Where is he?"

"With the carnival."

"What carnival?"

"The one at Fiesole. I thought it was rather a clever idea," I said defensively. "David knew one of the people— the man who runs the carousel. We were there the other day and Pete loved it. So I left him with . . . what is the man's name? Bartelli, or something like that."

"Clever? It was crazy, my poor demented girl. I do believe you need a few more sessions with the head doctors. As usual, it's my job to clear up the mess. I'll go get the kid and you explain to your boyfriend that his heroics weren't needed. He'll feel a bit of a fool when you tell him the truth, I expect."

"Oh, all right. Where is he?"

"In the storeroom with the rest of his junk." Bart added casually, "He may be in need of repairs. There's some first-aid stuff in the butler's pantry."

"Then get it," I said shortly. "I haven't any idea where to look." My hands were shaking. I jammed them in my pockets.

"You've changed," Bart said, giving me a speculative look. "The little mouse has grown sharp teeth. You know, I think I like you better when you fight back."

"That will have to wait," I said. I knew if he tried to kiss me again I'd do something foolish. "Hurry up, Bart, and let's get this nonsense over with. I want to go to bed."

"So do I, *cara.*"

iv

After we had found the first-aid materials, Bart said he'd go up with me and explain the situation to Alberto. "I left him guarding the door," he explained glibly. "Lover boy was frothing at the mouth. I thought we had a crazy man on our hands; had to lock him up."

The story was developing nicely. By now, I thought, Bart probably believes it himself.

Alberto sat on the top step, the rifle beside him, smoking a cigarette. When he saw Bart he snapped to attention, his brutal face doglike in its devotion. Bart spoke to him in Italian; then, turning to me, he said, "I don't suppose you understood. You never were any good at languages. I told him you'd patch up the chap's wounds and explain matters to him. I'll be back in an hour or so, and add my bit, and then we'll get rid of him."

"Why wait? I'll tell him—"

"He can't leave till I get back. I'm taking his bike."

"Why?"

"Because you did the job on those tires, my helpful little darling. They can't be patched. Now get the hell in there. And be convincing."

v

They had had the decency to leave him a light, the same battery-operated lamp he used for his work. The light wasn't very bright; the batteries must be running low. In the pallid glow I saw him, lying unmoving on the floor. Bart hadn't bothered to mention that he had decided it was necessary to tie the madman up. For a heart-wrenching moment I thought there might be one other minor detail

Bart hadn't bothered to mention, but when I bent over David, he opened one eye and inspected me briefly before closing it again. Only one eye was functional. The other was swollen shut, and the lower part of his face looked lopsided.

I began working on the knots that held his wrists behind his back. The only thing I succeeded in doing was breaking a nail. After a time he said, "Have you come to gloat, or to share my captivity? Not that it's any of my business, but I like to get these things clear in my mind."

"It's more complicated than that." Another nail bent painfully back, and I swore. "But we're on the same side. Pete is okay. They won't find him."

"Then what the hell are you doing here?"

"That's complicated too. You were one of the considerations, however."

"Is that right? I don't know that it makes me feel any better."

The knots were too tight. I went to the door. "Give me your knife," I said to Alberto. "Don't tell me you don't have one, you filthy clot. Knife. Give me—"

"The word," said David, "is *coltello.*"

Alberto finally got it through his thick skull. He wasn't thick enough to hand me the knife; he cut the ropes himself, and went out.

When I reached for him, David let out a bleat of distress and flapped his hands feebly. "Don't touch me!"

"I can't carry out the plan I had in mind without touching you."

He rolled over and sat up, his back against a steamer trunk. "If you mean what I hope you mean," he mumbled, "go ahead. I'll clench my jaws like a true hero and stifle my groans."

It was an inauspicious occasion for our first embrace.

But I needed it, the way an invalid needs medicine. David's lips wiped away the last lingering memory of Bart's kisses and made me whole again. It wasn't until I tasted blood and knew it was his that I pulled away. "It's my fault," I whispered. "If I had confided in you—I wanted to, David, but I was afraid—"

"It wasn't your fault, or mine. It was what somebody once called the general cussedness of things. If I had . . . What are you looking at me that way for?"

"You have no idea how nice it is to hear someone tell me it isn't my fault."

"Maybe I do. Kathy, I know how lousy this is for you—having to choose between your husband and the child—"

"Lousy? Wait a minute," I said. "Let's get a few things straight. Until about two hours ago I thought Bart was dead. I identified—not his body, there wasn't enough left of it to. . . . But I saw his wristwatch, melted and blackened, a ring I had given him. When I made a run for it with Pete, I thought Francesca was the one who had tried to kill him."

"How did you . . . Never mind, it doesn't matter." His one open eye was steady and pitying in the grotesque mask of his face. "You found out he was alive, so you came back. You still—"

"Love him?" Laughter bubbled in my mouth, wild, sick laughter. And then it died. "I hated him. I was glad when he died. That's why I fell apart after the accident, because I was glad, because I had prayed to be rid of him."

vi

There were other women, right from the beginning. There were his insane fits of rage about other men—not jealousy, but possessiveness. The final blow came when I found out he was dealing drugs. In a way it would have been easier to take if he had used the stuff himself. I could have viewed addiction as a sickness and tried to help him. But he never touched it, except for marijuana now and then. He despised the people who did. He used them, without mercy or compunction.

The night before the accident he was with one of his women. He didn't call, he didn't tell me he wouldn't be home. He came in next morning looking like a cartoon caricature of a cheating husband, even to the lipstick on his collar, and stinking of pot. I blew up. He knew I would. He threw a few things into a suitcase and stormed out of the house. The last thing he said to me was, "You'll be sorry. It's your fault. You never understood me, never tried. . . ."

He was always picking up hitchhikers. It was a way of taking chances, flexing his muscles, playing macho. The body they found, burned beyond recognition, must have been that of some vagrant he had picked up, deliberately choosing someone about his age and size. He must have planned it well in advance and waited for the right weather conditions—it wouldn't take long, not in January in Massachusetts. The storm had been forecast the day before. The schools were closed, there were few cars on the road.

And now I knew why he had done it. I assumed he'd be in trouble sooner or later, with the police or some of his business associates; he'd have no qualms about cheating them if he thought he could get away with it. But that wasn't why he faked his death. A few weeks earlier he had read of the plane crash and he knew that only a small child stood between him and the dignities he had always wanted and had falsely claimed. Il conte Bartolommeo, master of the Morandini estates. They must be worth more than I had supposed. The land itself had considerable value.

When Pete told me that it was Bart who took him from his aunt and uncle, it was like a lightning bolt that illumines a dark landscape. Suddenly I realized that everything could be explained by one simple assumption: that Bart wasn't dead. He stood to profit from Pete's death. He had access to the drugs Pete had been given. It wasn't a ghostly memory that had tormented me, it was Bart himself. He'd been here all along. That assumption even explained Francesca's peculiar behavior. When she equivocated about the child's future, she didn't know herself what Bart planned to do. He'd have brushed her questions aside: "Leave it to me. I'll make the arrangements." She didn't care enough to persist. She didn't suspect him. People believe what they want to believe.

My unexpected arrival forced Bart into premature action. He had been in no hurry before that, he could take his time. Six months, a year, building up the picture of a child tormented into recklessness, driven by grief and "hereditary madness." Sooner or later one of Pete's escapades would have ended fatally, and after a proper period of mourning the new Count Morandini would have assumed his title. There would be no problem with the police, even if his activities in the States had aroused suspicions. His presumed death had closed that file; five thousand miles away and a year later, who would make the connection? At least that's how Bart would reason. He shared that happy human faculty of believing only what he wanted to believe.

He had been prepared to close the file on me, too. When my letters arrived he had probably told Francesca I had no claim—that he had never married me. Even when I showed up at the door she tried to get rid of me, until she got the idea that I was carrying Bart's child. Unconsciously she had already written Pete off. Sickly, psychotic, accident-prone—he would never live to carry on the name. In her mind Bart was already *il conte Morandini,* and the imaginary embryo was the next heir.

What a deadly, disproportionate effect that one seemingly harmless lie had had on everyone involved! Francesca must have been nagging Bart for days to tell me the truth; he must have had a hard time fending her off, thinking up excuses why he couldn't. Matters came to a head when I told Francesca I was going home. "But it would be different if Bart were here," she had said. My decision had forced Bart's hand. He couldn't put Francesca off any longer.

That was what she looked forward to seeing on Friday—the great revelation, the joyful reunion of two lovers. Off we would go for a second honeymoon—with, of course, a proper wardrobe for the signora so she wouldn't disgrace her new family and her elegant husband; and before long the inconvenient holder of the title would disappear. The world is full of dangers—speeding cars, wild animals, poisonous plants. Sometimes unhappy children run away from home. Sometimes they are never found.

vii

It didn't take long to tell. David kept up a monotonous undercurrent of groans and curses as I tended to him, but he listened intently. Finally he said, "That should do it. Don't tell me any more, Kathy, it just makes me mad, and I haven't got time for that. We'd better get the hell out of here before your homicidal husband comes back."

"It's all right. He's going to let you go."

"Say what? He may not be very bright, but—"

"He's bright enough in some ways, but his vanity is so enormous, it leads him to underestimate other people. He thinks I'm still under his spell. I'm supposed to be explaining to you that this has been an embarrassing misunderstanding. You don't know anything about the danger to Pete. You jumped Alberto because you thought he was going to attack me. I have now set you straight on that and told you your services aren't wanted. As soon as Bart gets back . . ."

My voice trailed off. David was shaking his head, slowly, monotonously. "My dear girl," he said. "My poor, dear, innocent girl."

I covered my face with my hands. "I'm the one who isn't very bright."

"Most people would be in state of catatonic shock after what you've been through tonight. And it isn't easy to accept the fact that someone you once . . . Gets back from where? Where has he gone?"

"To Fiesole," I said listlessly. "I told him I'd taken Pete there, to one of the carnival people. David, I'm scared. I thought I was so clever, and yet I overlooked so many things I ought to have anticipated. When he gets back, without Pete, he'll be raging. He'll know I lied."

"But it was a brilliant idea, Kathy. Better than you realized. The carnival is moving on tonight; Lucca is their next stop. It will take him hours to track them down and discover Pete isn't with them. That means the only one we have to worry about is Alberto."

I said hopefully, "Didn't they teach you karate or kung fu, or something, in the Secret Service—or Interpol, or whatever organization it is you're with?"

I think the expression on his face was surprise. It was

hard to tell. "The only organization I'm with is the University of Colorado. Somebody probably teaches karate, but it isn't obligatory for junior faculty."

"The University of . . . Aren't you a policeman? Didn't you come here looking for Bart because of his drug dealings?"

David started to laugh, then stopped, touching his lip tenderly. "Talk about a Comedy of Errors," he muttered. "It would be funny if it weren't so catastrophic. I'm not a cop, honey. I wish I were. I'm Uncle Don. The baseball *star,*" he added.

"Pete's uncle?" I gasped. "But what—how . . . I'm sorry, I think my brain has finally given way. David—Don—"

"David is my middle name. And my last name really is Brown. I couldn't change that, because I had to have genuine credentials to show the contessa. I figured she wouldn't remember my sister's maiden name. It's a common name, after all."

"Then Pete's mother was your sister!"

"Yes." His face hardened. "I knew Guido pretty well, too. The last time Pete saw me he was about five, and I had a beard then. He couldn't possibly remember what I looked like. I was in Europe last year, on a grant—I'm on the tail end of it now—when Guido and Amy left Pete with Vera. I met them, for the last time as it turned out, in London later in the fall. I was still in England when I heard about the plane crash. I didn't know Amy and Guido were on the plane till Vera finally tracked me down, and by the time I got home Bart had already gone off with Pete. You can imagine the state Vera was in. She had lost two people she loved—Guido was as close as a brother—and then to have the boy snatched away too, when she was hoping they could keep him . . . They weren't even allowed to correspond with him. The contessa told them Pete's doctor had recommended a complete break with the past.

"I had gone back to England but I was in touch with Vera, and I didn't like the sound of things. Guido had mentioned his cousin—not that he anticipated trouble from Bart, the subject just happened to come up. He said Bart was a bad lot, mentioned a few unsavory episodes . . . Well, when I heard it was Bart who had come for Pete I started to wonder, and the more I thought about the situation, the more uneasy I became. So I figured I'd go to Italy and have a look. It took me a while to arrange the necessary references. I really am looking for old diaries, and I had even talked to Guido about looking through his family papers, but I knew that wouldn't cut any ice with the contessa, and I decided, just to be on the safe side, that I wouldn't tell her who I was. She was never particularly fond of the Brown family.

"Even before you arrived and I finally got to see Pete I knew the arrangement wasn't right for him, but I hadn't seen any signs of cruelty or mistreatment that would give me an excuse to intervene. It wasn't until the incident with the dog that I started getting funny ideas. I talked to Rosa, and she told me about the other 'accidents.' And then I really got cold chills."

As he spoke he was rummaging in the boxes. He didn't have to explain what he was looking for.

"And you assumed I was one of the bad guys," I said. That rankled, even though I had made the same error about him.

"Well, you see I knew one fact you didn't know." David lifted a cracked marble lamp base, shook his head, and put it aside. "I knew Bart was alive. In fact, I didn't know he was supposed to be dead. Car fatalities are only too common; the story didn't make the national news. I figured he'd be here, and I even saw him a few times—always at night, driving out in the Mercedes or walking in the garden. I didn't understand why he was keeping a low profile, but I was afraid to ask questions for fear of blowing my cover.

"Then you turned up, and Rosa told me the romantic story of the pregnant, brokenhearted young widow, as it was told to her. It was the first I'd heard of Bart's 'death.' I asked Rosa about the man I had seen; she told me there was nobody else here except Alberto's half-witted assistant. What was I to think? Obviously that your husband had staged his death and that, after a decent interval, you had joined him here. From Guido's caustic comments I gathered Bart might have excellent reasons for wanting to be thought dead. When I realized someone might be planning a fatal accident for Pete, I had no doubt as to who that someone might be."

"But you saw me with Pete. You should have known I—"

He sat back on his haunches. "I didn't want to believe it, Kathy. I didn't think you were actively involved. But I thought you were still in love with your husband, and people in love don't always have good judgment. If you cared that much about him you might follow his instructions blindly, without letting nasty suspicions enter your mind. I knew things were coming to a head when the contessa gave me the bum's rush, and when I found you in the garage I was afraid the final accident was in progress—that you were taking the kid to Bart. It wasn't until Alberto appeared and you cussed us both out that the light dawned. Forgive me?"

"I guess I'll have to, since you're nobly overlooking my refusal to trust you. What are you doing?"

He had amassed a collection of small heavy articles,

ranging from a brass doorknob to a miniature marble bust of some bearded dignitary. "Defensive weapons," he said, loading up his pockets.

"I thought you were looking for something you could use as a club or a—"

"Club? Honey, if I found a saber I wouldn't use it. I don't intend to get within arm's reach of that gorilla. He has already beaten the you-know-what out of me once tonight. And don't suggest any clever little schemes like luring him in and bashing him over the head. It would take a two-by-four to even stagger him. I know; I tried it."

"Then what—"

David pulled himself to his feet, leaning heavily on the table. I could see he had delayed this move as long as possible. "We are going to move furniture," he said. "I don't think he'll bother us unless we try to open the door, but let's keep it quiet, okay?"

It was impossible to be quiet. We had to push some of the larger objects, such as a massive mahogany sideboard, and they made loud screeches on the rough floor. If I had been Alberto, I'd have been curious. Luckily he lacked that characteristic. Dull obedience and a few flashes of innovative sadism were his whole repertoire. When we finished it would have taken a stronger man than Alberto to force the door open. A ten-foot-high barrier of furniture and heavy boxes barred the way.

"That should do it," David said, holding his heaving sides. "Let's go. Pray it didn't occur to them to lock the other door."

Crossing the room was an exercise in mountaineering—over boxes, under tables, between barrels and trunks. Alberto must have landed a few blows above and below the belt; David kept catching his breath and emitting eloquent nineteenth-century curses. Commiseration would have been a waste of time. He would certainly be in worse shape if Bart got hold of him again.

The door wasn't locked. Instead of opening it David held up the lamp, which he had brought with him, and studied me with sober concern. "Are you all right, Kathy?"

"Whatever happens," I said, "it's been worth it."

"Don't get mushy." He smiled, and brushed my tangled hair back from my forehead, his fingers lingering. "We'd better figure out where we're going before we rush out into the night. I don't know what is outside that door; I never came this way. What's the quickest route out of here?"

"There isn't any quick way out. I only hope I can remember how I came before. It's either the kitchen door or the front entrance, David. I'm not sure where the other exits are, and if they're locked we could find ourselves in a blind alley. Alberto's not the only one we have to worry about. Emilia is around somewhere, and so is Francesca; Rosa and the *tuttofare* have probably been told you're a desperate criminal; if either spots us, she might sound the alarm. The front door may be our best bet. At least I know how to unlock it."

"Okay. Then into the gardens—we can play hide and seek there indefinitely if we have to—"

"Only if we have to. I left my car off the road at the top of the hill. If we can reach it, we're home free."

"Good." His hand closed gently over my shoulder. "One heroic rescue per night is all I'm entitled to, Kathy. If we're separated, don't wait for me. Get out."

Darkening bruises and shadows made a caricature of his face, which had never been much to look at even at its best. At that moment it seemed more beautiful to me than the classic features of Michelangelo's masterpiece.

"The same goes for you," I said.

"Right. 'Neck by neck, stride by stride, never changing

our pace. . . . Not a word to each other. . . .' " He switched off the lamp.

We stood in darkness till our eyes adjusted. Gradually the shapes of the windows became visible, half hidden by piled-up boxes, and lighter than I would have liked. It was pitch-dark where we stood and I heard, rather than saw, David open the door.

"Stairs," I whispered.

"How many?"

"Damned if I know."

He let out a soft breath of laughter.

I sympathized with his decision not to use the lamp, but as we blundered through the warren of rooms and passageways I wondered if any prisoners in fact or fiction had ever carried out such a farcical escape. We barked our shins on sharp edges of furniture and tripped over chairs; ran into door frames and groped for openings. Even in daylight I had been bewildered by the absence of any coherent plan in this part of the house.

After David had fallen headlong across a low iron bed in one of the maids' rooms, producing a hideous howl of rusted springs, he switched on the lamp. He was grinning like an idiot, and if he was crazy, so was I; I wanted to laugh too. This wasn't James Bond or Jane Eyre, it was the Marx Brothers.

I knew why I felt so ridiculously lighthearted. It was David. Maybe Browning had a word for him. The only ones that came to my mind were totally inadequate.

"I'm afraid to get up," he said in a low voice. "Do you think there's something alive under here? Where the hell are we?"

I looked around the room. It was exactly like a dozen others on that corridor, but at least I knew which corridor it was. "I picked the wrong door. The one we want must be farther along. It leads to another storeroom, and that opens into a big room with windows overlooking the front, and from there you go into the corridor where Pete's room is. And from that—"

"I've got it." He heaved himself off the bed, amid another screech of rusted metal. "We'll have to use the lamp. I don't mind telling people I've been beaten and tortured, but I'll be damned if I want to admit I broke a leg tripping over a chamber pot."

It was easier with the light. David switched it off again when we reached the passageway stretching along the front of the house. From there the route was known to both of us.

As we passed the door of Pete's room David reached for my hand and squeezed it, and I knew he was thinking the same thing I was. Whatever became of us, the boy would never be locked in that room again. I had accomplished that much, at any rate. If I didn't return to the Grande Albergo, my letter would go to the police, and my disappearance would confirm the accusations I had made. From what David had told me, I felt certain Pete's aunt and uncle would hurry to be with him. He would be all right now. I only hoped the same could be said of us.

Down the stairs to the second floor, to lighted corridors at last. Not a sound broke the stillness. Francesca must have gone to bed. David gave me the lamp. His right hand went to the pocket of his jeans, where his "defensive weapons" made unseemly lumps. Down, farther down, to the wide landing. David stopped and looked over the balustrade. The bulbs in the chandelier shone on the polished marble of the floor of the hall, and reflected in the polished brass of door handle, bolt and chain.

"The door is unlocked, David! We can—"

"Sssh." His finger touched my lips.

Then I heard it too—a far-off rumble that rose to a roar and ended in a crash and a crunch of stone. David abandoned his favorite poets for a more emphatic comment. "Son of a bitch! He's back. I'd know the sound of that motor anywhere. I wonder what—"

Of course Bart would use the front door. Only tradesmen and servants went to the back. I heard the furious thud of his feet crossing the terrace; then the heavy oak panel exploded open. We had barely time to retreat a few steps, out of the light, but if he had looked up he would have seen us. David had taken the brass doorknob from his pocket. His fingers curled around it and I thought insanely, "Fast ball."

Bart didn't look up or pause. He was in a towering rage. Without stopping to close the door, he ran across the hall and disappeared from sight under the stairs. Another door crashed open.

"Run for it," David said, taking my hand.

We didn't have much time. Bart would be up the back stairs like a bullet, and when he found the door was blocked he would really blow up. He wouldn't waste time forcing it, he was smart enough to know what we had done. He must know every inch of the house, every door, every room.

Illogical though it was, I almost hated to leave the house. The front terrace and stairs were so open, so well lighted; and it was such a long way to the car. Then I saw the motorcycle lying on its side at the bottom of the stairs.

We made a bad mistake then. But the temptation was almost irresistible—fast transportation, practically at our feet. If I knew Bart, he had left the gates open. And there was no other functioning vehicle in the place.

David righted the bike and mounted. I jumped on behind, wrapping my arms around his waist. His foot hit the pedal; the still-warm engine caught instantly. The roar was loud enough to alert everyone for miles around.

We hadn't gone ten feet when I felt the machine lurch and slide. There was something wrong with the steering. Either it had been damaged when Bart threw it down or the furious pace he had set along the rutted road had done the job. We took the turn too wide, branches battering our heads, and narrowly missed the trunk of a tree. I missed it; David's knee didn't and the jar threw him even farther off balance. We slid off the drive at an angle, straight at the trees. At the last second David did the only thing possible—he let himself fall sideways, pulling me with him. We hit the ground, the bike hit a tree trunk and landed on top of us. By the time we had untangled ourselves I knew it was too late. A flashlight beam cut through the branches over our heads, and when David tried to stand, his knee gave way. He dropped down onto his side. "Run," he gasped.

I suppose I might have tried. The shrubs were thick and the shadows were dark. But they could have tracked me by the sounds I made, and it was a long way to the gate. The crack of a rifle and the whistle of a bullet through the boughs made up my mind for me. Twigs and pine needles showered down onto my head.

"All right, you've had your little run," Bart said. "I hope you enjoyed the exercise." He clamped a hand over my arm and yanked me to my feet.

The rifle was in his other hand. Alberto held the flashlight. In the same cool, pleased voice Bart went on, "You little bitch. I know you have the tastes of a peasant, but I didn't think you were that low. You must have been desperate to shack up with him."

I looked at David, blinking foolishly at the light shining in his eyes. It would have been hard to find a more disreputable specimen of manhood. "You're right," I said. "You are absolutely right, Bart. I was desperate."

He wasn't quite sure how to take that. The irony eluded him, but he must have sensed some undercurrent. His fingers tightened till I had to bite my lip to keep from crying out.

We started back to the villa. Bart kept jerking and shaking me, like a child venting his anger on a stuffed toy. It was stupid, and it hurt. But I was more concerned about David, stumbling behind us. Once I heard a slither and a gasp, and knew he had fallen. Alberto laughed.

When we reached the open space in front of the fountain Bart stopped. I had expected he would take us inside, but as he began arranging his tableau, pushing me down to kneel at his feet, ordering David and Alberto to take up a position nearby, I understood. Setting: a villa near Florence. I wondered how Bart had cast himself, as hero or villain. He wouldn't care, so long as he had the leading role.

I tried to get up. He pushed me down. "Where's the boy?"

"I told you. With the carnival."

"You rotten little liar, I looked for him there."

"Then you didn't look hard enough or ask the right people. I didn't exactly advertise his presence."

The faintest shadow of uncertainty crossed his face. That was why he had returned earlier than we had expected. He hadn't looked hard enough. Patience was never one of his virtues, and his arrogant manners wouldn't go over too well with the independent carnival people. No doubt he had started giving orders and they had told him what he could do with them.

"That won't wash, Kathy," he said. "How can I trust you

when you were ready to betray me? How long have you known this—this scarecrow?"

"I never met him until I came here. That's the truth, Bart."

"But you preferred him to your husband. What lies have you told him about me? What *were* you doing, if you weren't running off with your lover?"

Unfortunately, that was the difficulty. Either I was running off with a lover or trying to escape a killer. I couldn't deny one accusation without admitting the other. I tried to think of a third possibility, but there wasn't an idea left in my head.

David cleared his throat. "I'd like to say something."

"The only information I want is the location of the boy."

"I don't know where he is. If I did know, I wouldn't tell you."

This time I made it to my feet, shaking my head frantically at David. Neither he nor Bart paid the slightest attention to me.

"Why not?" Bart asked softly.

"Let's not fool around, okay? You're a sensible man; you know when it's time to retreat and regroup. The police have been informed that you're here. They know all about your background and they know what you were trying to do to the child. They could arrive at any minute. If you make tracks right now, you stand a good chance of getting away."

It was a sensible, reasonable speech. If he had been dealing with a sensible, reasonable man, it might have had the desired effect. Bart's reaction was to swing the rifle to his shoulder.

David's eyes widened, more in surprise than in fear; it had never occurred to him that Bart would do anything so stupid as commit deliberate murder in front of two witnesses. I wasn't surprised. David's speech had threatened Bart's most cherished images of himself: the great lover, the brilliant schemer. As Bart's finger tightened on the trigger I grabbed the barrel of the rifle. The bullet hit the ground. The recoil sent me sprawling, my ears ringing with the blast of the explosion.

When I got my eyes back in focus I saw that Bart was standing quite still, the rifle in one hand. Alberto had David in a wrestler's grip. All three were looking up, toward the top of the staircase.

The light behind her left her face in shadow and outlined her slender, erect form. The sweeping folds of her robe and the fur-trimmed neckline and the flowing sleeves gave her the look of a character in some dark Renaissance melodrama—the duchess pronouncing sentence on the traitors, the princess awaiting the return of her lover from the war. Emilia, all in black, hovering, might have played the malevolent duenna or housekeeper, or a witch crying doom on the ancient manor.

"Go back inside, Francesca," Bart said. He spoke English. I suppose his adopted language came easier and more naturally by now. Or perhaps he wanted me to know he was still in command.

"You have lost your senses," she said in the same language. "No matter what she has done, you must not risk your child."

"How do I know it's mine?" demanded my devoted husband. "She's had the scarecrow and the shrink since she arrived; the latest of a long list, I'm sure."

"You are obscene," Francesca said frostily.

Before she could continue, Emilia sidled forward and tugged at her sleeve. I didn't understand the hissing, hostile speech, but Bart did; a slow, unpleasant smile lifted the corners of his mouth. "Well, well. Who would have thought it? Guess what, my honorable little wife. Emilia says you aren't pregnant after all. What do you say?"

"Oh, what difference does it make?" I said impatiently.

Francesca started. "Is it a lie?" Her voice was not as steady as usual.

"You see, it does make a difference," Bart said, showing his teeth. "You don't suppose Francesca tolerated you for your own sweet sake, do you? She—"

"She'll stand by and watch you commit two murders?" I cut in. "What lie did you tell her to explain why I took Pete away tonight? She doesn't know you want him dead, that you tried—"

He reached for me. I had expected a blow, and tried to duck; instead of striking he caught me and pulled me against him, his hand spreading over my mouth and throat in a grip so agonizingly painful I couldn't move. David, who had stood meek and limp in Alberto's grip, brought his head sharply back. The chauffeur let out a yell and released his hold, clasping both hands over his nose. David started toward us.

"Stop right there," Bart said. "I'll snap her neck if you take one more step."

Francesca stood unmoving, aloof as a spectator at a play she found faintly disgusting. "Go back inside," Bart said. "I'll deal with this. It's my right—my honor that has been sullied." Still she didn't move. Bart's voice took on a softer, wheedling note. "She lied to you, *carissima*. You wouldn't take the word of a liar, a stranger, against mine?"

He knew he had won. His caressing voice poorly veiled the note of confident triumph. His hand tightened; fingers and thumb had settled into points of pressure against nerves and arteries. They contracted and relaxed, rhythmically, sensuously, and spots danced in front of my eyes.

Francesca straightened. She spoke slowly, articulating every word with such precision that even I understood.

"Alberto. The rifle. Take it from him. Bring it to me."

The chauffeur's heavy body swayed, forward and back, as if invisible hands were tugging at him from two different directions. Emilia let out a long, keening cry. That was the only sign of emotion—I almost said of humanity—either gave. Emilia was suddenly silent. Alberto started walking toward Bart.

Bart was even slower to react. He cried out to Alberto in Italian, stumbling over the words. His voice was high with disbelief. Alberto kept walking. Bart backed away. I was an impediment now; he tossed me aside, carelessly, without malice for once, as he might have brushed an object out of his way. Again I measured my full length on the gravel. I didn't even notice the pain, I was too stupefied. David raised me to my feet and we clung together, like children seeing monsters in the dark.

Bart's voice had lost all its trained beauty. It was a hoarse, breathless monotone. He appealed to Francesca, who stood like a marble statue, to Alberto, who plodded steadily forward, to Emilia . . . astonishingly, horribly, to me. "Kathy, tell her you lied, goddamn you, tell her, you got me into this, it's all your fault. . . ."

It was fitting that those were the last words I heard him speak. He had reached the steps and was backing up them, stumbling, his eyes fixed on Alberto. The chauffeur started up after him. His hand went out.

Bart raised the weapon. The muzzle could not have been more than a foot from Alberto's chest when he pulled the trigger.

Dark liquid spattered against the balustrade. The impact flung Alberto back, then forward, as his body rebounded from the stone railing. He fell, his arm still extended. Only the stiffened hand touched Bart, but it was enough to make him lose his footing. If he had dropped the gun and caught the balustrade he might have saved himself. Still clutching it, he toppled backward, and his sleek black head struck the sharp edge of one of the stone steps.

The dull, soggy sound seemed to go on echoing for hours. It was the only sound, the only movement; we were all characters in some unbelievable black farce, frozen in the final tableau as the curtain fell. The only figure of genuine tragedy was the woman who stood silent and motionless at the head of the stairs. She was a little more, and a little less, than human at that moment—the personification of some cold abstraction such as Justice or Retribution. For a moment she stood looking down. Then she turned and walked steadily into the house.

It was Emilia who crawled down the stairs, her face slobbered with tears, to raise, not her husband, but mine, into her arms, and cradle his head against her breast. His eyes were open. They were tarnished and muddy, like pools of stagnant water.

viii

I've often wondered if Francesca knew what would happen when she gave her servant his final order. She must have realized Bart would never endure such a challenge to his authority, especially in the house where he had always been master. I wonder, too, what intangible evidence tipped the scales in my favor. I'd like to think it had something to do with her feelings for me. Not love or liking or fondness, but something more important, at least to me. What was it she said? "I respect those qualities, if I do not admire them."

I will never know. I never saw her again. She never answered my letters. All I can do for her is respect her wish to be left alone.

David and I limped down the drive toward the gate. He was hobbling like a rheumatic old man and I was so exhausted every step was a supreme effort. Neither of us spoke. As David said later, it would have been impossible to invent dialogue that wouldn't have sounded banal and anticlimactic.

The gates were open, as Bart had left them. I said, "Why don't you wait here? I'll get the car."

"I accept," David said promptly. "Old baseball injury," he added, indicating the wounded knee.

I smiled feebly. But as I started forward he caught my hand. "Kathy," he said. "Don't be long."

The mountaintops were black against the dawn. I said, " 'There's the grey beginning. . . . I know my own way back. Don't fear me!' "

I heard his laughter, so different from that other laughter, as I started up the hill toward the sunrise.

**A woman discovers her mysterious link with the past
in a tale woven with suspense and romance . . .**

STITCHES IN TIME

from the author of *Ammie, Come Home* and *Shattered Silk*

BARBARA MICHAELS

New York Times bestselling author Barbara Michaels
brings back some of her best-loved characters in a
captivating new novel sure to delight both old fans
and new. Rachel Grant is a graduate student studying
the superstitions connected with women's crafts, who
believes that in past societies, women wove protective
spells into ceremonial garments to keep the wearer
from harm. But her theory takes on a horrifying
reality when an antique bride's quilt comes into her
hands, and she finds that her actions, and even
her thoughts, are being affected by something
beyond her control. Can Rachel free herself from the
quilt's malignant influence before it destroys both
herself and the man she loves?

Combining the ancient lore of needlecraft with a
contemporary story of magic and possession, Barbara
Michaels will enchant readers with this eerie tale of
a woman caught in an evil spell.

**"A writer so popular that the public library has to
keep her books under lock and key."**
—*The Washington Post*

Coming in May 1995 in hardcover from

📖 HarperCollins*Publishers*

ISBN: 0-06-017763-2 • $22.00

"Please don't leave angry," Ryan said.

"Do you want me to stay here and be angry?"

"I don't want you to be angry at all."

Cara tilted her head. "I confide in you that I want to buy the stable. You buy it. And now you want the luxury of not feeling bad about it. You must live in a world where you get everything you want."

Ryan shook his head. It would be so nice to tell her that the past year had been everything he didn't want. A failed engagement that was over so fast his family and friends never even knew about it. A failed business tangled up in that messy engagement. His friends and family didn't know about that, either, because he was too embarrassed to tell them.

"I didn't steal it. I bought it from Gary. And I'd already talked to him before you told me that."

"You could have told me."

"I didn't want to—" He was about to say he didn't want to break her heart, but that sounded so personal, even for someone he'd known her entire life.

Dear Reader,

Welcome back to Christmas Island for the fifth book in the series!

Christmas Island is in the Great Lakes region of the United States. Just off the Michigan shoreline, it has warm summers and snowy winters. It's a beautiful area with clear water, trees and rocky shores. Visitors travel aboard the ferry to the island, where they bike, enjoy horseback rides, shop in downtown boutiques and buy souvenirs of their excursion.

In *Under the Mistletoe*, Cara Peterson is finally ready to achieve her dream of owning a horse-riding camp encouraging kids to blossom. She makes a move to buy the Christmas Island Stable only to find someone else has just purchased it with a different plan. Worse, that someone else is Ryan Brookstone, a lifelong friend coming home to the island with the heavy burden of a secret.

I hope you'll love your visit to Christmas Island and enjoy reconnecting with characters from the first four books!

Happy reading,

Amie Denman

HEARTWARMING

Under the Mistletoe

—

Amie Denman

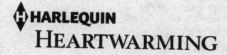

HARLEQUIN
HEARTWARMING

HARLEQUIN®
HEARTWARMING™

Recycling programs
for this product may
not exist in your area.

ISBN-13: 978-1-335-47556-5

Under the Mistletoe

Copyright © 2023 by Amie Denman

For questions and comments about the quality of this book,
please contact us at CustomerService@Harlequin.com.

Harlequin Enterprises ULC
22 Adelaide St. West, 41st Floor
Toronto, Ontario M5H 4E3, Canada
www.Harlequin.com

Printed in U.S.A.

Amie Denman is the author of over fifty contemporary romances full of humor and heart. A devoted traveler whose parents always kept a suitcase packed, she loves reading and writing books you could take on vacation. Amie believes everything is fun, especially wedding cake, roller coasters and falling in love.

Books by Amie Denman

Harlequin Heartwarming

Return to Christmas Island

I'll Be Home for Christmas
Home for the Holidays
A Merry Little Christmas
Last Summer on Christmas Island

Cape Pursuit Firefighters

In Love with the Firefighter
The Firefighter's Vow
A Home for the Firefighter

Starlight Point Stories

Under the Boardwalk
Carousel Nights
Meet Me on the Midway
Until the Ride Stops
Back to the Lake Breeze Hotel

Visit the Author Profile page at Harlequin.com for more titles.

This book is dedicated to my three sisters,
who have been my best friends all my life.
Like the Peterson sisters in the Christmas Island
series, we know what it's like to grow up in
a family business and how the bond of
sisterhood is a gift.

All my love,
Amie

CHAPTER ONE

CARA PETERSON WAS counting candy boxes, packages of parchment paper and bottles of vanilla and peppermint flavorings. Now that it was October, the summer candy season on Christmas Island was winding down, but the holiday sweet season was in full panic mode. Not that she was worried. She liked helping her sisters Camille and Chloe keep track of how many pounds of fudge and Christmas candy they'd sold the previous season and was making projections for an even bigger one this year. Cara thrived on being busy, a trait that served her well as the youngest daughter who was as much a workhorse as the animals she cared for at the stable for her second job.

She was the dependable person everyone counted on, so much so that she'd almost forgotten to pursue what she wanted for herself. Her life had become a predictable yet comfortable pattern, but a thrill passed through her chest when she thought about the fact that it was about to change. It would rock a few boats, but for a person who lived on an island, wasn't it about time?

"Can you take a break?"

Cara looked up and saw her friend Violet Brookstone in the open door of the storeroom tacked on to the back of Island Candy and Fudge. She held up one finger, finished counting the stack of pink-and-white striped cardboard boxes, typed the number into the inventory program and hit Save.

"Sure," she said. "Are we taking Daisy for a walk while the sun's out?"

Violet shook her head. "We're meeting the ferry. My brother's coming over with kitchen cabinets for Jordan's house, and I want to be there. I could use a backup opinion from someone who's always on my side."

Cara no longer had to try to conceal a blush or suppress a sigh when Ryan Brookstone came up in conversation. It had been almost ten years since she'd completely given up her preteen crush on her friend's older brother. The crush had simmered and required suppression for a few years, but when Ryan moved away permanently from Christmas

Island and found success building luxury houses on the mainland, it had gotten a lot easier to forget him—except for the times he came to visit on island holidays and special events. He was one of the many things Cara had pushed into the corners of her brain while she'd been busy helping her friends, family and community.

Cara grinned at Violet. "It's very nice of you to rush to the docks to see your beloved sibling."

Cara tried to remember how long it had been since she'd run into Ryan on Christmas Island. She'd heard he'd been back a few times in the past month to measure and consult on the improvements to Violet and Jordan's future home, but she hadn't talked to him since the Christmas in July Holiday Hustle, when they'd partnered up and almost won—bested only by Violet and Jordan.

"Ha," Violet said as she plopped into a chair by the door. "*Beloved* is technically true, but sometimes he forgets I'm not twelve. Ryan didn't like my decision to go with painted cabinets in a beautiful dark sage, and he assured me I'd regret not going with natural wood, but I reminded him I'm the one with all the good taste in the family and he'll have to trust me."

Cara smiled and nodded. "It's really nice of you to let him install those cabinets for free despite his big-brother bossiness."

"Right," Violet said with a chuckle.

A blast of the ferry's horn came through the open back door of the storeroom. "The two-minute warning," Cara said. "And I'm fully prepared to tell your brother I love the sage green whether or not I do. I'm that good a friend."

Violet laughed. "You won't even have to lie. Jordan's house is going to be magazine-worthy by the time we get married and I move in."

Cara called a goodbye to her dad, who was watching the front counter of the store, and she and Violet went out the back and walked along the shore to the ferry dock. They passed the back entrances of downtown restaurants and shops along the way. Mike Martin was filling up a bike tire from an air pump behind his bike rental, and he waved as they went by.

"I hope Ryan can stay the weekend this time," Violet said when they approached the docks. "He's been making quick trips, but I feel like I've hardly connected with him. He's

Mr. Big Business, but I think there's something on his mind."

"Running a business is time-consuming, as we all know," Cara said. Ryan had been his old friendly self when she'd seen him over the summer, but he'd treated her just like he treated everyone else on the island. Pleasant but definitely as if they were part of his past. He was one of the few island kids who'd moved away but tried to maintain a connection, probably because of his sister. Cara's older sister Chloe did the same, but the family candy business kept her tightly in the loop.

"There's his truck," Violet said as she and Cara stood at the top of the long sloping entrance to the island ferry's dock.

The dockhands tied up the boat and lowered the gate, and in just moments, Ryan's white pickup truck idled next to Cara and Violet. Even though his window was down when he drove off the ferry, he rolled it up as soon as Violet approached and sat staring ahead at the other cars exiting the ferry as if he couldn't see her.

Undeterred, Violet pounded on his window until he finally rolled it down, barely suppressing a grin.

Oh, how Cara had once loved that devilish grin, not that he'd noticed her as anything but his little sister's friend and a member of the island friend group.

"You know I want to see," Violet said.

The car behind them honked the horn.

"We're holding up the cars exiting the ferry," Ryan said. "A hazard to navigation."

"We'll get in," Violet said.

Cara wanted to object. She really did have bottles of flavoring and bags of sugar to count. But she'd promised to support her friend. Sort of. She sighed and got in the back seat of the pickup while Violet ran around and got in the front passenger seat. Clearly, Violet's plan was to create a detour in her brother's trip to the home site so Cara could corroborate Violet's excellent choice of cabinets.

"Hi, Ryan," Cara said as she leaned forward and poked her head between Violet and him. "Can you pull over downtown, let us see the fabulous pink cabinets and then drop me off at the candy store?"

Ryan turned and smiled at her, his face only inches from hers. "Dark sage green."

Cara laughed. "I was kidding. Violet told

me about your insistence on painted cabinets."

"Did she?" Ryan asked wryly as he drove onto Holly Street. "She has definite ideas."

"And?" Violet prompted.

"And I have to admit I don't hate the cabinets."

"That's a start," Violet said.

"But that could change when they're installed," Ryan added.

Cara was all about supporting her friend, but she hadn't planned to end up taking a back seat to a sibling dispute, friendly though it may be. "I really have to get back to work," she said.

Ryan pulled into the parallel parking space in front of the candy store. "I'll open one box so you can gang up on me with your opinions, and then I'm going straight to the home of the guy who's saddling himself with my little sister for eternity."

Violet gave her brother a peck on the cheek and then hopped out of the truck. Cara followed her friend and waited while Ryan pulled back the packaging on one of the boxes in the truck's bed, revealing a beautiful dark green.

"I don't have to lie," she said to Violet. "I really do love it."

"Me too," Violet said. "I'm going to put up a sign that says I'll open at ten instead of nine, and I'll ride up to the house with you."

Before Ryan could answer, Violet dashed across the street to her island clothing boutique to put the sign in the front door, leaving Ryan and Cara standing on the sidewalk in front of the candy store.

"So, the candy business is really...busy," Ryan said.

"Camille and Chloe have expanded it, and I'm along for the ride right now."

He nodded. "And you and your sisters will take it all over one of these days."

Cara felt a tiny quiver of rebellion. Not against her family, of course. She loved them and the candy business. It was more a resistance against assumptions. Why did everyone assume she would just be a candy girl—the island's nickname for the three Peterson sisters—her entire life? Hadn't anyone noticed that she spent at least half her time working at Christmas Island Stable and that she had also recently branched out into community service as a member of the village council?

"I wouldn't say that," she said.

Not that she should say much. Not until she at least told her family. But she was burning to tell someone. Ryan would drop off cabinets and leave. What could it hurt?

Ryan tilted his head and looked interested. "Not that there's anything wrong with that. Christmas Island is a slice of paradise."

"Says the guy who left and hardly comes back."

He leaned on the side of his truck. "Can't have everything we want," he said.

And that's where Cara thought he might be wrong. The thing she'd always wanted was finally a possibility, and it wouldn't be long before everyone knew.

She glanced across the street at Violet's boutique, but there was no sign of Violet.

"I might be able to get everything I want."

Ryan gave her a smile and his full attention. "That's great," he said. "Everyone should do that."

Which was exactly what she'd been thinking about lately. Ryan would know, right? He'd taken a risk to build a business and was, by all accounts, immensely successful. It was nice that he, with his experience, seemed to be encouraging her. It gave her a bolt of confidence. Her family and friends would encourage her, of course, but Ryan had no reason not to be truthful. She could tell him.

"I'm just about to buy a chunk of property on this island and do what I've always wanted."

Ryan's eyes widened and his mouth opened.

"Wow. That's…fantastic. What are you going to do?"

"If things work out as I plan, I'm going to turn the riding stable into a camp for kids much like the one I went to every summer on the mainland when I was young. My own business, Cara's Camp."

"The stable?" he said, his expression faltering. "Gary's stable where you work?"

She wanted to remind him he'd once worked there, too.

"Yes," Cara said. "Can you believe I've worked there more than ten years?"

"But, I…" His words trailed off, and Cara could understand why. Gary had owned that stable for practically forever. It was going to surprise a lot of people when she bought it.

She put one finger over her lips when she

saw Violet exiting the front door of her shop. "Listen, don't tell anyone, even Violet. Nothing is set in stone, and I haven't even told my family yet. I want to surprise them."

"Your, um, secret is safe with me," he said. "I promise."

RYAN DROVE HIS sister, Violet, the short distance from downtown to where Jordan Frome's home sat on a small hillside. From the front, it wasn't obvious that the home was being renovated, but inside, it was a construction zone. Jordan lived in it, but he didn't have much of a functioning kitchen, and the spare bedrooms were now one big room on its way to becoming a principal suite with an attached bathroom.

It was going to be a perfect house for his sister, and Ryan was honestly happy that she and Jordan had finally discovered their life-long friendship was true love. They had trust, too, and that was something Ryan had found out the hard way was difficult to build but easy to break.

He had to shake off his bad experiences of the past year if he was going to rebuild his life. Burdening his sister with his problems and admitting his failure to his old friends on Christmas Island wouldn't help, and the fewer people who knew about the lawsuit against his ex-fiancée, the better. This was a load Ryan needed to carry himself for a while, but the weight of his decisions had gained a metric ton half an hour earlier when Cara told him she hoped to buy the stable property.

It already had a buyer. In fact, it had a new owner.

Him.

Ryan sighed as he drove.

"Come on," Violet said. "Is it really killing you to admit I was right about the cabinets?"

He forced a smile. "I want to enlarge the window over the sink so it won't look too dark in there with your green cabinets."

"Even better. I like big windows."

"I'll order one from my supplier, and it should be in before the weather turns cold. Don't let me forget to measure it sometime this weekend."

"You're staying all weekend?"

He was planning to stay a lot longer than just one weekend, and he'd rehearsed his reason. "Your house project is keeping me busy, and the development I was working on an hour away from here is at a standstill because of a…technicality, so I was thinking of spending more time this fall and part of the winter out here on the island."

"Wow," Violet said. "That's great. Do you want to stay at my place?"

"Have you forgotten I'm allergic to your dog?"

"Oh. Well, maybe Daisy could stay with Jordan?"

Ryan shook his head. "It's okay. I'm looking for someplace to rent for a few months, just so I have a home base out here while I make sure you don't do anything wild, like knock down a wall and add a fireplace between the bedroom and bathroom."

"I do like those," she said.

"Speak now if you plan on that."

Violet laughed. "I'm trying to stay within a reasonable budget. And I do appreciate you doing the work for free."

"Consider it a wedding gift."

"Maybe I can return the favor someday by making a gown for your bride."

Ryan kept his expression neutral. His sister didn't know he'd entangled himself in a brief engagement, and there was definitely no reason to tell her now. The offer of a gown would have to wait a long time until he was ready to open his heart.

"Let's talk about the bathroom tile," he said.

After a tour of the construction progress and a consultation about the kitchen cabinets, Ryan was relieved to drive Violet back downtown so she could open her store. He needed time to think, and building something with his hands was how he found solace. It always had been. As a kid, he'd escaped to the garage and made so many birdhouses he'd gained a reputation as a builder by the time he was ten.

His family didn't own a home on the island anymore, with his parents having moved to Florida, but the downtown store that had been a souvenir shop and was now a thriving clothing boutique in the capable hands of his creative sister was still a legacy of the Brookstone family.

What would his legacy be? He'd thought it would be a distinguished construction company on the mainland, specializing in custom homes with quality finishes. And it had been. Until he'd decided to take a risk that he'd be paying for with his heart and his bank account for a long time.

Ryan tried to shake it off and instead focused on fitting the cabinets along one wall of the kitchen—the wall without a window—and measuring for countertops. That would be the next design adventure, going with Violet to the countertop supplier on the mainland. He'd have to make a plan with her to catch the ferry one of these early mornings before her store opened, unless she could get Cara to run the store in her absence.

Cara. The nice, sweet, youngest daughter in the Peterson family who was always around helping everyone. He'd even heard she'd filled a gap on the village council when they needed someone. But their hurried conversation in front of the candy store stuck with him like a splinter in his finger.

She'd said she was doing what she'd always wanted to do: she wanted to buy the stable where she'd worked for many years and—what had she said? Turn it into a kids' camp? When she'd spoken of it, her cheeks pinked up and her eyes brightened. Cara had always been a pretty girl, like her sisters. Her hair was long and brown, and her eyes were green. Something he'd noticed today for the first time. She was tall, almost as tall as his six feet, and her athletic body looked...well, she looked like a person who could handle a horse or a truckload of candy boxes or a kids' camp.

If her heart was set on acquiring the stable, her heart was going to be broken, and it was his fault. It had been pure happenstance that the moment he needed an affordable project that would take him home to Christmas Island, his lawyer heard about a ten-acre chunk of the island going on the market. He'd had just enough money, and it had seemed like kismet.

Cara wasn't going to think so.

When evening shadows reminded Ryan that it was time to head downtown to his temporary room at the Holiday Hotel, he couldn't help driving past the stable on his way. He rolled down his truck's window despite the light rain and heard the soft nicker of horses as he pulled alongside the century-old building for which he had big plans.

It wouldn't hurt to prowl around a bit. After all, he just had to sign the papers and the property would be his. Ryan softly closed his truck door so he wouldn't startle the animals, but as he approached the open barn door, he heard voices.

Cara's voice. Then he noticed the car. It was the hatchback her parents had driven for years, and it was parked on the other side of the barn entrance. He stopped and listened. Having grown up on the island, he knew everyone, and he recognized the voices of Cara's parents, Ron and Melinda, and her sister Camille.

"It's what I've always wanted," he heard Cara say. "I know it's a big risk, but I don't want to wait any longer. I could miss my chance to buy this property."

Ryan froze. Cara was inside the barn with her family, telling them what she'd started to tell him that morning, and she sounded as if she were trying to justify it to them.

Oh, goodness. He retraced his steps as silently as possible and went back to his truck. Mercifully, the light shower had intensified, and a sudden burst of rain covered the sound of his truck starting. If he was lucky, he could slink away tonight, but there would be no hiding from the fact that he was about to ink a deal that would break Cara's heart.

CHAPTER TWO

RAIN POUNDED THE ground outside the barn door, but Cara's heart pounded just as hard. She counted to five slowly. Her parents were rarely speechless, and her sister Camille never was. Why weren't they saying anything?

"What do you mean 'buy this property'?" her father asked. His tone was neutral, as if he were approaching someone threatening to jump off a bridge and he didn't want to scare them.

"I mean I want to buy the stable and all the horses," Cara said. "You know I've been talking about having my own camp for kids for years, ever since I started going to that one on the mainland. You know how much I loved that. I've always said I was going to have a camp of my own someday. And someday is now."

Her words trailed off into what sounded to her own ears like a pleading tone. She didn't want to plead with them for understanding. She didn't have to. She was twenty-four years old.

One of the horses nickered and raised its nose, sniffing the fresh damp air coming through the barn door.

"You'd leave the candy store?" Camille asked.

"Not completely," Cara said. "I could work for you in the winter when my camp is closed."

"But—" her father said, but her mother laid a hand on his arm.

"Honey, just because you want to buy something doesn't mean it's for sale. Have you actually talked to Gary about it?"

Her mother's tone reminded her of the time she'd declared she was going to save up her money and buy a horse to ride to school instead of a bicycle, and her mother had pointed out that the horse would be lonely all day while she was in school.

But she wasn't seven years old anymore.

"Of course I've talked to Gary," Cara said. *Indirectly.* She had a long and friendly relationship with the elderly man who'd owned the stable for almost fifty years. They'd often talked about her taking it over someday. Of

course, Gary had always added the fact that
he didn't think he could ever sell it and that
maybe she should do some extra chores so
she'd make it into his will.

They'd joked about it all the time. Cara was
the only logical buyer. She thought of Gary
as a benevolent sort of great-uncle, and she
knew he valued her as an employee of over
a decade and someone he could trust completely with his assortment of horses, barn
cats, two goats and one donkey.

A month ago, Gary had gone to stay with
his niece in Detroit while he had back surgery, but he'd said he was returning to the
island before Thanksgiving. Cara had received text messages almost daily the first
three weeks he'd been gone. He'd asked about
the animals and how she was managing on
her own.

Then the messages had started skipping
a day and then several days. He still asked
about the animals, even though he said he
knew she was taking good care of them.

It was the message three days ago that had
kept her awake staring at the bedroom ceiling upstairs in her parents' house. There was
one glow-in-the-dark star still stuck to the

ceiling from when she'd tried to make her bedroom feel like she was sleeping outdoors. She'd been eleven then, but she still loved the idea of sleeping under the stars.

That message that robbed her of sleep for the past three nights had said simply, *I'm thinking of selling and retiring, and I thought you deserved to know.*

"Gary has officially put the stable up for sale?" Camille asked, pulling Cara's thoughts to the question on the table.

"He's going to," Cara said.

"It's a lot of work and he's getting older," her mother said, her tone implying that she was trying to make sense of things. What on earth was so hard to understand? Why didn't her family pile on with congratulations and excitement? They could hire someone to count boxes in the candy store and stir fudge. Cara was certain she was replaceable as an employee at Island Candy and Fudge. She was practically spending all her time at the stable as it was. What would it matter to them?

"How can you afford to buy this property?" her father asked. He sat on a bench, and one of the barn cats hopped up next to him and tested his leg with her front paws. The cat climbed onto his lap and curled up, unbothered by the human drama taking place in the open space between rows of stalls. Cara had thought bringing her family to the barn to tell them about her plan was smart. She'd been sure of their excitement and enthusiasm and had even pictured walking around the grand old building with them and talking about improvements she could make when it was hers.

Cara squared her shoulders. She'd thought this was going to be the only hard part, but her family's reaction so far was a bucket of cold water on the warmth of her plans.

"My college fund."

She let the words hang in the air for a moment. Her grandparents had started a college fund for Cara and her sisters when they were born.

"The money is still sitting there, and I've been deferring going for six years now."

Camille's face relaxed into a partial smile, probably because she and Cara had privately wondered how much longer their parents were going to accept the deference excuse before they gave up on Cara attending a university. Maybe she was winning Camille over, but her parents' expressions were somber. Did they really think she was making a huge mistake?

"Your grandparents worked hard to save that money," her mother said.

"You could still go to college," her father said. "Even for just two years. You could even go online so you wouldn't have to leave the island."

"I know what I want," Cara said. "Every year when I'd go to that camp, I'd feel like I was someone special, not just the youngest Peterson girl. It made me feel confident. I want other kids to feel that way." She walked over to a stall door and ran a hand along the velvety nose of one of the horses. All twelve horses got their names from the song "The Twelve Days of Christmas." Turtledove dipped his head and nuzzled her as if he knew she needed the support and love.

Her family had always been her source of support and love in addition to animals.

"So, you plan to withdraw the college fund in your name, buy the stable, and turn it into a summer camp," her mother said, speaking slowly and pausing between each phrase.

Cara crossed her arms over her chest. "Yes."

"Do you...how do you plan to turn a profit?" Camille asked.

"I'll keep renting horses to tourists, plus charge parents to send their kids to camp. I've done the math. I can run weeklong camps every week in the summer and weekend ones in the spring and fall when kids are back in school. I could do a special winter camp during Christmas break and longer camps during spring break."

Camille was nodding and staring at an invisible dot on the distant wall of the barn. Cara knew her well enough to know she was doing the math in her head: adding up the weeks, how many campers there would be and what the cost per camper would have to be to make a profit. Camille loved business and had expanded the family candy store to reach an online audience so they could have profits year-round.

"When would you plan on starting this?" her mother asked. "In the spring?"

Cara shook her head. "Now. I'm going to call Gary this weekend to negotiate a price. I already have an appointment at the bank on Monday morning to talk about a property and business loan. My college fund will be a big down payment, but I'll need operating expense money, at least for the first year."

"So soon," her dad said. "You're moving fast."

"I've had years to think about it," Cara said. "Just because I'm the youngest in the family doesn't mean I can't do something bold." Her eyes stung and she willed herself not to cry. "I've thought this through for a long time. I've even looked at other properties on the island."

"You have?" Camille asked.

Cara nodded and felt a twinge of guilt that she hadn't told her sister about her visits to the few undeveloped lots left on the island. She'd been afraid to show her hand and reveal the dream that was in her heart because she was afraid people wouldn't think she could do it. She'd been afraid of exactly the dubious and lukewarm reception her idea had just gotten. When would people stop seeing her as the little sister?

"But this place is perfect," Cara insisted. "It's already set up for horses, and it has ten attached acres where I can add camping. Tents at first and then maybe cabins someday."

Her throat was thick. She saw it all so clearly. Did her family really doubt her?

It didn't matter now. She'd finally taken the bold step of telling them, and no matter what their reaction was, it was out in the open, and she wasn't backing down.

"Can't you understand that I might want to do something on my own?"

Her parents and sister exchanged a glance.

"But you won't be alone," Camille said. "I'll help however I can. We all will," she added, looking at their parents.

"Yes," her mother said. "We'll just...well, we'll just see how your meeting goes at the bank and...go from there."

Cara let out a long breath. Her parents weren't mustering enough energy to power a single light bulb, but they hadn't completely squashed her idea. She did know one thing, though. The pressure to be successful and not waste the college money her grandparents had carefully saved was high. She'd never let anyone in her family or community down, and she wasn't going to let herself down either.

It was too late to change his mind despite what he'd accidentally overheard the evening before at the barn. Ryan kept that thought in his head while he enjoyed brunch with his sister and Jordan and then put in a few hours of work at their house on Saturday afternoon. He wanted to come home to Christmas Island. Needed to, even though he couldn't admit that to anyone. And his plan to use the stable property as the centerpiece for a building development had come along at the perfect time.

For him.

For Cara, it had also been the perfect time. Almost. Ryan sat at the window of his hotel room and looked out over Holly Street. The view included Mike's bicycle rental in one direction with souvenir shops, the post office and a kite store leading toward the ferry docks. If he glanced the other way down Christmas Island's main street, he could make out the pink awning over the candy store owned by the Peterson family. He couldn't see his sister's boutique because it was on the same side of the street as the Holiday Hotel, but he knew it was there and knew every inch of the building.

The island was his hometown, the place where his grandparents had made their living and then his parents and now his sister.

Was it possible it would be not only his refuge now but also his future?

He pulled up the agreement his attorney had worked out with Gary for the purchase of the stable. In a stroke of luck, Ryan's business attorney—who was actively engaged in disentangling him from a disastrous decision—was a golfing buddy of Gary's attorney. The deal was swift and uncomplicated.

Cara hadn't had that luxury. But that was business—the early bird got the worm.

As he stared at the pink awning, his phone dinged with a message. He picked up his phone from the bedside table and saw the name Griffin May.

Dinner downstairs at six. Don't dress up.

Ryan grinned. His lifelong friend who happened to own the ferry line and the Holiday Hotel with his brother, Maddox, knew him well enough to know he probably wouldn't dress up for dinner anyway. Ryan had lived in work clothes his entire life, and his calloused palms had held a hardware store's worth of tools. He not only owned Brookstone Builders, but he spent his days on the job sites making sure nothing went wrong.

Things hadn't gone wrong on a job site. That had happened on paper when he let down his guard and let emotions get involved with business.

I'll be there, he texted back. Thanks.

As Ryan entered the bar and restaurant on the street level of the hotel, he felt thankful for the distraction from second-guessing all the decisions he'd made over the past year. Griffin May and his brother and business partner Maddox were seated at the bar and waved him over to a table in the corner.

"I'm almost glad your sister adopted a stray dog so you can't stay at her place. We can use a paying customer on fall weekends," Griffin said.

"You may get lucky," Ryan said. He picked up a menu and perused it even though he knew the contents and had his heart set on his favorite: beef stew with biscuits. "If things work out as planned, I may be spending a lot of time here this winter."

"Is Jordan's house in need of that much renovating?" Griffin asked. "I knew it was a bit neglected over the years, but I can't believe you'd give up your life of luxury in Lakeview to hunker down here for the winter."

"I've spent a lot of winters here," Ryan said. He didn't need to defend his decision, although he couldn't tell his old friends the whole story. "And I'm thinking this island may be the perfect place for my next building project."

"What's the project?" Maddox asked. He took all three of their menus and stacked them up to let the server know they were ready to order.

"Something creative," Ryan said.

"Like what?" Griffin asked.

"I'm not ready to reveal my plans just yet, because I need to finalize some details, but you'll find out soon."

"Is it a Christmas superstore? The kind of place that sells lights and ornaments and Santa trinkets all year long? Tourists would love that," Maddox said.

Ryan laughed. There was an entire town elsewhere in Michigan dedicated to Christmas all year long with multiple shops and themed restaurants. It was a big state, but he wasn't sure Michigan needed two such places. "No Christmas superstore."

"How about an indoor ski slope?" Griffin asked.

"With a pool," Maddox added. "Can you believe our guests here often ask if we have a pool? I try to nicely point out the giant lake out there," he said, gesturing toward the front windows. "Although it's usually too cold for swimming."

"I could build you an indoor pool. I've put several in mansions for clients," Ryan said.

Griffin and Maddox shook their heads at the same time. "We're putting all our construction energy into doubling our dock operation and the tourist depot in Lakeview. We don't need a pool."

Ryan grinned. "That's what people say who've never enjoyed the luxury of swimming in warm water while the snow falls outside the floor-to-ceiling windows."

The teen server approached and they placed their dinner orders. Griffin turned the conversation to his upcoming wedding to Rebecca Browne in just two weeks' time. Ryan had met Rebecca on many occasions when he'd been visiting the island, and he knew his sister, Violet, was close with her. Violet

had said something about making the bridesmaids' gowns.

"Violet inspected my black suit and assured
me it would be fine," Ryan said. "I hope she's
not messing with me, and I'll feel ridiculous
when you two are in blue or gray suits."

"Violet never jokes about clothing," Maddox said. "Camille told me the details are all
worked out, and all we have to do is wear white
shirts, black suits and shiny black shoes. The
ladies are providing the ties."

"Good," Ryan said. "One less thing I have
to think about."

"So, seriously," Griffin said when their
food had been delivered and they'd started
eating, "what is your mystery island building project? You can't just mention it and then
clam up."

Ryan sipped his drink. It was tempting to
tell his friends about how the stable would
be a centerpiece for a whole development.
The beautiful antique barn would anchor a
ten-acre property that would include single-
family homes arranged to mimic an old-
fashioned neighborhood. There would also
be at least one shop and one restaurant so it

would feel like its own community just outside downtown Christmas Island.

He had it all drawn out and designed right down to the old-fashioned street lights and maybe even a skating rink in the center. The moment Gary's attorney had told Ryan's attorney that the stable property could be for sale, Ryan had started dreaming. It hadn't hurt that the timing was just right. His attorney had just delivered disappointing news about an ongoing lawsuit he was involved in because of a foolish mistake—a business partnership that now threatened his entire business—and it had made Ryan want to run home to Christmas Island as fast as he could and hide. The initial shock was a year old, but the damage was a lasting reminder he should never have mixed business with a relationship.

"Not yet," he said reluctantly. It would be nice to talk about it, but the grim reminder that there was competition for the property made him keep his cards close to his vest, even with people he trusted. He hadn't thought he would ruffle feathers on the island by snapping up the stable before it went on the market. He'd thought public opinion would be squarely in his favor as a son of the island.

And it still could be. Cara might be just as happy with another location for her riding camp.

"I have to work out some details yet, and I don't want to run my mouth ahead of time. You could help me out, though, even if you might consider this request a conflict of interest."

"What?" Griffin asked.

"Do you know of any houses or apartments for rent for the winter?"

"What's wrong with this place?" Maddox asked. "On some cold January nights, you could be our only hotel guest. You could sleep in every bed if you wanted to and take showers in twelve different rooms."

Ryan laughed. "Tempting, but I could use a little more space than a hotel room, and a kitchen wouldn't be a bad amenity, too."

"Housing is tough on this island," Griffin said. "Not much to rent, not much in a buyable price range for the average guy."

Ryan kept his expression neutral, but the lack of available and affordable housing on the island was all part of his plan. He felt relieved knowing he was doing something valuable for the community where he'd grown up, and it took away some of the icky feeling that he was taking something away from Cara.

"But there's an empty duplex you could probably get for a few months," Griffin continued. "Hadley's grandma Penny lives in one half of it, but her friend MaryAnna rents the other half and is going to Georgia for the winter to be with her daughter and grandkids. She might let you stay in her half if you don't mind living in a senior-type duplex. It's one floor, and Hadley's grandma will probably crochet you five blankets before spring."

"Five blankets, huh?"

"At least," Griffin chimed in. "She's very productive and generous, but she might ask you to pick up her yarn shipments at the post office. Hadley usually does, but she's pretty busy these days with the baby." Hadley had recently married Mike Martin, the owner of the bike rental, and they'd had their first child.

"It might be perfect," Ryan said. By the time MaryAnna returned to the island in the spring, he should have his project underway and his roots reestablished on the island. Maybe his luck had finally improved.

"You're serious about spending the winter here, aren't you?" Griffin asked.

Ryan nodded. "Is that so hard to believe?"

Griffin shrugged. "Not really. I just thought you had a lot going on in Lakeview and beyond." He smiled. "It will be nice to have someone different to hang around with instead of my brother."

Maddox gave Griffin a mild shove on the shoulder, and the server came back to offer dessert. As much as Ryan had his mind on his construction business and its serious challenges, it also felt good to be home.

CHAPTER THREE

CARA SAT IN the small office just off the lobby area of the only bank on Christmas Island. The bank building was on the back street behind downtown, where tourists only noticed it for its ATM machine under a green awning. It was a small-town bank where everyone knew everyone, so Cara knew she wasn't going to keep her big news quiet for long once she sat across from the loan officer who was also a part-time teller.

"I have your preapproval from your on-line application," Gina Parker told her. The middle-aged woman, who Cara knew from serving with her on the village council, pushed a paper across the desk.

Cara picked up the paper but set it down quickly again so Gina wouldn't see her hand tremble. It was a large amount, and her heart thumped just seeing it on paper. The purchase price of the land plus enough capital to make the improvements she needed was the biggest risk she'd ever taken.

"With the down payment you have, you qualify for a large real estate loan, although I'll warn you the payments will be pretty steep on the amount you're requesting."

Cara had only been guessing, based on researching similar properties, about the amount she'd need to purchase the stable and ten acres. Her college fund would be absorbed fast, and she'd have to work hard to make the monthly payments. Failure was not an option. Not when she lived on the island and would be faced with it every single day.

"It helps that you have a good credit score from slowly building it over the past six years. Of course, it would be better if you'd had a car loan, but in this bank, we recognize that not a lot of people who live on an island have car loans. The bank is willing to take a chance on you, although you'll pay a higher interest rate."

"That's okay," Cara said quickly.

"I'm sure your family will be excited for you to get a home of your own but also a little sad to see you move out," Gina continued. "You have such a nice close family."

Cara nodded, but she felt warmth creeping up her neck. The support from her family after she'd made her big announcement on Friday night had been patchy at best. Her parents tiptoed around the topic at home and at the candy store, and her only relief had been escaping to the barn, where the horses had complete confidence and trust in her.

Her family would see. And so would the bank. It might take a year, but by next Christmas, no one would doubt her.

"Thank you," Cara said.

"This is only a preapproval based on your down payment and credit score," Gina said. "And now the fun part of looking for property begins, right? Are you thinking of building a house on a quieter part of the island, maybe where you could have a horse and a barn of your own?"

"Well," Cara said. Should she break the seal and just tell Gina what she intended to buy? She hadn't been untruthful on her loan application. It was a real estate loan, technically. It just happened to be real estate that came with acreage, a barn and twelve horses. Should she have applied for a business loan instead? She needed to ask Camille or Rebecca for their business savvy.

"I actually have my eye on a piece of property I have inside knowledge might be going up for sale," Cara said.

Gina's expression turned to intrigue. As a member of the village council, everything that happened on the island was of interest to her, which was something Cara had discovered since she'd taken over a vacant seat at the end of the summer.

Telling Gina her plans meant she was ready to broadcast them...and why not? Except for the fact that Gary hadn't officially put his property up for sale, of course. But he was going to; she was certain he wouldn't have teased her with that information. And why wouldn't she be his first choice for a buyer?

"It's the stable where I've worked since I was eleven," Cara said. "You know Gary is going to sell it one of these days, and I think I might be the perfect buyer."

Gina sat back in her chair. "You don't think he has family who will want to take it over?"

Cara shook her head. "He has one niece in Detroit—that's where he's staying now for his back surgery. We've been in daily contact, and he told me himself he's ready to make a change."

"Well," Gina said, "this is unexpected, but certainly an interesting turn of events. This preapproval is for a real estate, but you may want to come back in and talk about a business loan instead when you're ready to talk seriously about buying the stable."

Cara thought she was serious. Wasn't that why she was taking the bold move of filling out a preapproval online and coming in, even revealing her plans to someone she knew and worked with? She'd insisted her family keep it quiet over the weekend, but now she was ready to start telling people.

"I'll be back," Cara said. "Hopefully by the end of the week."

She folded the paper, tucked it in her purse and held her chin high as she walked out of the bank. She passed through the alley next to the Holiday Hotel and was about to turn on Holly Street to go to the candy store when she saw Ryan leaving the hotel and getting in his truck. The truck had the logo of his company—Brookstone Builders—on the door.

Ryan saw her and waved, but he closed his truck door and started the engine. He was probably going to catch the nine o'clock ferry, but he had a minute for an old friend, didn't he?

Cara strode up to his truck and motioned for him to roll the window down. "That thing I told you about on Friday night," she said.

His expression looked troubled, confused. It was only a few days ago. Didn't he remember?

"About me buying the stable," she clarified.

"Oh, that," he said. He put on his seat belt and adjusted the rearview mirror.

"I just wanted to tell you I've told a few people, so you don't have to keep it a secret. It's out there."

"You told people you were buying Gary's stable?" he asked.

"Yes," she said.

Why did he look irritated? Sure, she was his little sister's friend. Did he really think her ambitions were so uninteresting? Fine. She had been considering using his construction company to build the cabins for her camp when she was ready, but maybe she didn't need him. Or his approval. Or his attention. He'd never really paid any attention to her anyway, despite her helping him and handing him tools throughout the course of two summers when he'd worked as a handyman at the stable. Despite her bringing him treats from the candy store and holding the ladder when he'd climbed up to fix the shutters or the roof.

He'd never seen her as anything more than the youngest Peterson sister. Just like everyone else.

Well, that was about to change.

"Anyway," she said, backing up a step, "see you around."

She turned and strode down the street without looking back.

RYAN DROVE ONTO the ferry for the return trip to Lakeview. His truck was lighter without the weight of the cabinets he'd installed at Jordan's house, but his heart had gained a thousand pounds since his brief conversation with Cara.

"Come up in the pilot house?" Griffin asked. "Best view from the boat."

"Thanks, but I'll pass. I have to make some calls." Ryan held up his cell phone to imply he had important business to conduct, and Griffin waved and headed up the steps to the pilot house from where he would captain the ferry. Ryan knew from long experience that the crossing would be about twenty minutes. Instead of getting out of his truck and enjoying the fresh air as he usually would, he sat behind the wheel, staring through the windshield.

An hour later, Ryan reached his home thirty minutes outside of Lakeview. He didn't bother to go to his office. There was no one there, and he'd laid off the three full-time guys who'd worked for him for the past five years. With a strong recommendation from him, all three had found other work, but he still felt he'd failed them.

He parked in his garage and pulled his lawnmower outside without even going in the house first. He checked the oil, added gas, and was about to start the mower to cut the grass for the last time when his phone rang.

His attorney.

"It's good news for the first time in a long time," Mitchell said.

Ryan sat on the bumper of his truck. "Let's hear it."

"Now that your house is sold, you're not in as much debt as you were."

"That's great," Ryan said without enthusiasm.

"And the debt on that island property is good debt because it's business. You've got a solid plan."

"Are you really calling me to give me a financial report?"

"Not entirely. I'm also calling to tell you that Poppy's lawyer got the extension they asked for, so you're tied up at least another month, possibly two."

"But I can move forward with the island project, right?"

"Yes. That's under your new LLC funded by the sale of your private home."

"If I could go back in time and see her and her father for what they were," Ryan said, "I wouldn't have given her a ring or bought into their scheme."

"Lesson learned."

Ryan forced a laugh. "How much am I paying you to tell me that?"

"I'm worth it."

"Any chance of getting the diamond back?" Ryan asked. "I could pay my rent all winter and then some with the amount I threw away on that."

"You could make a vague breach of contract argument if you want to go there with Poppy."

"I don't want to go anywhere with her," Ryan said. He should have had his eyes open when he started dating her a year ago. That led to a whirlwind romance that had them engaged only two months later. Her father was in construction management and development, and Poppy seemed to really care for Ryan. She laughed at his jokes, picked out his clothes, took him home to meet her father and brother. And that's where he'd made the bad decision to invest heavily in a venture with them, which now had him facing major financial and possibly legal trouble.

"When are you moving back to the island?" his attorney asked.

"Soon. I have to make a few calls about renting a place, but I think I may have found something."

"People will be glad to see you investing in Christmas Island. Hasn't it been a while since they had new housing and businesses?"

"It has, but that doesn't mean all of them will like my plans."

"You don't need all of them. You just need the ones who vote on zoning and development. It's probably only three people on that island, and it can't be that hard for a nice guy like you to charm three people."

A chilling thought occurred to Ryan as he sat with his back to the tailgate of his truck. Cara Peterson was not going to be happy with him when she found out he bought the stable, and she'd recently gotten some role in island leadership. What was it? His sister, Violet, had told him, but he'd been too wrapped up in his own problems to pay enough attention. If he was lucky, Cara was on the downtown beautification team that took care of the hanging baskets and made sure the city employees emptied the garbage cans extra times on holiday weekends.

"I'll try to charm at least three people," Ryan said.

"Come into the office later today, and I'll have the documents for you to sign with the offer for the island property. We have a verbal agreement already, and Gary's lawyer overnighted the formal documents, so I have them now."

"I'll be there early afternoon."

With at least two hours until he needed to go anywhere, Ryan had time to mow the lawn and edge the sidewalks, leaving the property neat for the new owners. He walked through the house he'd bought after his first big construction project filled his bank account. The house had been too big for him then, and it certainly felt too big now. He'd only had the bare minimum of furniture since he was hardly home, and now that he'd sold off or put most of the furnishings in storage, the place was a cavern.

He was glad he had to go to his lawyer's office, and even gladder he had a project that would keep him busy for the next two years on an island far away from his problems. He knew he couldn't keep his legal and financial matters silent forever, but he had every intention of putting off the humiliation of his failure and the fact that he was the island son who'd gone off to make a fortune and then lost it all.

CHAPTER FOUR

ON THE SECOND and fourth Wednesday of the month, the Christmas Island Village Council met in a room in the back of the fire station. The blue carpet hadn't changed since Cara had visited the fire station with her third grade class for a lesson on safety. On the Wednesday after Cara got her preapproval amount from the bank, the second Wednesday in October, she saw Gina again at the meeting.

"We've got a lot to discuss," Gina said. "The Halloween trick-or-treat parade needs a little punch of excitement this year, and we're hoping that having young blood like you on the council will help us."

"I like it how it is," Cara said. "All the stores turn on their lights and hand out candy, and kids get to show off their costumes. Isn't that enough?"

"The newspaper in Lakeview is coming

over to cover the event. They haven't bothered in years, and you know one of our island goals is to offer more year-round activities for tourists in addition to summer and Christmas."

"We could...challenge the downtown businesses to a decorating contest. That way things will look extra festive all along the street."

"That's a good start," Gina said. She took her place at one of the rectangular banquet tables, and Cara sat down with the other six council members. With the sudden resignation of Mack Carter the past summer, the council had been down to only six members, and an even number was an invitation for trouble. When Gina and Shirley from the chamber of commerce had approached Cara and asked her to fill the rest of Mack's term, they'd told her she just needed to fill a seat.

But here she was coming up with ideas for the Halloween celebration.

Gina called the meeting to order and reviewed the minutes from the previous meeting in which they'd discussed ways to enforce a speed limit on some of the island roads during the heavy tourist season of the summer.

Accidents were rare, but there had been two notable collisions right before school started that raised an alarm with the island police and fire departments.

"Next up, we need to formalize who is on the zoning board. It's been Shirley, me and Mack for several years, but we need to put it down in the record that Mack's replacement, Cara Peterson, will also fill that role as she completes his term. Do we have any objection?"

She looked at Cara as she spoke, and Cara shook her head. She'd been put on the clean water commission at a previous meeting, and the extra committee assignments were part of the job responsibility.

"Then it's settled," Gina said. She called for a motion and a vote, and then moved on to new business.

"I already have one good idea for spiffing up the Halloween thing. Cara, go ahead."

"Oh," Cara said. "Sure. I was thinking we could challenge the downtown merchants to do a display in their shop windows but also on the sidewalk in front of their stores and restaurants. Maybe we could offer prizes for the top three places."

Shirley rubbed her hands together. "I love a competition."

"Any other new business?"

"Not business, but some interesting news," Shirley said. She leaned forward. "Gary is selling his stable."

"Really?" Roger said. "I thought he'd never part with it."

"I called him to ask how his back surgery went, and he told me all about it," Shirley said. "The good news is he's selling it to someone we know."

Cara noticed several people glancing her way, especially Gina. Had Gary really told Shirley he would sell it to her? He hadn't returned her text messages all week except to answer a direct yes or no question about one of the horse's medicines.

"An islander," Shirley said, drawing out the revelation now that she had everyone's attention. Cara felt as if she could burst into a volcano of confetti. Her heart pounded and she felt sweat on the back of her neck. "Ryan Brookstone," Shirley concluded.

Cara heard a loud gasp, and then she realized it came from her. "No," she said. "That's not right. Ryan isn't buying the stable."

"That's what Gary told me. Said he'd signed the paperwork and got his asking price," Shirley said.

"But I..." Cara began. She searched the room, looking for someone who would tell her she'd misheard. Shirley had misunderstood. It was a mistake. Gina gave her a sympathetic glance, obviously putting two and two together. Where was her sister Camille or her friend Violet when she needed them? How...absolutely *how* could Ryan have done this?

"Ryan doesn't even live here," Cara said.

"I heard he's going to rent MaryAnna's duplex while she's in Georgia," Shirley supplied.

Cara liked Shirley very much. She was an integral part of the island fabric and enthusiastic about anything involving Christmas Island. But Cara wished Shirley didn't sound quite so authoritative right now. It made her words sound true. And they couldn't be.

She'd told Ryan she was going to buy the stable, had confided in him before she'd even told her family, and then he'd turned around and betrayed her instantly, stealing from her the one thing she'd wanted.

She looked like a fool now. To her family and the few friends she'd told.

"I know you've worked there for a long time," Gina said. "So this change may come as a bit of a shock."

Cara nodded. She swallowed and concentrated on the two shades of blue running through the carpet at her feet. She was not going to cry in front of her colleagues on the village council. She was an adult, and she needed and wanted their respect.

"Ryan worked there, too," Cara said. "For two summers when he was seventeen and eighteen."

"Well, I have no idea what he plans to do with the place," Shirley said. "But if he needs changes to the zoning, that's going to come straight to us first. We'll be the first to know what grand plans he might have for transforming that property."

While Gina called for a motion for dismissal and read the roll call, Cara's mind was stuck on two things: Ryan might transform the property? It might not even be a stable anymore? Heaven forbid it was turned into a strip mall or an apartment complex.

The other thought that tapped at the side of her brain like a hammer was that she was now on the zoning board, and whatever plans

Ryan had for the property he'd somehow stolen right out from under her, he was going to need her vote.

The meeting ended and Cara stood. She smiled politely at her fellow council members, agreed to spearhead the downtown decorating contest and send out flyers, and then retreated from the fire station with shaking legs. She didn't stop walking until she'd gone three blocks from downtown and was standing in front of the stable. In her jacket pocket, she had a key ring with a key to every door, drawer and cabinet in the old building. Gary had trusted her with the health and care of the animals and with the combination to the safe he only used at the height of tourist season.

But he'd sold Christmas Island Stable to Ryan instead of her.

WHEN RYAN GOT off the ferry on Friday, he drove straight to the stable. He parked in the small lot alongside the barn and sat in his truck for a moment. It was exciting owning the property. He'd never owned anything on Christmas Island. When he graduated from high school, he moved out of his parents' home, did a two-year construction degree at

Michigan State and then started his own business by doing small jobs.

Now, at thirty, the only remnant he had left of Brookstone Builders was the two-year-old white pickup he was sitting in. Through the open window, he heard horses whinny.

His horses. Were there ten or twelve? He tried to remember the exact details of what came along with the barn. Cara would know, and he was going to need her help. Did she know yet that he'd bought the property? It was only a matter of time.

He opened the door of his truck and immediately heard fast-approaching hoofbeats. Had a horse gotten loose? He spun around and saw Cara on horseback, her long brown hair flying out behind her as she rode a big white horse. She pulled it to a stop, dismounted smoothly, glared at him for a moment and then led the horse into the barn.

She knew.

Ryan got his blueprints briefcase from the back seat and forced himself to walk straight through the wide-open barn door. The barn's construction was simple and functional. The front wall facing the street had an extra tall and wide door that horses and carriages could get through. There was a smaller door to the left and a window to the right. Inside, there were ten horse stalls down the right side and five on the left. An office was immediately to the left inside the big door, and there was a restroom, tack room and multipurpose room toward the back.

Cara was walking the horse she'd been riding up and down in the wide space between the rows of stalls, letting it settle down before putting it in one. She was talking to the horse, and Ryan thought he heard his own name connected with an unflattering word. He pushed open the office door and went in, leaving the door open. The room appeared to be just as Gary had left it, clearly intending to return. A coffee cup that said Gary on the side sat on the edge of the desk, and there was a sticky note with a short grocery list written on it.

Ryan wondered if Gary had gotten those eggs and crackers and cheese before he left for Detroit. There was no computer on the desk, and the office looked as if it could have been from the 1970s, roughly the time period when Gary had purchased the stable and begun a lifetime of running it.

Would Ryan be here in fifty years?

He spread the site plans across the desk, first carefully setting the coffee cup on a nearby shelf. Now that he was standing on the property, he might need to make adjustments to the drawings.

He opened a blind to let in more natural light and then stood, hands on both sides of the desk. It had to work. This was his only option for starting over, and he had all his money invested. He picked up a pencil and adjusted the circular road that would go around the houses. The stable would remain at the center of a semicircle, a horseshoe, really. It was perfectly themed, and given what he knew about the island, the houses would sell quickly. He could recoup some of his costs within eighteen months if he got going.

And he needed to get moving. It would be hard to build during the heavy winter months of January and February, and his bank was going to want evidence of progress before then. For fun, he added a window and some details to the porch of one of the houses. Perhaps he'd live in that one. He could customize it. Of course, his personal comfort was far down the list. Business decisions needed to come first.

"I said goodbye to the horses," Cara said from the doorway.

"What?" he said, looking up.

"I said goodbye. Rumor is that you bought this place, and I can see from the way you've moved in already that it must be true."

"It is true." In a move he regretted almost immediately, Ryan handed her a copy of the purchase agreement. She took off a riding glove and held the paper in front of her. Ryan watched her face change from stony anger to something worse. Pain. Hurt.

"You signed this two days ago."

He nodded. When she'd told him the previous Friday that she wanted to buy the land, he knew his deal was almost closed, and the paperwork had come through during the week.

"I told you in confidence that I wanted this, and you turned around and signed this five days later."

"It was already in the works," he said.

She threw the paper onto the desk. "A fact you could have told me before I made a fool of myself."

"Sorry."

"It doesn't appear that way. It looks like you have big plans."

"I'm keeping the horses and the stable pretty much as it is."

He thought this would appease her.

"Good luck with that."

"I need your help."

"I already quit."

"You can't."

Cara picked up the sticky note from the corner of the desk. Her scowl relaxed for a moment and then returned. "I got these groceries for Gary a week before he left. We were a team."

"We could be a team."

Cara flipped the paper over, took the pencil from Ryan's hand, and scribbled something. She stuck the yellow paper right on the house he'd earmarked for himself and marched out.

Ryan stared after her for a moment, and then he heard one of the horses stamp its feet. He couldn't manage the stable alone, and Cara was the only person who could help him.

He picked up the sticky note and read the words *I Quit* followed by her signature.

"Wait," he said, running after her. "Cara!"

He heard the door slam on a car that was

parked on the other side of the barn. No wonder he hadn't seen the Peterson family car when he pulled in. He picked up his speed and put a hand on her car door. Her window was down.

"Please don't leave angry."

"Do you want me to stay here and be angry?"

"I don't want you to be angry at all."

She tilted her head. "I confide in you that I want to buy the stable. You buy it. And now you want the luxury of not feeling bad about it. You must live in a world where you get everything you want."

Ryan shook his head. It would be so nice to tell her that the past year had been everything he *didn't* want. A failed engagement that was over so fast that his family and friends never even knew about it. A failed business tangled up in that messy engagement. His friends and family didn't know about that, either, because he was too embarrassed to tell them, and they'd just want him to fight Poppy and her lawyer harder, to fight for every penny that was his and what he'd unjustly lost.

But the fight was out of him, and he hoped that his lawyer was right about keeping the news quiet improving their odds.

"I didn't steal it, I bought it from Gary. And I'd already talked to him before you told me that."

"You could have told me."

"I didn't want to…" He was about to say he didn't want to break her heart, but that sounded so personal, even for someone he'd known her entire life. His sister had told him once that she thought Cara had a crush on him when they were younger. Saying anything involving Cara's heart seemed wrong, cheap somehow.

"I wonder if there's another good place on the island for your horse thing?" he said.

"Better than an established stable with twelve horses I know everything about? Gee, enlighten me about another piece of island property like that."

"I don't know," he said. It was time to be brave enough to ask what he'd run after her to ask. "You can be mad at me if you want," he said. "Even though I have good intentions for this property you might even approve of someday."

"Thank you for the permission to be mad," Cara said. "I don't like upsetting people. As everyone on this island knows, I'm the nice little sister in the Peterson family who's always there to lend a helping hand."

He knew she was being sarcastic—to a point. She *was* the youngest and *did* have a reputation for being on everyone's side. But she was also helpful. And he needed help.

"Would you do something nice for the horses even if you're not happy with me? I need someone to take care of the daily operations of the stable while I—"

"Shop for more island land to snap up?"

"That's not what I meant. I do need to work on my development plans, but I want the horses and other animals to have the best care. The kind they're accustomed to."

"I'm sure you'll find someone."

"There's no one better than you."

Her expression softened just enough to let him know she was listening and he was making a little progress.

"You can put an ad in the weekly paper," she said. "It just came out, so you'll only have to shovel the stalls and haul food and water for seven more days or until someone answers your ad."

"Please, Cara. Stay on and keep doing what you're so good at."

She was silent a moment. "I'd only be doing it for the animals. And I want a raise. I was due for one when Gary left, but we said we'd talk about it when he returned."

If Cara had really believed Gary was returning—and perhaps Gary had, too—the rug had been pulled from under her. She saw the stable's availability as an opportunity until Ryan had taken it away. No wonder she was upset. He'd lost bids for real estate back when his business was thriving and viable, and it hadn't felt good. He had to acknowledge, though, that it also hadn't felt personal.

Until the person pulling out the rug was his fiancée, Poppy. He'd learned a giant bitter lesson about mixing business and emotions.

"A raise. Yes. It's the least I can do," he said. He stuck out his hand, wanting to seal the deal but also to have some contact, a connection with Cara. She was an old friend, and he'd unintentionally damaged their relationship. Was everyone on the island going to see it this way? If so, he would be shaking a lot of hands and mending a lot of fences.

Instead of taking his offered hand, Cara put both her hands on the wheel. "See you at six tomorrow morning. You can help with the morning chores, and you might even learn something."

Ryan watched her drive away. He assumed she was either headed home or to her other job at the candy store. Did she still live with her parents? He thought about Cara's life for a moment. She would be around twenty-four, maybe twenty-five now. Was she itching to do her own thing just as he had been when he left the island for college and never returned? He didn't remember hearing anything about Cara going to college.

Which could mean her choices were to take her place in the family business or...build her dream business. It was apparent which she had chosen, and he was standing in the way.

Ryan went back inside and picked up the pencil Cara had tossed on the desk next to her resignation. He couldn't start clearing land or building yet. He needed to get some final paperwork in place and secure the permits for the development. He'd thought that would be an easy task, returning to his home island and proposing something he knew was needed. Housing for families and seniors and even young singles who wanted to live on Christmas Island. He'd considered asking Violet and

Jordan to choose one of his homes instead of continuing the renovation on Jordan's, but no one, not even his sister, knew about the plans yet. Besides, Jordan had recently come to peace with the family memories that lived in the little house on the hill, so Ryan didn't plan to bring it up.

He'd have plenty of takers for the properties once he got them built. Maybe even Cara would want to live there once she saw how nice it was.

CHAPTER FIVE

ANYONE WHO KNEW Cara knew she would say yes to Ryan. And not because she'd adored him as a preteen. She'd been over it for so long it didn't even sting anymore. She was an adult with two jobs and a seat on the village council. She'd also just negotiated a raise at one of her jobs.

Maybe her day wasn't completely like the big pile of manure behind the stable. Instead of going straight to the candy store, where she could bury herself in work, or to her bedroom, where she could sulk, Cara texted her sister. She didn't explain much as Camille got in the car and Cara began to drive the loop around Christmas Island.

"I'm happy to sit here and not have to do anything," Camille said. "Drive until you feel like talking."

On a small island where privacy was hard

to find, the interior of the family car had an important role.

"It's the vault," Melinda Peterson would tell her daughters as they were growing up. "Anything you say in the car can't be overheard by anyone else. It's the safe space to discuss anything you want."

Cara had not typically revealed much in the rolling vault, but she'd heard her sisters—especially the oldest, Chloe—unload some heartache as their mother did the school drop-off and pickup, or they got on the car ferry for a shopping trip on the mainland.

"I may or may not feel like talking," Cara told Camille as they drove out of town, "but I do want to invoke the sacred law of car confidences."

"You can count on it. I'll just be sitting here trying not to fall asleep. Planning Rebecca and Griffin's wedding while also thinking about my own in just over two months and wrapping up Halloween candy production while also starting Christmas candy is just… whew. A lot."

"If you fall asleep, I'll nudge you when I need you," Cara said. The island wasn't large enough for her to pour out all her emotions in one loop around it, and she remembered her mother taking an extra lap around when she and her sisters were in their teens.

Roughly twelve square miles, Christmas Island wasn't just the downtown shops, restaurants and hotels. Open year-round to tourism, the island was busiest during the spring, summer and fall when a reliable ferry service could be maintained on the lake before it froze for the winter.

Like the Peterson family, several hundred people lived on the island permanently, many of them with lovely homes on the perimeter with water views. Vacation homes of seasonal visitors took up the rest of the shoreline, but the inland acres of the island had room for development. Perhaps it was even better for her horse camp—"horse thing" as Ryan had called it, as if it were so unimportant to him that he couldn't even give it a more specific name.

"Horse thing," she muttered.

"What did you say?" Camille asked.

"Nothing. Just talking to myself right now."

"I'll wait."

Cara slowed the car as she approached the center of the island. The airport occupied a level strip at the top of a hill in the very center, but there was plenty of land around it. Some of the island roads were a bit primitive and had names only the locals knew, but there were paved roads illustrated on the tourist maps, too.

"That land," she said, pointing. "Well, I guess it has lots of trees, but no buildings or utilities or even a driveway for bringing in guests and horse feed." She sighed. That would take a lot of development on her part, but the five acres of land could be cheap enough to make it possible. It hurt her heart that there were no sweet, gentle horses already in residence that she knew and loved. No barn to house them.

It was starting from scratch.

Cara pulled off the road and got out of the car. She strode to the For Sale sign and took a picture of it with her phone. The island didn't have a Realtor, so people used someone from the mainland if they needed a deal to be negotiated. A lot of island land didn't pass through a Realtor, though. Families sold land to family members, or word of mouth made the sale in other cases.

Like Gary's sale to Ryan. Even though Ryan didn't even live on the island, he'd somehow

' found out about Gary's intentions before anyone else did—even her.

Camille got out of the car and stood next to Cara. "Why are we looking at these woods?"

"Because I need to reconsider the location of my camp."

Camille put an arm around her. "I heard a rumor yesterday that someone else bought the stable, but you didn't say anything, so I didn't bring it up. I hoped it wasn't true."

"It's true."

"Dad heard at the hardware store that Ryan Brookstone bought it."

Cara turned to her sister. "I worked with Mom and Dad all day today, and they didn't say anything."

Camille gave a small shrug and her expression was sympathetic. "They probably didn't know what to say, and you're not usually big on talking about your problems, which is why I wasn't terribly shocked when you wanted to go for a drive. I thought you might need someone to talk to."

"If only talking would help." Cara had years of experience as a listener, but she'd seldom thought she'd helped solve problems by being a sympathetic ear. Practical action solved problems. Emotions complicated everything. Which was one of the reasons she loved the outdoors and horses. Weather and nature were on a predictable cycle. Animals, too. Horses, barn cats and goats got fed at the same time every day, and their world was simple.

"I love your idea," Camille said. "Even though Mom and Dad had a moment there. They'll come around. They were just surprised."

"How were they surprised by me doing something I've said for years I was going to do?"

"You're the youngest. Maybe they don't want you to grow up and leave the nest. With Chloe married and living in Lakeview and me building our candy empire and getting married, maybe it scares them that you're ready to make decisions that are out of their hands, too."

"Well, they may get a reprieve," Cara said.

"You're not going to give up, are you? Maybe this property could work."

"The stable would have been perfect."

"Have you talked to Gary? Did he say why he sold it to Ryan and not you?"

Cara shook her head. "I kept texting him

earlier this week asking for a good time for a phone call because I had something big I wanted to discuss with him, but he never called. I assumed it was because of his recovery from back surgery, but I think he might have guessed I wanted to talk about the future of the stable."

"I don't know why he wouldn't choose you as his buyer."

"Maybe because I never got a chance to offer. We'd always talked vaguely about me taking it over eventually, but I realize now that me taking it over didn't necessarily mean I would own it someday. And maybe Gary still sees me as the little girl who started working there when she was eleven. He doesn't see that I've grown up. Didn't know I might have the down payment available. Maybe it's my fault for not being more direct and coming out and saying what I wanted. Story of my life."

"This isn't your fault. Whatever reason Ryan has for buying the stable probably has nothing to do with you. And you don't know what price or deal he made with Gary."

She might have known if she'd read past the date on the purchase agreement Ryan had put in front of her. But she'd missed her chance to read the fine print and answer some questions. Whatever. It didn't matter anyway.

Cara swept a hand along the frontage of the wooded land for sale. "Do you think this could be a camp for kids?"

"I think it has nothing but possibility," Camille said. "But you're going to need to acquire some horses."

Cara nodded. "The upside to that is that I get to name them anything I want."

"Good idea. You could name the horses for types of candy or flavoring. Ginger or Taffy might make good horse names, but I'm not so sure about Peppermint or Fudge. You don't want the horses to think people are mocking them."

Cara laughed and felt some tension drain away. Her shoulders had been tight and her jaw set since the Wednesday night meeting when she'd first heard about Ryan's purchase of the stable. She'd wanted to deny the truth or even persuade him to change his mind. But when she'd caught him reviewing plans in Gary's office—his office now—his ownership hit home.

Camille leaned on the side of the car. "What do you think Ryan will do with the property?"

"He has plans. I saw them on his desk."

"What was in those plans?"

"I don't know," Cara admitted. "I was more interested in handing him my resignation than gathering information."

"Understandable," Camille said.

"Although he did say he's keeping the horses."

"Let him feed and shovel for a while and he may change his mind and sell them to you for Camp Pine Tree here."

"I ended up agreeing to continue working at the stable until he finds a replacement," Cara said.

"You're nicer than most people."

Cara wasn't sure that was the compliment her sister probably intended. Being nice meant she had friends and a good reputation. But she wanted more.

"And it doesn't matter if you got a look at his plans or not. You're still going to be one of the first people to know."

"Are you suggesting I break into Gary's old office with the keys I have?"

"You can," Camille said. "But you're on the village council, and now you're on the zoning board, too. If Ryan wants to build something or make significant alterations to an existing structure, he has to get approval from the zoning board. We all like Ryan. He's an islander even if he did move away. But he better have a good plan that will win the hearts of the zoning board if he hopes to get anywhere with whatever plans the stable property is part of."

CHAPTER SIX

A WEEK LATER, the October wind buffeted the sides of the horse barn, but Cara didn't mind. Blustery fall weather meant the holidays were coming and then the long, peaceful winter on Christmas Island. Tourist season, with its chaos and excitement from May through September, was the bread and butter for her family's candy business, but nothing compared to quiet rides on island trails where deer stepped delicately from between trees and squirrels paused, unfazed, in the middle of the path.

She ran a hand along the neck of a big brown horse. "Won't be long before we'll go for sleigh rides," she said. The horse nudged her with its nose, and then its ears pricked up at the sound of an electric drill. "I'd ask him to be quiet," she whispered to the horse, "but the wedding is in two days and we need that carriage repaired."

The horse nodded as if it understood her,

and Cara gave it a final pat on its shoulder. She scooped up a kitten from a litter born over a month earlier and cradled it as she walked into the heated workshop area of the barn where the carriages, wagons and one elaborate Christmas-themed sleigh were stored.

Cara sat on a tack stool and covered the kitten's ears as Ryan used a circular saw to cut a board balanced between two sawhorses.

"Too loud?" he asked when he saw her shielding the kitten's ears.

"Kittens are sensitive," she said. "And the horses are tolerating you, but they hope you'll be done soon."

The truth was that she was tolerating him, too. He'd owned the stable over a week, and they had fallen into a routine where she showed up for work every day and they basically avoided each other. To her surprise, he hadn't made a single trip to the mainland in the past week and was still, she'd heard, staying at the Holiday Hotel.

Ryan laughed. "Since you speak animal better than I do, you can assure them I better be done soon if this carriage is going to take

Rebecca and Griffin from their wedding to their reception."

"I have confidence in you," Cara said. She meant that—when it came to working with wood and building things. Ryan was a natural and had been since he was a little kid. Why wasn't he sticking with his off-island business building homes instead of coming back to Christmas Island and poking around with a stable project?

Something didn't add up. She'd asked her friend Violet about Ryan's future plans, but Violet had assured her that she'd been in the dark. She blamed herself, being preoccupied with her relationship with Jordan and helping him remodel his family house. Violet admitted she hadn't had as much contact in the past year with her brother as she usually had, and she felt bad that she'd gotten out of the loop with him.

It wasn't easy to notice things, even when they were right under one's nose. "I wish I had noticed sooner that the carriage needed repair," Cara said. "Gary's had a lot on his mind, obviously, and I didn't think to look myself since we haven't used it in a few months."

"That's why I always do everything myself," Ryan said. He looked up from the board he was screwing fast, and Cara could have sworn there was regret in his expression. He hadn't let her into his confidence all week, and she didn't blame him. She'd done her work mechanically and had avoided unnecessary conversation. They had to work together, and they were both in Griffin and Rebecca's wedding party.

"Will we have time to paint those fresh boards?" she asked.

Ryan ran his hand along a board and picked up a belt sander. "Yes, but I have to sand first, and—" he nodded toward the ginger cat in Cara's lap "—it's going to get loud."

"Say no more," she said. She got up and went into the tack room, where she closed the door and found a soft place for the kitten to sleep. Instead of stretching out as she'd expected, the kitten hopped up and nosed around the corners of the room until it found a piece of leather to play with. She smiled at its antics as it tried to hold the leather between its paws and kick it while lying on its back. "You're adorable," she said. "I wish I could take you home with me."

Taking a kitten to her parents' house where Cara still occupied her childhood bedroom wasn't an option. The Peterson family had endured Cara bringing home living creatures from an early age, and she knew they were all relieved when she got a job at an island stable where she could get her fill of animals in the evenings after she worked her day shift in the candy store.

During the winter, the candy store's limited hours gave her more time at the stables, and she kept the horses and barn cats from being lonely as snow fell outside the windows.

"No snow yet," she said aloud, even though the kitten wasn't listening. "We have a wedding and then Halloween to get through, and snow wouldn't be good at either of those."

"If it snows, you do have a sleigh," Ryan said from the doorway. He leaned against the door frame.

"I didn't hear you open the door," Cara said. "That door usually squeaks like crazy."

He smiled. "I know. I oiled the hinges earlier today while you were downtown. I don't know how the horses could stand that noise."

"I'm sure you're discovering many things that need maintenance around here now that you're seeing it with an owner's eye," she said. She tried to keep her tone neutral. Although she took any criticism of the stable personally since she'd worked there for so long, she couldn't deny that Gary had allowed some things to slip over the years as he'd grown closer to retirement.

"Some of the windows could be reglazed. I think I was the last person to do anything like that when I was a teenager, and so it's been at least ten years, and I didn't get them all done those summers I worked here."

Cara remembered those two summers in vivid detail. Ryan had built a shed, repaired doors and windows, and added stalls. Even as a teen, Ryan had a reputation for building. His love of woodworking was famous, and he'd built so many birdhouses and mailboxes for people on the island that you couldn't go down any island street without seeing his handiwork.

The second summer he worked at the barn was the summer before he went away to college, and it was also the summer of her first crush. On him. At the grand old age of twelve, when she suddenly realized her older sister's friend Violet had an older brother with chocolate-colored hair and eyes, and he was sweet and friendly, even to a little girl who no one else seemed to notice. With two big sisters and a busy candy store to run, Cara had become a master at slipping under her parents' radar and disappearing to the quiet backyard or the horse barn where she worked three days a week feeding horses and shoveling out their stalls.

But Ryan had taken time to say hello and had shown her how to nail together the framework around a door. He'd helped her haul a heavy bag of feed, and he'd put a birdhouse in the spot where she'd pointed out that the birds looked lonely and hungry.

That birdhouse was still there, but she'd grown up a lot since then. No one knew about her girlhood crush that had remained alive for years, sparking into existence when Ryan visited the island even though he lived elsewhere most of the year. It was in the past, and she didn't have time for such silliness. Not with the big plans she had.

Cara straightened a row of tack hanging on labeled pegs. Everything in the barn was precisely in its place, something summer visitors noticed when they rented horses or took lessons. Their comments online about how neat and orderly the Christmas Island Stable was kept went straight to Cara's heart. She had earned that recognition.

He cocked his head to the side, and half a smile lit his face. "I remember showing you how to nail up some trim a long time ago."

Cara wanted to ask what else he remembered about the skinny girl with braids and boots who was always hanging around the barn. He'd given her a ride home one night when she'd overstayed in the barn and it was almost dark. Her parents had called the phone that hung on the wall outside the stalls. She was sure they were on their way to the car to come get her, but Ryan had assured them over the phone that he'd bring her home.

She shook off the memory. Trim and frames. That's what they were talking about. "And do you see any missing trim around here?" she asked. She'd applied those skills numerous times.

Ryan glanced at the window and door and then returned his gaze to Cara. "Not in this room."

"Not anywhere if I can help it. I've done

a lot of extra things around here during the quiet off-season."

Ryan pushed away from the door frame and came into the room. He reached down, picked up the kitten and then held it at eye level. "Hey, little friend."

"I thought you were allergic," Cara said.

"Dogs," he said. "I'm fine with other animals, but dogs get me almost every time."

Cara laughed. "Your sister's dog, Daisy, was going to live here at the barn, but she kept running back to Violet, so I gave up. One of these days, I'll get a dog that wants to live in a horse barn, but for now, it's just me, twelve horses, two donkeys and roughly ten cats, give or take."

"I thought you said the off-season was lonely," Ryan said.

Cara met his eyes. "I believe I said it was quiet, which is not the same thing as lonely."

Not for the first time, Cara wondered about Ryan's life on the mainland. Did he have a girlfriend, or was he too busy for relationships? She didn't have anyone, but choices on the island were limited. For all she knew Ryan could have spent a lot of lonely winter nights in Lakeview—or none. The topic was certainly none of her business.

"I better get back to work on the carriage," Ryan said, breaking eye contact with her. "But I hope I can count on you to paint it. Your skill decorating cookies and cakes is a lot better training for the fancy paint job it needs. I'm more a utilitarian painter."

"I already planned on it."

"OCTOBER IS BEING good to us," Cara whispered to her sister Camille as they lined up in the garden at the Winter Palace on the third weekend of the month. Christmas Island was full of her friends' weddings these days, with Hadley and Mike getting married over the summer, Griffin and Rebecca now, and her sister Camille marrying Maddox May in just two months.

"Lucky break," Camille whispered back. "But I'd be happy to have snow for my Christmas wedding."

Cara smiled. "Okay, but only the pretty kind with the big flakes and no wind."

"Of course," Camille said.

They waited for their cue to walk across the lawn between rows of white chairs with their fellow bridesmaid Violet Brookstone. Rebecca was behind them, standing just inside the garden entrance of the Winter Palace in the beautiful white gown that Violet had ordered and altered earlier in the summer.

"Maddox looks nervous," Camille said. She gave a slight nod to the garden arch where Griffin waited with his best man and brother. "I hope he's not thinking of being a runaway groom at our wedding."

Cara suppressed a giggle. "You'd catch him."

"Darn right I would," Camille said.

Everything was perfect, Cara thought. Bright blue sky, a hint of autumn chill without being cold, and colorful foliage in the trees outlining the garden. The perennials had all been cut back, but there were red, yellow, orange and purple mums surrounding an arch that had been there for years. Had it seen other weddings? Flora Winter had never married herself, but she was there on a cushioned chair in the front row for the wedding of her honorary grandson Griffin and his bride Rebecca.

Was true love ever going to find her? Cara swallowed. She wasn't usually emotional, but she'd have to have a heart of stone not to be moved by the beautiful ceremony.

"Ready?" Camille said. Violet Brookstone and Mike Martin were the first to go down the aisle, and Cara waited until Violet was halfway down the aisle before she turned and took Ryan's arm. As maid of honor, Camille would be going last.

"The carriage looks great," Ryan said quietly.

"That was your work."

"But your painting talent after I finished the woodworking two nights ago."

Cara gave a little shrug. "We have to work together." *Boy, was that true.*

They walked down the aisle in the October sunshine while the guests turned to watch the procession. Cara knew almost every person in attendance. All of Griffin's friends were islanders, but there were a few people he'd met in college and some people from the mainland associated with his ferry and freight business. Rebecca had no family, so her guests included college friends and a few foster siblings who could make the journey.

She'd have plenty of family now that she was officially a member of the Christmas Island community by marriage and by her own sweet personality that had won hearts since she stepped off the ferry.

As Cara walked with Ryan, she felt people staring at them. The island rumor mill would have reached everyone by now. Every person there would know she'd wanted to buy the stable, but Ryan had. And she was still working there, cheerfully mucking out stalls.

Would people think she was a fool? Or that it was just one more symptom of her usual loyalty, her propensity to please people and help them, even at a cost to herself? She tried pushing away those negative thoughts and concentrating on the beautiful love that had brought them all to the garden at the Winter Palace.

Throughout the wedding, Cara shifted her attention from the smiling people in the crowd and then back to the couple under the arch. On the clear air, she heard a horse whinny from the driveway, where the carriage awaited the end of the ceremony and would take the new Mr. and Mrs. May downtown to the Holiday Hotel for a reception.

Near the end of the vows, Cara saw a flash of activity from the front row and glanced over in time to see Flora Winter's little dog, Cornelius, hop down from her lap. Griffin's mother was sitting next to Flora, and she made a grab for the dog, but the terrier was too quick. Cornelius dashed right to the wedding party and bounced at Cara's feet, begging to be picked up.

Cara laughed. All eyes were on her instead of the bride and groom, so she handed her bouquet to her sister, scooped up Cornelius and scratched his ears so the wedding could go on. She made eye contact with Flora to let her know she was perfectly happy to hold the dog, and Flora smiled and laughed.

As soon as the bride and groom kissed and began their trip down the aisle, Cara ducked down the front row and handed Cornelius back to his owner.

"Animals love you," Flora said.

"And we love them right back," Cara said.

"We certainly do," the older woman said.

Cara grabbed her bouquet from her sister and followed the wedding party down the aisle.

"Nice save," Ryan said to her when he joined her for the recessional.

She didn't need his approval, but he was trying to be nice. Was he only being nice because he'd picked up the application for zoning permits from the village council the day before and had certainly learned that she was a voting member?

"All in a day's work," she said. "I was planning to be a low-profile bridesmaid, but Cornelius brought me the spotlight. I hope he comes to the reception so I have an excuse to take him outside and get some fresh air."

She'd always liked Flora and her dog that seemed to have been around forever. Flora typically spent all summer at her island home, but she had taken a few years off until the previous summer when she'd stayed the whole season again. Flora was a sweet old lady and was generous with her wealth.

Cara brushed a piece of dog fur off her dark green bridesmaid's dress, and it drifted off on an autumn breeze.

"Since Cornelius has chosen you as his favorite bridesmaid, you might be in luck with your escape plan," Ryan said.

"I used to save treats for him, and I gave him a few buggy rides so he could feel the wind in his fur," Cara said. "I'm surprised he remembers me from last year."

"Let's consider ourselves lucky that he ran up to you and not me. I would have had to turn down his affections or risk sneezing all over the groom."

A hint of self-deprecating humor from the man who claimed to have big building plans for little Christmas Island, starting with a stable renovation. She tried reminding herself that Ryan was still the same sweet brother of her friend that she'd known all her life, even though his plans conflicted with—killed— hers. Cara hadn't seen the plans yet, but she would as soon as he submitted them to the village council.

"Pictures," Camille called, saving her from her conversation with Ryan. "Just a few quick ones before they get in the carriage."

"We're up," Ryan said to Cara.

Cara moved to the assembled wedding party, which stood at the grand front door of the Winter Palace. A photographer behind a tripod motioned for her to take a place on the bride's side of the photograph. She glanced down the lineup of groomsmen, bridesmaids and the bride and groom—all people she loved and had known her whole life.

Christmas Island was the best place in the world, she thought as she smiled brightly for the wedding photos. Everyone deserved a taste of it, especially kids who needed a fresh start or some fresh air on horseback.

She was still going to do everything she could to get that for them.

She waved as Rebecca and Griffin got into the carriage that Cara and Ryan had improved over the last two days. The horses, Piper and Partridge, were a perfect match for each other in color—chestnut brown with black manes—and their steps synchronized as they carried the newly married couple down the hill toward the lake, where they'd turn to go downtown. The photographer took dozens of pictures of the departure.

"Ride?" Violet Brookstone asked. "Jordan parked a little ways down the hill so we don't have to hoof it downtown."

"I wish I had hooves," Cara said. "But I'll take a ride. The Peterson family car is pretty crowded with Chloe and her husband being here for the wedding."

She got into the back seat of Jordan's car, and Ryan climbed in next to her. Great. She had to be nice to him. Thank goodness it would be a short ride.

Violet turned around. "Were the dresses a huge success?"

Cara laughed. "You know they were. The wedding dress was perfection on Rebecca, and the dresses you made for us are too pretty to wear only once."

"And yet you picked up a dog wearing yours," Violet said.

"Just a little dog."

Everyone in the car laughed. Being around her friends and loved ones reminded Cara how important the island family was. Perhaps that was what stung her most about Ryan buying the property he knew she wanted. If Ryan had plans for the horse stable property that weren't good for Christmas Island, it would be easy for her to say no. She'd rather disappoint one person than let down an entire island.

The question that loomed before her, though, was what she would do about it if she had a choice.

CHAPTER SEVEN

THE LAST VILLAGE council meeting of October fell just two days before Halloween. Meetings at the fire station were, of course, public, but seldom was there any public participation. Cara remembered her father going to a council meeting a few years back when there had been a big proposal in the works to enhance the sidewalks downtown and ask the merchants to fund the project. Luckily, a compromise had been reached that used some state grant money, local taxes and a reasonable contribution from downtown businesses.

Christmas Island had beautiful sidewalks, and everyone was happy. As Cara listened to Gina pound the gavel and give the formal start to the meeting, she saw only one public participant in the row of six seats that were always allocated for villagers but rarely occupied.

Was Ryan Brookstone even a villager? He

hadn't lived there in years, but he did own property now, Cara reminded herself with a little shiver of irritation. He had a large folder in his hands, and she guessed it was the plans he'd had spread across the desk in Gary's office. Ryan's office now. She hadn't snooped, even though there were plenty of days in the past two weeks she was alone in the barn and had a key ring admitting her to every lock. Unless Ryan had changed the lock on the office.

She hadn't tested that theory. She was simply a barn employee until he found someone else. Cara showed up for an early morning and late afternoon shift, worked in the candy store in between and occasionally borrowed the family car for a slow cruise around the island, trying to convince herself that she could buy property elsewhere that would be just fine for her camp.

"Any discussion on the minutes from the last meeting?" Gina asked.

Cara snapped her attention back to the meeting. She couldn't keep mooning about the stable property that would never be hers now. She couldn't spend her days being bitter at Ryan. That would be wrong. She was a person who never put her feelings ahead of anyone else's.

The other members of council shook their heads, and Gina called the roll to vote to approve the previous meeting's minutes. The most noteworthy thing that had occurred during that meeting was her appointment to the zoning board.

"Before we get to new business, this is the opportunity for public participation," Gina said. She looked directly at Ryan sitting alone in the public chairs. "If anyone wishes to speak, they can state their name and address for the record and address the council."

Ryan stood. "Ryan Brookstone, 351 North Carriage Street, Christmas Island."

Just hearing him give the barn's address as his own was a knife in Cara's heart. And that was technically a business address anyway, not a residence. It was tempting to argue a technicality—that Ryan didn't actually live on the island, at least, not yet to her knowledge—but she knew that as a business owner, he would have the right to speak to the council.

She forced her shoulders to relax and composed a neutral expression as she waited for him to speak.

"I have recently purchased the Christmas Island Stable from Gary Scheid," Ryan began.

Cara noted that other members of council nodded.

"I have nothing but respect for Christmas Island, its citizens and its history," Ryan said. "I feel the same way about the stable where I had the privilege of working two summers when I was younger. Building projects and doing maintenance there helped me become the builder that I am."

Cara noticed that he referred to himself as a builder. Not an owner of a luxury home construction business. Just a builder. Did he believe humility before the council would give him an edge when it came to whatever he was going to propose?

"That's nice to hear, Mr. Brookstone," Gina said. Cara found it interesting that Gina, who was old enough to be Ryan's mother, wouldn't refer to him by his first name, even though she'd watched him grow up. Perhaps it was just the formality of the council meeting structure.

"Having said that, I want to formally present an application for new construction and use of the property."

Here it comes, Cara thought. The moment when she would find out why her dream had been destroyed by whatever his was. Why his plans had crept in and stolen the life from hers. Why Gary had betrayed their long friendship and working relationship and sold out to Ryan without even giving her a chance. Heat crept up her neck, and her throat felt thick just thinking about the dual betrayal, and she forced those thoughts aside and sat there like a statue.

She had to appear unaffected, or people might think her decisions on the council and zoning board were biased. She had already discussed a possible conflict of interest with Gina and Shirley regarding Ryan's plans, because she worked for him. They had assured her that a vote of the zoning board was only one step in the process, a stepping stone to full consideration by the seven members of the village council. Her opinion wouldn't make or break any deal.

"The most important thing I want to assure you all of is that I'm keeping the barn and riding stable pretty much as is. I may make some improvements to the building itself, some structural and some cosmetic, but

I have no plans to change the footprint of the barn or alter the business model of renting out horses for tourists."

Cara found it easier to breathe for a moment. He'd told her as much, but she hadn't completely believed him. Why should she? He also hadn't told her he was buying the property when she'd confided in him that she wanted to. How could she trust him? Now that he was revealing his plans to the village council, though, he had to be telling the truth. She believed.

"However," he continued, "there's an additional ten acres connected to the barn. It's undeveloped right now, with very limited utilities and lots of trees."

Beautiful trees, in Cara's opinion. And the rustic nature of the property would have been perfect for her camp. From Ryan's tone, though, she was guessing the rustic nature was not perfect for his plan.

"One thing I have observed about Christmas Island is that it's a perfect place to live. The natural beauty, great downtown businesses and friendly people make it pretty attractive to anyone looking for a permanent home, or even a vacation home."

He was certainly saying all the right things to flatter the people on the council. They were true but obvious things. Of course Christmas Island was idyllic and there was no other place she'd ever want to live.

But Ryan hadn't lived there in a decade. She wanted to interrupt him and ask why he'd suddenly returned and taken an interest in the island. But she kept her mouth shut. If it got around that she was bitter or jealous about his purchase of the property and return to the island, she might have to recuse herself entirely from the zoning board and any council decisions regarding his plans. Cara felt quite strongly that she would like at least some voice in those plans—and it wasn't just pettiness, she was sure of it. It was because she took her role as a council member seriously. People were counting on her.

"Go on," Gina said.

Ryan had hesitated in his prepared speech, and Cara realized it was because he'd glanced over at her. Was he looking for any kind of reaction?

"But housing is hard to find on this island. Especially affordable housing that will appeal to families. And that's why I'm presenting you with a plan this evening that will address this urgent need here on Christmas Island."

Cara wanted to scoff at his portrayal of anything on the island being urgent. It was a slow-paced island with a long history and few dramatic changes or events. Claiming there was some urgency was a bit colorful, but no one else on the board had reacted to his statement.

"I propose to build twenty single-family homes for sale or rent. I will offer three different floor plans for small families, retirees and large families. I plan to add some commercial space as well."

Silence met his proposal and Cara risked a glance around at her fellow council members. Did they love it? Hate it?

Twenty homes on ten acres. It wasn't unreasonable. And she had to give him credit for recognizing an island need...but Cara couldn't quite get past the reason. Why didn't Ryan continue his business model of building such housing developments on the mainland? Why, suddenly, had he returned to his hometown he'd abandoned a decade earlier?

"Do you...have any questions?" Ryan asked. He looked nervous. Cara could see his Ad-am's apple bob as he swallowed twice. He was facing a group of people that included one of his former teachers, friends of his parents and a person whose heart he'd broken by buying the land in question. Anyone would be nervous. But was there something else? Why did he seem so intent on this project that he rushed through the land's purchase—Cara would always believe that it had been rushed because the land was sold practically before it went up for sale—and now he stood before a council holding a large folder that shook just a tiny bit.

Maybe it's very heavy, Cara thought.

"Are those your plans?" Gina asked, nodding toward the big folder.

"Yes."

"You'll need to submit a formal request that will go before the zoning board for review, and they will then make a recommendation to the council at large at a future meeting."

"I see," Ryan said. "Would you like to see what I've brought?"

Was he hoping that his plans would be so pretty that they'd gain him some early favor with the council?

Gina shook her head. "That's not our process. You can see the council clerk tomorrow to submit the formal request. Until then, does any member of council have any questions?"

"I'll have questions about the nature of the rentals and whatever the commercial spaces are going to be," Shirley said. "But I'll save those until the zoning board has weighed in."

Ryan flicked a quick glance to Cara. He'd heard the minutes from the last meeting. He knew she was on that zoning board, and he was probably wondering if she'd be a friend or foe.

ON OCTOBER 31—the day after Ryan moved into his temporary digs on the island—Ryan's new neighbor, Penny, had been over three times, and it wasn't even dinnertime yet. Her first visit had been to make sure he knew how to run the electric stove and how to adjust the thermostat. Ryan assured her that he'd talked to MaryAnna, who had sent him a lengthy email with details about her side of the duplex, which he was renting until March.

Penny's second visit had been to bring him a blanket she'd crocheted for Christmas for her new grandson-in-law Mike, but she'd decided now that the two shades of blue didn't go with her granddaughter Hadley's couch, so she was one third of the way through making a new one for Mike. She bustled into Ryan's bedroom and spread the large blanket out on his bed herself.

"One more thing," Penny said as Ryan answered the door. "We have trick or treat tonight, and even though we're one street back from the heart of downtown, if we leave our porch lights on, the kids will come and get candy."

"Candy?" he asked. Of course he knew it was Halloween. He had vivid memories of trick-or-treating as a child with Violet. His parents had owned a home on a backstreet of downtown Christmas Island until they'd sold it and moved a few years after he left the island. Violet had moved into the apartment above her boutique, and Ryan had been on the fast track to having it all in Lakeview. Or so he'd thought.

"Four dozen will be plenty. There aren't that many kids on the island, and I usually start giving out two pieces as the night wears on so I don't have candy hanging around my house. It's a curse that I love the sticky toffee and chewy stuff, but they don't agree with my dentures. One year, I…well, you don't want to hear that story about the glories of aging."

"I'm going downtown in just a minute to visit the candy store," Ryan said. "Can I buy your candy for you while I'm there?"

"Thank you, but no, I've been ready for two weeks. I went shopping with my granddaughter Wendy and her kids."

"That's nice," Ryan said. He knew both of Penny's granddaughters, Wendy and Hadley. If he hadn't already heard the latest about them from hanging out with Griffin and Maddox, the pictures Penny had shown him on her first visit would have gotten him up to date.

He was quite sure his comings and goings would be noted by Penny, but that was a chance he was taking by renting half of a senior living duplex for the winter. The fact that there was no other place to rent on the island, even in the off-season, strengthened his argument for building additional homes and making some of them rentals. He just hoped the members of the zoning board and the village council would agree.

"I'm leaving my porch light on from five to seven," Penny said. "And you don't have to worry about attracting bugs this time of year. I'm setting a chair right inside my door so I don't have to run back and forth when a child rings the bell."

"Do you need help moving a chair?"

"I wouldn't turn it down," Penny said.

There was nothing about Penny that suggested she was a frail and fragile old lady, even though Ryan estimated she had to be close to eighty. He followed her next door and took one of the heavy chairs from her kitchen table and placed it exactly where she wanted it inside her front door. He shifted the rug to make sure it wasn't a trip hazard, and then he assured Penny he'd see her later and would be stocked up with candy.

As he walked the short five-minute trek to Island Candy and Fudge, he was torn between hoping Cara was there and hoping Cara was *not* there. She showed up to the barn early every morning and took care of the animals. If he didn't make an effort to say hello to her and find her working in one of the stalls, she would come and go without him even knowing she'd been there.

Except the horses' hay was fresh, their water and food full, and the manure neatly removed.

Cara was efficient and responsible, but she didn't spare any conversation for him. In fact, he highly doubted Cara would be in the candy store because, given the time of day, she was likely at the barn checking on the animals.

He paused under the deep pink awning over the candy store's entrance. Everything about the storefront and the entryway was familiar except for the elaborate Halloween display in the front window. Display windows framed the entrance. On one side, a large pumpkin made of orange chocolate and shaped to look like a carriage was being pulled by a team of chocolate horses. The window on the other side held a huge castle made of gingerbread and was decorated with orange and white icing to look like a Halloween ball was taking place. The windows were even lit from within.

"Wow," he said aloud.

"I know, right?" Melinda Peterson said. Cara's mom held open the shop door. "Cara suggested the window display competition for downtown merchants, and I may be biased, but I think she should be the clear winner. However, she's too concerned about being fair, so she refused to have our windows judged in the contest."

"That's too bad. I can't imagine anyone else has a better one."

Melinda smiled. "There really are some amazing Halloween displays. Is that what you're doing downtown today? Are you window shopping or filling out a judging ballot?"

"I'm here to buy candy for trick or treat. My new neighbor, Penny, and I are putting our porch lights on at five."

"She's a sweetheart and always buys too much candy, but she loves the kids. I should probably advise you not to buy any and just dip into her supply, but what kind of a businesswoman would I be if I talked you out of buying something?"

Ryan laughed. "Penny advised four dozen."

"Three is more than enough, but come in and decide for yourself."

He followed Melinda inside and was greeted by the familiar aroma of fudge and cookies.

"We have chocolate pumpkins with cream filling packaged in groups of a dozen if you like those. Or pretzels dipped in white chocolate with little eyes that make them look like ghosts. Kids like those." Mrs. Peterson pointed out Halloween items in the display cases. "You could also go with the cookies dipped in chocolate and rolled in nonpareils. That's Cara's favorite."

Ryan looked up from the case. "Even after working with chocolate all day, she still likes it?"

Melinda laughed. "You build houses all day, and I'd bet you still tinker in the evenings with smaller projects."

He had already eyeballed a better way to use the shelf space above the toaster in Mary-Anna's kitchen, and he planned to ask her permission to make a few small improvements as a favor to her for letting him rent her place.

"You're right," he said. "I'll take a dozen of the chocolate pumpkins and the pretzels and two dozen of Cara's favorite. I would guess she's an excellent judge of sweets."

"That will clean me out of those, but that's okay. I think everyone else on the island has already done their candy shopping, and it's only two hours until showtime."

Showtime, Ryan discovered later, involved bringing one of his kitchen chairs to his front porch and carrying Penny's chair outside so they could sit side by side under a shared afghan and hand out candy together. They pooled their candy, gave at least two pieces to each child who came by in a costume and discussed their favorite costumes of the evening. Penny's pick was a ladybug costume, but Ryan was the most impressed by a pint-size lumberjack.

Shirley from the village council and chamber of commerce came by to take pictures of the island-wide celebration, and she snapped a photo of Ryan and his octogenarian neighbor sharing a blanket and a bowl of candy. Cara walked past at the end of the evening just as Ryan and Penny were considering hauling their chairs inside and turning out the porch light.

Cara greeted Penny warmly, nodded a hello to Ryan and stooped to look at their dwindling candy supply. "Mom told me you bought all the chocolate-covered cookies."

"She said they were your favorite, and that was enough recommendation for me."

"But you bought them all and didn't leave any for me."

Ryan picked up a wrapped cookie from their

basket. "Would you believe I saved two of them just in case someone special came by?"

Cara laughed. It was the first time he'd seen her laugh or smile since she found out he'd bought the stable. He loved the musical sound of her laugh and the way her smile transformed her entire face.

"No, I wouldn't believe that," she said. "But it's ten minutes until seven, and you have other treats left, so I'll take one cookie. It's been a long day."

"You poor thing, working so hard," Penny said. "Do you want to curl up under our blanket with us?"

Cara patted the older woman on the shoulder. "Thank you, but I'm going home to warm up under the purple blanket you made for me on my eighteenth birthday."

Penny smiled. "The one with the pink and white shell border around the outside. I thought it looked just like candy when I made it."

"It does."

"See you in the morning?" Ryan asked.

"I suppose so. You know where to find me since I work for you."

Cara walked away and Penny gave him a

questioning glance. "I would have thought you and Cara were old friends."

"We are."

"But—"

Ryan got up and folded the blanket carefully, matching up the edges. "She's not that happy that I bought the stable from Gary."

"I see," Penny said. "I'm sure she was disappointed that Gary sold it after so many years. She worked with him a long time, and change is hard." Penny patted his shoulder. "She'll get used to the idea."

Ryan considered telling Penny the whole story and seeing if she was so optimistic after hearing it, but instead, he carried her chair inside for her and wished her a good night.

CHAPTER EIGHT

WHEN CARA ARRIVED at the stable the morning after Halloween and went to the closet where she kept her boots, there was a cookie on the little table. It was from her family's candy store, and she knew she'd made it herself because she always put on more of the nonpareils than her mother did.

"Good morning," Ryan said. He leaned on the door frame while she changed into her barn boots and put on her jacket. "It's getting colder throughout the day, and I wanted your opinion about barn temperature during the winter months. I only worked here during the summer, so I need your expertise."

"Gary replaced the furnace three years ago," Cara said. She shoved an arm into the sleeve of her dark blue barn jacket with the corduroy collar and deep pockets for storing apples and carrots. She'd had the jacket since she was twelve and was the tallest girl her age on the island. She hadn't grown much since and hadn't needed to. Even her boots were close to ten years old and had plenty of history, just like everything else in her life.

She liked the history, but she was ready to start something new.

"So, I should keep it set around sixty degrees? Is that where the horses are most comfortable?"

"As long as you keep the big doors shut, that will be fine. Until we get into the deep winter and unless it's windy. Then we reassess. Dancer will be the first one to start stomping his feet if he gets too cold."

"I'll remember that."

Cara slipped the cookie into her coat pocket.

"You're not feeding that to the horses, are you?" Ryan asked.

She gave him a slight smile. "No, I'm taking this coat home today to give it its once-a-month washing. I get the washer and dryer on Mondays at my house."

"Do you...sometimes think you'd like your own house?" Ryan asked.

Cara gave him a long look. He was broader in the shoulders and handsomer than he had been a decade ago when he'd worked in the barn for two summers, but other than that, this conversation could have transported them back in time. He used to lean in the door of her little cubby and talk to her before or after work. She was usually the one bringing him something from the candy store back then.

"You already know I have plans for my future that don't leave a lot of time or resources for a house for myself. Not like there are any houses available anyway on the island."

As soon as the words were out of her mouth, she wished she hadn't said them. She did not want to invite conversation about his development plans. It would be a conflict of interest.

"That's why I—"

"No," Cara said. "This is not the time or place to discuss your request for the zoning board. Anything you have to say can be said to the entire board, and any questions we may have you can answer in writing or by coming to a public meeting. We're not talking about this."

"If we were just two old friends, would we be talking about it?"

"We're not," Cara said.

"Not talking about it or not friends?"

Wasn't this arrangement difficult enough? She'd agreed to stay on at the stable and help him manage the animals because she cared about the horses, donkeys and cats. She had not agreed to be drawn into conversation about his grand plan to bring a development to the island on the exact location where she wanted a riding camp. Was he going to force her to be rude to him?

"Friends are judged by their friendly actions," Cara said. "I didn't see it as a friendly gesture when you burrowed your way between me and Gary and bought this place before I had a chance to see the asking price."

"I asked Gary why he didn't sell it to you," Ryan said.

Cara stilled but her heart raced. This was why she didn't want to talk to Ryan. She did not want to hear about how Ryan had outbid her without giving her a chance or how Gary had somehow…preferred Ryan to her. Her feelings were tender, and she wanted to save her emotional energy to rebuild her plans using a different piece of land. This was done. Her life at the stable was almost over… as soon as Ryan could find a replacement who would take care of the horses like she did. It couldn't be just anyone. Who would know that Goldy and Turtledove needed to be next to each other in the barn but couldn't pull a carriage together without battling? Who would know that Drummer and Partridge loved green apples and carrots but not red apples?

"We're not talking about this," Cara repeated.

"Don't you want to know why he sold it to me and not you?"

Cara crossed her arms. "Are you deliberately trying to hurt my feelings?"

Ryan stepped backward and his mouth opened. "No."

"Then stop talking about it. Let the paperwork you submitted to the village clerk—which I haven't looked at yet, so don't ask—speak for itself."

"I just thought you would feel better if you knew that Gary said he didn't think you—"

Cara shoved past him and picked up a bucket. "I love these horses, but I will quit this job if you don't stop talking to me at work. Don't you have things to do, like plan how you're going to storm the harbor with a fleet of ships you'll build yourself during the long slow winter here? You can't possibly get much done on your housing development during the winter, especially if you don't get the permits and get started soon."

"If I don't get the permits?" Ryan asked. The color drained from his face, and Cara suddenly realized he looked tired. The skin around his eyes was almost blue in the dim barn light. Wasn't he sleeping? Was there something on his mind? Once again, she wondered what had brought him home to the island for the winter, especially since what she said was true. It would be very difficult to build anything with limited ferry service and harsh winter weather.

"These things take time," Cara said. "No one on this island is in a hurry. I'd think you would know that. It hasn't changed in the years since you've lived here."

"Let me…let me buy you lunch today. As a thank-you for helping me out here. At the stable," he added quickly as if he didn't want her to think she was being bribed regarding helping him with the village council and zoning board.

"I'm having lunch with your sister," Cara said. She'd made the plan with Violet a few days ago because Mondays in November were quiet, especially if the weather turned cold. Which it had.

"Could I come along and buy lunch for both of you? I should catch up with my sister, and you're my number one employee."

"Don't you have plenty of employees on the mainland?" Cara asked. It seemed like a simple question to her, a teasing question. Everyone knew that Ryan had a successful business and obviously employed quite a few builders.

"Not any...not at the moment. It's...winter, as you already mentioned. Tough time for building in Michigan."

Those dark circles around his eyes weren't the only thing that had Cara wondering now. Was there something going on with Ryan that no one knew? Perhaps having lunch with him and Violet would tell her something about his current life. Not that it was her business, but if she was going to make decisions as a local leader, it might be her business to find out what might be behind Ryan's grand plans.

"You'll have to ask Violet if it's okay with her," Cara said.

"Is it okay with you?"

Cara wished he'd bothered to ask her opinion or permission before he snapped up the stable, but this was different. It was just lunch.

"If Violet asks, tell her it's okay by me as long as you're buying. We're going to the Mistletoe Melt at noon."

"WE'RE PLANNING TO talk about weddings, babies and dresses," Violet said. "Possibly dogs, cats and other animals. Sorry, but you invited yourself along."

She handed Ryan a menu and he forced a smile. Those were not his favorite topics, but at least he was spending time socially with Cara and, he hoped, breaking the ice with her at least a little bit.

"I will order lots of food so I have an excuse to keep my mouth shut and listen," Ryan said.

He noticed that Cara had changed her clothes since he'd seen her earlier in the barn. She wore dark jeans and a green sweater that matched her eyes with boots that looked fashionable, not the kind she would wear in the barn. Her long brown hair fell over one shoulder and shone in the wintry sun coming through the restaurant window.

Ryan focused on the menu instead of Cara's

green eyes that crinkled at the corners when she smiled at Violet.

"First topic," Violet said. "Griffin and Rebecca's honeymoon. Did you see the pictures they posted on social media? I wouldn't have thought there was an island more beautiful than this one, but Aruba looks like paradise."

"Especially in October and November," Cara said.

"Where should Jordan and I go on our honeymoon?" Violet asked, her head tilted as if it were a deep philosophical question.

"Depends on the time of year," Cara said.

"Which means you should set a date," Ryan added. "Mom and Dad keep asking me if I know anything, especially now that I'm back on the island, and I think they don't believe me that I'm in the dark."

"You were in the dark about my fake engagement to Jordan last summer, too, so you're not going to win the prize for most perceptive big brother," Violet said. "And weren't you going to eat instead of talking?"

Ryan grinned. His sister and Jordan had nearly pulled off a fake engagement to help Jordan's career prospects with the owner of the Great Island Hotel, and he and his parents had fallen into the trap, easily believing Violet and Jordan were in love—which they were.

"We haven't ordered yet," Ryan said. He couldn't help smiling. He loved his sister and their easy friendship, and Cara was one of those people who blended seamlessly into a group and helped ease the way for others. She'd always been like that, now that he thought about it. The pleasant, helpful, youngest sister of the Peterson candy empire who would dogsit, babysit, pick people up at the ferry dock, or hand you a hammer when you were up on a ladder. She'd done that countless times for him and always seemed to have a sixth sense of what tool he'd need next.

He could have used a perceptive helpful person like her on his construction site or in his office. Maybe she would have warned him to stay far away from bad deals and…well, Poppy.

If he would've listened, that is. He'd been blind.

He adjusted his glasses and concentrated on the five different types of salad dressing he could choose and the three different potato-based side dishes. Anything was better than thinking about Poppy.

"I'm thinking summer," Violet said. "Maybe late spring so the Great Island isn't quite so busy. If you're still going to be here, Ryan, perhaps you can run my boutique for me while I go on a fabulous honeymoon somewhere."

"I could run it," Cara offered.

"I always ask you. I feel that I've taken advantage of you. Besides, maybe you'll be too busy getting your camp going by summer. Camille mentioned you were looking at property."

"Looking isn't the same as acquiring," Cara said.

Ryan noticed that both Violet and Cara studiously avoided looking at him. Thank goodness for that lengthy menu. He pushed his glasses higher on his nose. Coleslaw or vegetable of the day? It was truly a riveting decision.

"And we're here to talk about dresses, weddings and babies," Cara said pointedly. "Any word on when the bridesmaid dresses for my sister's wedding will be in?"

"Not yet, but they had better be in soon. I'm trying not to panic about it," Violet said.

"Should we decide on sashes now that the wedding is only seven weeks away? We should nail down our decision to go with green satin or black velvet or a nice shiny Christmas plaid."

Ryan noticed his sister's humorous glance his way—he'd been warned—and then her bright smile redirected toward Cara. "You're right. I have pictures on my phone I'll show you as soon as we place our food order. Although I already have a favorite, you're the maid of honor, and I think Camille will lean heavily on your opinion."

"It's her wedding," Cara said. "I don't want to tell her what to do."

"She's stuck between the three choices, so you're going to have to help her out," Violet said.

Cara's expression faltered for a moment. "Okay, but if you think I'm steering her wrong, please say something."

"When it comes to clothing choices, you know I can't keep my opinions to myself," Violet said.

"Just clothing?" Ryan teased.

His sister swatted him with her menu and Cara laughed, and Ryan felt unaccountably happy that he'd crashed their lunch. It was nice being home on the island, and all he had to do now was make it work.

CHAPTER NINE

THERE WERE ONLY three people on the zoning board, and their recommendation was important. Without an approval from them, any proposals had few options for getting in front of the whole council. Gina, Shirley and Cara would be the first to see Ryan's plans in full, read his proposal and either approve it or ask for changes.

Gina had banking experience, and Shirley had been a business leader on the chamber of commerce for years and owned the island grocery store. Cara was the newest and youngest voice in the group.

"These designs are pretty," Shirley said at the zoning board's meeting during the first week of November. "I don't know what he means by commercial space here, though." She pointed to the center section of the large horseshoe-shaped row of homes.

"We'll have to ask," Gina said.

Cara was fascinated by the section of the drawings that included a detailed rendering of the existing stable and barn. Extra trim and shutters had been added as well as an outdoor arena—something she'd always tried to get Gary to add—but the familiar old barn looked much the same. It was a relief, like walking into her house and smelling her favorite casserole in the oven.

The horses weren't going to have much of an upheaval, and a little voice in her head also reminded her that her job would probably remain available just in case her grand plans of her own riding camp never worked out.

The thought made her sigh.

"You don't think we should ask about the commercial part?" Shirley asked.

"No," Cara said. "It's not that. I was thinking about the horses and how they'll like the outdoor arena."

Gina gave her a smile. Gina had been one of the first people to know about Cara's plans... and her disappointment.

"The houses are really nice," Gina said, changing the subject. "I know he said they would be for families, and I had the impression they would be affordable—did he say that?"

"It's here in the description," Shirley said. She pointed to the price ranges he predicted for the homes, their prices varying by size. "This island can use that. Some of the younger people might want to stick around if they could afford to live here. It would be good for business. You might even get one," she said, tapping Cara on the forearm as they all leaned over the plans. "You know, get out of your parents' house."

"I've...certainly thought about it," Cara said. "I'll be twenty-five in January, and it's time to start living my own life, right?"

"I wonder if Ryan plans to keep one of the houses for himself?" Gina asked. "He hasn't said he's moving back permanently or anything, and he's just renting MaryAnna's place for the winter, but you know my son works in Lakeview, and he saw the land transfer in the paper. Ryan sold his house over there."

Ryan sold his house on the mainland? Up until now, Cara had assumed he'd swoop in, build something profitable, and swoop back to his usual business. If he'd sold his house, what did that mean? Did he expect to make a big profit from the island project and get a bigger house, or was he really moving? Of course, he could be moving anywhere...but back to the island?

Why hadn't Violet said anything about it?

"Let's go through our bylaws and check sheet for approvals," Gina said. "I believe we're going to need clarification on a few things before we bring this to council at large, but we can check off some of the details. Cara, this is your first time reviewing building plans, so jump in and ask any questions. We appreciate you being on this board."

Shirley poured coffee for all of them and brought the cups to the table while Gina brought up the island zoning regulations and bylaws on her laptop. "It's divided into categories," Gina explained. "Environmental impact, infrastructure such as roads, sewer and power, code compliance for building and electrical, and then the more touchy-feely topics, like is the project a good fit for our island and do we need or want it here."

"Sounds like a long process," Cara said. Had Ryan taken a bold chance by selling his house and moving to the island for the winter? Did he expect the zoning permits to take time, or did he think being on the island would help him, especially if he used his charm and connections?

"It can be," Gina said. "And sometimes things go fast. We had to approve the addition of dock space and a new building for Griffin and Maddox May last year, but that was easy. This island definitely needed more ferry access, and the May brothers have a long-standing reputation for caring about the island's needs."

"Ryan has a good reputation," Cara said. "He's also from the island."

"But he hasn't lived here for ten years," Shirley said. "He has a right to live wherever he wants, and by all accounts, he's been really successful with building projects elsewhere. So, I guess we should be glad he's coming home, although it would be nice to know if he plans to stick around after this project is done."

"It would be nice to know that," Gina agreed, "But it's technically none of our business as long as he has a plan for property management, whether he's here or somewhere else."

"We're definitely going to need one of us to be a liaison with Ryan as we work through this approval process. Since Cara is already friends with his sister and works at the stable where she'll see him all the time, she's the obvious choice," Shirley said.

Gina nodded, but Cara couldn't help thinking she was actually the worst choice as liaison. What if she came out and told Gina and Shirley she'd once had a major crush on Ryan and she wasn't entirely sure it was dead. Despite him stealing the stable property out from under her, it was hard to ignore the years of friendship behind them and the way he sometimes looked at her as if he saw *her* and not just the youngest Peterson sister.

At least, that was what she imagined, but it was dangerous to trust those feelings from a person who had already taken something from her without apology or explanation.

"Apples are apples, Partridge," Ryan said. "I'm a human and I'm not all that picky about the color or variety."

The horse dipped its head and blew out a breath, getting slobber on Ryan's sleeve.

"I'm just saying Milkmaid and Lord Leapster didn't care what was in my palm, they just ate it. But you're being a diva."

He heard a chuckle, the human kind, behind him. He turned and saw Cara. She was already wearing her barn coat and boots, so she must have come in quietly while he started the morning chores. He didn't usually get there early enough to start without her, but he hadn't been able to sleep last night.

The zoning board was meeting for an initial review, and he'd chosen to waive his right to be there—and then second-guessed his decision all night. He hadn't wanted the three members of the board to feel he was pressuring them, especially since he knew them all personally, but he'd lain awake thinking he'd blown a chance to explain himself.

If needed.

But what could be needed? He had a rock-solid plan for a much-needed improvement to the island.

"Horses can be divas," Cara said. "But I think Partridge is overly sensitive about apple varieties because of the whole pear tree thing in his name. It can't be easy being named after a bird in a pear tree when you're a horse. You feel as if you're a fish out of water, right?" she said. She stroked the horse's nose and produced an apple from her pocket, which Partridge gobbled up immediately.

"This is why I need you to stay on working here," Ryan said.

"It's not the only reason," Cara said.

She looked as if she regretted her statement as soon as she said it.

"I mean…I know a lot more about running this stable than just the food preferences of the animals," Cara said.

"You've been here a long time," Ryan said. "I know you know this place better than I do, but I'm trying to learn."

"Even though horses and animals really aren't your thing," Cara said.

Ryan considered his response before speaking. Did Cara wonder why a builder would want an old horse barn, even if it did happen to sit on a valuable piece of property? Why not sell off the horses and tear down the barn to make room for additional rental or saleable houses?

His banker had asked the same thing. He'd asked himself the same thing. He and his construction business were in a fight for their lives, and making a sentimental decision wasn't something he had the luxury of doing.

"Why the stable, Ryan?" Cara asked, getting right to the point.

"My decision is a business one," he said. "This island thrives on tradition and sentimentality. People can buy houses on the mainland for less money, so what would bring them out here and make them want to put down roots? What makes a person who already lives here want to stick around and invest in a home?"

"Renting a horse for a good old-fashioned ride?" Cara asked. She crossed her arms and frowned at him. "Are you mocking people who chose to stay on the island, people like me, while you were out chasing your fortune on the mainland?"

"No," Ryan said. He reached out and touched the sleeve of her barn jacket. "I would never do that."

"You don't think it's silly to ride horses named after a Christmas song around an island that's Christmas all year round?"

"Of course not."

Cara turned and walked a few steps to Swan's stall. The white horse bobbed its head in greeting. "She's one of our oldest horses," Cara said. "Almost twenty. She was here when I started working here, and I feel as if we've grown up together."

"Except she's a lot older than you in horse years."

Cara shrugged. "It's all relative. I'm old enough to know what I want and so is she."

"I didn't mean—"

Cara turned to him. "Are you planning to stay on the island permanently or just until you get your project going?"

Ryan swallowed and let out a long breath. This was the question he'd been avoiding from his sister and his friends. It would be better for the future of the building project if people knew he planned to stick around and supervise the sales and rental of the homes himself as well as the operation of the stable. But there would be questions. People would want to know why he was moving back to the island, and he didn't want to—couldn't, at his lawyer's advice—spread much information about the lawsuit and the case against Poppy and her father. The fewer people who knew, the better. And that included his friends and relatives on Christmas Island.

He hardly wanted to admit, even to himself, how much his failure stung him personally, and he didn't want people to think he wouldn't have the means or ability to see the island project through.

Cara held up a hand. "It's not that I care personally or anything, but the other members of the zoning board and I have some questions about the future management of this project you're proposing."

This was what he'd been fearing. He didn't want to show his hand any more than he had to—but if he had to?

"Do you doubt that I'd be a good steward of island land and respect the place where I grew up?" he asked. Sure, he was avoiding the question, but he also did wonder if people had a reason to doubt him. Had they heard something? A cold shiver ran over him at the thought. Were people aware of and, worse, talking about the business deal he'd invested in that went bad? The lawsuit was technically public record, but a person had to know where to look and that it even existed first.

"No one doubts you," Cara said. "You're one of us. Right?"

He nodded and forced out an "Of course."

"But even so, we can't just issue you a blank check without asking about details.

We have a responsibility to the people of the island."

"And…and I respect that," Ryan said. The last thing he needed to do was alienate people in the place he planned to make his permanent home, and it would be especially foolish to put a burr under Cara's saddle any more than he already had by purchasing the stable property out from under her.

He had to tread carefully.

"I'd be happy to answer any questions the board has," he said. "Can I come to the next meeting?"

"Yes, but you can also talk to me," Cara said. "I was appointed to be the liaison with you because we're…because we work together."

This was either the best or worst news for him. Cara had previously placed a moratorium on any conversation about the development, so she couldn't be happy about her new role. But he was more comfortable talking to her than he would be talking to Gina or Shirley.

"I'm glad it's you," Ryan said.

"After I finish the morning chores and make sure the horses are comfortable, I could meet you in Gary's—in your office and review the questions from the board."

"That would be great," Ryan said. "Thank you for giving me a chance, even though I know you—"

"I'm not petty," Cara said. "This isn't about you buying the stable instead of me. This is about me doing my job on the zoning board and the village council."

"Of course," Ryan said.

Treading carefully was going to be an understatement.

CHAPTER TEN

CARA HUNG UP her barn jacket, hosed off her boots and changed back into her regular shoes and coat before heading for the office she still considered Gary's, even though Ryan had owned the place for one month now. It would be hard to erase the memories of Gary drinking the last cup of coffee from the pot, right down to the dregs, every day. She used to shudder at the thought of that bitter black brew, but Gary had been doing it for years, ever since he'd given up smoking her first summer at the stable.

One small fire in the hay pile from a cigarette had been enough for him, and he'd tossed out the cigarettes and added fire extinguishers to every other post in the place. "Can't be too careful," he used to say, "These horses have no one else to speak for them except us."

She'd thought she and Gary would go on caring for the horses forever, but when he'd decided to sell, she'd never have imagined someone else would get in front of her. Maybe she should have let Ryan finish explaining Gary's reasons, but it would hurt too much to hear it from anyone but Gary. She hadn't asked Gary, had been afraid to confront him and make him feel bad, especially because he was recovering from surgery.

It didn't matter anyway. What was done was done, and she was moving forward professionally—at least on the surface. She wouldn't let Ryan or anyone else know about the tears of frustration she'd shed in her bed at night over her plans for the horse camp that had been nipped in the bud. She never asked anything for herself; instead, she was always the quiet girl helping other people out.

Sometimes she wanted to scoop that attitude right out with the manure. Getting her own property and being on the village council were baby steps toward getting what she wanted, but the property wasn't working out, and serving on the council was putting her right in emotional danger.

"You're here," Ryan said, looking up from his desk. He jumped out of his chair as if he'd invited a royal dignitary and was surprised she'd shown up.

This was interesting. He needed her.

Ryan used his shirt sleeve to dust off the chair in front of his desk. "Please sit down. I made coffee."

Cara laughed. "Did you clean out that old pot?"

"I soaked it for two days in the sink to get the crusty sludge off the bottom," Ryan said. "It may have been a bit neglected."

"Or overused. Not a day went by without the aroma of burning coffee mixing with the smell of hay and manure."

"That would make a great scented candle," Ryan said.

"Espresso horse barn." Cara laughed. Ryan had always had a fun sense of humor, but this was the first time she'd seen it since he'd arrived back on the island. He was the old Ryan she knew but also a more serious one, as if something was weighing on his mind. She wondered if he found her to be the same girl he'd known.

She hoped not. That girl was basically invisible. She knew her family and friends loved her. It wasn't that she was treated unkindly. It was just that she was like a trusty workhorse, and she was ready to be the lead horse. Not a show horse. She didn't seek that kind of affirmation or attention. Instead, she wanted to use her gifts to help others in a way no one else was doing—not on the island at least.

She sank into the chair. Her feelings were hard to explain, even to herself. Somehow, she'd wrapped up all her own desires into the idea of the horse camp, and backing away from it, even temporarily, had dulled her vision of the future.

"Here," Ryan said. "It may not taste the same as Gary's coffee, but it's what I can offer you."

No one could replace Gary, although Cara couldn't help thinking that she might have been a good candidate for the job. No matter now. She had another job to do.

"So, about your plans you submitted to the zoning board. They—we have some questions."

Ryan sat in Gary's chair. "Fire away."

"What exactly do you plan for the commercial area?"

His confident gaze flickered. "Shops."

"What kind of shops?"

"I'm not entirely sure yet."

"I thought you would have worked that out before you committed to such a big project," Cara said.

"I was in a hur—"

He didn't finish the statement, but he didn't have to. His plans, although they appeared quite detailed and professional, were not entirely complete. He'd been in a hurry? Why? Nothing moved fast on Christmas Island and Ryan was an established builder. Certainly he hadn't gained the good reputation he had by rushing into things.

There was only one reason she could think of for the haste on this one—to hurry up and grab the land before someone else did. Before she did. The thought punched that already sore spot around her heart.

"Do you have an investor?" she asked. Shirley and Gina had not told her specifically to ask that question, but that would be a logical reason why Ryan would have put together a quick plan. To sell the idea to investors.

"Is that a required question on the zoning board's approval process?" he asked.

He didn't want to answer the question?

"I'm...new on the board, so I don't know

every single article and bylaw, but it did come up in our discussion."

Indirectly at best. She was going out on a limb here, asking a question out of curiosity. She needed to remember her role in this whole affair. She would never own the stable now, unless Ryan somehow failed or chose to bow out. And there was no way he was going to do that, quit on a project before he even got started. Unless…

She didn't dare to think that evil thought. If he couldn't get approval from the zoning board for a project he obviously intended to profit from, he might turn around and sell the property. Cut his losses.

"I have no investors other than myself," Ryan said. "I have a bank loan for the land purchase, and that loan is based on the ability to develop the land according to this plan."

Cara concentrated on her phone's screen. "Let me just jot that down so I can accurately relay this information to Gina and Shirley. As the liaison," she added. Having that title made her feel entitled to ask questions. Even awkward personal ones that went off script.

"Next question. Do you plan to live on the island permanently?"

"Permanently?" Ryan's voice squeaked a bit on the word.

"Yes, that was the question."

"*Permanent* is a big word."

"So, that's a no?"

"I didn't say that," Ryan said. "I…I plan to see the project through, if that's what you mean."

"And the future management of the property if you decide to move back home?"

"Home?"

She knew he'd sold his house in Lakeview, but did that mean he didn't have anywhere else to live? He could have an apartment or condo for all she knew.

Ryan sat back in his chair. "You know," he said, "no matter how long I've lived elsewhere or where I've been, I've always considered this island to be home."

Cara felt tension leave her shoulders. Maybe it was the way his eyes softened and a smile lit his face when he said the island was his home. Perhaps it was the flicker of the Ryan she used to know and adore. Perhaps it was just her loyalty to the island itself that was gratified by hearing that it was important and superior to other places.

She should stick to the list of questions. Going off topic was dangerous with someone she just wanted to reach out and hug—or push onto the ferry and tell him to go back to where he'd been.

"What do you love most about the island?" she asked.

His smile broadened. "Sunrise and sunset. Birds singing. Watching the last ferry leave on summer nights and knowing that almost everyone left on the island is someone I know."

"I love that, too."

Ryan leaned forward and put his forearms on the desk, bringing his face much closer to Cara's. "I also love the abundance of good skipping stones all around the island, even though you know from painful experience that I'm not that good at skipping them."

She grinned, remembering the Holiday Hustle from the previous summer that had come down to the final challenge in a race around the island. The top three teams were neck and neck on one of the island's beaches, and the challenge was to skip a rock thirty-two times. She and Ryan had been paired up and were in first place. Until Ryan's sister, Violet, and her now fiancé Jordan had shown up.

"No one can skip stones like Violet and Jordan," Cara said teasingly. "It's not fair to compare yourself to your more successful younger sister."

It was also not fair to look back on that beautiful summer day and wish she could do it over again, just for the fun of being with Ryan in a carefree race around the island. Before this whole business of the stable property had stained her feelings for him.

"I do envy Violet sometimes," he said quietly.

Cara waited, hoping he would elaborate. How well did she know Ryan anymore?

One of the barn kittens came in the office and hopped up on the desk, breaking the spell of the nostalgic conversation. Cara picked it up quickly and held the kitten while Ryan pointed to a spot on the drawing near where the animal had perched momentarily.

"As for the commercial section, it's not going to be huge. Maybe a convenience store or a sit-down restaurant." He looked up. "Don't worry, I'm not going to put in a grocery store and compete with Shirley."

Cara drew back, irritation replacing the happy feelings from moments before. "I don't think that's the—"

"And certainly not a candy store. No one would even want to try to compete with—"

"Really, Ryan?" Cara said, rising from her seat with the kitten clutched against her chest. "Are you accusing members of the zoning board of having their own personal interests involved in asking perfectly legitimate questions?"

"No, but I—"

"We have every right to fully vet the largest new development this island has seen in a long time."

Ryan nodded. "You do. And I hope you keep in mind that this *is* the largest new development this island has seen. Not every developer would want to take a chance on building on an island that is mostly seasonal and where it's difficult and nearly impossible to get work done in the winter."

"So, why are you?" Cara asked, the question leaping from her mouth.

"Why am I willing to take a chance?"

"No. Why are you suddenly coming back to a place where you haven't lived in ten years? It feels rushed and mysterious. You didn't even tell your sister you were moving back."

"That's business," he said coldly. "You see an opportunity, you take it. If you delay, you might lose out."

You might lose out. No kidding.

Cara gave the kitten a kiss on the top of its head and put it down on the floor. She wanted to cry, but she would not let the thickness in her throat show in her voice. She looked up and ran her eyes along the familiar beams in the old office. A horseshoe hanging upside down for good luck was nailed to a beam over the windows. Gary had told her it had been there when he bought the place, and he'd never taken it down.

Was Ryan just a lucky guy in the right place at the right time for this property purchase and development, or was there something more?

"I will go back to the board and tell them you were not able or willing to give me a solid answer regarding the commercial area and your future plans."

"Cara, that's not—"

"It may not actually matter. The board can't require you to live here against your will. Our concern is who would manage the property in the future, but you're a businessman. You know how to hire someone to do the work you cannot or will not do."

"You're making me sound like a villain," Ryan said. "I'm trying to do something good for Christmas Island and build housing that is desperately needed."

Cara nodded and tried to keep a neutral expression. She was having this conversation as a public servant. Her feelings could not and should not be involved. Especially if Ryan was going to be quick to accuse people of serving their own interests. For his sake, she wasn't even going to tell Shirley what he'd said about a grocery store, and she was going to try to forget his little crack about a candy store.

"I'm sure the board and the greater village council will see your project's value. Our board meets on an as needed basis and then refers our recommendation to the council, which meets twice a month. We should have a recommendation for the council at its meeting the second week of November."

"That's almost a week away."

"Is there a hurry?"

Ryan opened his mouth and then shut it.

"I'm anxious to get started while the weather's still decent."

Cara felt there was more to his timeline, and there was definitely something he wasn't telling her. She had no authority to probe any deeper as a zoning board member, at least not unless some other legitimate concerns came up from her fellow members, but personally, she had a lot of questions she'd like to ask Mr. Ryan Brookstone.

"The horses need exercise, especially during the off-season when no tourists are renting them. I suggest you put them on a rotation and take them out for rides every day the sun is shining."

"It's been a while since I've ridden," Ryan admitted.

"It's like riding a bicycle," she said. "And the horses are accustomed to skittish riders who don't know what they're doing. Let them lead."

The kitten still lingered in the doorway, and Cara scooped it up as she hurried out.

RYAN SAT ACROSS from his banker in Lakeview. He'd worked with the same man for five years, and those five years were marked with less tension than a fluffy pillow. The money had flowed, his debt-to-income ratio was text-book and his banker had never given him the look he was getting right now.

"It's just a little setback," Ryan said. "Trust me. I know how things work on Christmas Island."

Paul Willoughs didn't change his expression. "It's a darn good thing your mortgage is gone now and that's all tidied up. And you unloaded your rented office and warehouse space. So, now your only liability and, unfortunately, your only asset is a barn on an island."

"A barn with twelve horses and ten acres and a very good plan."

"Construction loans have deadlines. It's over thirty days since you acquired the property, and I might remind you that you assured us at the time that there would be no issues with permits and zoning. We took your word for it because you're from the island and because of your good and longstanding history with us."

"And you're not going to regret it," Ryan said. He'd put on a suit jacket and shaved for the first time in weeks for this meeting, hoping to convey an image of success instead of what he currently was. A purveyor of just the right kinds of apples to finicky horses, a man who was stepping gingerly around the powers that be on the island and a man who'd stepped on the toes of one of those people in power.

Who also happened to be his little sister's friend. And his old friend. And someone with very pretty hair and a cute nose and a way with people and animals that was just—

"How close are you to breaking ground on the new construction?" Paul asked. "I assume you've already gotten moving on the utilities."

"There is a road and water and electricity already available to the property," Ryan said. It wasn't a lie. The barn sat on the property, and it had a paved street leading right up to it, water, electricity and internet. The island wasn't the Wild West, if that's what Paul's impression of it was.

"Can you give us evidence of progress by December first then? That's when you had originally scheduled the first installment of the construction loan funds."

Ryan started to run a hand through his hair and then stopped himself, not wanting to appear nervous. The time clock for the payments on the loan would start when he took the first construction withdrawal, and he had built the timeframe with that knowledge in mind. The sale of his home on the mainland would only keep him afloat for so long. If he could start selling empty lots in the development to buyers who would then begin making payments for home construction, he could just barely crawl through the financial wilderness he'd created for himself. If his plans went accordingly, he'd have breathing room in his checkbook in about a year.

It was going to be a long year. And any delay in getting the project moving could potentially sink it right into the lake.

"Winter on the island is a tough time for breaking ground," Ryan said.

"Yes?" Paul said, a question in his voice.

"And I wonder if we could adjust the payouts back a bit. Say I didn't need the money for new construction quite yet based on site conditions and weather."

"And the fact that the permits weren't exactly handed to you on a Christmas cookie tray yet?" Paul asked.

"I'm working on that. I don't think it will be a problem." An image of Cara's face flashed before him as he considered how much of a problem he'd already created by alienating her. Or had he? Cara was saddened that he'd gotten the property instead of her. He'd stomped on her dream, but she could still move forward with it...just somewhere else. Did it even have to be on the island? He wondered if she'd considered building a horse camp outside Lakeview, where land would be cheaper and more accessible.

Should he suggest it to her? Even offer to help her look? The thought relieved his guilt and worry for just a moment until he remembered her loyalty to the island. Her family was there and she still worked in the candy store. But her older sister had married for love and moved to the mainland, and she was running a candy store branch. Maybe Cara—

No. He couldn't wish her away or drive her away. He was going to have to work with her and appease her and the zoning board if he hoped to get moving on this project.

Paul pushed back from his desk and glanced up at the wall clock. "I hope it won't be a problem. Reopening the loan and renegotiating the terms doesn't always work in your favor. It's best if you can find a way to stay on the track you planned for and signed on."

His banker was a nice guy, pleasant and courteous to work with, but his tone was all business at the moment, and Ryan couldn't blame him. At this point in his life, with a massive loss in his recent history and a lawsuit currently in progress and his only asset an island parcel with a big complicated dream attached to it, who could blame anyone for doubting him?

Heck, he doubted himself every day. The only way he knew to counteract that doubt and keep his sanity was through hard work. Moving forward, working harder, creating something valuable that people would want. He was itching to get started.

"Understood," Ryan said. He rose from his chair and reached across the wide banker's desk to shake hands. "I'll come through. I always have."

Paul shook his hand. "If I don't see you beforehand, I hope you have a nice Thanksgiving. I assume your family is on the island and you'll celebrate with them?"

"My sister, Violet, is there. My parents moved

to Florida a while back, but basically everyone on the island feels like family."

"Lucky you," Paul said. "We're going to the in-laws in Traverse City unless I can persuade my wife that we can overeat and watch the parade on television from the comfort of our home this year."

Ryan smiled. "Good luck."

As he left the bank, he thought about the Thanksgivings he'd celebrated. Nearly every one had been on Christmas Island and included a dinner and tree lighting ceremony at the Great Island Hotel. The first year his parents had moved to Florida, he and Violet had flown down to be with them in their new place, but they'd all agreed there was no place like the island for holidays and had moved their family event back there ever since.

That house in his future development that he'd already thought of as his own would be a perfect place to host the family party, if he ever got it built.

He made a few stops in Lakeview and then drove past his former home just for curiosity's sake and saw a moving truck in the driveway. Should he stop and ask the new owners if they needed anything? Would they wonder what the extra light switch by the patio door operated? He'd never gotten around to adding the landscape lights he'd intended. He'd thought there would be time for that.

He drove past, not wanting to interfere with moving day or face an awkward conversation. He had plenty of those at the moment.

"You've got an empty truck," Maddox May commented when Ryan drove onto the Christmas Island ferry at the mainland dock. The dock had enjoyed many improvements in the past year, including a passenger depot, an enlarged parking area and better lights and signage. More improvements were planned, as well as the major expansion of the island dock, and the May brothers were on their way to having a ferry empire.

"Didn't come on a shopping expedition today," Ryan said.

"You must have been checking on your construction empire," Maddox said, flashing him a grin.

It was tempting to unburden himself and just tell his old friend that there was no empire. No business. No excavators, warehouse, employees and only the truck he was currently driving. How long would it be before everyone knew anyway? Why not just tell his island friends that he'd decided to sell it all off and put all his eggs in the Christmas Island basket? It was a semitruth, though, and it would come with questions he just didn't want to answer. Not while the wound was still so fresh and not while the outcome of the lawsuit was still undecided.

His lawyer hadn't been in his office that morning, and the assistant couldn't offer an update. He needed to be patient and wait. Story of his current life.

He forced a smile. "My current empire is right behind the stable on the island."

"Isn't that where the manure pile is?" Maddox asked.

Ryan laughed. Maddox wasn't wrong. "We may have to find a new location for that necessity."

Or it was an unfortunate but apt metaphor for the current state of his affairs. Ryan followed Maddox up the steps to the pilot house and stood next to him for the ferry crossing just as he'd done a hundred times. As the island's details came into view with the white church steeple, the elegant homes along cliffs on both sides of downtown, a deep U-shaped harbor that was empty at this time of year and a colorful downtown where he knew every shop and shop owner, Ryan resolved to do everything in his power not to end up buried in that pile behind the barn.

CHAPTER ELEVEN

CARA CHECKED BIRDY'S hooves as part of her daily routine. The horse was technically named Four Calling Birds, but Birdy seemed to suit the eight-year-old filly with a sweet, feisty temperament. The horse seemed restless, and Cara was accustomed to that feeling when tourism quieted down and there were fewer people in the candy store and almost no riders lined up to rent a trail horse outside the stable door.

"You need a ride," Cara said. "And the sun is shining today, so I think we can make that happen."

"It's not her turn."

Cara glanced at the stall door where Ryan stood. He wore a barn coat that had been Gary's and a red-and-white striped ski cap that made him look like a rustic candy cane.

"I made a spreadsheet as you advised so I could make sure the horses got equal exercise. Her turn is tomorrow after Three French Hens's."

"We call him Frenchy."

"And it's his lucky day today, so I'm sorry we'll have to disappoint Four Calling Birds."

"Birdy."

"Yes. Unless—"

Cara checked the last of Birdy's hooves and then began rubbing her down with a brush. Ryan let that word *unless* hang in the familiar-scented barn air, but Cara wasn't in the humor to take his bait. She had a job to do, and that job wasn't finishing sentences for her boss. In the past two days, Ryan had been especially attentive and friendly to her. He gave her the first cup from the coffeepot, he offered to unload the wheelbarrow into the manure pile out back, and he'd even made a bed out of an old horse blanket for the kitten that loved to wander into his office.

And now he was wearing Gary's coat. Was he settling in or staking his claim, or was there something else going on—like he needed her goodwill? The first few weeks he'd been back on the island, he'd seemed more sure of himself. But in the past few days, he'd seemed a bit—was it desperate or just unsure of himself?

She knew all about being unsure of oneself. She'd finally gotten to the *sure* stage, which had lasted about three days, thanks to Ryan.

"Aren't you going to ask me how we can avoid disappointing this fine horse?"

"You can exert yourself and take her for a ride after Frenchy," Cara said.

Ryan's expression flattened from *I've got a brilliant plan* to *Oh, I hadn't thought of that.*

Cara wanted to laugh. "That wasn't what you were planning to suggest?"

"I was going to suggest you go with me. We ride together."

Her first and strongest inclination was to decline. There was work to be done in the barn, and then she had work to do in the candy store. It was almost the second week of November, and the Christmas candy business her sister had worked so hard to create online was emerging as a substantial part of their yearly revenue. The fudge and specialty candy orders were huge and a bit exhausting.

The price of success.

What price was Ryan paying for his good fortune of being able to nab what, to him, was the perfect island property for his new plan? Did he consider riding with Cara as just part of his business decision, especially because she had a vote he needed, or did he take any pleasure from the thought of spending an hour leisurely riding horses along quiet island trails with her?

"It would give you a chance to ask me any more questions the board has, and I actually have answers to at least some of the ones you posed a few days ago."

So much for using the ride as an excuse to enjoy her company.

"You could put those in writing in an email to the board," she said.

"But personal discussion seems better. In case I need to clarify something."

Personal discussion. That phrase clearly had more than one interpretation. She brushed out a tangle in Birdy's mane as she considered his suggestion, letting him stew for a moment while he awaited her answer. If he was accustomed to calling the shots and having things happen on his timeline, it was good for him to be reminded that was a luxury not everyone enjoyed.

"You could just tell me now," she said.

"But the horses need a ride, and there can't be too many nice days like this left before it turns cold," Ryan said. "I know I haven't lived here in a while, but trust me, I remember what it's like to live on Christmas Island." He lowered his voice and gave her a serious expression. "I remember everything."

A shiver went down her spine at the emotional tone in his voice. It wasn't possible for him to remember how she'd felt about him the last summer they worked together in this very barn, because she'd never told him. He hadn't known. Besides, she'd been twelve.

Shaking off the idea that he had inferred anything personal by that statement, she decided she was curious about the answers he had for the board. That was enough justification to say yes to a ride. She never turned down a chance to hit the trails on the back of a horse, but this felt different—almost as if she were opening a door to Ryan that led someplace where she didn't know the terrain.

"I'm on the clock," she said casually, "but exercising the horses is an important part of their care. I'll grab a hat and gloves, and then we can saddle up. If you still remember how."

He grinned, and suddenly he was eighteen

again, and she wanted him to stay that way and be the cheerful builder of birdhouses instead of the man who sat in Gary's chair and frowned over plans spread over the well-worn desk. Of course he'd grown up and was an adult with responsibilities.

She pulled on leather gloves—a Christmas gift from several years ago from her parents—and a warm ski cap that controlled her hair and kept her ears warm and then joined Ryan to lead the horses to the tack room.

"I'd prefer Birdy if you don't mind," Cara said.

"Is that because you hope Frenchy will toss me off and leave me beside the lake road?"

Cara laughed. "Birdy is actually more likely to do that if she gets the thought in her head and you rub her the wrong way. I'm looking out for you here."

"Thank you."

They blanketed and saddled the horses and Cara checked the bits and reins as she always did for riders who rented them. It was good practice no matter how experienced she was and Ryan had been.

"I'll follow your lead," he said as they mounted up and walked the horses away from the barn.

IT WAS LIKE riding a bike. Cara was spot-on with that assessment, but it didn't make his seat any less sore. He was accustomed to working long days outside and using his muscles, but horse-riding muscles were different, and his legs were already feeling it.

Cara, on the other hand, rode like a champion, as if she and the horse were part of the same movement with each step. Half an hour into the ride, Ryan was very glad he'd only suggested a one hour ride so the horses wouldn't get too chilled. He could manage another thirty minutes if they turned around sometime soon.

"Break time?" he asked Cara, who rode next to him on an island road. They'd come out of a trail through the woods and were on a paved road with no traffic.

"Do you need a break?" she asked with a tiny tilt to her lips that he found rather appealing. Her cheeks were pink with the November air and her eyes bright. Long strands of brown hair flowed out beneath her blue hat. For a moment, he didn't see Cara Peterson as the youngest sister in the candy family and the friend of his little sister, Violet.

"Are you going to make me admit it?" he asked.

Her smile grew. "I don't have to." She swung a long leg over her saddle and lowered to the ground in a graceful move.

He swung a leg over without groaning, he was pleased to say, and thumped to the ground. He took the reins and starting walking before his legs could protest. Cara walked next to him. The horses were on their outsides, and they walked side by side. Ryan noticed a sign alongside the road about fifty yards ahead. Was it a For Sale sign?

"Frenchy seems to like you," Cara commented. "He's never directly unpleasant to riders, even tourists who've never ridden, but he's definitely more cooperative with some people than others. I could tell he trusted you."

"I'm trustworthy," Ryan said.

Cara didn't answer, and he considered himself lucky. She had reason to doubt him, considering the timing of his land purchase. Someday, he'd be able to explain why he'd moved so quickly.

"So, tell me what answers you have for the zoning board," Cara said.

"For one, I am planning to live on the island."

She stopped leading her horse and turned to him open-mouthed. "You are?"

He nodded.

"That's hard to imagine when you've been gone so long."

"People move back. Your sister Camille moved back, and she was gone for years."

"Seven years," Cara said. Her expression lost some of its doubt. The Camille argument had come to him in a flash, and it was a good one. He could just let it rest at that, but he wanted Cara to trust him and have a larger reason to believe him.

He sucked in a breath and let it out slowly. "I sold my house in Lakeview." She was the first island person he'd told. He hadn't even brought it up with his sister or his friends, knowing it would spur further questions, albeit friendly ones, he imagined.

"I know," Cara said.

"You…know?" Ryan sputtered.

She nodded. "Gina told me and Shirley at the last zoning meeting. Land transfers are public record, and she has a connection in Lakeview who saw it when it hit the paper there."

It would never make the Christmas Island paper, but Ryan knew islanders often subscribed to the online version of the mainland paper, and it was only a matter of time.

"If you all knew I'd sold my house, why did you want to know if I was going to live here on the island?"

Cara shrugged. "Just because you sold one house over there—" she nodded her head to the mainland visible in the distance across the blue lake "—doesn't mean you're not going to buy another one. Or get a swanky low-maintenance condo or move in with…someone."

Ryan felt a cold hand squeezing his heart. If they knew about the house sale and hadn't said anything, what else did they know? And what did she mean by "move in with…someone"?

"I'm not moving in with anyone," he said.

"Okay."

"Or buying a house or condo."

"All right," Cara said neutrally as if he'd just said he preferred French fries to onion rings with his lunch.

"In fact," he said, feeling the need to justify himself even though part of him was irked that he felt that way, "I plan to take one of the houses I'm building for myself."

"You do?" Cara asked, interest finally showing in her eyes.

"Yes. I've already picked it out and planned next year's Thanksgiving dinner with Violet and my parents, if you want to know."

"That's nice. But I didn't ask you that."

"Yes, you—"

"I simply asked, on behalf of the zoning board, if you were planning to live on the island or have your new unnamed development run by a manager of some sort."

Unnamed. Yes, he was aware of that, but he'd deal with it later when he was ready to start selling lots. For right now, calling it the stable property sufficed.

"Now you know."

"Thank you," Cara said. She continued along the road, leading her horse as if their conversation was no big deal, even though Ryan felt as if he'd opened the first lock in a combination series that would lead to him revealing far too much.

He started walking, following her along the road and matching his breathing to his footsteps. In for two steps, out for four. It was a trick he used whenever he needed to calm down and focus his brain on an important job or while solving a difficult problem. Unfortunately, the horse's steps, four to his two, interfered with his counting, and he had to give up.

He caught up with Cara and walked alongside her in silence.

"And the other question about the commercial properties?" she asked.

"I'm still working on it, and maybe you could help me," Ryan said.

"You want me to tell you what should be in your development?"

Maybe this was a mistake. If Cara was a spiteful person, she might tell him a riding camp was what should be in his plans instead of fancy houses and a store. She might even tell him to go jump in the lake.

"You're a leader in the community, so I thought you'd know what would work, what's lacking on Christmas Island."

"A movie theater," Cara said. "With buttery popcorn and big reclining seats."

Ryan laughed. "I don't have room for that."

"Bowling alley."

"Smaller, but still not exactly the direction I was going."

"Indoor pool so we can stay fit all year round. With a rec center."

They'd just come up on the roadside sign advertising the plot of land for sale.

"Also a great idea, and I agree islanders would love it, but you do know I only have ten acres, and I want to keep the horse barn, add an outdoor arena and build as many houses on decent-sized lots as I can, right?"

Cara shrugged. "I've started to have big dreams lately, unattainable though they may be."

"I don't think your idea of a riding camp for kids is unattainable."

He expected a retort or at least for her to brush off his statement. Wasn't he the one currently standing right in the way?

Cara looked over and made brief eye contact. "Thank you."

"I mean it."

She stopped and let her horse pick at some grass alongside the road. "My family was a bit chilly toward the idea. I think it was mostly because of the way I was going to make the down payment."

"Were you planning to rob a bank?"

"They think I was planning to rob myself by using my college fund."

"Ah, I wondered."

"I suppose you didn't think a candy girl like me could come up with the cash."

"I didn't know your situation, but Gary said…"

Cara hadn't wanted to hear Ryan's explanation about Gary's choice to sell the land to him instead of Cara before, and he hated to lay it on her now. Unless she wanted to hear it.

"He hasn't called me," Cara said. "We've texted a bit, mostly about the horses. If we ever have a conversation about why he sold you the land without giving me a chance, it should be in person or at least in a phone call and not a text."

"I can see that," Ryan said. It had been a text from Poppy that had utterly destroyed his world. Not that a phone call would have changed the outcome.

"What did he tell you?" Cara asked. She kept the reins in her hand but gave him all her attention.

"He said he'd always thought about leaving

it to you in his will because he knew you'd never have the money to buy it, but when he went to visit his family, he didn't want to cheat his own nieces and nephews. He sold it to me before he could change his mind, but I could tell the decision ate him up."

Cara blew out a long breath. "I wish he'd asked me. If we'd had a direct conversation about it, I could have told him I might have a plan. We could have worked it out. But now, well, I guess I've learned a lesson about not directly asking for what I want."

"I'm sorry, Cara," Ryan said.

"You weren't sorry enough to turn him down and tell him you knew I wanted it."

"The timing—"

Cara held up a hand. "There's no sense beating a dead—ugh, I hate that expression."

"Is all hope lost, though?" Ryan asked. There had to be a solution. Wasn't that what he was good at? Making plans, putting ideas into action and concrete structures. He'd thought it was his superpower, building things, until he'd discovered that he had a very powerful kryptonite in the form of emotions getting involved. Poppy. If only he'd seen that coming.

Emotions right now made him want to slice his land down the middle and give Cara half of it to build her camp. But that would be a financial disaster for him because he needed to squeeze revenue from every corner of the property to dig himself out of the hole he was in. He couldn't be blinded by feelings again, no matter how different Cara was from Poppy or how long he'd known her and her family.

Ryan had to put his own business first if he hoped to hire back the guys he'd laid off and restore Brookstone Builders to what it could be—what it once was.

Determined as he was to keep his head and heart separate, he couldn't resist one little suggestion that was staring them both in the face.

"This looks like a nice piece of property," he suggested. "It has lots of big trees and a nice secluded feeling. It looks like at least five acres. Wouldn't this work for your camp?"

It seemed like an utterly logical suggestion, so why had Cara's pleasant expression turned sour as if she'd eaten something she hated? He had no idea what the asking price of the land was or how much Cara was willing to spend. In fact, he didn't know her business plan at all, and it was none of his business. He was treading on thin ice with her as it was, and trying to nose into her business would guarantee a cold fall through that ice.

"Let's talk about your business," she said. "And what commercial venues you're actually going to put in there that the zoning board will appreciate."

"Okay," Ryan said.

"Five minutes, and then we're getting back on the horses. I don't want them to get cooled off too much walking on this road."

"Five minutes. Okay. I'm thinking a convenience store, as I might have mentioned before. Snacks, drinks, some groceries—"

"There's a grocery store right downtown."

"Maybe not actual groceries. Maybe more like grab-and-go sandwiches and…toothpaste and stuff like that."

"Okay," Cara said. "There are restaurants downtown, too, but you could argue another one could be useful during the high tourist season. I think you might want to dig a bit deeper, though, into your actual reasons. Why do you want stores at all? Why keep the stable? Why not just build houses if that's your thing?"

Ryan felt as if someone had lain down a challenge, and he was walking under bright spotlights. Why did he want those things?

"When I first heard the property might be available—"

"Wait," Cara said. "Did you have this plan already, or did your hearing about Gary's selling cause you to make the plan?"

The truth was he'd been casting about desperately for some face-saving project he could latch on to at the time, something on the smaller side that he could finance with the sale of his house. The added bonus of retreating to the place where he'd grown up had been impossible to resist.

"It all sort of happened at the same time."

"I see. And what appealed to you about it?"

He couldn't tell her the whole truth. Not yet. She'd think he was a fool for getting involved in a bad deal and a bad relationship and tanking his own business. Would she vote against him with the zoning board out of a lack of confidence, or would he just feel small—which was almost worse?

"Christmas Island. The community. I haven't been living here lately, but it's home."

"Okay," she said. "So you want to evoke a

sense of community with your development. Like an old-fashioned postcard with the barn and houses and a cute little general store."

Was she mocking him or putting the whole plan quite succinctly?

"Um, yes."

She nodded. "It could work."

Without another word, she swung into the saddle and turned back toward town. Ryan mounted up and followed, convinced he'd avoided disaster with Cara's opinion of him and maybe even gained a little favor. She was being polite to him because she worked for him and because he was an old friend in that tight-knit group of kids who'd grown up on the island. But was it just tolerance and good manners, or did she look forward to seeing him every day just a little bit?

He needed her vote, but the more time he spent with her, the more he wanted her approval.

CHAPTER TWELVE

ON THE SECOND Wednesday of November, Cara joined her sister and their friends Rebecca and Violet in the back of Violet's store for a momentous occasion.

"Wait a second," Violet Brookstone said, jumping up from the velvet ottoman in the changing area in the back of her boutique. "I have to put up the Closed sign and lock the front door so nobody wanders in and sees the dress before the wedding."

Camille laughed. "I highly doubt Maddox is lurking out there hoping for a glimpse of his bride six weeks before our wedding."

"You never know," Violet said. "If he knew how gorgeous you look in that dress, he'd be tempted to trespass. Any man would."

Cara stood behind her sister as Camille viewed herself in the triple mirror. Her older sister Chloe's Christmas wedding had been spectacular, and Cara hadn't been at all surprised that Chloe stole the show in her gown. But Camille's wedding dress was also perfect. Cara smiled. Both her older sisters were Christmas brides on Christmas Island. Her heart skipped when it occurred to her that people might expect the same of her...someday.

Right now, there wasn't anyone she knew that she'd marry. And she had too many other plans demanding her attention. She was quite happy being a maid of honor and cheering her sisters on as they found true love. It was one of the nice, safe things about being the quiet, youngest sister.

"Wow and wow again," Cara said. "Rebecca slayed us all in her wedding gown, and now the expectation for Christmas Island brides is going to be set so high no one will ever want to get married on this island again."

Camille laughed. "I hope that's not the case. Maddox and Griffin want to start hosting more weddings at the Holiday Hotel, especially during the winter when the Great Island Hotel is closed. It's good income and also really fun, and our sweet shop gets to make the cakes."

"Lucky us that no one wants to take a wedding cake on a ferry boat," Cara said.

"It could be done, but it's not ideal," Camille said.

"It's snowing," Violet said as she came back into the room. "Just a few pretty flakes coming down, but now I'm in the Christmas spirit."

"Me too," Camille said. Her gown was sparkling white satin with long sleeves and a narrow red sash at the waist. It would have been Christmas perfect as it was, but the white velvet jacket with emerald green beads around the collar and cuffs completed the look.

The back door opened. "I'm here," Melinda Peterson announced, but then she stopped in her tracks when she saw her daughter. Snowflakes sparkled in the older woman's hair and on her shoulders, but she didn't even seem to notice. "Oh, honey. Oh, my goodness. You're so, so beautiful." Tears streamed down her cheeks, and Cara could see Camille's eyes getting watery.

She grabbed a tissue. "No tearstains on the dress."

Violet knelt and examined the hem. "I'm happy with it. I'm glad we went a half inch shorter than planned in case there's snow on the ground. You don't want to try dancing with a wet hem. Ick."

"It's perfect," Melinda said. "That jacket is amazing, and I hope you'll wear it again after your wedding."

Knowing her practical sister Camille, Cara guessed she'd already considered that.

"Are you trying on bridesmaids gowns tonight?" Melinda asked.

Rebecca, Violet and Cara shook their heads in unison.

"They didn't come in yet," Violet said.

"But the wedding is in only six weeks," Cara's mom said.

Violet sighed. "I know. I called the company and said a few mildly salty things, and they assured me we'd see the gowns next week." She squared her shoulders. "That will still give us plenty of time for any alterations, which I will do myself, of course. I should have just made the dresses in the first place, like I did for Rebecca's wedding, but with all the work on Jordan's house, I—"

"Stop," Camille said. "It'll be okay. And if the dresses never come in, we'll recycle the bridesmaids' gowns from Rebecca's wedding."

Cara laughed. "I was hoping to wear that again."

"It's not going to come to that," Violet said. "Now everyone admire Camille for three more minutes, and then we're putting this gown in a safe place until the big day."

Cara's mom snapped pictures with her phone, although Camille told her she couldn't share them with anyone before the wedding, and then Violet helped Camille out of the gown.

"Want to order pizza?" Rebecca asked. "Griffin is having a guys' game night with his brother and nephew, so I'm free for dinner."

Melinda grinned. "Ron has leftovers in the fridge, so he won't starve. I just want to get home before too much snow comes down. I can't afford a slip and fall during the busy Christmas candy season."

"I'm in for pizza if we could get it here pretty quickly," Cara said. "I have a zoning board meeting at six thirty and then a village council meeting at seven."

"Violet and Camille, we're ordering pizza out there, okay?" Rebecca called through the dressing room door.

"Pepperoni," Camille called.

"Black olives," Violet added.

"Works for me," Cara said.

"Me too," Melinda added.

"That's easy," Rebecca said. She dialed the only island pizza delivery open in mid-November, ordered two large pizzas and then plopped onto the velvet love seat in the back room of Violet's boutique. "They weren't busy and said the pizza would be here in less than half an hour, so you'll make it to your meeting with plenty of time."

Cara's mom and her friend Rebecca gave her a serious look, and she guessed what was coming.

"How's the zoning thing about Ryan's…the stable property going?" Melinda asked gently.

"I'm only one opinion," Cara said. "The true vote lies with the full council."

"And?" Rebecca asked.

"It's complicated," Cara said. "I shouldn't really talk about it outside the zoning board meetings or the village council meetings, which are public record, and you're free to attend if you want, but I'll tell you it's not the slam dunk I think Ryan was expecting."

"Why not?" her mom asked.

"It's a big development. There are at least twenty things to check off on the zoning application. Plus, he has the issue of asking for the property to be rezoned from recreational to commercial."

"Gary ran a business there," Rebecca said. Knowing Rebecca with her head for business, numbers and logic, she probably had the zoning map of the entire island in her head. She had been instrumental in guiding the May brothers with their business expansion the previous summer and autumn and could probably help Ryan out a lot if she wanted to.

"But Gary's business was grandfathered in because it was there before the village codified the zoning regulations. Ryan has to go through the process just like anyone else would have to," Cara said. She didn't mean to sound defensive, as if she had to justify herself to her family and friends.

Her mother nodded. "He certainly does. And we don't have to talk about this, honey."

"It's okay. I'm trying to be fair and unbiased in my role on the board, and I'm over being mad at him for buying the stable."

"You are?" Camille asked.

"I hauled it out with the manure a few days ago so it would stop weighing on me."

"I'm still mad," Violet said as she emerged from the changing room with a dress bag held up high so it wouldn't drag on the carpet. "He never even told me, his only sister, he was doing that. I still haven't figured out what the secrecy was about or what the hurry is."

Cara shrugged. "You'd have to ask him."

"I have, but he either clams up or finds a very subtle way of reminding me that there's a lot of work left to be done on Jordan's house before I consider it move-in ready, and I should spend my extra energy on that," Violet said.

"There is a lot of work to be done," Camille agreed. "But I love that you're working together to fix it up. That's a great start in life."

"Well," Melinda Peterson said, "I'm proud of you for doing the right thing, and I hope you haven't given up on your idea about the horse camp."

This was the first time her mother had brought it up, and Cara was surprised she had raised the topic in front of her friends. Did that mean she had warmed up to the idea of Cara spending her college fund on some property, or did her mother think the topic was safe now that there was no immediate purchase on the radar? With the stable property gone, it definitely slowed and even totally stalled Cara's ambitions.

"I haven't," Cara said. "Camille went with me to look at some land for sale up by the airport. I'm thinking about it."

She noticed the quick look her mother shot Camille, and it was clear Camille had not mentioned the land visit to their mother. They had been in the vault, and the whole family respected the sacred silence of the car.

"Good," her mother said. "If your father and I can help, just let us know."

"I will," Cara promised. Maybe things would work out.

As she sat in the village council meeting over an hour later, the warmth of the time with her mom and friends and the cheesy delicious pizza cooled off as soon as she saw Ryan enter and take one of the lone public seats in the front row.

He wasn't going to like what he heard.

HE KNEW HE'D answered the questions the best he could right now. Cara was his liaison, and she was on his side...wasn't she? Still, Ryan waited out the lengthy reading of the minutes from the previous meeting and then new business, which included a discussion about an island-wide promotion to encourage tourism on the upcoming Thanksgiving and Christmas holidays, and a preliminary discussion of plans for the next fiscal year and what improvements with tax dollars might be included.

"Committee reports," Gina announced.

Finally. This was where the zoning board and whatever other committees were involved in island leadership would report out to the group. He had his fingers crossed the zoning board would hand over his permit requests for a vote of the larger group.

The leader of the island's safety board brought up the matter of a new fire truck, and some discussion followed regarding the bidding process for such a purchase and a needs study. The parks and recreation board chair reported that the committee had finalized plans for the temporary ice rink to be installed near the marina. A fall through the ice on one of the island's inlets where residents frequently met to skate had caused a public demand for a safe skating place.

Ryan was happy to know Christmas Islanders would have a safe space to skate and that the rink would open by the first of December, but he was ready to lose his mind waiting for his building permit to come up.

Shirley raised a hand when Gina asked for any other committee reports. "The zoning board has an update."

Update. That did not sound good. It didn't sound at all like a submission for a vote, which was what he desperately needed.

"Concerning the matter of the unnamed housing development proposed by Ryan Brookstone," Shirley said. Ryan noticed she did not look at him, which he considered a bad sign. And once again, the issue of the property being unnamed seemed to ruffle feathers. He should ask Cara for a good suggestion. Maybe he'd catch her between horses at the barn in the morning or, better yet, stop in the candy store in the afternoon and get a treat to take back to his neighbor, Penny.

"The zoning board is working through the permit application along with the request to change the zoning designation from recre-

ational to commercial, but our board had a
few questions for Mr. Brookstone that remained unanswered. He will have the opportunity to amend his application before
the next board meeting in two weeks, and
we may bring it forward for a vote at the December meeting if everything is in line."

Ryan stood up. He was right there. Sitting
in the front row. If they had questions... And
why hadn't Cara gone back to Gina and Shirley with the answers he'd provided? She'd
seemed satisfied with them. Or was she stalling his plans?

"Public participation will come later in the
meeting," Gina said. She gave him a look
over her reading glasses, and he sat down.

Gina waited a good fifteen seconds and
then adjusted her reading glasses and read
from the agenda. "Public participation."

Ryan wanted to jump out of his seat, which
he'd just taken, but he tried to appear professional and collected. He stood slowly and
tugged at his shirt collar.

"State your name and address for the record," Gina said. "And you have five minutes
to address the council."

He reminded himself to breathe. "Ryan

Brookstone, twelve and a half Lake Lane, Christmas Island." He remembered giving the barn's address the last time he spoke, but now he had half a rented seniors' duplex. Was he moving up in the world? "I just want to say—" he turned toward Shirley and Cara, who were seated to the right of Gina "—that if there is anything I can clear up or any assurances I can give the zoning board or the council at large regarding my plans for the project at the stable property, I am available right now or any time at your convenience, and I am anxious to get this project moving so it can be an asset to the community."

Gina's expression could be summed up as curious, Shirley's as skeptical and Cara's as a complete mystery. Her cheeks were pink, as they had been the day they went riding, but there had been a cool breeze that day. Why was she flushed now? Did she know something she wasn't telling him?

She didn't owe him anything. He reminded himself of that fact. But lately the ice between them had seemed a bit less jagged and fragile.

"Thank you," Gina said. "I'm sure the zoning board will keep that in mind."

Ryan didn't move. Was that it? Was he just

being dismissed? He'd kept his savings in a passbook account in the bank where Gina worked when he was a kid. He'd gone on grocery missions a hundred times for his mother, cash and a list in hand at Shirley's store. They knew him. Why couldn't this be a simple rubber stamp?

"Anything else, Mr. Brookstone?" Gina asked.

"I…I guess not."

He sat back down, and the meeting adjourned. He heard the council members chatting about how the snow was really coming down, and they were all shrugging into their winter coats and pulling on their hats as if they were in a hurry to get home. Ryan only had about a block to walk, and there was no reason to rush home to sit there by himself, frustrated and listening to the evening game shows through the wall that adjoined Penny's apartment.

Zipping his parka, he stepped around the empty seats allotted for the audience and held open the door for Gina to pass through. Cara was right behind her, and Ryan continued to hold the door for her. Gina got in her car, but

Cara started toward her family's home a few streets over.

The first block of her walk would match his, and Ryan fell into step alongside her as the thick snowflakes fell around them.

"It's getting slippery fast," he said, not wanting to startle Cara, who may not have heard his muffled steps in the fresh powder.

"It's beautiful, though," she said. "I love the snow all the way up until March, and then I'm ready for it to stop and be spring."

Ryan laughed. "We've got a long way to go before March is here."

"It'll go fast," Cara said. "With the holidays and my sister's wedding and then Valentine's candy to make. Time flies."

"That's what I'm worried about," Ryan said. "Can I ask what is causing the delay on my application? I thought I'd given you adequate answers, but Shirley seemed as if she didn't—"

Cara stopped and faced him, and snowflakes began turning her blue hat white under the streetlight. "Didn't what? Didn't get the answers? Are you accusing me of purposely not reporting back to the committee with what you said?"

"No," Ryan blurted. Okay, maybe. But he certainly felt like a jerk for thinking that now. With the snow sparkling on Cara's lashes and the beautiful stillness all around them, the last thing he wanted to do was argue with her. He reached out and put a hand on her parka sleeve. "Cara, I…" He didn't know what to say. His desperation to save his company and save himself didn't mean he was going to throw away or further damage his relationships with people he'd grown up with and who were part of his life again. People who would be part of his future life if he got what he wanted.

Cara glanced at his hand on her arm, but she didn't shake it off. Instead, she seemed to sway a bit closer to him, or was it the dizzying effect of the snowflakes swirling around?

"I should get home," she said.

"I'll walk you."

"It's only one more block."

"Then," he said, and hesitated a moment. "Would you stop in and have a cup of coffee with me?"

The duplex he shared was visible, its porch light gleaming through the snow. Aside from Penny and a fleeting visit from his sister, Ryan hadn't had company—except for his own thoughts and regrets and worries. Maybe if he and Cara sat down on neutral territory, a place owned by neither of them and with no history for either one, they could make some progress on the obstacle between them and between him and his goals.

He was sure she would say no. He'd practically accused her of stonewalling him, and it was snowing heavily. Anyone else would tell him to forget about it and go on their merry way.

"Do you have a coffeepot? I assumed you just came to the barn every day and used that one."

"There's a pot on the kitchen counter. It belongs to MaryAnna, but she told me in the rental agreement to use anything I want."

"She's a nice lady. Do you know she used to be a professional watercolor artist before she retired to the island? She had a gallery in Petoskey."

Ryan smiled. "No, but that explains the artwork hanging all over the apartment, all scenes from Christmas Island and really quite good. You should come in and see them."

Cara glanced up at the snow, and a flake landed on her nose. She brushed it off and smiled. "Okay."

CHAPTER THIRTEEN

IT HAD BEEN entirely her choice and saying no would have been the easiest thing to do. But Cara followed Ryan to the threshold where matching side-by-side doors divided his half of the duplex from his neighbor Penny's. No doubt Penny would hear the door, but Cara didn't think she would rouse herself from her easy chair and peek out, expecting only Ryan coming home late.

Not that it would matter if she were seen entering Ryan's house. They were both adults, unattached, old friends. A friend of the family, really. Hadn't she spent an hour with his sister earlier in the evening eating pizza and talking about weddings? But then the zoning meeting and council meeting had put up a wall against that friendliness.

Inside the door, Ryan stopped to take off his boots, and Cara did the same. Thick snow clung to the tops of her boots, and she put them carefully in the rubber boot tray inside the door next to Ryan's and a pair of small rain boots with flowers painted onto the rubber. MaryAnna must not have needed those boots in Georgia.

"The kitchen is this way," Ryan said, even though its location was obvious in the small apartment. A living room to the right, kitchen straight ahead and a bedroom and bathroom on the other side of the living room. It was a mirror image of the place it adjoined. She'd been in Penny's apartment before, not anything unusual on a small island where the year-round residents looked out for each other. Cara remembered dropping off candy for Christmas, picking up a blanket being raffled for charity and displayed in the candy shop's window, and taking food over one winter when part of the downtown was out of power but Cara's house was lucky enough to have it.

In the small kitchen, Cara took the chair by the radiator, and Ryan filled the pot at the sink. "I could just do hot water, and we could have tea or cocoa instead of coffee," he said.

"Cocoa sounds nice," Cara said. "I have a

sweet tooth even after growing up making candy almost every day of the year."

Ryan got a box of instant cocoa packets from a cabinet. "Cheater cocoa okay?"

"I'm not fussy."

While the pot gurgled, Ryan sat across from Cara at the table. She waited. Clearly, there was a reason he'd invited her in, and she was certain it was about his zoning request. There was no other reason he'd choose to spend time with her alone unless it was for business at the stable or because he needed her help with the village council.

"It's nice to just talk," he said. "And we don't have to talk about my application. I don't want to put you on the spot."

Interesting. But she wasn't getting suckered in by the way the dim light in the kitchen reminded her of early mornings and late evenings working with him at the stable back when they were young.

"Let's get that out of the way first," she said. "The board needs time to consider the impact of water usage and evaluate the trunk line going to the property."

"That's all?"

"It's a big deal," Cara said. "But it's not all.

The water department is basically one full-time guy and a seasonal helper, so getting his opinion isn't going to take long."

"There must be something else," Ryan said.

On the kitchen counter near a back door, a birdhouse Cara recognized as being from the park by the marina lay partially disassembled. Seeing it took her back to when Ryan had been known as the kid who loved to build stuff. He'd sought out projects large and small around the island and had repaired things at the stable that summer that Gary hadn't even known needed fixing.

It was one of the things she liked about him, one of the things that had drawn her to him as if she were on a boat drifting toward shore...

He'd always known what he wanted. That was the essence of Ryan Brookstone. It was his quiet confidence that she'd found irresistible. Did he still have that quality? He did seem focused on getting what he wanted—this housing project—but where was the quiet confidence, the sense of purpose that always showed itself in his posture and his easy smile?

"I think I...I mean we, the zoning board, wonder what you really want."

"What do I want?" he asked. Emotions ranging from surprise to frustration crossed his face, and Cara almost regretted asking...but no. Her question must be right on the mark if it elicited such a strong reaction.

Ryan got up and retrieved two thick mugs, blue and red, from the counter. Cara noticed the cabinet doors were off, and all the contents were stacked neatly on the counter below.

"Is there something wrong with those cabinets?" she asked, giving Ryan a slight reprieve before tackling her more difficult question.

"I told MaryAnna I would rebuild them while I'm here. They've started to sag, and the shelves are too high and too deep for her. It's the least I can do in exchange for a place to stay on an island that doesn't offer much in housing, as we both know."

"I know."

"Then why are you questioning why I'd want to build a housing complex?"

"No one is questioning that. It's what you do for a living," Cara said.

She got up and took her mug to the counter, standing elbow to elbow with Ryan in the small kitchen as if they were…what? A couple? They were not a couple. All her preteen fantasies about him noticing her while he was busy building something were staring her right in the face. He was building something a lot bigger than a birdhouse now, and if he noticed her at all, it was only because he needed her.

In her quest to be someone more than just the youngest Peterson sister—a quest that she'd made very little progress on aside from her service on the village council—Ryan and whatever interest he did or did not have in her would only stand right in her way.

"I'm sorry I'm in your way," he said, as if he had read her thoughts. He moved aside so she could reach the pot filled with hot water. Then he tore open two packets of hot cocoa mix and poured one in each cup. Cara followed up with the hot water.

As if they were a well-oiled team. Which they were not.

Ryan took two spoons from the drawer next to the sink. "I wish I had little marshmallows to offer you, but I—"

"It's okay," Cara said quickly. "It'll be fine just as it is."

Ryan leaned against the counter and stirred his cocoa instead of taking one of the chairs, and Cara did the same. Their cocoa was too hot to drink, and they needed to fill at least two minutes with conversation.

"I wanted to come home," Ryan said quietly.

Cara held her breath, hoping he would elaborate. Was this the moment when he said he'd missed the people, especially the ones who were special to his heart? He'd already basically told her this, although she suspected there was more. She waited, stirring her drink, and finally she decided she needed to take charge of the conversation.

"Is that what you want me to tell the zoning board?" she asked.

Ryan took a sip of his drink instead of answering, and she knew from the way he flinched that it was still too hot and he'd burned his mouth. But he didn't look at her.

"You can tell them what you want, but it's the truth." He stirred his drink faster and then turned around and placed it on the counter. He put both hands on the edge of the counter and then looked up at Cara. "Do I need to have a good reason to come back to the place

I grew up and want to do something good for the island?"

At the expression in his eyes, something inside Cara melted. If her hands weren't clasped around the hot mug, she would have touched him. Perhaps just laid her hands over his as they gripped the counter's edge. She might have put her hands on his cheeks and cradled his face—the handsome face she'd once dreamed would look at her with something—recognition, attraction…love?

If she didn't leave right away, she would be too tempted, and she would end up disappointed.

"I should go," she said.

She put her untouched mug of cocoa in the sink, tugged on her boots and walked out into the snow, where the cold reminded her that she had a long road to go if she wanted to do what was best for herself instead of spending all her time pleasing other people.

HE'D WANTED TO kiss her. The next morning, Ryan stood in the punishing November chill on the open ferry deck, hoping to blow some sense through his brain. The last time he'd let his emotions get involved in something that was an important business deal, he'd destroyed his own world. The destruction wasn't even over. The civil suit his attorney had filed against Poppy and her father had finally reached the deposition stage, where they would take statements from the parties involved.

It was humiliating that some of those statements would come from men who'd worked for Ryan and trusted him. They were out of work now. Facing the holidays with either no jobs or new jobs during the very slow construction season in Northern Michigan. And now they'd have to testify about anything they knew about the project Ryan had staked everything on. Not that they knew much. He didn't involve even his longtime dedicated employees in his decisions.

He didn't involve anyone. Except for once. And look what a mess he was in now. It was a good reminder that whatever feelings might populate the air between him and Cara, they needed to stay far away from the reality of business decisions. He couldn't afford another mistake, or he would truly have nothing to his name.

The civil suit, if it was successful, would generate enough money to pay his legal fees and add some breathing room to his bank account. It was also about principle, although principle wouldn't put his men back to work. The island housing project could do that, but he couldn't ask them to wait forever, and his bank sure wasn't going to wait.

The cold wind off the lake didn't clear his head; it just made his ears cold, so Ryan finally got back in his truck and waited out the rest of the ride back to the island. The truck's bed was filled with construction supplies for his sister's future home with Jordan. Luckily, Violet and Jordan were footing the bill for materials, and Ryan's main function was physical labor.

Thank goodness he had a project while he waited out the zoning board and held his breath, anticipating the next meeting.

There was a knock on the window of his truck, and Ryan saw Griffin May standing at his door.

"You didn't come up in the pilot house today," Griffin said.

"Too cold," Ryan said. The truth was he wasn't in the mood for company, even the company of his old friend. Maybe Griffin would understand better than anyone else.

He ran a business, and the ferry business had almost gone under a few years back. Griffin had dropped out of college to come home and save it with grit and hard work. With his brother, Maddox, they'd undertaken a risky but bold move to expand the business before they knew they were the recipients of a large inheritance from Flora Winter.

Griffin would understand the desperation to save a business and the difficulties posed by the island location, but Ryan couldn't unburden himself. Not yet while things were still up in the air.

"Understood," Griffin said. "Got a big package for your sister that's marked urgent. It came to the depot this morning. I thought it might be something for the project at Jordan's house."

"I'm not expecting anything to come from parcel delivery," Ryan said. "Must be for her boutique. Will it fit in the cab?"

Griffin nodded. "We can slide it into the back seat if there's not much else back there."

A short time later after Ryan drove off the ferry, his first stop was Violet's boutique. Whatever was in the package, he didn't want to leave it in his truck and take a chance on forgetting it, especially if it was urgent as the glaring labels implied.

"Thank goodness," Violet said the moment she saw him at the back door. She wasn't looking at him; it was the big oblong box in his hands that had all her attention. "Cara!" Violet said, yelling back into her shop and totally ignoring Ryan. "The bridesmaids' dresses are here."

Cara appeared behind Violet, but her gaze didn't fix upon the box. She looked straight at Ryan. He hadn't seen her at the barn that morning because he'd left for Lakeview on the first ferry. The snowfall from the previous night had been pretty but hadn't added up to much. Still, the air was frosty and Ryan's ears burned with the cold.

Violet grabbed the box and negotiated it through the door, but Cara lingered. "You should come in and warm up for a minute."

His own sister was more interested in her package than in him, although in her defense, he was an adult who'd lived on his own for a long time. Violet didn't need to take care of him any more than he needed to watch over her. But they usually still did. Coming back to the island and getting to see his sister almost every day was one of the things that appealed to him about the move.

Cara didn't have to spare him a glance or invite him in. She was probably either visiting Violet or helping out in the store as she sometimes did in the afternoons when she didn't have a pressing project in the candy store. But Cara held the door open for him.

"Daisy's upstairs if you're worried about your dog allergy," Cara said.

His allergy to dogs was widely known, but it was touching that Cara remembered. Honestly, his hesitation about going inside the boutique was more aligned with his feelings about Cara than his worries about the dog. There was something between them, but there couldn't be. It would put them both in a bad spot, and the last time he should have listened to his gut, he'd failed to do that. He wasn't making that mistake again.

"Just for a minute," he said. His ears really were cold, and he wanted to ask his sister a question about the bathroom remodel at her future home before he tore out the old tile. "And then I'm going to unload the truck up at Jordan's house."

Violet was using a box cutter to very carefully cut the tape on the package. The back room of her boutique contained fussy furniture and a changing area, but it was also toasty warm. Ryan wanted to sit down, but the velvet couches and chairs didn't seem welcoming to a man in work clothes.

"Oh, good," Violet breathed. "When you order things, even when you have a fabric swatch in advance, you can't be sure how the color is going to look. But this," she said, holding up a red dress in front of the window where the natural light washed over it, "this is what Camille had in mind. Don't you think?" she added, turning to Cara.

Cara nodded. "I think she'll be happy. Are all three gowns in the box?"

Violet rummaged past the tissue paper. "Yes. Whew. What a relief. Even if they aren't a perfect fit, I can handle that. I was just worried. You hear horror tales about orders that end up in California or just disappear forever. It would be tough getting a whole new order this close to Christmas."

"I can text Rebecca and see if she can come try hers on," Cara said.

"Good idea," Violet said, and Cara pulled

her phone from her back pocket and sent off a quick message.

"I should go," Ryan said.

Violet waved a hand at him. "It's not bad luck or anything to see bridesmaids' dresses before the wedding, so there's no harm in you sticking around and warming up if you don't have anything else to do. I can count on you to keep your mouth shut and not tell the whole town what the dresses look like, right?"

"I've already forgotten," Ryan said.

Cara held up a dress in front of her and looked in the full-length mirror. The vibrant red contrasted with her creamy skin and dark hair, and she looked beautiful. She'd always been pretty, like her sisters but taller with darker hair. As he watched her consider her own reflection in the mirror, his mouth was dry.

It must be the winter air.

"I love this color," Violet said. "Maybe I should choose red for my wedding."

"When is your wedding, Violet?" Ryan asked, teasing his sister who had yet to select a date despite his parents' numerous hints. "If you gave me the date, it must have slipped my mind."

Violet grinned and swatted him. "You'll be the first to know."

He laughed. "Like I was first to know you were fake engaged to Jordan last summer?"

She screwed up her face. "Do you tell me all your secrets?"

Ryan drew in a breath. She had him there. "Nothing to tell."

His sister flicked a tiny glance at Cara, who was looking at her phone. "If you say so."

There was no way of asking Violet what she meant by that. Did she suspect he had business problems? That there was some reason beyond sentiment that he'd moved back to the island? Worse, did she think there was something going on between him and Cara just because they spent hours together every day?

This was exactly why he needed to compartmentalize and stay focused.

"Rebecca's on her way. I wish Chloe could be here, but she probably won't come over until the weekend."

"That's okay," Violet said. "I'm going to wait until closer to the wedding to fit her gown because of the baby."

"It's so early, I don't think she'll be showing at all yet," Cara said.

This was all news to Ryan, and his face must have betrayed him.

"They were keeping it quiet, but Chloe's almost three months now, so it's no secret anymore," Cara said.

"Oh," Ryan said. "That's great."

He was no longer cold. In fact, the air in the back of the shop felt superheated. Maybe it was all the talk of weddings and babies and dresses and secrets. Chloe was his age, and now she had a husband and would have a baby. What did he have?

Twelve horses, two donkeys, assorted cats and kittens, a semisturdy barn with a lot of history and ten undeveloped acres that could make or break him.

"Even though it's early, I want to make sure I leave room in the bodice, just in case," Violet said. "A lot can happen before Christmas."

His sister was right about that. In his case, he hoped a lot of productive things happened before Christmas. The zoning board could stop being picky and recommend his project to the village council so he could show enough progress to make his banker happy. That was a priority on his Christmas list.

The front doorbell chimed with a customer,

and Cara left to go greet them, leaving Ryan and his sister alone in the back of the store.

Violet tilted her head and studied him, probably noting his pink ears and cheeks.

"It's hot in here," he said as a proactive measure.

"Do you think so? I think it's just right."

Ryan swallowed. Coming back to the island, he'd thought he'd be walking back into situations where he felt comfortable, easy, as if he'd never left. But he felt as if he were walking along rafters, picking his way carefully so he didn't fall through.

"Did you, uh, want to salvage any of that white tile in the bathroom before I take a hammer to it?" he asked.

Violet shook her head. "No. I don't think it's worth it."

"Agreed," he said. He knew he sounded distracted. He heard Cara out front talking to someone about wool versus nylon for a winter coat. She had a lot of talents. The barn, the candy store, helping in the boutique, being a town leader now...

"Is something going on between you and Cara?" Violet asked.

"No," he said quickly.

"Aside from the fact that you stole her horse camp location, and now she has the power to kill your project with her spot on the zoning board."

"Did she say that?" he asked. Was it a topic of conversation behind his back, and if so, how long would it be before people knew the ugly truth?

"Of course not. You know her better than that."

Did he?

"Ryan," Violet said, moving closer to him and giving him a hug. "I think you're going through a tough time right now, and clamming up about it can't be helping."

The warm hug felt so good he considered telling Violet everything. She was his sister. She would understand and sympathize. But that wasn't how he operated. He solved his own problems, and relying on himself was the only safe bet.

He mustered a smile. "I live in senior housing with all the blankets I could ever need, and I have twelve horses that sometimes even like me. What more could I want?"

CHAPTER FOURTEEN

THANKSGIVING AT THE Great Island Hotel was tradition. The elegant, old-fashioned hotel on a bluff about a mile from downtown Christmas Island officially closed for several months during the winter because it was too hard to heat such a large structure in the harsh island winters, and tourists were few. But they put on a fabulous feast in the formal dining room every year as a gift to the community.

Cara's oldest sister, Chloe, loved every single thing about the island, each tradition, all the trimmings. Camille had been away for seven years, so she was rediscovering some of the traditions as an adult and loving them with a fresh newness. Cara had never left. She'd tagged along with the family for twenty-four of these dinners, not that she could remember the earliest ones.

Cara followed her parents through the lobby of the hotel. Jordan Frome, Violet's fiancé and one of the hotel managers, greeted them at the entrance to the formal dining room.

"Are you working or having fun tonight?" Cara asked.

"Working here is fun," Jordan said. "And I promised Violet and her brother that I'd sit with them as soon as I can. It's nice having a family to sit with this year."

Cara's heart melted. Jordan's own parents and grandparents had passed years ago, and even though he was part of the friend group on the island of people his age, including Violet, now that he was engaged to her, the holiday clearly felt different to him.

Cara smiled. "I should stop taking my family for granted, right?" she said quietly, giving him a little nudge.

"You should do whatever you want, but you can't escape your fate as a candy princess," he said. "I really hope that one of these years, one of you sisters will show up with a candy crown."

Cara laughed. "Chloe is the most likely person to do that, but she couldn't make it tonight because she's having Thanksgiving with her husband Dan's family."

As Cara waved goodbye to him and walked down the long central aisle of the dining room with its mirrored columns and softly glowing wall sconces highlighting the seasonal decorations, she thought about what Jordan had said: "You should do whatever you want." She'd had a front-row seat to his struggle with that same concept last summer. He'd wanted to escape the stigma of his family's poverty and move up in the world of hospitality, even coming very close to accepting a job at a sister property of the Great Island Hotel in another state.

But his love for Violet had kept him on Christmas Island, and judging from the joy that rolled off both of them like waves, he didn't regret it. Was true love so powerful that it could make you change your mind about something you'd always thought you wanted?

Cara arrived at her family's table, where her parents were already seated. There were four seats, one for Camille also, but Camille was standing over at the May table, where Griffin, Rebecca, Maddox and Maddox's son, Ethan, were seated. Camille had a hand on Maddox's shoulder, and she reached into their bread basket and grabbed a roll, eating it and chatting with what was soon to be her new family.

"It looks like it's just us," Melinda Peterson commented when she saw Cara watching Camille at the May table.

Cara smiled. "When they run out of rolls in the basket, she'll be back."

Her dad laughed. "Who says we're sharing?"

From a nearby table, Violet waved at Cara and made a motion for her to come over. Her parents had not flown in for Thanksgiving because her dad had a head cold and didn't want to fly. Her table included Violet, her brother, Ryan, and her fiancé, Jordan, but there was one extra chair.

Cara got up and started toward Violet, but the oddness of her position made her legs feel leaden. The family tables were changing, but she was still at the same old Peterson table.

Not that it was bad. She adored her parents and enjoyed working with them, but wasn't there something else waiting for her? In the past year or so, she'd felt the need for change. Wasn't that why she'd said yes to serving on the village council? Wasn't that desire to define herself a large part of her plan to build a camp where other young people could figure out who they were?

Sitting in the third chair at the family table for another Thanksgiving made her feel stuck, but going to Violet's table, where Ryan had just claimed a chair, leaving one for Jordan and one empty one—how did that feel?

"Cara," Ryan said. "Happy Thanksgiving. Are you sitting with us?"

Cara paused midstep. She wasn't family, even though she'd been a longtime friend of Violet and currently worked for Ryan. The fact that Ryan even asked the question made her wonder…did he want her to? Was it an invitation?

"I'm at the Peterson table tonight," Cara said. "Camille has already abandoned mom and dad, so I better stick around. Like I always do." *Ugh.* Why did she add that last part? It was in her brain, but it sounded bad aloud.

"You look fabulous," Violet said, filling in the awkward silence. "That green sweater dress is perfect for you."

"As you knew it would be when you made me try it on in your store," Cara said.

"Was I wrong?" Violet asked.

"No," Ryan said. "You look beautiful."

Violet swung her attention to Ryan and then back to Cara. What had just happened?

"Finally," Violet said. "I thought you only had good taste in houses and architecture and those birdhouses you populated the island with. Now I know you can appreciate a quality dress."

Cara was grateful that her friend tried to deflect away from Ryan's odd comment about Cara looking beautiful. She expected Violet would bring it up later—perhaps with Ryan and certainly with Cara, but the moment was smoothed over. Not that Cara would be able to forget the way he looked at her.

As if he saw her.

She straightened her spine and added an inch to her height, and then she took a moment to look around the large dining room. She spotted Gina sitting with her family near the windows that overlooked the lake.

"I should go say hello to some people," she said to Violet, "before I eat too much and just want to go home and stretch out on the couch."

"Catch up with you later, and if you spill anything on that dress, turn it inside out and wash it on cold. No dryer."

Cara smiled her thanks and then walked over to Gina's table, where Gina reached up and caught her elbow. "Cara, you know my husband, Richard, and this is his mother visiting for the holiday from Lakeview."

Cara shook hands and said hello.

"Cara is the newest member of the village council, and she's already getting her feet wet with some challenging business on the zoning board," Gina explained to her family. "Never a dull moment on this island."

"No, there isn't," Cara agreed. "I'm also trying to start my own business."

The moment she said it, she was struck by her own boldness but also by how nice it sounded, just to say the words aloud and claim them.

"Good for you, dear," Richard's mother said. "What kind of business?"

"A horse riding camp for kids, where they can have fun and be themselves."

Gina nodded. "Your loan preapproval is good for sixty days."

Sixty days. And she'd already used up half of that being angry with Ryan because he bought the stable property. Sure, she could reapply, but was she serious about doing this or wasn't she? It was time for action.

"Oh, I guess I should do something then, right?"

"I hope you will," Gina said in her no-nonsense way. "But you can always restart the process if you're not ready."

She was ready. Didn't anyone except her see that? But, then again, if they looked closely at her, they'd see a young woman who appeared to be running in place instead of moving ahead.

What was she waiting for?

"It was nice to meet you. Enjoy your dinner," she said, and then she went back to the table her parents had vacated to go to the buffet and pile their plates with a Thanksgiving feast. She looped her purse over the back of her chair and strode toward the buffet with a renewed sense of urgency about her plan. Ryan Brookstone had the property she'd wanted, but she had herself and her plans. She'd moped about losing the perfect location for weeks. She was going to put Ryan and his plans out of her mind and focus on herself.

Cara piled her plate full of mashed potatoes and green beans, skipping the turkey and stuffing and only going for the things she liked. She drizzled gravy over the whole plate and marched back to her table to relish the food.

RYAN MECHANICALLY FILLED his plate at the buffet and walked back to his table. The empty chair next to him with its empty white space on the tablecloth loomed as if it wanted to tell him something. A year ago, he imagined bringing Poppy home to the island and introducing her to his family, his friends and the island traditions. His relationship with her had accelerated quickly when he'd met her and her father during the planning process for a mansion he was building for one of their friends.

It had seemed too good to be true. Was that the reason he'd never told his family he was dating someone and had bought a ring? His pride thanked him for sparing himself that embarrassment, especially considering the engagement had lasted a matter of weeks before he'd realized he was being used and had gotten himself and his company into a dangerous place. There was still hope he'd win the suit and recover some of his losses, but the less said about all of it, the better. He would deal with his own mistake instead of burdening anyone else with his problems.

Ryan put his coat on the empty chair.

"That was interesting," Violet commented as she cut into the piece of turkey on her plate. "Your comment to Cara."

Ryan scanned the entrance to the dining room. Where was Jordan? If he came and sat with them, the conversation could be about his home renovation instead of something personal.

"It's not wrong to tell someone they look beautiful. Especially someone I've known all my life, just like everyone else on the island."

Violet tilted her head. "Is Cara just like everyone else on the island?"

A hotel server paused over their table with a water pitcher and filled their glasses, and Ryan used the interruption to ignore Violet's question.

"Of course Cara isn't like everyone else," Violet said, undeterred by his silence. "She's nicer. The evidence is in the fact that she comes to work at your barn every single day and probably does a great job despite the fact that she should have been the person to buy that place, not you."

Ryan sucked in a breath. No one had been bold enough to say that to him. Except Cara.

"Don't look so shocked," Violet said. "You have a right to do what you did, even though everyone expected Cara to be the heir apparent to that property."

"Isn't she the heir to the candy store?"

Violet wrinkled her nose at him, and he recognized that look from arguments they'd had as children. She wasn't going to let him off the hook now that she'd started.

"You're changing the subject, but I'll say this. Cara doesn't have to work in the candy business all her life just because her family does. I wanted to continue with the family store, even though I did make some big changes turning it into a boutique, but you didn't. You went and made your own fortune."

Ryan wished he could tell her that the supposed fortune he'd made was gone, but he wasn't ready now or possibly ever to admit that.

"Aren't you glad I'm back so you can torture me over Thanksgiving dinner?" Ryan asked.

Violet reached over and touched his shoulder. "I am glad you're back, but I see those shadows under your eyes, and I wonder what you're not telling me."

"Sorry that took me so long," Jordan said. He slid into the seat next to Violet and kissed her cheek. "I tried to get to the table as fast as I could."

"Because you're hungry," Violet said.

He grinned. "Be right back."

He got up and Ryan jumped up, too. "I'll go with you to the buffet. Those mashed potatoes are great."

He knew he wasn't fooling Violet, who would certainly notice he hadn't finished the food on his plate, but he didn't want any more questions. Jordan would be a nice buffer. As he passed the Peterson table, Cara looked up at him and made eye contact, but then she returned to her conversation with her parents. They had a spare chair at their table, too, and he noticed that Cara had put her red coat on it.

He scooped mashed potatoes from the buffet table and stalled until Jordan had piled his plate and started back toward the table where Violet sat waiting for them. Ryan steered the dinner conversation to every practical topic he could think of involving Jordan's home renovation, even little details about light bulbs, cabinet handles and switch plates. He couldn't avoid his sister forever, but he could avoid her tonight, when the holiday and the traditions and the food and candlelight were making him feel sentimental. That must be the reason he'd slipped and told Cara she was beautiful. Would he have said the same thing to Camille or Rebecca or anyone else he'd grown up with?

He didn't want to think about his feelings, but his glance strayed to Cara's table several times, and Violet caught him looking at least once. It was a relief when Jordan suggested they put their coats on and move outside for the tree lighting ceremony on the front lawn. Around them, other diners were donning coats and moving toward the exit.

"See you outside," Violet said as she took Jordan's arm and walked with him. Ryan zipped his dark blue parka and joined the line of islanders making their way toward the lobby where the big front doors would open onto the porch and lawn.

No lights were visible on the many pine trees dotting the Great Island Hotel's lawn as Ryan descended the steps from the porch. Griffin and Maddox were right ahead of him with Rebecca and Camille, and Ryan stuck with them, planning to stay with their group since Violet would likely be with Jordan.

He was surprised when, a few moments later, Violet took his arm and waited with him. "I love this moment," she said. "Even though it's always Christmas on this island, the tree lighting seems like the official beginning of the season every year."

Ryan tucked her arm farther through his and soaked up the atmosphere. Around him, there were nearly one hundred people, the vast majority year-round island residents with a few visiting relatives tossed in. For the past ten years, he'd been the visiting relative, but now he was an islander again. Had it not been for his bad experience with Poppy and his business disaster, would he be here tonight? Probably. But it would be different. He breathed in the night air and scent of pine. Maybe that hard lesson had been good for him, because even though he'd been thinking negatively about it, his problems were the catalyst that had brought him home now.

It certainly hadn't occurred to him to be

glad about it before, but it didn't sting his pride any less to think of it that way.

It had been completely dark for over an hour, and as the clock counted down toward seven, Jordan emerged from the crowd and stood in front of Violet. "I have a surprise for you," he said. "But you have to close your eyes and follow me."

Violet let go of Ryan's arm and laughed. "Okay, but you won't let me trip and fall on my face in front of the whole island, will you?"

Jordan took her hand. "I would never let you fall."

The way he said it convinced Ryan that his sister was in good hands and had made a wonderful match with someone she'd always known and trusted. Jordan and Violet were some of the lucky ones. Ryan watched him lead her away with one reassuring arm around her.

Would he ever trust anyone enough to walk through a crowd with his eyes closed?

"He already proposed," Rebecca said, "so I wonder what the surprise is?"

"I think I can guess," Camille said.

As they waited for the tree lighting, Cara joined them and put an arm around her sister.

"Mom and Dad miss Chloe," he heard Cara say, "but I cheered them up by telling them that next year she'd be here with their grand-child."

"Good move," Camille said. "You're good at knowing what to say, and if you keep it up, you'll overtake Chloe as the favorite."

Cara laughed. "Too much pressure there."

As Ryan listened to Cara and her sister talk, it made him think about Cara's role in her family and her community. She was a sup-porter. Always there to help out. Wasn't she helping him run the horse barn even though it had to hurt her feelings every day when she saw him at Gary's desk? If he took a risk and told her why he'd hurried his purchase of that land, what would happen? Knowing Cara, she'd listen sympathetically, but would it do any good to tell her when it wasn't going to change anything? It wouldn't make her feel better. It would make *him* feel better to get it off his chest.

He wasn't that selfish.

Griffin's phone rang and he answered it, giving the caller only one-word answers. "Okay...yes, got it...I'll get there soon."

"What was that?" Rebecca asked.

"The pilot brought a guest over to the island, and he drove her to the Holiday Hotel and told her to wait in the lobby. I'll go as soon as the lighting is over and get the person a room. Must be someone's last-minute surprise holiday guest."

"Look," Camille said, nodding toward a table decorated with red and green lights. Jordan had led Violet to stand behind the table. The crowd around Ryan fell silent, and he could feel the anticipation in the night air.

"Open your eyes," Jordan said loudly enough for his voice to carry to the spectators on the lawn.

Ryan watched his sister open her eyes and smile. Had she guessed she was going to get to have the honorary position of flipping the switch to light all the trees? If she had, she did a great job of looking surprised and awed. She took Jordan's hand, and together they hovered over the switch while the audience counted down from ten.

White lights illuminated dozens of trees on the lawn, and a few seconds later, the remaining trees lit up red and then green. Ryan cheered and clapped along with the crowd, and people around him hugged and kissed as if it were the stroke of midnight on New Year's Eve.

Camille gave him a big hug and kissed him on the cheek, and when she stepped back, Cara stood alone. He waited a heartbeat, and then she opened her arms, inviting him to step into them.

He'd hugged her before. They were all close growing up. But this time felt different, because it didn't feel as if he were hugging an old friend. His relationship with Cara was...new. She worked for him. He needed her. And he'd taken something away from her that she'd wanted. Her opening her arms to him felt as if she were saying he could trust her and even depend on her.

And he wanted to.

Her hair and jacket smelled just a bit like hay and something sweeter—could it be a candy aroma from the store? He smiled as she stepped back. Those were Cara's two worlds. The barn and the candy store. But she wanted something more than that.

The fact that he wanted to take her hand and walk with her through the illuminated pines and tell her the chain of events that led up to him suddenly buying land and moving back to the island—just the temptation of that and the comfort he believed it would bring him frightened him and made his heart hammer.

He wanted to run before he betrayed himself by telling the humiliating story and asking for...what? Help? Forgiveness?

He was the only person who could help himself out of the jam he was in, and pressuring Cara to move his building application along out of pity would be unfair and unkind to her. It would put her in a terrible position.

He dragged in a long breath and noticed Cara doing the same thing. His mind was reeling, but what was she thinking? Did she see something in his expression that changed the air between them?

Cara opened her mouth and began to speak, but Ryan interrupted her.

"Happy Thanksgiving," he said, and then he turned and walked through the glowing trees, brushing past the emotion of the holiday and his own situation before it got to him.

CHAPTER FIFTEEN

CARA ARRIVED EARLY at the barn after a restless night. She'd eaten too much. That was all. Her lack of sleep had nothing to do with Ryan's hug. Or the way he'd looked at her. She'd redirected her thoughts at two in the morning to her own future and plan. It was the day after Thanksgiving, a traditional day of shopping, and she was going to honor that holiday by shopping for the right piece of land on the island, even if she had to get creative and beg someone to sell her something.

Ryan's car wasn't there, but his office door was open. Had Gary still owned the barn, she would have had no reservations about going into the office and helping herself to the coffeepot. It could be an hour or more before Ryan showed up, and her sleepless night needed an antidote.

Cara filled the carafe with cold water and hit the Brew button. She leaned against the counter and enjoyed the scent of coffee percolating. That aroma mixed with horse smells felt like home to her. When she got her own camp and her own office, she'd try to recreate the smell of the old barn mixed with coffee.

The building plans which she'd seen in depth were spread across the desk, reminding her that she'd have to make a decision the next week about her vote. She'd thought Shirley would balk at the convenience store idea Ryan had, but Shirley loved competition in any form. She was fine with it. It was Gina who seemed to have reservations, but she hadn't voiced anything specific.

Cara perused the plans while the coffee dripped into the pot. She wasn't snooping. Ryan had shared the plans with the zoning board. It was public record.

There was a blue folder she hadn't noticed before. Was it part of the development plans? She glanced at the door and listened. There was no one in the barn, and all was silent except for the gentle noises of horses moving around in the early morning. Cara flipped open the folder's cover and saw the name of a law firm at the top.

Ryan had consulted a lawyer about his plans? She read the first paragraph and then read it again. Heart pounding, she closed the folder and stepped back from the desk.

"Helloooo?" a female voice called from the main part of the barn.

Cara's heart felt as if it might jump from her chest. She strode from the office as if it were any normal day and she hadn't seen that paragraph implying there was a lawsuit involving Ryan and two people she'd never heard of.

A woman in an expensive full-length camel tweed jacket stood inside the barn door looking as if she were afraid to take another step and risk getting dirty. Her flaming red hair was sleekly cut and styled, and the purse on her arm would buy a year's worth of candy for the average household.

"Hello," the red-haired woman said. "I'm looking for Ryan Brookstone."

Cara walked toward her with the intention of being friendly even though the woman didn't look inviting. "Ryan isn't here yet, but he should be here pretty soon."

"Who are you?" the woman asked.

"I...I work here."

"What do you do here?" the woman asked.

Cara had a lifetime of customer service experience, but visitors to the candy store didn't usually ask her in a suspicious tone what she was doing there.

"Perhaps I can help you with something," Cara said, "while you wait for Ryan."

"No."

"Are you looking for a horse rental?"

The woman laughed. "Of course not."

Cara smiled. "My mistake. But you are in a horse barn."

"Hmm," the woman grunted.

"I'm Cara Peterson."

There was a long pause in which Cara wondered if the unexpected guest would be willing to stoop to the lowest common denominator and give her name.

"Poppy Newland."

Cara sucked in a breath. That was one of the names she'd noticed in that document in the blue folder. Poppy wasn't a common enough name for it to be a coincidence. Was this woman suing Ryan for something, and she'd come all the way to the island about it?

"How did you get to Christmas Island?" Cara asked. "The ferry isn't running this early."

"I arrived last night on a plane, but the whole town was empty. I had to sit in the lobby of a hotel downtown and wait until someone arrived to get me a room."

Cara almost smiled, imagining the stranger who was clearly accustomed to being waited on as she cooled her expensive heels at the Holiday Hotel. So, that was Griffin's phone call last night just before the trees were lit at the Great Island Hotel.

"The man at the hotel didn't know where Ryan was staying, but he told me I could find him here."

Islander loyalty. Griffin knew exactly where Ryan was currently living, but he didn't know this woman.

Who was Poppy, and why did she come all the way to the island to see Ryan? Had Cara misread that one paragraph? Perhaps there was some...relationship between them. He'd never mentioned anyone and neither had Violet, so if Poppy meant anything to Ryan, it was likely just in a business sense.

Bad business if there was a lawyer involved.

"Is there somewhere I can wait?" Poppy asked, impatience in her tone.

Cara considered putting her in Ryan's office as she would with any other guest, but she didn't know this woman or her objective in visiting. Would Ryan want her to see the plans on his desk or, worse yet, open the blue folder? Despite her differences with Ryan over the purchase of the horse barn, she had islander loyalty running through her veins, too.

"I'll get you a chair," Cara said. She held up a finger. "Be right back."

Cara ducked into Ryan's office, grabbed a chair and then closed the door behind her and locked it. She placed the chair right in front of Drummer's stall door. The big brown horse reached over the door with his nose and sniffed Poppy. The woman shuddered and moved her chair closer to the center aisle, where Drummer couldn't reach her.

"The horses are all named for the song 'The Twelve Days of Christmas,'" Cara said conversationally. "That one is Twelve Drummers Drumming, but we just call him Drummer."

"Did Ryan think of those names?" Poppy asked.

"Oh, no," Cara said. "They've had those names a long time. A few horses have come and gone in the years I've worked here, but we've kept the naming theme."

Cara remembered the sad times when Five Golden Rings had been retired to the mainland and the winter when Ten Lords a Leaping had died. There was a new Goldy and Lord Leapster, and she'd grown to love them, but she never forgot their predecessors. Looking at Poppy's wrinkled nose and stiff posture, she doubted the visitor would be interested in hearing about the beloved horses.

Instead of trying to entertain the person who was not there to see her anyway, Cara went to the tack room and donned her boots and barn coat. She wanted coffee, but she didn't want to unlock that office door and allow Poppy a glimpse inside, because she might ask to wait in there. Inside the tack room, Cara sent a quick text to Ryan to tell him he had a visitor.

His response was swift.

Griffin warned me. Be there in ten.

"Warned." Just that little word told Cara there were things about Ryan's past she didn't know, but if those things would impact his future plans on the island, she might want to find out.

RYAN WAS GRATEFUL to Griffin for not revealing his address and for waiting until morning to tell him a beautiful redhead named Poppy was at the Holiday Hotel asking about him. He'd had enough on his mind as he'd tried to sleep. Namely, that hug with Cara. And the way Cara had looked in that green dress. And the sentimental holiday vibe that had clung to him all the way back to his duplex, where he'd said goodnight to Penny after driving her home.

He'd been spared overnight, but now that he knew Poppy had made her way to the barn at the crack of dawn and had encountered Cara, there was no time to lose. Who knew what Poppy would tell Cara? That thought had him shoving his feet into boots and barreling out his rented front door.

On the very short trip to the barn, driving today instead of walking to shave off precious minutes, Ryan considered the disaster that could ensue if Poppy twisted a story and sold it to Cara, who not only worked for him and kept him awake thinking about her but was a powerful vote on his plans.

Poppy knew all about zoning plans and permits and how it could destroy a project before it even got started. Bitterness rushed through him as he parked and speed-walked to the barn door. What if she was sitting at his desk perusing his plans right now?

When he shoved open the barn door, his first feeling was relief to see his office door shut and Poppy sitting on a chair in the middle of the aisle while Cara groomed Swan at the far end of the barn, too far away for conversation.

"There you are," Poppy said, standing.

Just seeing her was a gut punch. There had been a time when she'd made his heart flutter, but her deceit had cooled any warmth he ever felt for her. How had he been foolish enough to spend big money on an engagement ring—money he was never getting back no matter how the lawsuit turned out?

That was the second most expensive hard lesson of his life. Occupying the top spot was the deal he'd signed onto with Poppy and her father, Herman.

"What are you doing here, Poppy?" he asked. He stood in front of her, arms crossed. The smell of her expensive perfume mingled with the horse barn smell, and Ryan took a step back so he could only smell the horses.

That was a comforting aroma, one he'd grown accustomed to over the past month. He almost smiled, imagining Poppy shampooing her hair five times to get that smell out after spending time in the barn waiting for him.

"I came to see you, obviously. It wasn't easy, and I spent my holiday getting out here. I'd think you'd be a little happy to see me."

"Why?"

Poppy took a step toward him, and her perfume again replaced the cozy barn smell. She put a hand on his arm. "I thought we could talk." She glanced toward Cara, who was doing an award-winning performance of appearing to ignore them. "Is there someplace we could go?"

Ryan gave her a long look. How had he never noticed those hard lines around her eyes and mouth? Despite her beauty, there was a layer of ugliness underneath. He'd tried to believe it wasn't her fault, that she'd been manipulated by her father, used just as he had been. But everyone made choices, even hard ones. He blamed only himself for his stupidity, and he relied only on himself to escape from the consequences.

"We can use the tack room," he said. He

walked past her and stopped in front of Cara. "Do you mind if I use the tack room to discuss something with my…with Poppy?"

Cara mustered a congenial smile. "It's your barn."

"Do I smell coffee?" Poppy asked as she followed Ryan.

Ryan shook his head. "No."

He noticed Cara sucking in her lips as if she were suppressing a smile, but he strode past and motioned for Poppy to enter the utilitarian tack room. Surrounded by the saddles, tack and familiar worn boot bench, Ryan felt as if he belonged there, but Poppy absolutely did not.

"Ryan," she said, moving close to him. He stood his ground without backing up, even though he fought his instinct to do so. Poppy put her head on his shoulder, but he didn't move, keeping his arms at his sides. "Can't we be friends? I know things didn't work out with my father's plan."

"Didn't work out?" Ryan asked. "How about, it was a total disaster I'll be paying for, for a long time?"

"It doesn't have to be that way. Daddy wants to make things right with you and bring you back in."

"No."

"Don't you see what this could mean? We could have a second chance."

"Why are you here, Poppy?"

"To see you, of course. Why else would I come out to this barren little island?"

He wanted to argue that Christmas Island was far from barren. It was very much alive in every way.

"This is my hometown," Ryan said.

"But not your home. Not now anyway. Running back here with your broken heart—"

"I did not come back because of a broken heart. You broke everything else in my life, but not my heart."

"Oh," Poppy said. "Well, I was heartbroken when you called off the engagement."

"You called it off."

Poppy continued as if he hadn't spoken. "And now this lawsuit against us. You can't be serious about pursuing it all the way to the end and hurting me and my family. My father is just—"

"I'm very serious," Ryan said, keeping his voice low. He didn't want Cara to overhear snatches of this conversation and draw any conclusions. If he'd told her about this before, he wouldn't have so much to fear from Poppy giving something away. He silently berated himself for keeping his business so close to his vest that no one knew anything or, worse, knew his side of the story.

"But your lawyer is being very nasty," Poppy said. "He's digging things up that have nothing to do with the failed Crystal Glen development."

Ryan almost smiled. His lawyer was trying to demonstrate a pattern and prove willful negligence and dishonesty. It wouldn't be too hard given what he now knew about Poppy and Herman. "I would guess those things he's unearthing have everything to do with your past behavior."

"It's not fair to lump me in with my father," Poppy said.

"I wish you'd thought of that before you walked into my life and wrapped me around your finger so you could use me."

When he thought of the thousands of dollars of ruined construction supplies that were sitting outside in a locked-off area because of a dispute over ownership of land Herman supposedly had the deed to, it sickened him. He would never forget being removed from that property by law enforcement and having to abandon trusses, wood, siding and truck-loads of construction materials. He'd been a fool for what he thought was love, and the money he'd invested was gone.

Or was it? The fact that Poppy had come to the island and was up to her old games…did that mean she and her father were nervous?

"You should leave. The ferry schedule is limited this time of year, and I don't want you to miss your chance to get off this island," Ryan said.

"Is that all you have to say to someone you once gave your heart to?" Poppy said.

He had to give her credit. She was sticking to her script despite his cold reception. That was how good an actress she was. Or how desperate. Either way, picking up the pieces of his own life didn't involve letting Poppy break him again.

"I'll drive you to the dock," Ryan said. He didn't relish being in the car with her, but he also didn't want her talking to Cara or any-one else. Who knew how much damage she'd already done? Griffin hadn't said anything, so maybe he was lucky, and Poppy had kept her opinions to herself. If she had, it was only because she was trying to save herself.

Ryan was starting to realize that keeping secrets wasn't the path to redemption for him, but if his mistakes were going to become public knowledge, that information was going to come from him, not Poppy.

CHAPTER SIXTEEN

CARA DROVE UP the driveway to Rebecca and Griffin's home. The Winter Palace was decorated for Christmas, and it made the ornate Victorian mansion even more beautiful. The island home of the Winter family had been a showpiece of Christmas Island for over a century. It was often pictured on brochures showing the island's history and tradition. With its three stories, multiple porches and gorgeous architectural details, the home was formal but still inviting. Flora Winter had spent summers there for over eighty years, and she had recently given it to Griffin and Maddox May, islanders she considered the grandsons she never had because of her unrequited love for their grandfather.

"Come in," Rebecca May called from one of the porches overlooking the approach. "Kitchen door is unlocked. I'll meet you down there."

Cara had been in the home countless times. The previous summer, she'd chatted with Ryan there at the annual Summer Solstice Bike Ride. He'd been subdued that night, she recalled, saying something about a bad feeling involving the owner of the mansion he was building.

Could that mansion have anything to do with the visit from Poppy that morning? Cara hadn't stuck around and waited for Ryan to come back after he'd taken off with Poppy. She had arranged a meeting with Rebecca at the tree lighting ceremony, and she didn't want to put her plans aside because of whatever drama was going on in Ryan's life.

She was focusing on herself and her future and not letting anything get in her way.

As she entered the warm kitchen, Rebecca came through a door from the parlor and gave her a hug. "Sit," she said, pointing to the kitchen table. "I've got cinnamon rolls and tea, paper, pencils and my laptop for making spreadsheets. We're in business."

Cara laughed. "I certainly hope so. That's why I'm here."

Rebecca placed cups and saucers on the table and then opened the oven door to check on the cinnamon rolls. "They're ready," she said. She slid on oven mitts and pulled the pan out, and then she turned to Cara. "And I'm ready to hear every detail of your horse camp. I know the basics, but I want to help you put it all on paper."

"You're making me nervous," Cara said, laughing. "It's hard putting yourself out there and telling someone your exact hopes and dreams. When I got the preapproval for a loan, I didn't include any details about what I actually wanted to do with a piece of property. I think Gina assumed I'd buy or build a house, but I'd be willing to live in a tent at my own camp if that's what it takes."

"We'll run the numbers and then decide if you're living in a tent," Rebecca said. "When you got your preapproval from the bank, was it for a business loan?"

Cara moved a roll onto her plate and poured hot water over a tea bag in her cup. "Not exactly. I just wanted to know how much I could borrow based on the amount I had in my college fund. Turns out, it's quite a lot, but I know getting an actual loan is going to take a lot more planning and getting details worked out."

"Your sister Camille is great at business. I don't want to step on her toes by helping you."

"She's the one who told me to ask you. She said you were the smartest person she knows and also that you've helped Griffin and Maddox with their ferry and hotel empire lately."

"Empire," Rebecca said, giggling. "They wish."

"Someday," Cara said. "Camille is also very busy right now with the Christmas candy shipping out and her wedding coming up. We both consider you an honorary sister, so that's why I'm here."

"I'm a candy girl now?" Rebecca asked. "I've come a long way from an orphan being shuffled from house to house."

One of the things Cara had always admired about Rebecca was her willingness to open her heart to people despite her difficult past. She wasn't afraid to talk about who she was and what she wanted in life.

"I'm glad you ended up in this house, and I appreciate your help," Cara said. She drew a thick notebook from her bag. It contained notes, sketches, photographs, articles and artifacts she'd been collecting for years, ever since her first visit to the horse camp on the mainland when she was a kid. "Here we go," she said, opening the notebook's cover.

For the next hour, Cara shared her entire plan for cabins, horses, campers, food, adventures, safety and activities in her planned horse camp. She'd talked with her family and friends about the general idea and why she wanted to create a place for kids to enjoy nature and figure out who they were, but she hadn't laid out the details on paper for anyone else to see.

It was scary but exciting.

Rebecca's kindness and business sense made it easier, and Cara folded up her notebook, now possessing spreadsheets and a strong belief that she could make it work. Rebecca suggested fees campers would have to pay to make the venture solvent, and Cara had a clearer vision for her future than ever before.

"How about names?" Rebecca asked.

Before Cara could answer, Griffin opened the kitchen door and swept in with the cold late November air. "That was an interesting visitor," he said before he saw Cara sitting on the other side of the kitchen table.

"Who?" Rebecca asked.

Griffin clammed up for a minute, and Cara guessed it was because of her.

"If you're talking about a red-haired lady named Poppy who spent the night in your hotel, I already heard about it. Saw her, in fact."

"I didn't give her Ryan's address last night, but I did tell her he could be found at the horse barn this morning," Griffin said. He helped himself to a cold cinnamon roll left on the plate.

"I could warm that up for you," Rebecca offered.

"Thanks," he mumbled with a mouthful, "but it's fine. I wonder what she wanted. Girlfriend, you think?"

Cara sat back, determined to keep her mouth shut about the little she knew. Ryan had a right to his privacy, even though her curiosity wanted answers.

"If she was a girlfriend, he would have been waiting for her when she arrived," Rebecca said.

"She could have surprised him," Griffin said.

"But she would have texted him or at least known where he lived," Rebecca said. "She doesn't sound like a girlfriend to me, at least not a current one."

This was interesting. Cara had seen Poppy's name on the legal document, and she'd acted as if she had some claim on Ryan, perhaps a prior one, but there had been no affection or spark between them that she had seen. Not that she was completely spying on them as she groomed a horse, but the barn wasn't that big. She doubted she'd miss the fact that Poppy was a long-lost love of Ryan's.

After they'd gone into the tack room, Cara had tried not to eavesdrop, but she couldn't help overhearing some of the conversation, at least Poppy's side of it. Her voice was higher and louder. Whatever Ryan had said, it was in a low tone and didn't appear to produce the reaction Poppy had come for.

He'd marched her out the door and hadn't even offered her coffee.

"She came to the barn and they talked, but I don't know anything about her or how long she's staying," Cara said. She couldn't sit there and say nothing. It would look suspicious, as if she knew something and was hiding it.

"She's not staying," Griffin said. "Ryan practically marched her onto the ferry and sure didn't kiss her goodbye."

Cara was relieved that she wouldn't be seeing Poppy around the barn, but why had she shown up, and why did she seem either angry with Ryan or desperate to get him back? She'd heard enough of Poppy's words to know there had been something in the past between them that was clearly over now.

She wanted to get back in his office and read the whole lawyer's document instead of guessing about its contents, but it was none of her business. Unless the lawsuit impacted his ability to come through on his plans for the new island development. Should she snoop in the name of the zoning board's good intentions?

"Maybe she was in a hurry to get back to the mainland to do her Christmas shopping. Black Friday isn't the same on an island," Rebecca said.

"I'll give you a free ride on the ferry if you want to go shopping in Lakeview," Griffin said, kissing the top of Rebecca's head.

She smiled up at him. "I already have everything I need right here."

RYAN SADDLED UP Ten Geese A-Laying. "Ready for some exercise, Goose? I don't know which one of us needs it more right now."

Goose dipped his head and nuzzled Ryan, who gave him an apple to munch while he zipped up a heavy coat and pulled on a hat. Ryan mounted up and walked the horse out of the barn. The day after Thanksgiving was cold but clear. Poppy would have a chilly ride back to Lakeview on the ferry, but it had been her choice not to bring her car across. Maybe she didn't think they had roads on the island. She certainly didn't think much of Christmas Island, but she was usually unimpressed by things that weren't either very expensive or in her range of experience.

Enough of her, he thought as he walked Goose down the back street toward the edge of the island where he could pick up the perimeter road and trot along to a connecting road that would loop him back to the barn. He knew every road and trail on the island from his youth, and they hadn't changed.

As he passed by the Winter Palace on the island's exterior road, he glanced up at the beautiful home where he'd attended parties dozens of times. Rebecca and Griffin lived there now, and they already had the holiday decorations up. Wreaths and garlands made the place look like it was in a Christmas movie. While he gazed up at the house from the saddle, his attention fell on a woman walking across the driveway. She was up the hill but visible, and he would recognize Cara anywhere, especially because he noted her car in the driveway.

What was Cara doing there? She'd finished the morning round of chores at the barn, but he expected she'd be at the candy store until the evening chores as usual. He pulled on the reins and stopped at the bottom of the driveway, wanting to talk to Cara but uncertain what he would say. Maybe it was smarter to move along and save any questions she might have for another day that was further removed from the irritation of Poppy's visit.

He'd almost moved on when her car emerged from between tall pines and stopped at the bottom of the driveway. She unrolled the driver's window, and Goose stuck his head in and gave her a kiss. Cara laughed.

"You're out riding without me," she said. "Not that you can't do that, of course," she added quickly. "They're your horses."

"I needed a ride," Ryan said.

Cara tilted her head and studied him. "Is everything all right?"

There was no avoiding it. Cara had certainly overheard some of the conversation with Poppy, and who knew what Poppy had told her before he'd shown up in the barn? He wasn't ready to tell Cara the whole story—maybe he never would be—although it might help his case with the zoning board if they knew how desperate and committed he was to making the island project a success. Even if he won the lawsuit and had the chance to put back together some of his company, he had no desire to move away again.

Not when he'd found peace on the island.

"You know," he said, swinging down from the saddle and keeping a loose hold of the reins, "I think I ate too much at the hotel party last night, because I had disturbing dreams that lasted until about an hour ago."

Cara smiled, but she didn't get out of her car. "Was there a grouchy red-haired lady in those nightmares?"

"There was. She wanted to drag me back to a chapter of my life that is, thankfully, closed, but this refreshing ride in the cold air has been a very nice wake-up."

"Horses are rehabilitating. That's why I... well, you know. In fact, I just met with Rebecca, and she helped me with my business plan for my camp."

"So, you found some land?" Ryan asked hopefully. If Cara could find a suitable place, he could stop feeling so guilty for buying the stable. It would remove a layer of tension between them and leave room for...what? Friendship? They had that, of course. They were friends just as he was with all the other islanders in their generation. Anything more was a risk he wasn't ready for. The unpleasant visit with Poppy was a stark reminder of how he was better off sealing up his feelings and sticking with building where everything was under his control.

"No," Cara said. "But I'm not giving up, no matter what I have to do."

She patted Goose on the nose but didn't look at Ryan, leaving him wondering if she would stand in the way of his permits in hopes of forcing him to give up and sell the stable property. He hated himself for thinking it of Cara, and he blamed it on the fact that he'd just spent an hour with someone ruthless enough to do it.

Cara wasn't Poppy, but he also wasn't the fool he'd been when he'd made a risky investment that nearly ruined him. If he didn't succeed now, he was really in trouble, and the nasty chain of events begun a year ago would continue haunting him.

He had to do something, but it was going to be one more incredibly hard thing in a long line of recent painful things.

"Cara, can I buy you lunch? Just us?"

"Why?" she asked.

"I need to tell you something." Finally. The surprise Poppy visit had scared him into realizing someone else could tell his story, and he may not be the hero of the telling. He needed to control his own narrative, and he had to trust someone. Cara was in a position to help him or hurt him, and he was going to have to take a risk. "But it's private. I don't want everyone knowing, but I think you should."

"I don't know—" she began.

"Please," he said.

She hesitated a moment and then nodded. "I'll pick up lunch and meet you at the barn."

"I could do that, I wanted to buy."

Cara gave him a lopsided smile. "You're on a horse. I'll get the food and meet you back there. I can promise to listen, but that's all."

"Thank you," he said. He swung up in the

saddle and pointed Goose toward the road
that would wind back to the Christmas Island Stable.

CHAPTER SEVENTEEN

SHE WAS NO FOOL. Ryan wasn't inviting her for a romantic lunch or even a friendly one. Something in him had been shaken loose by Poppy's visit, and he now suddenly felt the need to have a sympathetic ear. And not just any ear. He may not know she was the swing vote on the zoning board, but he knew she was one of three votes.

Cara got containers of the Friday special, mac and cheese, from the Holiday Hotel and made it to the barn at almost the same time Ryan led Goose to the center aisle, where he unsaddled the horse and rubbed him down.

"Office?" Cara asked, holding up the bag of food.

"Sure," Ryan said. "I believe there's an untouched pot of coffee burning away in there, too."

She couldn't help smiling. "Even better."

Cara unlocked the office door and took the

seat across from the desk. The blue folder still lay on top of the drawings, but she didn't reach for it. Reading that first paragraph had been an intrusion, and it was up to Ryan to tell his story now—whatever it was.

"I think the cold weather makes Goose hungry," Ryan said as he came into the office several minutes later. "Me too."

"Horses aren't that much different from people," Cara said. "Although I often prefer their idiosyncrasies over human dramas."

Ryan nodded and offered her a smile. "So, you met Poppy."

"I wasn't necessarily talking about her, but yes. I encountered Poppy and gave her a chair. She didn't have much to say to me because she probably thought I was just any old stable hand."

As she said the words, she thought bitterly that she actually *was* just a stable hand. She had no stake in the stable, no future chance of buying it, no longer the heir apparent to Gary. She fed horses and mucked out stalls for a weekly paycheck because of her loyalty to the animals, but there was no future in it. The plan she and Rebecca had solidified was her future.

"You're not," Ryan said.

"It doesn't matter. Poppy wasn't here to see me. She came out to the island to see you."

Ryan rolled up the building plans and snapped a rubber band around them, and then he moved the roll and the blue folder to a counter, leaving the desk open as a dinner table. Cara put the food containers on the table and then got up to pour a coffee for each of them. They sat down and opened their mac-and-cheese containers.

"I was engaged to Poppy for a short time last year," Ryan said.

Cara paused with food halfway to her mouth. She'd suspected there was a relationship, but an engagement? How had that remained secret?

"She and her father were friends with some clients I built luxury homes for, and that's how we met. She seemed to think I was a real prize, and our engagement happened practically overnight."

"You never told your sister or any of your friends on the island, did you?" Cara asked.

He shook his head. "I told myself I was keeping it quiet for all kinds of reasons. I was busy. Mom and Dad were in Florida. I wanted to wait until I came back here to tell people in person. I had lots of reasons for not telling anyone. But looking back on it, I think I know the real reason I didn't want to say anything. It seemed too good to be true. And it was."

"I'm sorry," Cara said.

Honestly, she wasn't sorry. Not just because of her feelings for Ryan but because she'd met Poppy, and it was obvious Ryan deserved someone a lot nicer than the woman who'd stalked into the barn that morning.

"That's not the worst of it," he said. "I'd appreciate it if what I'm about to tell you remains just between us."

Just between us. *As if there were an us*, Cara thought, but she nodded. "Okay."

"Poppy and her father persuaded me to invest in a big real estate project they were doing. They handled all the planning, and I would get the building contracts. It was worth a fortune to my company, but I had to invest big first. I bought hundreds of thousands of dollars' worth of construction materials and had them delivered to the site, and I was only waiting for the green light to begin digging foundations when, suddenly, we were locked out of the site."

"Locked out?"

"I showed up one day, and there was a fence and a No Trespassing sign. When I tried to enter, I got escorted out by the sheriff."

"Why?" Cara asked.

"Poppy and her father didn't actually own the land. The property deed was dubious at best. Maybe they had good intentions going in, although I doubt that now, but they were operating under an umbrella of lies."

"They lied to you?"

Ryan nodded. "I believe Poppy thought I'd be too blinded by our relationship to ask too many questions. And I was. I'm still kicking myself that I didn't insist on having evidence that this project was viable before I sank a huge investment into it."

Cara took her time chewing her food and then stirred her coffee. There were eerie similarities between the failed project with Poppy's family and the currently stalled one on the island. Except that, this time, Ryan hadn't bought materials in advance, and he wasn't engaged to anyone involved in the project.

"What happened to your construction materials? Can you use them here?"

"They're still sitting there out in the elements being slowly ruined. They won't be usable, and it makes me sick. The property remains locked because the dispute isn't settled."

Cara thought about that document in the blue folder. This was the lawsuit, but Ryan wasn't the party being sued.

Ryan closed the lid on his take-out container after eating only half of the food. He got up and picked up the blue folder from the counter and placed it in front of Cara. "Proof that I'm telling you the truth."

Cara felt her lunch go cold in her stomach. "I've known you all my life. You don't have to prove to me that you're not lying." Did he really think so little of their friendship?

"Maybe not you, but other people may get wind of this, and I don't want them thinking I was involved in something unscrupulous."

"You were involved."

He scrubbed a hand through his hair. "Yes, but my crime was stupidly trusting people, not doing something illegal. It's all in there."

Cara laid a hand on top of the folder, but she didn't open it. "You want me to read this so that if it comes up with the zoning board or the village council, I can say I know the whole truth and you're innocent of any wrongdoing, and that will clear the way for your permits on this project."

When she put it together aloud, it hurt. He hadn't confided in his friends Griffin and Maddox. Had not told his sister, Violet. He was only telling her, not because he cared about her as a friend or even something more, but because he needed her help. He'd taken the property she wanted, kept her on to literally do the dirty work in the stable, and now he opened up to her only because she could be useful to him.

Good old useful, dependable Cara Peterson.

"Please, Cara. I can't fail again. I laid off all my workers and even sold my house. This property and its future are all I have."

And all I ever wanted.

Cara forced her fingers not to tremble as she opened the folder. Ryan slipped out of the office, leaving her alone to read the details of a lawsuit he had brought against Poppy and her father in which he detailed their deceit and his losses and demanded remuneration. The suit had been filed four months ago. Cara knew these things took time, but was it getting close to a resolution? There had to be a reason Poppy had suddenly shown up and attempted to sweet-talk Ryan. Maybe she thought she and her father were on the brink of losing.

Either way, Ryan's legal problems were none of Cara's business, except for the fact that the document demonstrated his innocence in the matter but also how desperate he was to succeed in the Christmas Island project.

She had a lifetime of experience helping other people and putting their needs and desires before hers, but this time, it hurt a lot more.

FOR THE NEXT five days, Ryan walked on eggshells. He was afraid to ask Cara what she thought when she read that document. He was afraid Poppy had talked to someone on the island, and he waited for rumors to get back to him.

Most importantly, he was waiting for the next meeting of the zoning board. Had he submitted enough evidence to the committee to gain their approval? If they had reservations about his intentions or his plans, would

Cara stick up for him now that he'd shared his secret with her?

She came and went and cared for the horses as usual, but his conversations with her were passing and casual, leaving him worried she thought he'd been a fool to be drawn in by Poppy (he was) and that he was a fool for taking a chance on another property without having all his ducks in a row.

Maybe he was. But this project was different. It was his alone, and it was his hometown. How could it go wrong?

On the fourth Wednesday of November, Ryan came out of his office in the morning and found Cara examining the front hoof on Eight Maids A-Milking. She didn't look up, but she said, "I think Milkmaid is getting an infection. I noticed she's been favoring her foot, and I think it's time to call in the vet."

"Is the vet clinic behind the hardware store open today?" Ryan asked. He was out of touch with the daily operations of the island.

"Every Wednesday, weather permitting," Cara said. "That's why I brought it up. I've been keeping an eye on her, but I don't want to let another week go by, especially with it being almost December and the major snow-storm forecast for later this week."

"Good thinking." Ryan wanted to add that he didn't know what he would do without Cara, because as much as he cared about the horses and could generally manage feeding them and cleaning their stalls, he hadn't noticed any limping from Milkmaid. He wanted to tell Cara how much he valued her help and appreciated her expertise, but he didn't want her to think he was flattering her just hours before the zoning meeting.

"I'll call Dr. Murphy," Cara said. "I have his number saved in my phone, and I'll ask him to stop by here today before he leaves the island."

"Thank you." Ryan leaned against the stall door. "I've been thinking about names for my building project." It was the closest he could come to bringing up the subject without directly asking her how she was going to vote and if she was on his side. "I'd like to do something with the words *horse* or *carriage* or *sleigh* in the title because the horse barn is the central feature of the housing development."

"Okay," Cara said.

"What do you think?"

"I think that's really nice."

Nice. That was it? "Which of those words do you think would work best?"

Cara finally looked at him. "It's Christmas Island, so probably *sleigh*. It combines Christmas with horses."

"Sleigh Bell Circle?"

"Maybe. Your design is more a horseshoe than a circle, but circle implies connection and completeness, and that's a good thing."

"At your meeting tonight," Ryan ventured, "will you tell your board that that's the working name?"

He really wanted to ask her what else she was going to say at the meeting and what his chances were, but Cara only gave him a brief nod while she dialed her phone. He listened to her half of the conversation with Dr. Murphy and then went outside to walk the property. The air had that feeling that a snowstorm was impending. As a kid, he'd always gotten so excited at the possibility of being snowed in so he wouldn't have to go to school.

Given the forecast, Ryan got in his truck and drove to the ferry dock. If he picked up drywall supplies, he could do some inside finish work on Jordan and Violet's house, no matter how much the snow fell outside. He needed to keep busy so the waiting on his approvals wouldn't rob him of any more sleep or sanity.

Cara was off the phone when he went inside. "Would you be able to be here when Dr. Murphy comes later today?" he asked.

"Sure," she said. "I always like to hear what he says and get instructions on caring for the horses."

"Thanks. I'm going to Lakeview for building supplies."

She tilted her head as if she wanted to ask a question.

"For Violet and Jordan's house," he said.

"Oh. That makes sense." She gave him a small smile. "Getting stocked up before the storm. Good idea."

"Can I call you later to find out what the vet said?"

She hesitated. "Yes, but I'll be at the meeting tonight. Are you coming to the public part of the village council meeting?"

He wanted to. He wanted to sit in the front row and plead his case, answer questions and get his project moving. Being passive and waiting around magnified the torture of wondering if and when he could redeem himself and his company. Had he taken a more proactive role in the project with Poppy and Herman instead of trusting other people, he might not be in this predicament.

But all he could do now was trust that Cara, Gina and Shirley would see the value of his project and recommend the permits to the council at large. He'd bared his soul to Cara, and he hoped that risk would pay off.

"I'm not sure I'll be able to. I'll be on the last ferry, but then I have to go unload my truck at Jordan's house and get the materials inside so they won't sit out in the weather and get ruined."

"That would be terrible," Cara said. Her look of understanding told him she was thinking about his other materials that were sitting outside behind a fence, no use to anyone anymore.

He reached out and touched her arm. "Thank you," he said.

"For what?"

"No matter what happens with my project and my lawsuit and my future. If I have to go back to building birdhouses and starting over,

I just want you to know I appreciate you putting your feelings aside and being fair to me about building on this land that you wanted."

Cara's face flushed, and she moved backward just enough to break the contact between her arm and his hand. "I haven't necessarily taken my feelings out of consideration. And because I work for you and am your liaison, I'm not voting. Moving your project to the full council will be decided by Gina and Shirley."

"But...but you can't. There are only three votes, and if either Gina or Shirley—" He broke off, not wanting to sound desperate or, worse, sound as if he were pressuring Cara.

"If the project has merit and you've done all the paperwork correctly, it will pass without my support," Cara said.

Ryan felt as if a stiff breeze had blown open the barn doors. Mixing emotions with business had been fatal for his company, and Cara had just admitted her feelings might be involved. But he and Cara weren't romantically involved. Their relationship was friendship. Business. That was all. That hug they'd shared a week ago had shaken him, but had it had any effect on her?

There was no safe way to ask, not when he had so much on the line.

"I know you'll do what you believe is right," Ryan said. Had he made a huge mistake by opening his heart and trusting someone? He'd thought he was pleading his case, but by trusting her with the details of his humiliation, he'd made it more difficult for her to be objective because he'd involved her in his pain.

CHAPTER EIGHTEEN

CARA HAD TO shake the feeling of frustration that had clung to her since the previous night's zoning board meeting. They hadn't voted. The water department hadn't made a final determination of the effect twenty more houses would have on the island's water system. The three members of the zoning board could have allowed the proposal to move forward to the village council with conditions so it could have its first reading into the meeting minutes. Gina had offered it as an option if the three members were strongly unified, but Gina herself expressed some reservations, and Cara was ashamed to admit, even to herself, that she hadn't fought for Ryan.

Not because she didn't believe in him or his plans. But instead because her mind was clouded by her feelings for him. She couldn't do the right thing for the island by cutting corners just because she sympathized with

Ryan. Wasn't that what had gotten him into trouble? Mixing emotions with business decisions?

She didn't relish telling him how it had gone and revealing the fact that his proposal might have moved forward with strong enough support. Gina and Shirley weren't stonewalling him. They truly didn't see the hurry in approving his plans.

Cara opened the barn door after finishing the morning chores of feeding and watering the animals. Several inches of snow covered the ground, but it wasn't a blizzard. The weather app on her phone predicted the winds would shift, and most of the forecast snow would miss the island. She donned her snow pants, boots, parka, hat and gloves and got in her car. After the meeting last night, one of the council members had told her about a piece of land going up for sale in a remote part of the island, and she couldn't wait another minute before checking it out.

She could get first crack at it, but she wanted to see it before getting her hopes up. Given how quickly the stable property had sold, there was no time to lose. Cara brushed snow off her windshield, shivering in the stiff wind that drove snowflakes down her collar. Her plan was to do a drive-by of the property and maybe walk around it. Did it have any improvements and amenities that would make it hospitable for a fledgling horse camp? If she didn't have to begin at the ground floor, it would save her time and money.

She started her car to let it warm up and then went back in the barn to fill a travel mug with hot coffee. As she snapped a lid on her cup, she heard the barn door open and close.

Rats. She wasn't quick enough.

"Good morning," Ryan said, a look of expectation on his face. "The weather forecast was right about the snow."

"It'll stop soon," Cara said.

His expression turned dubious. "That's not the forecast I saw."

"They changed it," Cara said.

"Okay," Ryan said. "Then I won't worry about getting snowed in at Jordan's house. I delivered my supplies last night, but it was late when we got it all unloaded."

Cara held her breath, waiting.

"Thank you for your text about Milkmaid's hoof. I'm glad she'll be okay."

"Me too."

Ryan waited another moment, but he finally said, "How did your meeting go last night?"

"It didn't...didn't have the result you were hoping for. Not yet anyway. The water department hasn't given us their final report, and we can't give a final approval until then."

At Ryan's crestfallen expression, Cara felt a stab of guilt that she hadn't fought for him. Would she be delivering good news right now if she had? Would he thank her for sticking up for him? Would he give her a hug? Would it change anything about their relationship? No, it wouldn't. Was that why she hadn't done it?

"Not even a temporary permit? I know I can prove the environmental impact will be manageable. It's something I've done plenty of times, and I've always worked well with local infrastructure."

"Sorry," Cara said.

"When will that report be done?"

"Hopefully in two weeks, in time for our next meeting."

"Two more weeks," Ryan said. "The second week of December."

"You can't build in this snow anyway," Cara said. "Does two more weeks really matter?"

"I have to have proof that I...well, it's hard waiting."

Didn't she know it. She'd been waiting to get her project going for a long time.

"Proof of what?"

"My bank is nervous after my recent failures. I have a timeline I need to stick to, or I'll be in trouble."

Cara thought about her loan preapproval that was half used up already. "I have to go," she said.

Ryan gave her a tired smile. "Be careful getting home in this snow. I'm glad you're not going far."

"I'm actually taking a little detour to see a piece of property for sale on the other side of the island. I heard about it last night."

"In this weather? Can't you wait until tomorrow or the next day when they have time to clear the roads?"

It was nice of him to care about her, and he wasn't totally wrong. She hadn't told her parents about her plans, because she knew they would have said the same thing, but she just needed one look at the piece of land and that would satisfy her curiosity until the skies cleared.

"It's supposed to stop snowing soon. And waiting is hard," she said, using Ryan's own words and heading off any further protest from him.

As she drove out of town and took a familiar road that led to the other side of the island, Cara started to doubt the weather app. The snow thickened, and her windshield wipers smeared ice and obscured her view. Maybe she should turn around, but she was partway there already, and finding a place to turn around on the road might get her stuck in a ditch. She slowed her speed but forged ahead.

A deer ran across just ahead of her, but she didn't slam on the brakes and slide off the road. She was wise about winter driving, which was why she thought she'd be okay. *It's only another mile*, she thought. Just past a new house, a water tower and the road that turned off toward the airport. There. She put on her flashers and pulled as far to the side of the road as she dared without getting two tires in the ditch.

There was no For Sale sign, but she knew this place. Someone from off the island had owned it for years and used it only a few weeks every summer. Had they even come the last few summers? It had one cabin and one barn, both painted red and visible through the snow. Cara knew there was also a driveway and a stone patio with an outdoor fireplace sitting on the ten-acre plot. She'd been here with Chloe five or six years earlier when they drove someone out from the ferry dock. With no taxi service on the island, locals often gave people a ride if they happened to be in the right place at the right time to help someone out.

Cara got out of her car and pulled up the hood of her parka. It wouldn't hurt to have a closer look at the barn. Would it be suitable for a few horses? She trekked through the deep snow and peered in the barn windows. There was room for at least two cars, and there appeared to be a smaller room on the back and a loft overhead.

The barn wasn't nearly large enough for her plans, but it could be a start. She circled the barn, walked around the clearing and noted the lovely tall trees all around it. Ideally, she could keep those trees and build cabins between them.

Cara didn't peer in the windows of the cabin because that felt too intrusive, even though it was obvious no one was there. The only tracks in the new-fallen snow were hers, although they were getting obscured quickly by fresh flakes. She tripped over a fallen tree under the snow and picked herself up, brushing off snow and resolving to be more careful. The flashers on her car were a beacon leading her back to the road.

She opened her car door and kicked snow off her boots against the bottom of the door frame, and then she slid in. The car was covered in snow, which insulated the vehicle and made it so quiet inside she could hear her own heartbeat. She ran the wipers to knock off the fresh flakes and then put the car in gear and tenderly pressed the gas.

Her wheels spun, fighting for traction. She let off and then tried again. The wheels spun at first, but then the car moved forward a good ten feet before the rear end slid around and went right into the ditch.

Stunned, she sat there, hands on the wheel. The front of her car was tilted slightly up, and the huge snowflakes were, ironically, beautiful on the glass. She got out of the car and circled around to the back, where she tried shoving the car out of the ditch.

"It's a two-person job," she said aloud. She was starting to sweat inside her heavy coat, and one thing was abundantly clear. She needed to call someone who had a truck. Griffin and Maddox May had trucks, as did plenty of other islanders.

Ryan had a big four-wheel-drive truck, and she wouldn't have to endure a lecture from him about the road conditions because he'd already gotten that out of the way. Wasn't it his fault anyway that she was out here looking at property while he stayed warm in the barn she'd wanted?

He could come out in the cold and pull her car out of the ditch.

He *would* come and get her. She was sure of that.

THE HORSES WERE RESTLESS, and Ryan believed they were picking up on his emotions. He paced the barn, already feeling snowed in even though he could get home if he wanted to. But home, despite its coziness and friendly neighbor, was also claustrophobic. He wanted to be outside doing something useful instead of playing a waiting game. Permits, holidays, weather. Everything seemed to be conspiring to keep him from getting his business back together and his future on track.

A gust of wind shook the barn door, and it rattled. Ryan walked over and checked the latch. It was secure, but the wind was strong. The snow was not slowing down as Cara had believed. It was getting worse. He hoped the power wouldn't fail, because he didn't want to have to go outside and fire up the generator. Did it even have its gas tank filled?

He should have prepared better. Owning this property and being responsible for the animals that depended on him was serious.

"Maybe I better stay the night with you guys," he told Goldy. "I could sleep in a spare stall."

His phone rang, and Ryan felt a cold hollow in his chest when he saw Cara's number.

"Are you okay?" he asked instead of saying hello.

"Stuck," she said. "My car slid into the ditch at the land I drove out here to see."

"Where are you?"

"Just past the water tower and the airport turnoff."

"I'm on my way."

"Thanks, I—"

"Are you sure you're okay?" he asked.

"Fine, I just—"

"I'm glad you called me."

He wasn't the only one on the island with a truck, and he certainly wasn't the only person who would rescue Cara in a winter storm. Everyone had everyone else's back on Christmas Island. But she'd chosen to call him.

He geared up with his winter parka and grabbed his truck keys from his desk. He looked around the barn. Should he take anything else? He grabbed a heavy chain and a shovel and threw them in the bed of his truck. Then he put the truck in four-wheel-drive mode and crawled out of his parking space.

Emotions swirled through Ryan, mirroring the flakes beyond his windshield. He loved winter on the island and had happy memories of snow days, building snow forts and ice-skating. Because of the size of Christmas Island, even when residents needed to drive somewhere in the snow, it wasn't far. He knew the airport turnoff and the water tower, and Ryan estimated it was less than three miles, but it felt longer.

Ryan was the lone vehicle on the snowy road, but there was a warm spot inside when he thought about the fact that Cara had chosen him to call. Was it simply a practical decision? She knew he didn't have a family to care for; she knew he had a truck. She was his employee.

But maybe there was more. Maybe Cara felt the growing connection between them that went beyond their friendship as fellow island kids, beyond a work relationship. It was trust. He'd trusted her with the story of his humiliating failure. She'd shown her trust in him with one phone call.

He didn't see the airport turnoff until he passed it, and then he slowed even more, squinting to see Cara's silver car through the snow. When he saw it, he stopped in the middle of the road and put his flashers on. He wasn't taking a chance on getting too close to the side of the road, as Cara had. He left his truck running and got out, but he didn't see Cara in or near her car. Snow blinded him as he moved toward the property she'd come out to see. Had she taken refuge somewhere?

"I'm here," a voice called, and Ryan stopped and turned. Cara stood under the porch roof of the small house. Relief washed over him, and he loped through the deep snow and up the porch steps. He wrapped his arms around her and hugged her close.

"I'm glad you're all right," he said, stepping back, grateful for the snow that crept down his collar and cooled his neck. "You're okay, aren't you?"

"I'm fine. I'm just standing here because it's out of the wind, and I didn't want to sit in my car."

"Smart move."

"And I'm trying to imagine," Cara said.

"Are you building an igloo or an ice sculpture in your mind?"

She laughed, but the sound didn't travel. Deep snow and more falling every minute dampened her laughter and held it there under the porch roof for only Ryan to enjoy.

"I'm trying to imagine what it would be like to live here and start my camp. A sunny summer day would be one thing, but this is definitely a hard trial for the property."

"What have you decided?" Ryan asked. He wanted to hear about her plans and be supportive, but it was a major sore spot between them. Would it always be that way? In two years when his housing development was fully operational and Cara had her horse camp going, would they meet on the street downtown and exchange a friendly wave?

He didn't want to wave to Cara from afar and have casual run-ins with her at the Mistletoe Melt or on the ferry. It was nice seeing her every day and having her be part of his life. Something in his chest changed when he saw her smile.

"I've decided I've got a few days to think about it, because I don't know what kind of a fool would come out here and try to take it away from me in this weather."

Ryan smiled and brushed snow from her hair. Cara didn't move away from his touch. Instead she took off a glove and wiped snow from his eyebrow, her finger tracing a warm line over his eye.

"We should go before it gets worse," Ryan said. Or before he pulled her close for another hug and kissed her pink cheeks and lips. She hesitated, her fingers still lingering over his cheek, but a tree branch cracked and unleashed a shower of snow near the porch, spurring them both into action.

"Should we try to pull out my car?" Cara asked.

"I brought a shovel and a chain, but I don't

think I'll have any success getting traction. There won't be much traffic past here, so I think we should leave your car until tomorrow."

"I'll get my purse and turn off the flashers so they don't drain the battery," Cara said. "I think you're right about not trying to pull it out of the ditch today."

Ryan opened the passenger door of his truck and waited until Cara climbed in before closing it, taking one last look at her car and the snowy property before getting in the driver's seat.

"Do you want to go straight home? I could drop you off."

Cara looked at the time on the truck's dashboard display. "It's only a few hours until feeding time for the horses. We could go to the barn. I'm worried about the power going out, and I don't want the horses to be nervous with all this wind."

"I like that idea," Ryan said. He didn't try to turn the truck around but went farther up the road and turned on the first road he knew would take him to the perimeter road around the island and, eventually, back to the barn.

The truck slid going around the corner, but

Ryan got it under control and then slowed even more. Cara cleared her throat and gripped the door handle. "Would you like me to drive?" she asked.

Ryan glanced over and smiled. "You can if you want."

"I'm kidding."

"I'm not," Ryan said. "This truck is the only thing I have left of my former business except for debt, and I'm not emotionally attached to it."

"The truck or the debt?" Cara asked.

He laughed. "Neither one. Coming home and starting over may turn out to be the best thing that ever happened to me."

"Had you thought about coming home before all that happened?" Cara asked.

"A hundred times. But I wasn't brave enough to do it."

He should shut up and concentrate on driving before he said too much and opened his heart any further. He'd already put more trust in Cara than he had in anyone in a long time, and it made him feel exposed. He was the man who put roofs and doors on things, not the guy who opened windows.

"I always thought you were brave for moving away and doing your own thing," Cara said. "Wrong, of course, because you were missing out on all the wonderful things going on here on the island, but brave."

"At this speed, we have at least fifteen minutes before we get back to the barn, so you could enlighten me about all the things you believe I've missed."

"It would take longer than that," she said. "But I am glad you're back."

Ryan wanted to reach over and touch Cara, but he fought that desire and kept both hands safely on the wheel as he battled the deep snow on the road back to the stable.

CHAPTER NINETEEN

CARA ALMOST HATED to leave the warm cab of Ryan's truck. He didn't know about her family's tradition of keeping car conversations in a protected vault, but he had shared a little with her anyway.

And she had, too. Admitting she was glad he was back was one of the last sentences spoken before they reached the barn, but it lingered in the air. She was glad he was back. The feelings he'd inspired in her growing up were still there. He was still Ryan, the handsome, confident man who was capable of making something out of nothing, who cared about the people in his life.

The shadow of doubt that hung over him from getting stung hard by failure only made him more human and appealing.

"The power's still on," Ryan said, nodding toward the light on the front of the barn. It usually only came on from dusk to dawn, but snow had darkened the sky so that it lit up even in the afternoon.

"Should we get the generator ready anyway?" Cara said. "Gary showed me how, and I did get it started three years ago when the power went out. I'm not sure it's been touched since, though."

"Let's check on the animals first, and then maybe we better see if we can get it running. Just in case."

They went inside and spent time fussing over the horses and kittens. Ryan replaced the batteries in two flashlights he found in his office and Cara made a fresh pot of coffee. She brought up the weather app on her phone and held it up for Ryan to see. He blew out a breath. "I'll take you home whenever you want to go, but I'm going to spend the night here. I don't want to take a chance on not being able to get here in the morning."

"I'll stay with you," Cara said.

"You don't have to do that."

"I want to," Cara said.

Ryan grinned. "You don't trust me to mix the feed correctly?"

"I do trust you, but the horses like me better."

They both laughed, and the moment was

friendly and sweet as if the tension of the past month had melted despite the snowstorm.

The lights flickered, breaking the spell. "Generator," they both said at the same time.

The gas-powered generator was in a small building outside the main barn, partly for safety reasons and also because the machine was loud. The lawnmower and other tools were stored in the shed, too, and Cara helped move items aside so she and Ryan could get to the generator.

"The gas stored in these containers shouldn't be too old," she said. "I remember filling them up near the end of lawn-mowing season, but then we only mowed one more time, so there should be a lot left."

"Good," Ryan said. He knelt and checked the oil and gas. "Can you find a screwdriver?"

Cara dug around in a tool chest, found the tool and handed it to Ryan. It was just like old times, like that summer when she'd handed Ryan tools and hoped he'd notice her, even though she was all of twelve and he had certainly just seen her as a nice kid.

Had anything really changed?

He smiled at her, looking directly into her eyes. "Thanks. Luckily, we have a generator just like this at my...well, we had one like this that we would take out to job sites."

He pulled the cord three times, and the generator came to life with a loud roar. Ryan let it run for a minute, and then he switched off the gas. "Let's hope we don't need it, but we're prepared if we do."

They went inside the barn. "Hungry?" Ryan asked. "I could go downtown and pick up supplies for the night. No one is going to be delivering in this weather."

"Next year, hopefully you'll have a convenience store and restaurant right out the back door of the barn," Cara said. "If you get snowed in, you won't have far to go."

"Hopefully," Ryan said. He leaned against the interior wall and crossed his arms. "I know I shouldn't ask this, but isn't there anything I can do or...you can do to move the permits along faster?"

Cara hesitated, not wanting to tell him about the private conversation in the zoning meeting—that they could force it forward with enough support. None of them had wanted to stick their necks out, not even her.

"I wish," she said. What did she wish? That she had spoken up? That she didn't know his motivation that made her feel torn? That he'd confided in her because he liked her, not just because he needed her?

"It's okay. I understand. If I were in your position, I wouldn't want to rush and betray the island's future by a risky vote."

"You make it sound so impersonal," Cara said.

"Business should be impersonal."

"Tell that to my family who makes candy for a living and delights in seeing people's emotional reaction to it. And what about my camp? Yes, I want it to be a viable business, but it's also personal. Everyone has a story to tell and something to gain…or lose…and that's why they need to get out of their own way sometimes. That's what I want to help kids with."

Ryan was quiet for a minute, and only the sounds of the horses filled the muffled silence in the barn. Two of the kittens chased past them, rolling around on the floor and then getting back up again to pursue a piece of hay.

"I need to get out of my own way," he said, finally breaking the silence.

"How?"

He swiped a hand down his face. "By doing what's in my heart."

Cara opened her mouth, but she found she couldn't make a sound. Was she in Ryan's heart?

"But not tonight," Ryan said. "Right now, I need to get us some food, and then we need to get ready for a long snowy night."

"I'm ready," Cara said softly.

"I'm not."

He walked toward her, paused and then pulled on his hat and gloves and strode out into the afternoon that looked more like night.

While he was gone, Cara noticed he'd pulled out the box of Christmas decorations from storage. She pawed through them to take her mind off the snowstorm. There was a wreath to hang around the nameplate of each horse, and she went around the barn putting one on each stall door. Golden tinsel garland was carefully wrapped around pieces of cardboard. Cara remembered helping Gary take the decorations down the previous January. Who would have guessed then that Ryan Brookstone would own the barn by the next Christmas?

As she thought of Gary, she found his favorite decoration in the bottom of the box. It was a bundle of mistletoe made of green silk flowers with a big red bow. Gary hung it on a peg right over the front door every year, jokingly saying that someday the prettiest woman on the island was going to come through that door.

Cara got a step stool and was reaching up to hang the mistletoe when the door opened and Ryan nearly ran into her. His hat and coat were covered in snow, and snow swirled in around him until he pulled the door shut. He looked up to see what Cara was doing, and she knew the moment he saw the mistletoe, because his face, reddened by the wind, flushed even more.

"It's Gary's mistletoe," she said. "He insisted on hanging it here every year out of sheer hope."

Ryan clutched a bag of food to his chest and opened his mouth as he looked up at Cara. If she leaned down just a little bit, their lips would meet. Was he feeling the same attraction she was? He continued looking up at her, lips parted, and time stood still as the wind whistled outside.

Cara leaned down, and suddenly, the door behind Ryan flew open on a gust of wind. One of the kittens was at his feet and nearly tumbled out into the snow, but Ryan picked it up with one hand and locked the door with the other.

"Not so fast, little girl," he said to the kitten. He held it up and gave it a kiss under the mistletoe while Cara stepped down from her stool, determined to keep her feet securely on the ground during the long night ahead.

A WEEK AFTER the snowstorm, Christmas Island planned a holiday tourist event weekend. Everyone said how lucky they were that the storm's timing had allowed time to clear the streets and reopen the ferry and airport so shoppers and day tourists could come and get a megadose of Christmas during the first full weekend of December.

Cara did her barn chores as quickly as possible all week long so she could pull double duty in the candy store to get ready for the impending weekend, especially since her sister Camille was distracted by details of her upcoming wedding. Cara was glad to be so busy. Pulling sugar, stirring fudge and packaging candy canes, cookies and chocolate as fast as they could make it took her mind off the tension between her and Ryan.

They'd spent the night in the barn, her in the office on the small love seat and him with blankets in a spare horse stall. When morning broke after the snowy night, they'd fed the horses, cleared the sidewalks, and Ryan had driven her home in the blinding sunlight bouncing off the white snowdrifts.

The contrast of sun and snow matched the contrast of Ryan's actions toward her. He cared, but he kept his distance. He drove out in the storm to pick her up, but he talked about keeping emotions under lock and key.

She promised herself she would stop thinking about him and instead poured her energy into chocolate Santas in three different sizes. It helped her keep her mind off Ryan, because he spent nearly all his time at Jordan and Violet's future home working on finishing the spare bedroom and bathroom and adding details to the kitchen cabinets. Cara heard about it from Violet, but Ryan avoided her.

Was he upset that she hadn't done more to get his permits? That was a problem that would be cleared up in another few days. To adjust for the holidays, the zoning board moved up its biweekly meeting, and Gina shared with Cara that she saw no reason to hold up Ryan's project any longer. The water department had approved the plans, and everything else was in line. If Gina and Shirley knew Ryan's building business had failed and he was barely able to finance this project, would they have reservations?

It wasn't Cara's story to tell, and she had not betrayed him to another soul. It also hadn't gained him any advantage to tell her about Poppy and the bad business deal. So why had he told her? She wanted to believe it was because he cared about her as at least a friend and perhaps more, but he'd been distant since the night of the storm.

He was going to get his heart's desire, even if he didn't know it yet, Cara thought. Would that warm him up toward her? It didn't matter. He had his plans and she had hers.

"I love the front window," Camille said as she came into the candy store on Friday afternoon before the big event. "It had to take you forever to decorate it."

"Who needs sleep in December?" Cara asked.

"I'm so excited about my wedding! It's all I see when I close my eyes at night. I'm probably going to sleepwalk right through Christmas *and* my wedding."

"I'm pretty sure you'll want to be awake for that," Cara said. "Why don't you go help Violet put up the lights in front of her store? The fresh air will wear you out, and you'll sleep like a baby tonight."

"Ryan's over there helping her," Camille said. "I saw him before I came in." Camille put on an apron and gloves and took over the batch of fudge Cara was stirring on the big marble table, gently pushing Cara aside. "Take a break for a minute. You've been working two jobs basically all your life, and you'll have to do triple duty while I'm on my honeymoon."

"It'll be our dead season right after Christmas. I'll be fine."

"But we have to get there without dropping," Camille said. "I'm curious about how Ryan is doing with the barn."

"He's in a holding pattern on that, but he's staying busy at Jordan's house."

"Uh-huh," Camille said. "And how are you two getting along?"

Cara shrugged. "I just work there."

"And?"

"And I just work there. He hasn't found anyone to take over helping in the barn, and I can't do much about my plans in the middle of winter, so it's horses and candy for me in the meantime."

"Did you forgive him for...you know?"

"That was business," Cara said. "That's all."

And Ryan had said himself that business and feelings don't mix.

"That's all? You used to like him."

"I like everyone."

"I mean, you used to like him in particular," Camille said.

"That was a long time ago when I was a kid. I'm not depending on someone else for my happiness these days."

Camille nodded. "Wise."

"Thank you."

"So, you're not voting against him on the permit thing?"

"No," Cara said. "I never did. That was a group decision, and there were reasons." She wanted to play it cool, but her voice rose as she defended herself.

"Sorry," Camille said. "No one would have blamed you for taking a bit of revenge, at least not the people who knew you planned to buy that place from Gary and got upstaged without warning."

Some shoppers walked past the candy store's door that was propped open because of the heat inside. "This is a vault car conversation," Cara said. "And none of it matters anyway, because I'm taking the plan Rebecca helped me with to the bank on Monday, and I'm going to officially apply for a business loan and make an offer on that property up by the water tower."

"Good for you," Camille said. "I'm glad. And that place comes with a little cabin and barn, right? So it's not totally starting from scratch."

"Exactly. It'll be fine."

Not as fine as an established barn with horses she knew by heart, but it was her new version of fine.

CHAPTER TWENTY

ON THE SECOND Wednesday of December, Ryan sat in the front row of the village council meeting fighting a sense of déjà vu and dread. Cara had been avoiding him for days except for her message telling him the zoning board and council meeting had been moved up because of the oncoming holidays. She suggested he should be there, but she didn't say why.

Gina made eye contact with him as she gaveled the meeting to order, and he considered that a good sign. The council sped through the reading of the minutes from the previous meeting, a painful reminder to Ryan that he hadn't succeeded in securing the permits his banker was asking questions about almost daily. Gina called for public participation, and all eyes on the council swung to Ryan, but he didn't have anything to say. What could he do? Ask for their confidence in him or at least their mercy? All he knew was that Cara had told him to be there, so there must be some decision.

He held tight and didn't raise a hand or stand when Gina asked for new business. There was no one else in the community chairs, and Ryan felt very exposed. He trusted Cara not to make a fool of him, but his stomach hurt just thinking about how much it would hurt if he got turned down again. It had been over two months since he'd bought the stable, and he'd been spinning his wheels.

"Committee reports," Gina said. "Recreational committee first."

Ryan listened to four different committee reports before Gina called on the zoning committee. Cara was the one to lean forward and speak.

"After careful consideration, we are recommending the Sleigh Bell Circle project submitted by Ryan Brookstone to the full council for a vote on the rezoning of the property to commercial and the permits for construction of twenty new family homes and two commercial buildings in addition to the preexisting barn on the property."

"Discussion?" Gina asked, looking around

the table where all seven members of the Christmas Island Village Council sat. Each of them had a folder of information that they opened and perused.

Ryan held his breath. What if someone else raised an objection? Clearing the zoning board was only the first hurdle, but he couldn't help but be encouraged. The hope left him feeling warm, as if he had been finally welcomed back to the island.

It would be better if he had someone to share that joy with. Someone who understood his sacrifice and challenges. *Someone like Cara.*

A sensation hit Ryan like a hammer falling off the top of a ladder at a construction site. He cared about Cara. Wanted to spend time with her. Had feelings that swirled in his chest and confused his thoughts, making him forget his surroundings and whether or not he'd had dinner and what day of the week it was.

Cara Peterson. The pretty girl who'd always been around and who had awakened something in him over the past few weeks. He'd tried denying it, but now he started to recognize it as affection, caring, complicating...

"If there's no discussion, I need a motion for a vote."

"Moved," Shirley said.

"Second," Cara said. She looked straight at him as she spoke, and the electric current of his newly awakened feelings zapped through him. Did she feel it, too?

Gina called roll, but Ryan knew he'd already won. Cara believed in his project, believed in him. He heard the yes votes around the table and acknowledged Gina's congratulations when she informed him he could proceed, but all he could think about was going back to his lonely duplex with its borrowed furniture and blankets and celebrating alone.

He smiled and accepted the polite applause from the council and then sat down. He couldn't just leave now that he'd gotten what he wanted. Ryan stayed glued to his chair, feeling like a stone statue with a river of lava running through it. There was so much he wanted to do now that he could. Even with the winter weather, he could begin moving in rented equipment. He could draw on his building loan to order materials. There were plenty of days when the ferry would run, all the way up until the lake froze later in January as it typically did.

There was no time to lose, but Ryan didn't move a muscle until the meeting adjourned and Cara got out of her seat. He rose to his feet, but his feet didn't move. What would he say to her? Thank you for helping sway the vote in my favor even though I robbed this project right out from under you?

Before he could move, Cara came up to him and held out her hand for a businesslike shake. "Congratulations and good luck," she said in a tone she would use for any person she had a professional relationship with.

They had more than that, didn't they? Although, he had to admit he'd been the one to squelch any thought of mixing emotions with business.

He held on to her hand longer than necessary. "Thank you."

"You're welcome."

"Can I buy you a coffee or glass of something? I…don't want to go straight home tonight."

"I don't know," she said.

"Now that the vote is over, no one will think I'm buying your vote," Ryan said.

Cara's expression cooled. "I certainly hope no one would think so little of me."

"That's not what I meant."

"You should go home," Cara said.

"Wait. Just one cup of coffee, something better than our ancient pot at the barn."

Using the word *our* added a layer of meaning to his invitation, and the way Cara's brows rose told him that she'd noticed it just as he'd noticed her use of the word *unanimous*.

"It's not a good idea," she said.

"Then walk out with me."

"Okay," Cara said slowly, a question in the word.

They walked outside into a cold, clear December night. Christmas lights decorated trees and shrubs, and wreaths hung from lampposts on the backstreet leading toward his duplex and her parents' home.

"I'm sorry I've been operating in scared rabbit mode," Ryan said.

Cara kept walking and she was illuminated under a street light.

"Everyone operates that way, to an extent. But you can stop being afraid now. The council has given you its blessing. You have everything you need and want."

"But I—" he began, but then he stopped himself. He'd been about to tell her that the barn wouldn't mean anything to him without her there, but it would be cruel to tell her that now, and why would she believe him? "I don't have everything I want. I hurt you to get what I wanted, and you...mean something to me."

"What do I mean to you?"

He wanted to be able to put it in words, but it was more complex than reading a blueprint and knowing where doors and windows should go. He hadn't felt this way in a long time.

"I'm trying to figure it out," he said.

Whatever the right answer might have been, he was pretty sure from her expression of sorrow and disappointment that his words had fallen short. Was there a way he could show her instead of telling her?

"Good night, Ryan," Cara said. She turned and walked toward the far side of town and Ryan stood in the cold clear night watching Cara go in and out of the glow of streetlights on her way. She was illuminated one moment and dark the next, like the roller coaster ride he'd been on for months.

He should be happy and relieved now, but

how could he celebrate getting what he wanted when she should have been the one to have it?

THE NEXT MORNING, Ryan was gone. He'd sent her a text telling her he had to go to Lakeview and he'd be gone all day, maybe longer. He'd asked her to take good care of the horses, especially Turtledove, who seemed lonely.

The horses were always lonely during the winter, which is why Cara tried to take them out for exercise. She usually walked them slowly through downtown, hoping to meet people and remind the horses they were an important part of the community, even when the tourists went home.

That's how Christmas Island worked. The tight-knit community pulled together, complained about but relished the wildly busy tourist season all summer and again in December, and then they settled into a rhythm of ice-skating on lake inlets and dinner at each other's houses to get through the long winter.

This winter was going to be long. Cara would work her two jobs, go to the Winter Solstice Party, celebrate her sister's wedding and continue to dream about that piece of property that was okay. It would suffice. It was better than nothing, better than giving up on her dream.

She didn't see Ryan all day long, and the next morning he also didn't appear for the morning chores. Cara put on a pot of coffee in the office Ryan had left unlocked and wandered through the barn while it brewed. She fed the horses and gave several of them a good rubdown.

As she poured her coffee in Ryan's office, she noticed the plans and folder weren't on his desk. Had he taken them with him to Lakeview or stowed them in his duplex?

Cara spent the afternoon, a Friday, preparing for another busy weekend. The second weekend of December didn't host the major festival like the previous one, but the weather held, and it was going to be a busy shopping event as soon as the first ferries arrived on Saturday morning. She also had a lot of preparation to do, because the Winter Solstice Party at Rebecca and Griffin's house was a double event this year—also serving as the bachelor/bachelorette party for Camille and Maddox. It wouldn't be a wild party, more a celebration of the upcoming wedding, but

Cara had promised to help Rebecca with all the details.

She had all week, but she had a lot to do, including another meeting at the bank about her loan application—a meeting which was exciting but also left her feeling exposed. Did she really have a solid enough plan and a substantial enough down payment to make it work, especially since she had little infrastructure and no horses to start with? Doubt crept in as she iced sugar cookies, but she fought it off by making extra swirls on the snowman cookies and an intricate pattern of silver edible baubles on the stars.

She refused to replay her conversation with Ryan in which he'd seemed to think he owed her something but was also holding back, proving he didn't have a clue what was in her heart.

Cara had had enough of people overlooking her, which was why she was moving forward as fast as possible on her land purchase. If she didn't start believing in herself and showing that to people, why would they believe her?

The front door of the candy store jingled, and Cara glanced up automatically, expecting to see an early tourist who'd come over on the Friday ferry.

It was Ryan. He wore his usual heavy blue parka, and his face was bright with the cold.

"Did you just get off the ferry?" Cara asked.

He nodded. "It was sunny, but wow, it was brisk. Should be a nice weekend, though."

"I hope so. I've decorated ten dozen cookies, and someone needs to eat them soon."

"I can help," he offered.

Cara smiled. She didn't know why he was there, and he didn't owe her an explanation for being gone a day and a half. She was his employee and he'd notified her. But Ryan was also an islander and a friend. "You can have two," she said, indicating a tray she'd just finished. "And I won't judge you if you pick out two of the biggest ones. They're good."

"Did you have one?" he asked, grinning at her as he chose a gingerbread man sugar cookie.

"A tiny one, just one of the little presents."

Ryan took a bite and then another. He finished the gingerbread man and swallowed, but he didn't select another cookie. "Speaking of presents," he said. "I wanted to give you something."

"Christmas is two weeks away."

"It's not a Christmas gift," he said. "It's an offer."

"I already have two jobs."

"It's not a job offer. It's something I should have done a while ago, but I was afraid. All I could think of was the quickest way to escape my problems in Lakeview and start putting my business back together. And that way was contriving a reason to come home to Christmas Island and build something I thought would be a sure thing."

Cara put down her bag of royal icing and wiped her hands on a damp cloth. She didn't know where Ryan was going with this, but he looked as serious as a person could get despite the blob of green icing on his bottom lip. She wanted to dab it away or at least tell him it was there, but she needed to hear whatever he was going to say.

"I've decided to sell you the stable property for the same amount I paid for it," he said. "I had my lawyer draw up the agreement." He produced a thick envelope from an interior pocket of his coat and offered it to her.

"You have got to be kidding me," she said. Her heart pounded in her chest, and she couldn't take her eyes off the envelope for a moment. He was handing her everything she wanted. It was her chance to prove to Gary, her family and everyone else—including herself—that she was ready and capable of stepping out of the shadows and going for her dream.

It was in that envelope.

Cara slowly raised her eyes to Ryan's face. She loved that face and the way his dark hair curled over his ears, and his eyes glistened from the winter wind. She loved Ryan.

"No," she said. "I'm not taking your offer."

"What?" he blurted. He swiped a hand down his face and the bit of green icing disappeared. "It's what you want."

"It's also what you want," she said. How could she take that away from him and exchange her happiness for his? What had changed his mind? That's what she wanted to know, needed to know.

"It was," he said.

"And now?"

This was the moment when he could change everything between them by telling her he cared about her. He believed in her. He...loved her?

"Why are you making this hard?" he asked. "I'm offering you what you should have been able to get six weeks ago. I'm sorry I stepped in line in front of you. I was thinking of myself, and I didn't really think you were—"

He stopped talking, but Cara had heard enough.

"You didn't think I was serious about it? Able to do it? Ready and willing to sacrifice everything for what I wanted, especially after a lifetime of helping other people get what they want?"

The candy store was always warm, but Cara's ears and face were downright boiling.

"I didn't mean that," he said quietly.

"Then what did you mean?"

He still held the envelope out in front of him, but Cara had made no move to take it. She noticed it shook a little. She should make this easier for him, say something conciliatory. That's what people would expect Cara Peterson to do.

"I was gone almost ten years," he said. "That's a long time to be gone with just visits here and there. I thought the island would somehow…fix my problems, but now I know it's not the answer."

Was he leaving? Now that he'd gotten his permits, was he going to chicken out and go... where? She didn't want him to go. Seeing him every day had become a habit. A nice habit. She'd let go of her childhood crush a long time ago, and it had come back to life in a different way.

"What is the answer?" Cara asked.

"It's me figuring out myself and what I want."

Cara gave a humorless laugh. "You've always known what you wanted since you could pick up a hammer. That's one of the things I l-like about you."

His breath hitched. He'd noticed her stumbling over that word.

"Take this," he said. "At least read it. You don't have to give me an answer today."

It was the most tempting piece of paper she'd ever seen. She could grab it, say goodbye to Ryan and the wasted last two months, go straight to her bank and start the New Year right. Everything she wanted was right in front of her.

"No," she said. "I'm not going to be your grand gesture that makes you feel better, Ryan. I can't find happiness at the expense of someone else."

He stood there, hand outstretched, envelope barely trembling for a moment, and then he crumpled it in his hand and walked out.

CHAPTER TWENTY-ONE

RYAN MADE HIMSELF look at that envelope as it
sat on his desk all evening. Cara came and did
the evening care and feeding of the horses,
but he didn't leave his office. He couldn't face
her. Not after what she'd said: "I can't find
happiness at the expense of someone else."

Ouch. He'd tried that, but he was trying to
undo it now. Couldn't she see he was trying
to do the right thing? His lawyer thought he'd
lost his mind and had given him dire warn-
ings about the effect of taking out a huge loan
and then suddenly repaying it. There would
be fees, interest, damage to his credit.

Heck, his credit was already in the toilet.
How much lower could he go anyway?

Instead of beating himself up all the next
day, he showed up early to Jordan's house. He
couldn't begin construction on his project, not
while the offer of selling it to Cara was still
on the table. What if she changed her mind?

All he could do was pour his energy into his sister's future home.

"Sorry I can't stick around and help," Jordan said. "The Great Island Hotel is staying open until New Year's this year, and people are booking rooms and loving the Christmas decorations and special holiday dinners. I hate to say it, but I'll be glad when Christmas is over."

"Shh," Ryan said. "Don't say that too loud on this island."

"I'll trust you with my secret."

"I'm going to need some help putting up drywall on the ceiling later, but I can ask Mike for a hand. No one is renting a bike in December."

Mike had been putting some work into his own downtown bike rental business, and he'd already asked Ryan to help him with a plan. Two of the other merchants who shared a building had also approached him about a remodeling project, and the Great Island Hotel had asked him to take on some renovations.

He'd put off giving definite answers, but if he was going to sell the stable to Cara and renege on that project, he'd need the work. Was there a way to stay on Christmas Island without his grand idea of a housing development?

The drawback would be seeing Cara all the time. Whether she relented and bought the stable or not, he would have to deal with his feelings for her. He didn't trust himself to give those feelings a name. Not out loud anyway. But he couldn't deny that he thought about her all the time. He'd tried to put her happiness before his own. But what happened if she wouldn't let him show her he cared? What happened if she didn't have similar feelings for him?

That would be too difficult to live with.

Ryan carried in his toolbox and started in on a project that would take him days and take his mind off Cara.

"Do you have a date for the wedding?" Jordan asked him before he left for work at the hotel.

"Yours?"

"Very funny. Violet's working on the calendar date. I meant a social date for Camille and Maddox's wedding. You can't be Violet's plus one because she's mine."

Ryan ran through the list of women he

knew on the island, and he could only think of one.

"Is there some law against going alone?" he asked.

"I don't know," Jordan said. "I never had to go to anything alone because Violet was always there for me. I can't believe it took me forever to realize we were in love. It's funny when you think about it."

Jordan left for work, and Ryan attacked his project with all his energy.

THE WINTER SOLSTICE PARTY on December 21 was for ten people. Not hard, Cara told herself. The venue was beautiful and familiar. Everyone in her generation had enjoyed visiting the Winter Palace. Their whole group had been together just six months ago for an evening of food and bike riding on the summer solstice. The longest day of the year seemed like a long time ago now.

So much had happened. Last summer, Cara had been in the holding pattern of her daily life. And then she'd taken the spot on the village council, which gave her a confidence boost to push her toward achieving her dream of her own camp. That dream bubble had burst, but it was filling up again. And not because Ryan had offered to sell her the stable.

Her answer was still a firm no. She hadn't even told her family he'd offered, even though Camille had pointedly asked her what was eating at her. Cara had almost broken down and told her sister because she didn't want her to think she was worked up about her upcoming wedding or the tasks she'd agreed to take on.

"We're having cake, right?" Camille asked the afternoon before the party as they worked together in the candy store.

"Of course," Cara said. "Your wedding cake will be exactly what you want. Two layers of white, one chocolate, and one spice."

"I mean the one for the Winter Solstice Party. That's going to be especially meaningful this year."

"Ganache," Cara said, ignoring the comment about the party being meaningful. She had about as much sentiment and emotion on her plate as she could manage. "Chocolate fudge cake with gallons of dark chocolate ganache poured over it."

Camille fanned herself and sat down. "I

know you're exaggerating, but I'm not sure I can wait another day for that."

Cara laughed. "You're going to have to."

"I'm glad we're not calling it a bachelor or bachelorette party and we're not getting T-shirts stating our role in the wedding," Camille said. "Can you picture me wearing a shirt that says Bride on it? Winter dinner party is a much better theme, and I'm glad we'll all be together, guys and girls."

Cara had a moment when she thought her life would be easier if they did divide up and she didn't have to endure a dinner party with Ryan involved. He was too attractive, too interesting, and their worlds were too entangled. She'd managed to avoid being drawn into conversation with him at the barn, partly because Violet had told her he was working long hours at Jordan's house. There had been only one day when they'd come face-to-face and nearly run into each other. Ryan's cheeks had colored and his breathing had quickened. Cara knew hers were the same.

"The offer still stands," Ryan had said.

"And my answer is still no. No, thank you," Cara had said as gently as she could.

She had walked away before Ryan could

ask her why she was turning down something he knew she wanted, but if he didn't understand there was something more going on, she wasn't going to explain it to him. What should she say? She cared about him and didn't want to destroy his prospects and be the reason he had no reason to stay on the island? That's not what she wanted. There was no way to have both.

Cara brought her thoughts back to the present, in which Camille sat on one of the candy store's red-and-white-striped stools. "I've planned a fun game."

"With prizes?"

"Of course. I'm texting everyone an assignment with an item they have to bring tonight. The items will be the basis for the fun game."

"Is it a scavenger hunt?" Camille asked.

Cara smiled. "I'm not giving away anything, but I will tell you it doesn't involve going outside or leaving the Winter Palace. It's too cold for that."

"That's a relief." Camille was quiet a moment, but then she got up and came over to look more closely at the cookies Cara was dipping in white chocolate. "What's going on with the Ryan situation?"

"There's no situation."

"Come on. Even though you're the no-drama member of the family, I can see there's something on your mind."

"I'm thinking about my horse camp and the business plan I submitted to get a loan to buy property. It's a big deal, and of course it's on my mind."

"What's Ryan going to do?" Camille asked.

"What do you mean?" Cara looked up quickly and dripped white chocolate across the counter.

"Without you."

Cara didn't move. Did Camille know something? "He never had me."

"Working in his barn," Camille said, grinning. "What did you think I meant?"

Cara let her shoulders fall. It was hard keeping her thoughts and feelings to herself. She'd always been good at it. She was a listener. A sympathizer. A suggester of solutions. Being on the other side of that was much harder than she'd ever given it credit for. She'd thought she had the hard job.

"I can't work for him and have my own place, too," Cara said. "It will be next summer before I get anything going, so I could help him out until then, I guess. I keep hoping he'll find someone else, but that's tough during the off-season on an island."

"He could manage the horses himself," Camille said. "He's not busy building his empire right now and can't until the ground thaws, so I'm surprised he doesn't just do it himself."

Cara had honestly not thought about that. When Ryan had first moved back to the island, he'd been new at caring for a dozen horses along with two donkeys and a bunch of cats and kittens. She'd told herself she was staying for the animals to ensure the continuity of their care. But Ryan could have taken over after a week or two. He may not have done things exactly as she had, but he would have managed.

He'd kept her on. Why? Did he not want to deprive her of a paycheck? Or was there something more?

"He must like you," Camille said.

"He likes having me do all the dirty work."

"Do you do all the dirty work?"

Cara thought for a moment before she answered. Ryan had become very efficient at shoveling out stalls and making trips to the manure pile. Her work had gotten lighter and left her more time for taking the horses out for quick walks around the yard or short rides in the cold weather. How had she not really noticed the change? She hadn't pushed a wheelbarrow or hauled a heavy bucket more than a dozen times in the past month.

"We share the hard work," she said, even though she realized it wasn't exactly true.

"Hmm," Camille said.

"Two hours until party time, and you need to go home, curl your hair and put on your favorite Christmas sweater," Cara said.

"Maybe you should also curl your hair and put on your favorite Christmas sweater," her sister said. "Just because I'm getting married in four days doesn't mean it has to be all about me."

Cara laughed. "I'll see you at home in a little while."

Cara finished her cookies and gathered party supplies, which included dozens of candy canes and a big bag of assorted Christmas candy. She sent individual texts to the ten people invited to the Winter Solstice Party, asking them to bring a specifically wrapped item, and then she went home to change her clothes and share a ride with her sister.

This year, the Winter Solstice Party felt like a turning point for the island friends. They were all grown up, starting new adventures and, in her case, wishing she had a reindeer with a light-up nose to show her the road ahead. As a member of their friend group, Ryan would be at the party, and with each passing day, it was getting harder for Cara to keep herself from falling in love with him.

CHAPTER TWENTY-TWO

RYAN WAS THE last one to the party. He'd been delayed trying to comply with Cara's request to all the guests, and that's why he'd walked into the living room at the Winter Palace and found everyone paired off on couches and love seats.

Every other guest was part of a couple except for him and Cara. She wasn't sitting down. Instead, Cara was on her feet fussing over the trays of cookies and finger foods. When he walked through the door, she paused midstep and looked at him, but then she quickly said, "Good. You brought the bag. Take it to the kitchen and put it on the counter by the back door with the other ones."

Ryan didn't know why he and everyone else had been instructed to bring a single wrapped ornament that represented them—either new or from their personal collection—for a gift exchange. They were also instructed to bring it in a grocery bag from the island store so no one would see them come in with a wrapped gift and identify the wrapping paper.

Cara had some secret party game up her sleeve, and that was fine with Ryan. If there was something to do at the party aside from sitting around and chatting, he'd be happy. His life was currently a blur of trying to stay busy so he didn't have to think too much. He didn't want to think about the lawsuit his lawyer said was winding down, but he couldn't guess the result. He didn't want to think about the risk he'd taken buying property on the island. He didn't want to dwell on his living situation in a senior duplex instead of a nice home of his own. But he really didn't want to face the reality of how he'd pushed Cara away just when he finally realized he wanted her close.

Games were good. The more, the merrier. If he had to play Pin the Tail on Rudolph, he would gladly do it until he could make a graceful exit. He went into the kitchen and put his grocery bag with the others on the back counter, and then he swiped a red plate and sandwich from the tray on the table and grabbed a glass of punch.

"Don't tell me this is the famous Winter family punch recipe," he said as he went into the living room.

Rebecca scooted over on the couch she shared with Griffin and made room for him. "It wouldn't be a holiday on this island without it," she said. "Flora gave me a private lesson in making it, so I consider it my solemn duty and lifetime responsibility to honor the tradition."

Ryan sipped the punch. "Well done," he said.

"You're not supposed to eat the food yet," Violet admonished her brother. "We're having a sing-along first and then eating, and then we have games, thanks to Cara."

"We'll stay busy," Cara said. She didn't look at Ryan, but he wondered if she had a similar reason for wanting to remain occupied. Were there things in her life she needed a distraction from, like her two jobs, her sister's wedding and the agony of waiting for her loan approval? Did she also have tangled feelings in her heart for him, or had he ruined whatever spark had been growing between them?

Rebecca pushed off from the couch and

went to the piano bench. She opened a thick spiral-bound book of piano music. "Serious Christmas carols, romantic ones in honor of the wedding coming up or frivolous silly ones?" she asked.

Ryan noticed a glance between Cara and Camille. "Silly ones," Camille said. "With all the weddings this year—" she nodded toward Mike and Hadley and then Rebecca and Griffin and then her fiancé Maddox "—we should give love a break and do all the snowflake and jingle bell songs until we get too hungry."

"Love it," Rebecca said. "First up, 'Frosty the Snowman.'"

Rebecca played a lively intro to the familiar song, and Violet and Jordan harmonized perfectly as usual and led the verses, with Griffin tapping out the drum part at the end on the side of the piano bench where his wife sat.

"'Jingle Bells,'" Rebecca said.

Ryan knew every word of every song. It was impossible not to when you grew up on Christmas Island. What he had forgotten, though, was how much he loved the spirit of the holiday. Warm lights and decorations surrounded them, the aroma of good food wafted out from the kitchen, and his best friends harmonized—some better than others—on familiar songs. Why hadn't he just been honest with himself and moved home because he wanted to, not because he felt forced to by his circumstances? And why had he kept his miserable secret to himself? Everyone in the room would have understood and sympathized, but he'd only been brave enough to share it with one person, and he had to admit to himself that his reason had been motivated by desperation almost as much as trust.

"'The Twelve Days of Christmas,'" Cara suggested in the brief lull between songs. She glanced over and caught Ryan's eye, and he knew she was thinking of the horses. Their horses. Her cheeks were flushed and her eyes bright. Did she also feel the magic of the holiday, and would it be enough to give them a fresh start? What would it take to prove to her that he cared about her?

THE FOOD, courtesy of Rebecca's planning, was perfect, and the house was festive and gorgeous. The company? Cara sighed as she carried a tray of bingo cards and candy to the living room. She loved every person in the room. They were all relatives by blood or

marriage, or old friends, and one of them...
well, she couldn't deny it to herself any longer. She was letting her heart get into dangerous territory with Ryan. Which was exactly
why they were going to be very busy playing a game of bingo in which they filled their
cards with little wrapped candies as markers.

After that, she had a trivia game based on
famous lines from holiday movies, and then
the gift exchange guessing game. By the time
the group completed all the activities she'd
lined up, it would be time to kiss everyone
good-night.

Almost everyone. When the farewell hugs
took place, she hoped to be busy in the kitchen
wrapping up leftovers to help out Rebecca.

"The winner of the bingo game will get
first choice in the gift exchange later," she
announced. "I need a volunteer to call the
bingo numbers."

To her surprise, Ryan raised a hand. It almost made sense, but she didn't want to think
about why. He was the only other person there
not seated with a spouse or fiancé. Maybe he
wanted to stay busy, too.

"Perfect," Cara said. She moved aside so
he could sit at the table where she had a tablet

propped up with a bingo number app on the screen. "You know what you're doing?" she asked him quietly while everyone else was busy picking up bingo cards in the shape of Christmas trees and handfuls of small pieces of candy.

"I worked those church fundraisers growing up just like you did," he said. "This is more fun, though, with the Christmas theme."

All the island kids had helped with the games and bazaar booths at the church fundraiser held on the same fall weekend every year. They'd gotten their fill of caramel apples and freshly fried donuts in exchange for helping out. She remembered running around all weekend, having fun at the festival.

"Thank you," Cara said. "I printed the cards from an online template and swiped the candy from the store."

"I can only imagine what you have planned next," Ryan said softly, his eyes friendly and sweet. They were friends. And coworkers. And two people who had something big in common—they were both trying to reinvent their lives and had bumped up against each other's ambitions in the process.

"I...plan to win the bingo game if you call the right numbers."

"I'll do my best."

Something about the exchange made Cara think she and Ryan could be a great team if they were on the same side. But there was no way to do that. He'd offered to sell her the stable, and her answer was still a clear no.

When the bingo cards filled up a while later, Jordan was the first winner, and Violet reached over and ate one of his foil-wrapped candies. "It's okay now that you've won, right?" she asked and everyone laughed.

"Jordan gets first pick in the gift exchange," Cara announced. She collected the bingo cards and handed out little take-home bags for the candies. Next up, Cara kept the group busy by playing snippets of ten different holiday movies and handing out cookies to the first person who named the movie correctly. She was happy to be busy, so she didn't dwell on the way Ryan looked at her or the way her heart raced when she thought back over the last ten weeks of seeing him almost every day. The horses, the morning coffee, the snowstorm, the mistletoe...

When it was time for the final planned

event of the night, Cara went into the kitchen and put all the wrapped gifts in a box. Returning to the living room, she piled the gifts on the coffee table, and everyone sat around.

"You all know which one is yours, but you don't know who brought the other ones. When it's your turn to pick, you choose a gift and open it, and you have to correctly guess who brought it. If you're right, you keep it. If you're wrong, the person to your right gets the next guess."

"This is fun," Hadley said. "And I didn't cheat and look at what Mike brought."

"Me neither," Rebecca said.

"Jordan goes first," Cara said.

Jordan took a moment to decide and then selected a small box wrapped in silver paper. He opened it and found a miniature piano Christmas ornament. He smiled. "Rebecca."

"Do I say?" Rebecca asked, looking at Cara.

She nodded. "If your name is suggested and it's right, go ahead and confirm."

"It was me," Rebecca said.

"You go next," Cara told Rebecca.

Rebecca picked up a green box and opened it to reveal an ornament with a black dog and a wreath. "Hadley!"

"You got it," Hadley said.

Hadley opened the next box with a boat ornament. "Uh-oh," she said, looking at Griffin and Maddox. "Which one of you is it?"

"You have to guess," Cara said.

Hadley closed her eyes. "Maddox."

"Sorry," Maddox said. "Not mine."

Hadley passed the boat to Mike who sat on her right. "I've got it easy," Mike said. "Griffin."

"You're right," Griffin said.

"Do I try again?" Hadley asked.

"Go ahead," Cara said.

Hadley opened another box and found a candy cane ornament. Her gaze shifted from Cara to Camille and back again. "Camille," she said.

"Yes!" Camille said.

Ryan shot Cara a quick glance. Had he thought she'd choose candy for her ornament?

"You're up next," Cara told Camille.

Camille opened a box with a bicycle ornament inside and she smiled broadly. "Mike."

"Got me," he said. "I already opened one, so it looks like my turn goes to Cara," he said.

Cara grinned. "Okay." She opened a box wrapped in green fabric and tied with a red velvet bow. Before she even got to the contents, she guessed whose it was from the wrapping. Inside was a sewing machine ornament.

"Violet."

"Too easy," Violet said. "I should have thought of some very complicated aspect of myself that no one knows."

"On this island?" Griffin said. "That would be tough."

Violet reached for a gift and opened it. The ornament in the box was a little boy with a dog. She looked up at Maddox. "This one is yours."

He nodded, and Camille threw her arms around him and kissed his cheek. Maddox had chosen his son, Ethan, as the representation of himself, and Cara felt tears prick her eyes at the sweetness of it.

Maddox chose a box. "Wish me luck," he said, and then he laughed when he saw it. "A house. That has to be you, Ryan."

"It is," Ryan said. He reached for one of the few remaining boxes, and Cara held her breath. He'd chosen hers, and anyone at the table would have guessed it was hers by the contents. But it felt right that Ryan had been the one to open the box that contained a prancing horse Christmas ornament.

He held it up and smiled at her.

"Hey, how did you know it wasn't mine?" Jordan asked.

Everyone laughed as Cara opened the last ornament and revealed a silver key representing a hotel room key. "Let me see," she said, tapping her chin.

"That wasn't easy to find," Jordan said. "But you know it's me."

"It's the key to my heart, right?" Violet asked. Jordan turned and kissed her. "Should we tell everyone?"

"Tell us what?" Camille and Ryan asked at the same time.

Violet laughed. "We have to now." She turned her smile on the group. "We chose a date for our wedding. The third weekend in April, which is right before the Great Island Hotel opens for the season."

"Perfect," Rebecca said with a hand over her heart.

"It'll be a spring wedding in the garden if the weather cooperates, and I'm considering doing something really wild and wearing a light violet-colored wedding gown."

Ryan went over and kissed his sister on the top of her head. "You can do anything you want," he said. "Congratulations."

Not long after the gift exchange, Mike and Hadley left to pick up their baby from Hadley's sister Wendy's house, and then Jordan and Violet left. Cara busied herself in the kitchen putting one piece of leftover chocolate cake on a plate and covering it with plastic wrap for her sister to take home. She thought it was Camille coming into the kitchen, but then she turned and found Ryan.

"You did a wonderful job making this fun for everyone," he said. "You always do things for other people."

"We all do," Cara said. "We're like a big family."

"But you deserve more. You're amazing."

She shook her head. "No one deserves anything. Life is what we make it and what we choose for ourselves."

"Cara, there's something I haven't said, and I can't keep it from you any longer. If you don't want to hear what I'm going to say, then tell me to leave now."

He leaned on the counter right next to her, his sleeve touching hers. He smelled like the outdoors, pine trees and a hint of the horse barn. It was hard to resist. She moved toward him a fraction of an inch and it was all the invitation he needed. He put an arm around her shoulders and pulled her to his side. She felt his lips touch her temple, and the happy emotions of the holiday mixed with the magic of his touch was too tempting a combination, even though she might regret letting her guard down later.

Would it hurt to let herself go for just a moment and give in to her heart?

"Go ahead," she said.

"I'm glad I came home to the island so I could reconnect with you. I'm ashamed to confess I never knew before how strong and smart and unique and beautiful you are. I didn't see it, but I can't unsee it now. You're so much more than I ever imagined."

The pure vulnerability and honesty in his words took her breath away.

He saw her.

Cara turned her face and, wordlessly, touched her lips to his in a sweet, tender kiss she was sure she would never forget. All her life, that kiss would be part of Christmas, the aroma of good food and candles, and her nostalgia for the holiday. She expected the kiss to be brief, just an acknowledgment of feelings ignited by the wintry night and the warmth of the occasion, but Ryan's lips lingered over hers in a string of kisses she didn't want to end.

"Oh," she heard someone say, and then the kitchen door clicked shut.

Ryan drew back just enough to break the kiss, but he kept an arm around her. Cara knew the voice that had interrupted them. Her sister. She tried to think of what she would say to Camille on the way home, but her thoughts came to a screeching halt with Ryan's words.

"I love you, Cara."

She opened her mouth but couldn't think of anything to say. She wanted to tell him that of course he didn't. It was just his imagination or the holidays or…something. How could Ryan Brookstone be holding her in the kitchen at the Winter Palace telling her he loved her after sharing a long tender kiss?

How on earth had she gotten here from where they were just two months ago?

"We've always been friends," he said. "And then when I came home and circumstances put us together all the time…my feelings started to grow. I was confused. I doubted myself. I didn't want to give in or mix up what I felt for you with what I needed to do with the housing project, but I don't care anymore about anything but you."

She should say something. She needed to say something, give him an answer or an indication. Did she love him? Desperately. But could she trust that this was the real thing and not a combination of external factors that had thrown them together and mixed his feelings for her with coming home, relief at getting his permits, holiday spirit, nostalgia for the island and their youth...?

"Aren't you going to say anything?" Ryan asked. He cupped a gentle hand on her cheek. "I'm not sure of anything much, Cara, including what happens tomorrow, but I'm sure of this."

"That's just it," Cara said, her voice thick with emotion. "You've had a lot of upheavals lately and you might be feeling—"

"I know what I'm feeling."

Cara stepped back just enough to break the physical contact.

"What are you feeling?" Ryan asked.

Cara picked up the plate with the cake she'd

wrapped up for her sister. She should take it to her, get in the car, not keep everyone waiting. What were people thinking with her and Ryan in the kitchen alone for so long? She was making everyone uncomfortable, drawing attention to herself.

"I'm feeling that I should go home right now. It's been quite a party, and I—"

"Trust yourself, Cara. Everything else can wait. For once, say what you want in your heart," Ryan said.

She stared at him, completely shattered by the fact that he knew what was stopping her. He understood her as if he saw into her heart.

"I want…" she began, but she knew the truth was that she wanted him even though she was afraid to take what was being offered to her. Was she ready to satisfy her own heart, finally?

"I need to go home and…think," she said.

Ryan's shoulders sank, but then he picked up her hand and kissed it. "I'm not going anywhere, and I'm not going to change my mind."

CHAPTER TWENTY-THREE

RYAN WENT HOME, but he didn't go to bed. Instead, he made a pot of coffee and sat at his kitchen table with his laptop and the rolled up sheets of blueprints with his housing development plans. It was the only way to prove to Cara he loved her and to find a way forward for them. If she bought an alternative property, he'd always know he'd robbed her of her plans. If he sold her the stable property—which she'd already declined—she'd always know she'd robbed him.

They had to do it together.

He redrew almost everything. The barn would remain as it was, but the pasture would be expanded. The restaurant and convenience store could stay, although their function might change. It was the houses. They weren't houses anymore. They were cabins. Fifteen cabins with lofts and porches, rustic but comfortable. There was only one house remaining, and it was a perfect two-story with four bedrooms. A family home.

He redrew the blueprints and used a computer program to design the cabins. He changed the name of the whole development and saved the new designs. It was nearly five in the morning when he got to the barn and plugged his laptop into a network cable for the printer. It was only a black-and-white printer, but it would suffice.

It took him an hour to print and piece together a large blueprint, along with a stack of detailed drawings. He folded some of the cabins so they were three-dimensional and set the whole thing up on his desk with a sign he fashioned out of paper and sticks.

Cara's Camp.

Ryan stood back and looked at the plans. It was beautiful. And, if he'd done anything right, he'd be sharing it with Cara. She needed time. He realized that after last night's kiss. He'd been thinking about kissing her for weeks, but had she? Was she ready for the relationship he now realized he couldn't live without?

He didn't want to be there when she saw the plans. If he gave her space to consider it, he thought his chances would be better. So, he left the office lights on and the door open, and he walked out of the barn an hour before he knew Cara would show up to feed the horses.

His eyelids were sandpaper and his stomach an acid pit from a night of coffee-drinking and worrying, but this was how it had to be. His acidic stomach was nothing compared to what his lawyer and banker were going to say, but there had to be a way. He would find a way.

Christmas was in three days, and it was either going to break his heart watching two island friends get married, or it was going to be the beginning of his own love story.

He got in his truck and closed his eyes for just a moment before turning the key. He'd done what he could. If he just went home and had a nap, maybe there would be a miracle when he woke up. He let his shoulders relax for the first time in hours, the weariness of redrawing plans and hunching over his laptop finally dragging him downward toward sweet relief.

Ryan dreamed he was in his childhood home, tapping away at his latest creation. A birdhouse in the form of a rustic cabin with a cat on the porch and a horse tied to the railing. The cat might have to go, he thought, because it might scare away the birds, who'd finally come home to a place where they felt happy and safe.

Tap, tap, tap. In his dream he was putting the final touches on the roof, hammering on the shingles. Where should he put this birdhouse? He'd already populated the island with his creations, but this one was special. It had to go someplace where it would be truly loved.

A blast of cold air followed by someone calling his name awakened him, and Ryan's heavy eyes struggled open.

"Are you okay?" Cara said. "I tapped on your truck window, but you didn't move. Did you sleep here last night?"

"Cara," he said. His mind was still asleep, focused on his dream. "The birdhouse is for you. It's perfect for you."

"What birdhouse?" Cara put a hand on his forehead. "Ryan, I'm worried about you."

Her cool hand on his forehead and her scent jolted him into reality. He took her hand and kissed the inside of her wrist and then held it against his chest.

"I'm fine. I stayed up all night working on something, and then I guess I fell asleep."

"You must be freezing. Come inside the barn."

"I haven't been out here that long."

Cara shook her head and her look of concern turned to curiosity. "What's going on, Ryan?"

"I didn't want to do it this way."

"Do what?"

"Show you what I worked on all night."

Her hand was still in his, and Cara pulled him out of the truck. "You're coming inside, and I'm making you some coffee, which you're going to drink until you start making sense."

"It'll make sense," he promised as he gained his footing and closed the truck door. He still had her hand, but he wanted her in his arms. It took all his power to resist wrapping them around her and instead give her the control and the space to make sense of what he was proposing.

Proposing. He hadn't thought about it during the night, but his entire plan was a proposal. Their life together, their house. Their cat on the porch with a horse tied up outside.

Cara tugged him toward the barn, and he

followed. Inside, she headed straight for his office. He wanted to slow her down, hit pause and prolong the moment, but Cara was on a mission.

She stopped as soon as she walked into the office. He came in behind her, but he leaned against the wall, watching her take in the sight of his plans. She paused over the sign and looked at him, but she didn't say anything. She moved around the desk, noting the cabins, the outdoor arena and even the reimagined store and cafeteria.

Cara got to the house at the top of the horseshoe-shaped property, and her lips parted. When she looked up at him, her eyes shone with tears but also understanding.

"I...told you I wasn't buying your property," she said cautiously.

"I know. And I'm not selling it to you anyway. I've gotten pretty attached to this barn and the horses. I don't want to let them go."

"But what are you saying? What is this plan?"

Ryan pushed off from the wall. "It's a proposal."

Cara sat down hard in the office chair, and

Ryan went over and knelt beside her, taking both her hands in his.

"It's a proposal for us to do this together. This place was meant to be a horse camp, and you were meant to be here. But so am I."

"How can this work? You need to build and sell your houses to make back your investment, or you can't rebuild your business. You'll be ruined. I won't be part of ruining—"

Ryan smiled and shook his head. "The only thing that would ruin my life is not being with you."

"But—"

Whatever Cara was going to say was cut off by the phone ringing.

"Answering machine," Ryan said. "We have too much to talk about. About our future."

Cara kept her hands in his, but she didn't look him in the face. The phone rang four times, and then Gary's voice came on with a recording asking the caller to leave a message. The office phone at the barn was so seldom used that Ryan hadn't bothered to change the outgoing message.

"Brookstone, it's Mitchell, and I've been

calling your cell and you're not answering, but you're going to want to hear this."

"My lawyer," Ryan said, a lead weight settling into his stomach. Of all the rotten timing. For pity's sake, he was in the middle of telling Cara he loved her and wanted to spend the rest of his life with her, and his lawyer was calling with probably bad news that would lurch him right back into the nightmare of a year ago.

"I wanted to tell you in person," the voice on the machine said, "but you're going to have the best Christmas of your life, because the suit has settled out of court. I don't know what kind of holiday spirit got into Poppy and her dad or if they've just moved on to the next victim, but they're settling with you, and you're recouping everything, minus my fee of course. Call me, or better yet, get on a boat and get over to my office so you can sign the deal."

Relief took all the strength from Ryan's legs, and he sat on the floor, his back against the desk. "I can't believe it. It…it's…unbelievable."

"You got what you wanted, so now you're

free," Cara said. Why did she sound sad? Hadn't she just heard what his lawyer said?

"Congratulations," Cara added. "I'm happy for you."

"For us," Ryan corrected her.

Cara shook her head. "This drawing is really nice, but doesn't that call from your lawyer change things for you?"

Ryan reached up and hooked a hand on the edge of the desk. He pulled himself to his feet, his head still swimming from a sleepless night, his lawyer's news and the proposal he had for Cara—wait…he hadn't actually proposed.

"Cara," he said. "That call from my lawyer only changes one thing, and that's the financial part of my plans. I recently figured out that money was never my real problem in the first place. It was trust and letting myself fall in love with someone. Money doesn't change that."

A horse whinnied and stamped its feet. "They're hungry," Cara said. "I should go feed them."

"Give me a minute and we'll go feed them together." Ryan couldn't resist any longer. He pulled Cara into his arms. "I told you I loved you last night, and I'm banking everything on the hope that you feel the same way."

He heard a tiny sniff and then a whisper. "I do."

Joy raced through him, and he pulled back so he could kiss her.

"I love you, Ryan, but I was afraid to let myself. I wanted to reach out and claim you as mine, but I…well, I'm not used to taking what I want and putting myself first."

"I think you should get used to doing what makes you happy," Ryan said.

"Only if you do, too."

He laughed. "That sounds like something we can work on together."

Cara grinned. "Did you know I had a secret crush on you those summers we both worked here?"

"When you handed me tools I didn't even need?"

She laughed. "I've always been very helpful."

"And now it's time you took some help from someone who wants your happiness more than anything else." He traced a finger down her cheek. "I said this new plan was a proposal, and that's exactly what I mean. Do you see this house?"

Cara turned and looked at the perfect home perched where it could oversee the whole camp. She put her finger on the birdhouse on a post in front of the house and smiled. She nodded.

"It's our house. Will you let me share your dream and be my wife, Cara?"

A horse whinnied louder and Cara smiled. "I'd say that's a yes."

"You're sure?"

"Yes," Cara said, her expression serious and her eyes bright. "I've never been more sure."

Ryan held her tight. "You can change anything on the plans you want to. This is just a rough draft."

"I don't want to change a thing," Cara said. "Except perhaps the name. I can't call it Cara's Camp. It's our camp."

"How do you feel about naming it after one of our horses? Two Turtledoves or Five Golden Rings?"

"I'd have to think about it," Cara said, giving him a quick kiss. "You're definitely on the right track, though, with a Christmas theme."

"Speaking of golden rings," Ryan said,

picking up her left hand. "I believe I know just what to get you for Christmas."

Cara pulled him close and held him, and he knew it was going to be the most magical Christmas of his life.

EPILOGUE

Camille's Wedding

"FIRST CHLOE AND then Rebecca and now you," Cara said to her sister Camille as she helped her pin her veil in place.

"And next you," Camille said.

"In the summer," Cara agreed, "but we're keeping it casual, not making a big fuss."

Camille laughed. "I feel like that's what every bride says, and then the wedding seems to spiral into dresses, cakes, live bands, party favors and every person you know hopping on a ferry."

"That's the fun of it," Cara said.

"And don't you dare have a barn wedding," Camille said. "I know you, and I bet you already thought about it, but remember Violet has definite ideas about wedding gowns, and she's not letting a white train drag across a stable floor."

Cara laughed. "Enough about me. This is your big day, and it's time we get out there and send you down the aisle to marry the two loves of your life."

"I hope I'll be a good mom to Ethan."

"You already are. And he's going to love having an aunt who owns a riding stable."

The small church on Christmas Island had seen a century of weddings, but Cara couldn't imagine a more perfect one than this. Both her sisters had gotten married at Christmas, and she'd thought about continuing the family tradition. However, she was committed to doing what she wanted lately, and she knew she did *not* want to wait another year to marry Ryan.

And it was going to be a busy year. Now that Ryan's lawsuit had settled, he was able to come through on a promise he'd made to the island. The ten acres Cara had almost purchased for her horse camp were still available, and Ryan's lawyer was drawing up the documents for Brookstone Builders to buy the property and go through with the plan for twenty affordable homes. Cara's heart swelled with joy knowing that Ryan could put his business back together as they began their lives together.

She joined the other bridesmaids—Chloe in her gown, which Violet had expanded the waist of at the last minute, Rebecca and Violet—and they marched happily down the aisle. At the altar, Maddox, his brother, Griffin, and his good friends Ryan and Jordan stood at attention as Camille's parents walked her down the aisle.

In the front row, Flora Winter dabbed at her eyes with a tissue as another one of her honorary grandsons got married. Seated all around her were dozens of Christmas Island residents, old and young, whose lives were bound together by island sunrises and sunsets, holiday traditions and the lake whispering along the shoreline.

Cara caught Ryan's eye several times during the ceremony as he stood on the other side of the groom. Violet's wedding would be next and then hers. Christmas Island was always magical, bringing holiday spirit to residents and visitors all year, but it seemed especially magical with the church filled with red and green ribbons and flowers and all the people Cara loved most.

After the wedding ceremony, everyone went outside, where a light Christmas snow fell.

"It's showtime for us," Ryan said. He and Cara hopped in his waiting truck and drove to the stable, where they quickly hitched up two horses—Partridge and Swan—and got back to the church with the carriage just as the bride and groom finished having their pictures taken by the wedding photographer.

Sitting next to Ryan in the driver's seat, Cara jingled the bells, and her sister, Maddox and Ethan got in the carriage's seat. The photographer took more pictures, and everyone waved as the carriage drove down the street to the Holiday Hotel, where the reception would bring the island together for a Christmas celebration of love.

Ryan slipped an arm around Cara and handed her the reins. "Merry Christmas, Cara."

"Merry Christmas, my love," she said.

Cara tipped her cheek up for a kiss as they drove the carriage down Holly Street with snowflakes and the sound of jingling bells in the air.

* * * * *